Moonlighting

Ola Wegner

Moonlighting

Cover Photo by Janusz Wilczynski, www.wilczynski.art.pl

Email address: OlaWegner@gmail.com

Chapter One

Elizabeth Bennet rolled on the other side in bed with a sigh, her eyes wide open. The silver light of the full moon crept into the room, despite the drawn curtains. One did not require a candle to make out the surroundings through the darkness. The weather had been disagreeable for the last couple of days, but today, the sky turned cloudless.

She threw the covers aside, found her slippers and walked to the window. The heavy velvet curtain moved to the side, and she gazed at the moon. It was bigger than she had ever remembered.

An unfamiliar sound caught her attention. She closed the curtains and listened. When it repeated itself, she thought it resembled a muffled cough. Worried that her sister's state had worsened, she pulled a robe over the nightgown and hurried to Jane's room.

Elizabeth placed a hand on her sister's forehead and found it cool, her breathing even. There was a hope that tomorrow, Jane would feel well enough they could leave Netherfield.

Elizabeth had never been so happy in her life at the thought of going back home to Longbourn. With the exception of Mr. Bingley, the company at Netherfield was hardly pleasant. Thankfully, Mr. Darcy had left early this morning before breakfast, having to go to London on some urgent business. She had not needed to bear his condemning stares or his hostile silence directed towards her during the meals and the short time they had spent together in the library.

Back in her room, she felt drawn to the window again. Again, she pushed the heavy curtains farther away and looked up at the full face of the moon. She reached forward to open the window. The pleasantly cool, fresh air swept over her face, and she inhaled deeply.

On impulse, she ran to the closet to retrieve her ankle high leather boots. She put on the warm woollen stockings and laced her shoes. She had her hair in curling papers for the night, but she refused the thought of removing them. Wrapped in a bed coverlet, she left the room.

As she walked through the dark, silent house, she considered how to get out at this hour. The main door was surely locked. She directed herself to the drawing room, and walked outside through the glass terrace door.

She could still feel the afternoon rain in the air, but it was surprisingly warm for November. She ran a short distance from the house and stopped in the middle of the yard. She tilted her face to the moon and stared at it, trying to figure out the shape of eyes, nose and mouth of the so called "man in the moon".

A cold shiver ran down her back, and she felt someone's presence close by. Her heart fluttered as she turned around. She let out a slow sigh of relief. There was a large, unusual looking dog sitting in front of her. His black eyes fixed directly on her.

She could not be sure of his intentions, but nothing in his behaviour indicated that she should be afraid of him.

"What are you doing here?" she asked in a warm tone she usually used when playing with her father's dogs. "Should you not be near the stables?"

The dog stared, his black eyes glistening at her.

She smiled. "You are friendly, are you not?" she leaned forward and pulled out her hand from behind the coverlet.

The dog waved his tail vigorously and let out a short bark.

"Yes, you are." Elizabeth crouched down and the animal approached her. "You are friendly, yes... you are." she patted the animal's large head.

The dog sniffed her, and his rough tongue licked her hand.

"You do not look like any of the dogs that belong here." she clasped her hands around the animal's head and took a long look at his face. She frowned. "As a matter of fact, you do not look like any other dog I have ever seen ... even in books." she scratched him behind his large spiky ears. "You look more like a ...wolf." she shook her head. "But it is not possible, there have been no wolves in England for many centuries now, everyone knows that."

The animal turned his head to the side and nudged her arm, clearly enjoying Elizabeth's attentions and demanding more.

"You like that." she laughed, scratching him harder. "You are beautiful." She leaned to hug the dog. "Such thick, and at the same time soft fur you have."

The animal purred in obvious pleasure and started sniffing Elizabeth's neck and chest.

"You are affectionate, are you not?" she stroked his back. "Nice dog, very nice… good boy… yes, good boy… I would wish to keep you…" she sighed. "But Mama would never allow it… Besides, I doubt whether your owner would wish to part with you." she stared into his dark, intelligent eyes. "Such a treasure."

The animal licked her cheek and started sniffing her neck again. Elizabeth giggled as she felt his wet nose touching the sensitive skin on her throat.

"I have to go, I am afraid." she lifted herself reluctantly after a moment. "It is getting rather cold." she wrapped the blanket more securely around herself.

The dog barked twice and threw his head in the direction of the house.

Elizabeth raised her eyebrow. "You think that too, do you? You are very smart. Well, you are right. It is not my intention to catch a cold like Jane."

She started walking back to the house, and the animal followed her close by.

"You must go now." she whispered when she reached the terrace door. "You know I cannot let you inside. You are all muddy, and they do not like the mud in here. I know something about it, trust me." she stroked the large head. "Especially Miss Bingley, you know. She would be undoubtedly very much displeased seeing you in the house. And we do need to be civil to her – even if we do not like her – for Jane's sake. I am almost sure that my sister is falling more ~~in more~~ in love with Mr. Bingley."

The dog licked her hand. Elizabeth kneeled down and gave him one very last hug.

"Go back to the stables now." she whispered. "I will try to find you tomorrow before breakfast so we could play again." she patted his back. "Now, go, go…"

The animal seemed hesitant to leave, but at last after the last lick at her palm and a playful nudge at her legs, he slowly ran away.

Back in her room, Elizabeth walked to the window to close the curtains. She stilled when she saw that her new friend sat on the grass and clearly looked up straight into her window.

She frowned and waved her hand at him, indicating him to go away. But he didn't move. She shrugged and closed the curtains tightly, not allowing the moonlight to disturb her sleep anymore.

When she climbed back into a bed, she fell asleep surprisingly quickly, and slept soundly, dreaming the whole night. The dreams were pleasant, she was sure of that, but she could not remember any specifics when she woke up in the morning.

***

"Miss Elizabeth!" Elizabeth heard and turned around to see Mr. Bingley as he dismounted his horse.

"Mr. Bingley." she curtseyed with a smile.

"I see you enjoy very early walks, Miss Bennet." The young man said as he gave the reins of his horse to the stable hand.

Elizabeth shook her head. "Not so much, sir. I only wanted to have a closer look at your stable before breakfast." she said, pointing with her head at the nearby well kept buildings.

Mr. Bingley raised his sandy eyebrows up his forehead. "My stables? I have never thought you to be the Amazon, Miss Elizabeth. I have never even seen you to ride a horse."

Elizabeth laughed at her host's half stunned, half amused expression. The gentleman had to be in good spirits this morning.

"You are right, sir." she acknowledged. "I do not ride." she stressed. "I only wanted to see your dogs."

"My dogs?"

"Yes." she nodded. "You see, yesterday I went on a short walk after dinner to have some fresh air before sleep. I kept close to the house, and I met a very friendly dog. He was so adorable, and I thought to play with him again today." she could not stop the enthusiasm from her voice.

"That is rather strange, Miss Elizabeth." Mr. Bingley looked down at her with an unusual for him frown. "All the dogs are locked up for the night, I assure you."

"Yes, I thought the same, but he did not look like any of the dogs I have seen before."

Mr. Bingley stilled and looked sharply at her. "He did not…"

Elizabeth shook her head. "No, he more resembled the wolves I saw in the books as a child."

There was a moment of silence before Mr. Bingley said very slowly. "And you do say that he was adorable." he looked at her incredibly.

"Yes, indeed, very friendly, gentle and sociable. He walked me back to the house, and later stood in front of my window..."

To her surprise, Mr. Bingley interrupted her decidedly. "I do not keep such dogs, Miss Elizabeth."

She gave him a doubtful look. "Are you sure? It was a very large dog, with dark colouring, very smart too. He truly looked like a wolf, but he was so gentle and domesticated... "

"No, Miss Elizabeth." Mr. Bingley interrupted her again, but this time his voice was gentler. "I keep no dogs such as you describe, and positively it could not be a wolf, because as you know the last wolves were seen in England during the times of William the Conqueror at least." he laughed, but his cheer seemed unnatural to Elizabeth. "I am sure it was just a dream. People dream strange things when the moon is full."

Elizabeth frowned. "Mr. Bingley, I am sure it was a real dog."

Bingley shrugged. "So perhaps it belongs to one of the farmers around here. Now tell me, how is you sister? Is she feeling better today?"

Elizabeth answered Mr. Bingley's enquiries about Jane, pleased that he was so much interested into her sister's well being. Still, she was sure he tried to draw her attention away from the subject of his dogs. That was rather strange. Why should he hide the fact of owning the rare breed of dogs? It was not like the dog she had met was dangerous and should be kept locked away. She was convinced, as well, that no farmer or tenant in the neighbourhood could have such a dog. It was all very confusing.

***

Almost a week later, the two eldest Bennet sisters were on their first walk to Meryton since their return from Netherfield. For the last few days, the weather had kept rather cold, which prevented them from longer walks, especially taking into consideration Jane's recent illness.

"What an elegant path!" Mr. Collins exclaimed. "There is a similar one leading from Rosings Park to my humble home."

Elizabeth rolled her eyes. Their cousin, Mr. Collins, who had come to visit them, and intended to stay for several weeks, was the worst possible company imaginable. She could not imagine a greater punishment than spending time with the parson. Even Mr. Darcy was better. At least he spoke little, and did not demand constant attention like Mr. Collins seemed to require.

"We are approaching Meryton." Jane noted calmly.

"What a lovely town!" Mr. Collins exclaimed anew.

Elizabeth felt Jane take her hand and give it a squeeze, followed by a reassuring smile. Elizabeth rolled her eyes and smiled back at her sister. Mr. Collins was currently looking for a bride, and did nothing to hide – or at least be discreet – about his plans. On the contrary, he made no secret of it. Elizabeth dreaded to think that he had set his mind on her very person; especially now, when Jane, the first when it came to beauty and sweetness among the Bennet sisters, was already being courted by Mr. Bingley.

They walked into the busy main street of Meryton, and wandered for some time, looking at the shops' window displays. They were approached by one of the officers, Mr. Denny, whom they had previously met several times at the gatherings and parties. He introduced a new officer to them, Mr. Wickham, who was to join the militia soon.

Elizabeth took an instant liking to gentleman. His manners were amiable and engaging; his looks dashing, still slightly boyish, with ready smile and a thick mop of sandy hair. He would be an excellent addition to the company at the parties and assemblies, she decided after a five minutes of conversation with him.

Unfortunately, their meeting was ruined with the appearance of Mr. Darcy. He came on horseback, together with Mr. Bingley, who dismounted promptly to talk with Jane. Mr. Darcy, in turn, stared at her in his usual cold and condescending manner from atop of his black stallion. A long moment passed before his eyes moved from Elizabeth to the gentleman standing by her side, Mr. Wickham.

Elizabeth could not help but notice the sudden change in Mr. Darcy's face, which sobered his already sullen features. He dismounted quickly, and rudely pushed himself between Mr. Wickham and herself. Elizabeth opened her mouth to protest the intrusion, but Mr. Darcy gave her such a domineering look that she closed her mouth and said nothing. She could not see much from behind Mr. Darcy's broad back, but soon Mr. Wickham walked away without a word of goodbye to anyone at all.

Mr. Darcy waited till Mr. Wickham disappeared in the crowd of people, before he turned and looked down at her.

Elizabeth pressed her lips tightly, angry at him for frightening the amiable Mr. Wickham away. She felt that his eyes looked for hers, but she stubbornly looked to the side. She did not intend to speak a single word to that man. Her chin held high in the air, she stepped closer to Jane and Mr. Bingley. As she joined their conversation, she pretended that Mr. Darcy did not stand by her side the entire time. She let out a sigh of relief when the gentlemen bid their goodbye and rode away. Mr. Darcy was not only plainly unsociable and rude; his behaviour indicated some unusual incomprehensible… oddity, she decided.

***

Later that day, closer to the evening, Elizabeth felt that she needed to escape the house, if only for a short time. Her mother insisted that she keep Mr. Collins's company every single moment. Elizabeth was terrified to think that there was only one reason behind this. Mrs. Bennet wanted the parson to make her an offer, and had already given her blessing to the match. Elizabeth dreaded the thought of this man even proposing to her, not to mention being married to him. Her toady, greasy, always sweaty cousin was the last man in the world to whom she wanted to be a wife.

She spotted the moment when Mary engaged Mr. Collins into a conversation about the sermons she had been reading lately, and quietly left the drawing room so that nobody apart from Jane noticed her disappearance.

She tiptoed upstairs to fetch her bonnet and warm pelisse, and a few minutes later ran outside. It was not her intention to walk far, as it was close to dusk. She just wanted to be alone for a few short minutes.

Just as she walked past the small park behind the house, she thought she heard some animal noises. Curious, she followed the sounds.

As she strode into the clearing between the trees, she stilled and gasped, her eyes widened. Two dogs fought with grim vengeance. Never in her life had she seen such ferocity and wrath in a fight. Her eyes widened when she recognized the dog that she had become acquainted with at Netherfield.

"Stop!" she cried before she considered whether there was any sense to it. "Stop that at once!" To her surprise, the animals listened to her, and stopped, if only for a short moment.

The dark eyes of her dog friend stared directly at her for a split of second. The moment was used by the other dog, who jumped at him with his sharp white teeth bared.

"No!" she cried.

She looked around, desperately searching with her eyes for some object which would allow her to interrupt the fight. Spying a large stone, she grabbed it, and without a second thought, threw it at the other dog.

Her aim was sound. It hit the yellowish dog right on the head. He stopped his attack, stepped away and swayed.

Elizabeth grabbed a long stick and waved it at him. "Go away, bad dog, go away!"

She could see the blood on the animal's head before he put his tail under himself and ran away.

When the attacker disappeared in the trees, she ran to her friend.

"Are you hurt badly?" she put a gentle hand on his head.

The dog squeaked quietly and stumped slowly into her arms.

Elizabeth ran her hands along his back and sides, checking for injuries. Her hand found the torn place lower on his chest.

She probed it gently, feeling warm blood on her fingers. "Come… we must take you to some safe place and clean this wound." she took the animal gently into her arms and stood up. He was very heavy, she could barely carry him. She nearly knelt under his weight. But she gritted her teeth in determination and strode slowly towards to the stables.

As she found a clean, quiet place at the end of the building, in one of the empty stalls, she put him gently in the corner on the soft hay.

His eyes opened and he licked her hand. She stroked his head to comfort him and at the same time examined his wound. It did not look well, and it bled heavily.

"Do not move." she whispered. "I must go back home but I will be back soon to help you."

She managed to enter the house unnoticed, and only on the staircase she heard Jane's voice.

"Lizzy where have you been?"

"Hush..." she put her finger to her mouth. She took her sister's hand and pulled her with her to their room.

"Mama has been asking for you." Jane whispered.

"Jane, please tell Mama that I have a headache and needed to retire early." Elizabeth walked into the dressing room, looking for something which could be used as bandages. "I must go back there and help him."

Jane's smooth forehead creased. "Help who, Lizzy?"

Elizabeth, in quick words, explained the situation.

"Lizzy, you do not know this dog well enough. He may be ill and dangerous." Jane cried, her eyes widened. "He can bite you, and you may die from the wound."

"Oh, Jane, he is very friendly and gentle." Elizabeth assured. "He would never bite me."

"But you said yourself that he fought with the other dog, so he cannot be as docile as you previously thought." her sister reasoned.

"Yes, but I am sure he was attacked by this other dog. Jane, I cannot leave him there… He will bleed to death."

Jane shook her head. "Lizzy… I am not sure about that…"

"Please, tell everyone I went to bed. I will be back as soon as I clean his wounds…"

She collected her sewing items and two of her oldest, most worn nightgowns, and walked past her sister to the hallway.

"Lizzy…" Jane tried to stop her, but Elizabeth shook her head.

"I must go." she squeezed Jane's hand. "Please tell everyone that I am already in bed, sleeping."

The main door was already locked for the night, but she got out through the window in her father's study.

A few minutes later, slightly out of breath, she entered the stall when she had left her friend.

She tried to comfort him first and stroked his head, speaking to him in soothing tones. His sad, pained eyes locked with hers when she cleaned and stitched the wound, the gentlest she could. For once in her life, she was glad that her mother had insisted so that she and all her sisters learn to sew.

She tore her nightgown into long strips, and secured it as a bandage against the injury.

Elizabeth stayed with the animal till he fell asleep. His head was supported on her lap, and she stroked him as it seemed to bring him relief. It was very late in the evening when she slipped back into the house.

When she came back early in the morning to check on her patient, he was gone.

Chapter Two

For the next few days, in vain, Elizabeth walked the path between Longbourn and Netherfield, hoping to meet her dog friend once again. But there was no trace of him. No servant at Longbourn saw him in the stables. She could not help but feel worried about him. Had he managed to return his home safely before dawn? Had his attacker found him and killed him in his weakened state?

She looked through her father's books on animals, hoping to learn more about what possible breed he could be. To her disappointment, she found no dog who resembled him. There was a little likeness between him and the dogs bred in Germany. But if anything at all, he looked more like a wolf. But wolves in Herefordshire in 1811… it was utterly impossible. Moreover, his behaviour indicated that he was well acquainted with the people and domesticated, so he could not be a wild creature from the forest. Not to mention there was hardly any forests near Meryton.

The news reached them from Netherfield that Mr. Darcy had been injured as he fell off his horse. Elizabeth was surprised to hear that. The man was an excellent horseman, she had to admit that at least. When her Aunt Philips came to visit, she said that Mrs. Hurst had called the doctor for Mr. Darcy, but he refused to be examined. It only strengthened Elizabeth's opinion about Mr.Darcy's peculiarity. His erratic behaviour was perhaps interesting to study, but she cared too little for his person to take the trouble.

***

"Miss Bennet!" she heard as she stepped out of the bookshop.

"Mr. Wickham." she smiled at the handsome countenance of the officer. "We have missed your company at Mrs. Philips' two days ago. She assured us that she had extended the invitation for all the officers."

"I am sorry, Miss Bennet." Wickham bowed elegantly, and only then did Elizabeth see a scrap of the white cloth sticking from his hat. "I did not feel well enough to attend."

"What happened?" Elizabeth asked with concern.

Wickham lifted his hand to touch his forehead and smiled. "That is nothing… I assure you. Just a slight accident during our military training."

"I am so sorry to hear that." she said sincerely. "I hope you are feeling better now."

"Oh, yes." he assured her. "Just my head aches some from time to time. I would be hardly acceptable as a dancing partner in such a state, I am afraid."

"So perhaps you should not be walking at all." Elizabeth suggested.

Wickham shook his head. "No, no, I feel much better today." he smiled warmly at her.

Elizabeth smiled back a bit shyly and averted her eyes. "I am to meet my sisters at the milliner's shop." she said after a moment.

Wickham offered his arm in an elegant gesture. "May I accompany you?"

Elizabeth nodded and smiled.

They walked for a while in silence before Wickham spoke. "May I ask whether you are well acquainted with Mr. Darcy?"

She looked up at him with surprise. "No, not at all. I met him at a few parties and spent three days with him under the same roof, though we spoke but little.

"I see." he said, and looked in the other direction as if lost in his thoughts.

Elizabeth bit her lower lip as she glanced up at him. "Forgive me, sir, but… you and Mr. Darcy… I had the impression that you knew each other, that morning when we were introduced."

"You noticed." Wickham stopped and turned to her. "I have not seen nor spoken to Mr. Darcy for many years now, though once we were good friends. We grew up together."

Elizabeth's curious eyes rested on him. "What happened?"

They resumed their walk, and for the next several minutes, Elizabeth listened with sympathy to the story of Mr. Wickham's life, and how terribly he had been mistreated by Mr. Darcy, the man who had ruined his chances for a career in the church and refused him a living promised by the old Mr. Darcy. What person could do such a thing on purpose, with cold calculation? Her tender heart tugged at Mr. Wickham's story.

"But he should be exposed for what he has done to you, refusing you the living that his father had yet promised to you." she cried with conviction.

"He certainly should, but it is not I who shall do that. I am not resentful by nature, Miss Bennet. I am not like him. Besides, I like to consider myself quite lucky in my current situation in life. Had not all these happened to me, I would have never come here to the south of the country, where I had the opportunity to meet such agreeable company."

Elizabeth let herself blush a little under Mr. Wickham's intense gaze. "I can only admire your resolve, sir. I doubt I would be able to act like this in your circumstances, after what you have suffered."

They were now close to their destination. Mr. Wickham released her arm and looked down at her.

"Miss Bennet, let me warn you." He paused as if looking for the right words. "Keep your guard when in Darcy's presence. He is not what he seems to be. I do not refer only to what he did to me. I have something entirely different in mind."

Elizabeth lowered her eyes with a frown of her own. "I am not sure of your meaning, sir. Still, I must admit that I found Mr. Darcy's overall behaviour strange at times. I heard that he refused to see the doctor when he fell off his horse. It is rather unusual, will you not agree?"

Mr. Wickham gave a little laugh. "His behaviour is more than unusual, I can assure you, Miss Bennet. I would even say that there is nothing normal and natural about him." his expression sobered. "Think twice before you let him come closer to you." he said, before bowing and disappearing in the crowd.

Elizabeth stared after Mr. Wickham with a frown for a long moment. She still felt cold shivers running down her spine. She did not like the feeling..

***

Elizabeth assessed her own reflection in the mirror. She looked pretty in her own usually critical eyes. Even her typically unwilling to be pinned straight, thick hair managed to be curled in fashionable ringlets. Like her sisters, she wore a new dress, made especially for the ball at Netherfield. She smoothed the silky, creamy material with trembling fingers. She put her hand to her bosom trying to ease the flutter of her heart.

"Lizzy, we are waiting only for you!" she heard Lydia's cry from the downstairs.

"I am coming." she cried back, and having collected her elegant cap and long evening gloves, ran out of the room.

The short drive in the family carriage was uneventful, and soon they were entering the elegant foyer at Netherfield manor. She was pleased to see that Mr. Bingley showed an instant interest in Jane, engaging her into conversation.

She walked further into the brightly illuminated rooms. As the smallest of all the Bennet sisters, she needed to stand on her tiptoes to recognize the guests. She hoped to see Mr. Wickham, but so far there was no sign of him.

"Miss Bennet." she heard behind her back.

She turned around to see Mr. Darcy, who… smiled at her.

She did not return the smile. She frowned at him, and performed only the slightest curtesy.

She looked to the side, purposely avoiding looking at him. She hoped he would simply go away if she did not speak to him.

"You are looking for someone?" he asked in a pleasant, engaging voice.

Elizabeth's frown deepened. She did not understand why he was so unusually polite, to her of all people.

"Yes." she raised her eyebrow in a challenge. "Mr. Wickham."

All the pleasantness disappeared from Darcy's face in an instant.

"You should be more careful with your dealings with the gentleman." Darcy murmured darkly through tightened lips. "He is not what he seems."

"I believe he could say the same about you, sir." she said, raising her brow, and without another word, walked away.

Some time later she was deep into the conversation with her dear friend, Charlotte Lucas, when Mr. Darcy appeared by her side again.

He bowed respectfully. "Miss Elizabeth, the music will start in a moment. May I ask for the first two dances?"

Elizabeth was glad to say that the first two dances she had already promised to her cousin, Mr. Collins.

But Mr. Darcy was not discouraged. "So perhaps the next two?" he asked politely.

"I…" Elizabeth searched her mind frantically to find some believable excuse when she felt Charlotte stamping hard on her slippered foot.

She gave a soft sound which Mr. Darcy had to understand as her consent.

"Thank you." he bowed and walked away.

"What were you thinking?" she demanded angrily looking at her friend.

"Do not be silly, Lizzy." Miss Lucas whispered. "The man is so rich. You would lack nothing as his wife."

Elizabeth's eyes widened. "His wife? Charlotte, I barely know him. Besides, he does not like me at all. I have no idea why he asked me to dance with him."

"He must admire you, Lizzy." her friend stressed. "You are the first lady in the entire neighbourhood he chose as his dancing partner." Charlotte pointed out.

"Charlotte, please. He is the most disagreeable man of my acquaintance, apart from Mr. Collins perhaps. I heard only the worst things about him, and his behaviour is sometimes more than unusual… He is odd."

She wanted to say more, but then Mr. Collins approached them. In his usual ridiculous manner, he reminded her that the first dance was about to start. With a heavy heart, she took her place in the row of couples, facing the parson. After only a few steps, she was convinced that he was the worst possible partner, not only in this room, but in the entirety of England as well.

After the humiliation of dancing with Mr. Collins, she was almost relieved to stand with Mr. Darcy. She perceived him to be a better dancer, and she was not disappointed.

At first she decided not speak a word to him during the dance, but then she thought it would be a greater punishment for him to actually engage him in a conversation. He always spoke so little to anyone, so he clearly detested the activity.

"Do you like dancing, Mr. Darcy?" she asked archly.

"Not particularly." he answered listlessly. "Dancing is something that I was taught to perform, but never learned to care for."

Elizabeth glanced up at him. It was a strange answer, but then she recalled his oddity, thinking it was something that she should expect from the man beside her.

"I see." she looked at him steadily from behind her long eyelashes. "If you so dislike the activity, I cannot see the reason why you decided to endure it for the next half an hour."

"It is very simple, Miss Bennet." He took her gloved hand, stronger than was needed and walked around her to the next movement. "It allows me to spend this time in your company. Dancing is a small price for the opportunity to be near you, I assure you." he acknowledged calmly as he passed her to another partner.

Elizabeth's mouth fell open, and she gaped at Mr. Darcy in amazement.

Elizabeth kept silent because, truthfully, she did not know what to say to this.

"I see that I managed to silence you, Miss Bennet. I dare say it is an accomplishment indeed."

She looked at him sharply with a frown. Then her expression relaxed, her eyes danced in her face, and she laughed.

Mr. Darcy smiled too. When she looked up at him, his expression was peaceful and pleased. He led her confidently through the figures, thought at times, she thought, keeping her too close to himself than propriety would have allowed.

When the music ended, he walked her back to the chair, took her hand again and bowed over it.

"It was a pleasure, Miss Elizabeth."

Elizabeth nodded slightly, still confused with his gallantry.

"May I inquire about Mr. Wickham?" he asked as he stared into her eyes with quiet intensity. "From what you said, I understand that he told you something about me."

"Yes, he did talk about you."

"I believe it was something unfavourable."

Elizabeth searched his eyes before she spoke slowly. "He told me how you disregarded your father's will and refused him the living in the Church that he was promised, reducing him to his current state of poverty."

Darcy did not look ashamed, or even disconcerted, as Elizabeth expected he should have been, hearing about his own misdeeds. He looked relieved.

"Miss Bennet, I assure you it is not the truth." he said with firmness. "Mr. Wickham fabricated this story, in my understanding, to turn you against me, and for other reasons I cannot divulge now."

Elizabeth did not know what to say and whom to believe. "Mr. Darcy…" she started hesitantly but was interrupted.

"I wish you every good fortune and happiness in life." he said in one breath, "You deserve it." he added ardently.

She stood up and shook her head, confused even more. "But sir, you spoke as if we were never to see each other again."

"You are right. I believe we shall not see each other in the future. I am going to London tomorrow, and later north to my estate."

He stepped forward and whispered heatedly. "I will always remember you as the kindest, most handsome and most generous woman of my acquaintance." His very dark eyes bore into her for a moment, before he bowed again and hastily walked away.

For the rest of the evening, Elizabeth was dumbstruck. She did not see Mr. Darcy again. He disappeared, and did not attend the dinner. The man was a puzzle. One time rude, unsociable and offending, another time the most amiable gentleman. Her suspicions about his character went as far as suspecting him of some slight mental instability. How otherwise could be his strange, changeable behaviour explained? She did not know as well what to think about what he said about Mr. Wickham. Who should she believe?

So engrossed in her thoughts was she, that she even overlooked her mother's coarse and her younger sisters' shameful behaviour during the evening. They were among the last of the families who were to leave the house and still their drivers seemed to take ages to bring their carriage.

Elizabeth had enough of waiting in the hot, overcrowded foyer, so she wrapped her elegant pelisse tighter around herself and slipped outside unnoticed.

The brisk air enveloped her, and she breathed in, her eyes closed. She gave a little gasp of surprise when she felt a strong nudge against her leg.

She looked down and her face broke into wide smile.

"It is you!" she cried softly, leaning to her dog friend. "Where have you been? Are you well now? Let me see." She removed her long gloves and started to look for the place where the animal was wounded.

"You have healed nicely... and somebody removed the stitches."

The dog licked her face, and only then did she notice that something fell out of his mouth.

"What do you have here?" she picked up an article that looked like a tightly folded, packed with something, sealed letter.

She turned slightly to catch some light from the house, and recognizing her own name written in an elegant firm hand on the front cover of the letter, Miss Elizabeth Bennet.

"Where did you get this?" she looked down at the dog. "Who gave it to you?"

Her friend barked twice, and threw his head in the direction of the manor.

Slowly, she turned the letter in her hand. There were initials at the back side, F. D.

"F. D." she murmured. "Is it your master?"

The dog barked again, wagging his tail.

Elizabeth frowned. "I am afraid I do not know any F. D."

Her friend nudged her skirts, as if demanding her attention. She crouched in front of him, and scratched him gently behind his ears the way he liked.

He pushed his head against her hands for a moment when Kitty's voice was heard nearby.

"Lizzy, Lizzy... Where are you? We are waiting only for you."

"I have to go." she hugged him one last time, stroking his strong back. "Come to my home tomorrow... Do not disappear like before." she added before she ran away to the awaiting carriage.

When they drove away, she could see that he followed the carriage for some time.

***

Only the next day, after the very late breakfast, as the entire family overslept after a ball, Elizabeth found enough privacy to read the letter. She settled herself in the far, secluded corner of the garden and opened the package.

The gasp escaped her when the beautifully crafted, oval medallion on a long delicate chain fell on her skirts. The piece was a little masterpiece, the front side depicted some fairy tale like landscape, with forest, mountains and lake, all that carved in the gold surface with painstaking care.

She turned the medallion in her hand; there was inscription in some strange letters. She could not make it out, but then she remembered a book from her father's library about the old English alphabet, from yet before the Norman conquest. Yes, it very much looked like Runic alphabet. Her forehead creased in confusion; nobody used this language for at least eight hundred years.

She could barely tear her eyes away from the beautiful medallion, but forced herself to read the note which accompanied it.

Miss Elizabeth,

Forgive me the impropriety of this letter, but I am at a loss as to what else I can do to protect you. I should stay by your side myself to keep you safe from any danger, but for your sake I must disappear from your life. I beg you not to trust Mr. Wickham. He is a liar and a vile type. I have my suspicions that he has set his sights on you. His only aim can be to use and hurt you. Despite appearances, he is not a man to be trusted.
What he told you about me is all untruth. I am not perfect and without flaws, I assure you, but his story how I mistreated him is a lie. He fabricated it, I believe, to take revenge on me. Last summer he tried to seduce and force into marriage my fifteen year old sister, hoping to gain access to our considerable family wealth, and her own sizeable dowry. I managed to prevent it, and he cannot forgive me this.
I beg you to stay away from him, and never allow yourself to be with him alone.
I wish you every happiness in your future life.

Your devoted friend,

Fitzwilliam Darcy

P.S.: I also want to thank you for tending to my friend's wounds. As you see he has healed well, thanks to your prompt assistance, I believe. I wish you to accept this small token of my gratitude for saving my friend's life.

Chapter Three

Two days after the Netherfield ball, Mr. Collins proposed to Elizabeth, who to her mother's great displeasure, refused him. The parson proved to be neither much devastated nor heartbroken by the rejection. Exactly two weeks later, he proposed to Elizabeth's best friend, Miss Charlotte Lucas. This time he was accepted.

Due to her refusal of Mr. Collins' suit, Elizabeth was exposed to a few weeks' of open hostility on her mother's part. Mrs. Bennet was only placated when Mr. Bingley made a proposal to Jane in the first days of the New Year. All she could talk about thereafter was what wealth and finery her Jane would have as the future Mrs. Bingley, and what opportunities it would create for the others girls. There was no question, after all, that Mr. Bingley had many rich, single friends who were also in the need of a wife. And who could be more suitable for them than her own fair daughters?

The winter months were pleasant enough for Elizabeth, and very busy. Their mother insisted that Jane should not feel inferior to Mr. Bingley's sisters when she would enter their family. Consequently, it was decided that Jane would receive at least a dozen new gowns; not to mention the new bed linens, nightgowns, robes, gloves, stockings, bonnets and numerous petticoats. With the help of Mr. Gardiner, the finest of materials were purchased quickly in London at very reasonable prices. What took time, however, was discussing the models and patterns which would suit most Jane's figure.

Elizabeth's skill at sewing was considerable. It was true that she much preferred to walk or read rather than to sit in the parlour with a needle. However, for her beloved sister, she was more than willing to resign from all the pleasures. She wholeheartedly agreed with her mother this time. Jane deserved all the best. She did not want her elder sister to feel as a poor relative against Miss

Bingley's silks and finery. Many hours a day in winter months, she spent stitching Jane's new dresses.

During her work, Elizabeth's thoughts returned more than once to her friend dog and to his owner. She should have guessed earlier that it was Mr. Darcy's. They even looked alike, with that dark colouring and black eyes.

She had not confided to anyone about the letter and the medallion, apart from Jane, of course. The piece was so beautiful that she liked to look at it every day in the privacy of her room. She especially liked to gaze at the landscape picture depicted on it. She knew that the only right thing for her to do was to return the medallion to Mr. Darcy. Jane agreed with her, pointing that it was highly inappropriate for a gentleman's daughter to receive such a gift from a strange, unrelated man.

Neither she nor Jane could guess the cost of the medallion, but it looked expensive. They discussed the possibility of sending it back to Mr. Darcy's townhouse, but eventually rejected it as too risky. As Jane was sure that Mr. Darcy would return to Hertfordshire in a few months to stand with Mr. Bingley at their wedding, Elizabeth decided she would return the piece to him at that time. She would make sure to find the opportunity to explain everything to him, apologize for how she had misjudged him and return the medallion. She anticipated meeting both Mr. Darcy and his dog.

Elizabeth had succeeded in avoiding Mr. Wickham's company. The cold weather and the time spent preparing Jane's trousseau stopped their frequent trips to Meryton. Meeting him at the assemblies and parties turned out to be unavoidable. Still she had been careful not to speak with him alone, following Mr. Darcy's instruction. She did not doubt the truthfulness of Mr. Darcy's note. He could not fabricate such a story about his own sister, after all.

At the end of February, the letter from Kent came, reminding Elizabeth about her promise made in December, to visit her friend Charlotte, now Mrs. Collins, in her new home. At first, Elizabeth had been more than reluctant to go. There was so much work yet to be done before Jane's wedding, and she wanted to assist with everything.

However, Jane insisted she accept the invitation. After a few days of careful consideration, Elizabeth wrote back to Charlotte. She confirmed her arrival in Kent, together with Sir William and Maria, in the middle of March.

***

Elizabeth walked briskly through the lushly green and fragrant countryside. It was only the end of March, but everything was already blooming here in Kent. Almost to the last hour before her departure from Longbourn, she had worked hard, finishing Jane's silk evening gown. No, she was happy with the opportunity to enjoy the outdoors.

Elizabeth checked her pocket watch to see that it was already late, near tea time. She hastened her pace, not wanting to make Charlotte wait for her.

When she entered the small foyer at Hunsford cottage, she heard some unfamiliar male voices in the parlour. Clearly, Charlotte was receiving unexpected guests. Her hand moved to her hair, to check whether all the pins were still in place before she walked inside.

Her eyes widened when she saw Mr. Darcy. What was he doing here?

Charlotte stood up. "Lizzy, come join us." She gestured to her. "The gentlemen have been asking about you. I started to worry that you may have lost your way."

Elizabeth shook her head with a smile. "It is such a beautiful day, I simply walked farther than usual." She knew that her voice sounded very nervous.

Mr. Darcy stepped to her and bowed his dark head. "Miss Bennet, it is a pleasure to see you again." he said seriously, but his eyes were warm as they rested on her.

Elizabeth averted her eyes to the side under his steady gaze as her heart began to flutter in her chest.

Only then did she notice the other gentleman. He stepped to her as well and bowed his head. "I see that I must introduce myself, madam, because my cousin is reluctant to do so. Colonel Fitzwilliam, at you service."

He took her hand gently and simulated a kiss over the top of it.

Elizabeth smiled at the gentleman. He reminded her of Mr. Bingley, perhaps because of his fair colouring, though he was considerably older than her sister's betrothed.

"It is pleasure to make your acquaintance, sir." She curtseyed.

"I must say that I was very curious to meet you, Miss Bennet." Colonel Fitzwilliam said. "I have heard so much about you from Darcy."

"You have?" she said slowly as she looked up at Darcy again. "I believe that Mr. Darcy is my severest critic."

She winced inwardly when she heard what she had just uttered. Truly, she did not know why she had said that. She always managed to say some nonsense in Mr. Darcy's presence.

Colonel Fitzwilliam continued to speak after Charlotte gestured for them to sit down and rang for more fresh tea. "On the contrary, Miss Bennet, I assure you. I believe that I have not ever heard him to praise any woman as highly as you.

"We arrived only last evening. When Darcy heard from our aunt that you were currently staying as a guest at Hunsford, he was determined to pay you a visit today."

Elizabeth smiled shyly, and said nothing to that. She dropped her eyes to her lap. She did not notice that Colonel Fitzwilliam looked intently from ~~her~~ his cousin to her, and back to his cousin.

Colonel Fitzwilliam's sandy eyebrows arched high on his forehead as he observed Miss Bennet's intense blush and his cousin's delighted expression as he stared at the young lady.

He cleared his throat. "Miss Bennet, I hear that your sister is too be soon married to Mr. Bingley."

***

The next day, the party from Hunsford was invited to dine at Rosings Park. Elizabeth briefly considered whether she should take the medallion, and try to return it to Mr. Darcy, but she decided against it. She doubted there would be a private opportunity for that in the room full of people, especially under Lady Catherine's watchful eye.

Elizabeth could hardly feel comfortable in the course of the meal, and spoke very little. She was seated beside Mr. Darcy, and it was all that she could concentrate on. His large frame, his strong hand placed on the pristine tablecloth next to her, his masculine smell; all that affected her more than she liked to admit. Even Lady Catherine found her behaviour strange, and enquired about her unusual quietness.

Later in the evening, she was asked, or more precisely, ordered by the lady of the house to play. With relief, she relocated herself to the quiet corner of the room, where the pianoforte stood. She was rather glad to escape Lady Catherine's immediate company.

She chose to play a melancholic tune. She knew it by heart, so her eyes fixed on the moon which peered inside the room. It was almost full in shape. She would probably not be able to sleep tomorrow night again, due to the full moon.

Her view was suddenly blocked by a tall figure, and she raised her eyes.

"Do you mean to frighten me, Mr. Darcy?" she asked, lowering her gaze back to the keyboard. "I am well aware that your sister plays very well. Lady Catherine and Miss Bingley praised her skill many times. My performance must be seriously lacking, compared to hers."

"You cannot be more wrong, Miss Elizabeth." Mr. Darcy assured her, his voice solemn. "My sister does play very well, but it is partially due to the fact she is often left to her own company. She practices many hours a day to fill her time with some occupation, I believe."

Elizabeth stopped playing and looked up at him. "Has she no friends?"

"I do not trust her with strangers... You must know that Pemberley is situated far from the towns and other estates. We do not have many neighbours. There are no suitable young ladies her age in the neighbourhood whom she could befriend."

"I see." Elizabeth started playing again. She did not know how to respond. She was not sure why he was telling her all that, but she desperately wanted to speak with him about the letter and his gift.

She bowed her head over the keys, so she would appear to be entirely concentrated on the music. It took her a moment to gather her courage before she spoke in low voice.

"Mr. Darcy, there is a matter I would like to discuss with you." she glanced up at him. "You must have some idea what I refer to."

"We can meet during one of your walks." he responded quickly, in the same hushed tone.

Elizabeth nodded in relief that he understood her before she started a new movement. "Every day after breakfast, I walk to the grove at the back of Hunsford Cottage."

"I know the place." Darcy said, and Elizabeth was sure that he wanted to add something more, but then Colonel Fitzwilliam joined them.

"I see, Miss Bennet, that Darcy did not exaggerate when speaking of your playing."

Elizabeth forced a smile. "You jest, sir. I am well aware that my playing is seriously lacking. I admit that this is entirely my fault, as I never took enough trouble to practice."

"I disagree, Miss Bennet. I have hardly heard anyone to play with such feeling."

She thanked Colonel with the smile before she started a new song.

Mr. Darcy started speaking with his cousin about his trip to London the next day on some urgent, unexpected business. Elizabeth felt that he mentioned it for her sake, so she would not wait for him tomorrow. She was actually relieved to hear about his plans, for it gave her a few days to prepare herself for the conversation with him.

She managed to play to the end of the song somehow, without making too many mistakes. It was hard to do as she felt Mr. Darcy's intense gaze on her the entire time.

Thankfully, she did not have to play more, because Lady Catherine called her back to her, to lecture her on her playing. Elizabeth was offered the opportunity to use the old pianoforte at the governess' room at Rosings any time she wanted since she would not be in anyone's way there.

***

"Pretty girl, very pretty." Colonel Fitzwilliam said when the cousins shared a bottle of brandy later that evening in the privacy of Darcy's room.

Darcy gave him a well levelled look. "Your point?

Colonel took a sip. "Oh, nothing. I am just surprised."

Darcy shrugged. "I do not understand."

"Simply, I did not know you had your taste in rosy, busty blondes." he laughed, staring at the other man. "Give her a babe on each hip, dress her in a cotton dress, apron and a cap and she may pass admirably for some tenant's wife."

Darcy glared at him. "If you do not have anything interesting to say, concentrate on your drink."

"Darcy." The colonel put his drink on the small table and leaned to his cousin. "She is a human."

"I have noticed."

"She seems kind, lively, intelligent." the colonel noted after a moment.

Darcy nodded. "She is all that, and much more."

"So leave her alone, if you care for her."

Darcy stood up and walked to the fireplace. "You know that I must marry one day, and rather sooner than later."

Colonel gaped at him. "You cannot be serious. You are considering marriage."

Darcy turned to him. "Why not? I am eight and twenty, I must have a son. It is high time. The pack demands it." his expression tightened. "You said yourself she is strong, healthy. She will do well."

"She is a woman, not a cow." the colonel pointed out dryly.

Darcy gritted his teeth. "I have my responsibilities."

Colonel Fitzwilliam narrowed his eyes at him. "So you have decided."

"If she wants me." Darcy acknowledged quietly.

"Of course she will." The colonel stood up and walked to the other man. "You are intelligent, well read, rich and good looking. You can be kind and attentive when you want to make an effort, even charming. She is too young and inexperienced with men to protect herself against your seduction. She does not stand a chance. My point is that you should not let her fall in love with you. It is not too late yet."

"I will not hurt her."

"I know… not on purpose, of course, but you cannot help some things about yourself and your family. You must know how difficult it was for your mother to adjust. She was far too delicate for this life."

Darcy's face tightened. "Elizabeth is different, not so frail. She is stronger than my mother ever was. She will have a better life with me than if she was to marry some silly idiot like Collins. My parents loved one another; we would be the same."

The colonel shook his head, "Think about what you intend to do to her. You cannot know, cannot remember the time from the beginning of your parents' marriage. Your mother suffered, she tried to escape a few times before you were born."

Darcy looked at him darkly. "How do you know about that?"

"My father told me. He said that Lady Anne had nearly gone mad before she accepted her fate and her place beside your father."

"I will do everything to make it easier for Elizabeth." Darcy said with sincerity in his voice. "I will help her."

"At least tell her before the wedding."

"You know I cannot do that. It is against our laws. She cannot know until she is absolutely bound to me."

The colonel raked his hand through his dishevelled hair. "Darcy, have some pity on her if you care for her. Think how she will feel the day after your wedding night. She will be terrified."

"Richard, please. I am not a monster." Darcy cried, losing his patience. "I am perfectly able to control myself. I can control my change."

"Can you really? I doubt it. Especially when very strong emotions are concerned. And you feel strongly about her, you cannot deny it."

"She will not know, not even suspect." Darcy insisted. "I can control myself and hide it from her as long as necessary."

"You mean till she will be with your child." the colonel exclaimed. " Good God, you want to trap her the same as your father did with Aunt Anne!" he accused.

"My mother was not trapped." Darcy said through clenched teeth. "She loved my father. My parents…"

"My father's version is slightly different." The colonel interrupted him angrily. "It was simply too late for her. She was already carrying you when she learned the entire truth. After you were born, she could neither leave you alone at Pemberley, nor escape with you. You would not survive on your own without the pack, among people only."

The heavy silence fell into the room. The men did not look at one another till Darcy walked to the window to look at the moon.

"I understand what you are saying, Cousin, but…." Darcy shook his head. "I care for her. I loved her last Autumn already, but I decided to remove myself for her sake. But now when our paths crossed again, I cannot deny myself. It is preferable for me to marry a full blooded human anyway. We must weaken the blood, adapt, learn to control the change more effectively, so to survive in this new, changing world. I am aware that it will be difficult for her, but she is brave, courageous. She will manage to come to terms with it in time. I will do everything to make it up to her. She will lack nothing."

A moment passed before the colonel spoke again. "You will do as you please, but consider it all one more time."

Darcy stared into the fire. “There is nothing to consider. I cannot struggle against it. In time she will be happy. You shall see.”

Chapter Four

The next day, early in the afternoon, Elizabeth walked out of Hunsford Cottage. As she stopped by the small gate, thinking in what direction she should walk today, she heard a bark.

She turned to the sound, and her face lit up. "It is you!" she cried and ran to the dog. "Mr. Darcy brought you here!" she crouched in front of the animal, "I am so pleased to see you!" she laughed, rubbing him behind his ears.

The animal leaped onto her, his forelegs supported on her shoulders. Elizabeth was sure that he was as happy to see her as she was to see him.

"Stop that!" she giggled, as the dog licked her nose. "No!" she shook her head with a laugh when he lapped at her cheek. "Shall we run?" she asked as she raised herself to her feet.

The dog barked twice, circled her and wagged his tail.

"Then come." she cried and sported first down the lane.

They ran and played for nearly an hour before Elizabeth grew tired and sat under the large tree with her back supported against it.

The dog lay down beside her, his head on her lap.

Her fingers raked absently through his soft fur as she stared at the meadows spreading in front of them.

"I do not even know your name." she said.

The animal's eyes met hers and he licked her hand.

Elizabeth let out a small yawn. "Forgive me. I am sleepy." She yawned again. "The walls at the cottage are so thin, I could not help but to hear the sounds coming from Charlotte's bedroom last night…" she paused, "There are things you do not want to know about your friends… All I could think was what he was doing to her to elicit such… sounds? She sounded so distressed. " she shook her head. "Poor Charlotte. Think that it could be me." she shuddered, "Truly repugnant."

Her fingers combed through his soft fur. "Sometimes I wonder how it is to be with a man." she sighed, "Not with Mr. Collins, of course… Perhaps Jane will tell me something after her honeymoon, though I do doubt it. She can be very secretive about her private matters, and I must respect her wishes on this. I certainly have my reasons not to ask Charlotte after last night. Poor Charlotte. She has to touch him, I suppose, if only a little." Elizabeth twisted her lips in revulsion, "It must be unpleasant to say the least."

The animal nestled his head more comfortably on her lap. Elizabeth responded by stroking his strong back. He had to enjoy her ministrations, because a low rumble escaped him.

"You are purring like a cat." she leaned and kissed the top of his head. "Would you mind if I nap for a little while?" She removed her bonnet, put it aside and laid back on her side. "Will you stay with me?" she murmured as her eyes closed.

When she woke up, the sun was considerably lower in the sky. Mr. Darcy's dog sat beside her, his black eyes resting on her.

"Have I slept long?" she whispered as she rubbed her eyes. "You stayed with me all that time, did you? Good boy."

The animal got up, walked to her straw bonnet abandoned on the grass and pushed it with his head in her direction.

Elizabeth smiled, and shook her head. "Sometimes I think that you understand absolutely everything." She took the bonnet from the ground. "And you glare at me the same as your Master when he is displeased with something." She tugged at the animal's ears gently. "Will you walk me back to the parsonage?" she asked as she secured the blue bow under her chin.

The animal barked and ran forward.

"I am coming, I am coming." Elizabeth said, straightening her skirts.

As they approached the cottage, Elizabeth saw her friend standing on the path leading to the front door.

"Lizzy!" Mrs. Collins cried. "Where have you been for so long? I have been concerned."

"I lost the sense of time." Elizabeth walked to her friend. "Forgive me."

Charlotte pointed to the animal that stood by Elizabeth's skirts. "What is that?"

"A dog."

"I can see that." Mrs. Collins frowned. "Do not tell me it is yours."

"No, of course not. It is Mr. Darcy's dog. He allows me to play with it."

Charlotte leaned down. "He does not look like any dog I have ever seen. What breed is it?"

"I am not sure. Mr. Darcy must have brought him from the north."

"Most likely." Charlotte straightened herself. "Well Lizzy, let us go inside. I have to show you something." she squeezed the other woman's hand. "I am so very excited about it!"

Elizabeth looked at her friend with curious eyes. Charlotte was hardly ever so very enthusiastic about anything.

"Yes, of course." she agreed promptly. "But would it be possible to get some food, or at least water for the dog."

Charlotte looked hesitantly at the animal. "I suppose so… Take him to the kitchen, there still should be some meat left from yesterday. Tell the cook I said to give it to the animal. Mr. Collins has no taste for mutton these days."

Elizabeth grinned. "Thank you. I promise not to take long."

Charlotte gazed at the dog for a moment, her nose wrinkled. "I shall wait for you with tea in the parlour."

Elizabeth took the dog to the back of the house and asked the grumpy cook to prepare what was left from Mr. Collins' meal.

The dog refused to even look at the previous day's mutton. He did not scorn the bowl of fresh water though.

Elizabeth walked him back to the garden. "Now, you must go back to Rosings Park." She petted his back. "Will you meet me tomorrow? In the grove?" she laughed as the dog licked her face. "Stop that." she giggled when his wet nose touched the side of her neck. She took his big head into her hand and pushed him away from her. Her dark green eyes met his black ones. "Remember to bring your Master to me when he comes back from his business in London. I must talk to him. It is very important." She sighed. "I need to apologize to him and give something back to him." She lifted to her feet. "But now go! Go! I am sure they will give you a better meal at Rosings than here."

When Elizabeth returned to Charlotte, she found out that during her absence, Lady Catherine had visited. She had given her friend a bolt of fine muslin for the new dress.

Elizabeth was astonished to see that the material not only had a beautiful warm, peach like colour, but was of fine quality as well. Charlotte was very excited to have a new dress made of it. She very much wanted to have it ready before Easter, which was quite late this year, in the middle of April. There was little time left, only two weeks, but Elizabeth was sure that with the help of the maid, they would manage to finish it on time.

The muslin needed to be washed first, as it was very dusty. Elizabeth guessed it had lain on the bottom of some trunk at Rosings Parks for many years. However, apart from being dirty in places, it was in excellent state.

That same day, the servant washed it, and it was draped in the garden to dry throughout the night.

***

The next few days, Charlotte and Elizabeth worked constantly on the dress, with the exception of the meals. First the muslin needed to be carefully ironed; next Elizabeth took her friend's measurements and made paper patterns based on the dress that Charlotte fancied from the fashion plate in the magazine.

For the third day, she planned the worst part, cutting the material. There could be no mistake, because too much of the cloth might have been wasted, or even the whole gown ruined.

Elizabeth strew the peach colour muslin on the freshly scrubbed floor and pinned the paper forms to the material. She took the scissors and with sure hands, began to cut. Over the years, she had helped her mother make many dresses, and she did not hesitate now.

After some time, she was left alone as Charlotte was called to her duties. When she cut out the front and the back of the dress, she took a short break to have some tea. Refreshed by it, she began to cut the parts of the skirt.

Like this, kneeling on the floor with large scissors in her hand, she was found by Mr. Darcy, who unexpectedly stood into parlour's doorway.

She guessed how surprised he must have been, seeing her like that, but he recovered quickly, and bowed respectfully.

"Miss Bennet."

Elizabeth rose slowly, red faced. "Mr. Darcy." she dropped a curtesy, trying to hide the large scissors behind her back.

"Pray tell me, what are you doing?" he stared down at the floor covered with the peach muslin.

"I am making a dress." she stated simply.

He stared at her incredibly. "By yourself?"

Elizabeth barely contained herself from rolling her eyes.

"As you see." she managed a small smile and lifted her chin higher. It was nothing she should be ashamed of, after all.

She realized that she should not be surprised with his reaction. Most certainly, his sister had never been forced to sew her own dresses. She could afford the best of seamstress.

"Mr. Darcy!" Charlotte ran into the room, followed by the servant who had informed her about the arrival of the guest. Her eyes darted back from the gentleman to her friend, who stood between the folds of peach muslin, still holding the scissors in her hand. "We did not expect you, sir."

"Pray forgive me, Mrs. Collins" Darcy said, his eyes on Elizabeth. "I see that I am interrupting."

"Oh, no!" Charlotte cried out impulsively. Clearly, she did not want to alienate Lady Catherine's nephew. "We were about to take some refreshment, were we not, Lizzy?"

Elizabeth nodded. "Yes, indeed."

"Let us sit in the dining room." Charlotte gestured, indicating the room on the left of the entrance door.

Darcy bowed and made a gesture for Elizabeth to walk first. She sent him a tight smile, and put away the unfortunate scissors, before she walked with a straight back past him.

The dining room, as Charlotte referred to it, could be in truth qualified as a small breakfast room. But Elizabeth liked the simple, white painted room with yellow curtains much more than a formal parlour with its dark wallpaper and heavy furniture.

When they sat, Charlotte rang for tea and engaged her guest in conversation.

"Have you just returned from your trip to London, Mr. Darcy?"

"No, I have not." he looked at Elizabeth again. "I was in London for only one day. I returned three days ago."

Charlotte's forehead creased, and she looked back from Mr. Darcy who stared at her friend, to Elizabeth who had her eyes steadily lowered to her lap.

"I see." Charlotte said. She looked at Elizabeth once again before she stood up abruptly. "Forgive me, Mr. Darcy. I will see to the refreshments."

Darcy raised himself respectfully, and sat again when Charlotte closed the door with quiet click, leaving the couple alone.

A moment passed before Darcy spoke. "I have been walking the grove the past few days, hoping to meet you." He looked agitated. "I was worried you may have been ill."

Elizabeth blushed. "I am well, as you see." She met his eyes. "It was my intention to speak with you, sir, but I was occupied with matters here."

"Yes, the dress, I understand."

"Yes, indeed. Mrs. Collins received the muslin from you aunt. She could not manage to make a dress on her own in such a short time; and I have helped to make many dresses for my sisters."

"I see."

Elizabeth observed his frowned expression. "I understand that you must be surprised with it, sir. I am sure that you sister never needed to sew her own dresses. But you must see that both my and Mrs. Collins' parents' resources have always been limited, so it was expected for us to learn to sew and…"

Darcy shook his head. "No, pray forgive me." he interrupted her. "It was rude and inconsiderate of me. I truly admire your skill. I know that you can sew exceptionally well."

Elizabeth gaped at him in surprise. "You do?"

Darcy glanced at her. "Yes… I admired your handiwork yet at Netherfield. Your…" he cleared his throat, "embroidery."

She frowned in confusion. She could not remember that she had embroidered anything while she nursed Jane at Netherfield.

"I did not know that the gentlemen pay attention to such matters, or even notice them."

Mr. Darcy did not answer, as the maid entered, bringing tea and biscuits.

"Mrs. Collins apologizes, but she has been detained with urgent matters in the kitchen." the young girl said, put the silver tray down, the very best Charlotte possessed, and left the room hastily.

Elizabeth flushed in embarrassment at her friend's obvious matchmaking scheme. She glanced at Darcy, but he seemed not to notice anything.

She stood up and occupied herself with preparing tea, making a lot of unnecessary clatter with the china.

"Milk?" she asked.

Darcy nodded.

"Sugar?"

Another nod.

When his tea was ready, she walked around the table to him. He took the cup from her with one hand and put it aside. His fingers wrapped around her wrist and he stared steadily at her face.

Elizabeth stood next to his chair, her eyes downcast, her hand in his. She raised her eyes slowly.

"I wanted to apologize…" she sighed, "to you… that I believed Mr. Wickham."

He shook his head. "No… there is nothing to apologize for." He stood up and pulled her closer, "Wickham is a charming cad, and you have a tender heart." He made a move with his hand as if he wanted to touch her face, but then he brought his fist to his mouth and only stared at her.

She smiled. "Thank you." She removed her hand from his, and walked back to her seat.

Elizabeth drank her tea, and from behind her eyelashes observed as Mr. Darcy did the same.

A moment passed before she gathered her courage again and spoke. "There is one more matter that we have to settle, sir."

Darcy looked at her, worry in his eyes. "There is?"

"Yes." she nodded. "You must know what I am talking about."

He stared at her with heavy frown.

"Your gift." she probed. "The medallion you enfolded in the letter. I cannot possibly accept it."

His expression softened. "Why not?"

"Sir… I think I do not have to explain it to you. You are a reasonable man. I understand that you were grateful because I helped your dog, and perhaps on the spur of the moment gifted me with this beautiful piece. I do appreciate it, but I feel I need to return it to you. I thought I would not have the opportunity until my sister's wedding in a May, but I am happy that it can be accomplished now. If you allow it, I will go to my room now and…"

Darcy shook his head, "Do you like it?"

"Yes, very much." she admitted.

"Then, please keep it."

"I cannot." she said firmly as she stood up. "You are not my brother, or a relative, and it is highly impropriate for me to receive anything from you."

He stood as well and walked to her, blocking her view. "Would you accept it, were you promised to me?"

Elizabeth's soft mouth fell open. " I…." she swallowed.

He lifted his hand, and with his fingertips, touched the puckered surface of her lower lip. "Would you?"

Elizabeth felt herself getting dizzy from his nearness, scent and touch. "Yes, I would but…"

His eyes bore into hers and he murmured. "So please keep the medallion for now, and give me some time to make it happen."

Elizabeth went red and silent. She was afraid to open her mouth. Did he mean what she thought he meant, or was she imagining things?

"How is your dog?" she changed the subject, as she stepped away from his and sat on her chair.

"My dog?"

"Yes." she nodded eagerly. "Did you bring him with you today? I missed him for the last days."

Darcy slowly returned to his seat. "Oh, no. I needed to send him away for now."

"Away?"

"Yes, at home in Cumbria."

"Cumbria?" Elizabeth's eyebrows raised high on her forehead. "I knew that your are from north of the country, but I did not expect that you live so far away."

"Yes, large part of my lands are virtually across and on the other side of the Scottish border. It is beautiful there, if somehow desolated. But I do like it."

"Of course." she took a sip of her tea. "I wonder what breed he is? I have never seen such a dog."

Darcy smirked. "To be precise he is not a dog, but a full blood wolf."

Elizabeth gaped at him. "I have thought that the wolves in England were gone many centuries ago."

"No, there are still a few families… I mean packs, but only in the far north of the country and in Scotland."

"Still, he cannot be a wild animal, he was so gentle when I played with him."

Darcy smiled broadly. "He is accustomed to people, but he has to like you a lot if he let you touch him."

"What is his name?"

He looked at her. "Who?"

She frowned. "Your dog of course."

"Oh…" he paused as if surprised. "He has not got a name."

"He has not got a name?" Elizabeth parroted.

"I have never thought to give him one."

"How do you call him then?"

Darcy shrugged. "I do not have to call him anything. He knows when I need him."

"That is unusual."

He smiled again. "Yes, it is."

Elizabeth stared at her companion for a moment in open confusion.

"Your tea is getting cold, sir." she said, as she took a sip of her own.

Chapter Five

"Lizzy," Mrs. Collins said as she walked into the parlour. "I want you to go out today, take some fresh air. You have helped me enough. I feel guilty that I involved you so much into this dressmaking business. You should be a guest here, and not sit all day long labouring needle in your hand."

"Charlotte." Elizabeth glanced up at her friend from her sewing. "I enjoy helping you. I am pleased that you will have such an elegant dress."

"No, no." Mrs. Collins stepped to her friend and took the folds of peach muslin away from Elizabeth's lap. "You must go for a walk today. I am sure Mr. Darcy is at his wit's end, waiting for you in the grove every day in vain."

A light blush graced Elizabeth's countenance. "I am not sure I comprehend your meaning, Charlotte." she said, staring at her hands, placed primly on her lap.

"Oh, I think you do." Charlotte sat opposite her, sewing basket in her hand. "Sometimes I think that you tease and torture the poor man on purpose, staying all these days indoors, and refusing to meet him."

"That is not the truth! I only wanted to help you with the dress." Elizabeth cried, and then she added quietly after a moment. "Though, I must admit I needed some time to think … away from his company."

"I see." Charlotte looked at her friend with perceptive eyes. "Let me only tell you that I think that Mr. Darcy seems to be very much interested in you. It would be unwise to discourage him."

"I do not intend to discourage him." Elizabeth assured. "Still, I feel a bit scared."

"Scared?"

Elizabeth's forehead creased. "Perhaps not scared but concerned," she nodded. "Yes, concerned about my own feelings for him. I believe I have started to like him," she bit her lower lip. "A lot."

Charlotte leaned to her and spoke in a lowered voice. "Elizabeth, it is in your best interest to learn to like him. A smart woman falls for a man who is rich, influential and deeply in love with her, for her own good."

Elizabeth said nothing to that, just looked out of the window.

"Now, Lizzy." Mrs. Collins said. "No excuses. Run to your room, take your bonnet and gloves, and go to him."

A small smile curved Elizabeth's lips. She stood up, put a light peck on her friend's cheek and dashed out of the room.

She darted the short way to the grove, the anticipation mixed with apprehension whether she would meet him there, hastening her pace.

She stopped and her hand went to her chest to ease its flutter. Mr. Darcy was there, his fine, tall figure visible from far away. He stood with his back to her, hat in his hand, one heavily muscled leg stepped forward.

Elizabeth padded in his direction, careful where to put her feet, mindful not to make a noise by stepping on some dry twig.

"You came." He turned to her, his voice rich and joyful. "At last."

Her breath caught in her throat, her eyes widened. "You heard me coming?"

"I have very keen senses." He stepped to her with a broad smile. "You came. I waited and waited every single day." His expression clouded. "I feared you avoided me for some reason."

Elizabeth shook her head with a smile, her eyes downcast. "I was occupied finishing the dress." she whispered.

"Is it done?" he snapped.

"No…" her eyes lifted at him, "But I stitched the most difficult parts. I trust that Charlotte can finish it now on her own with the help of the maid."

"I am glad to hear it. I know how devoted a friend you are, and I admire you for it, but I do not like when something keeps me away from your company."

Elizabeth frowned. "My friends are very dear to me."

"I am well aware of your kind heart." he said in warm voice. "I am only jealous of time you have spent with the others, and not with me."

The blush on Elizabeth's face deepened and she averted her eyes, her gloved hands clenched in front her.

For a moment, she could only hear his quickened breathing. "Did I say too much?"

"No… it is just…" she looked straight into his eyes. "I am not sure what to expect from you, sir."

He closed his eyes. "I am a fool." he muttered, and then took her hands into his and pulled her closer. "I love you." he announced. "Will you marry me?"

Elizabeth blinked her eyes repeatedly and she stared at his determined expression. His proposal was so very forward and direct, entirely bare from compliments and the kind of pleasantries expected in such a situation; and she did not know how to respond.

He stepped a bit closer, so their bodies touched lightly, and spoke in a fervent whisper. "Almost from the beginning of our acquaintance, I have felt the deepest admiration and regard for you. I…"

Elizabeth frowned and stiffened.

"What is the matter?" he enquired gently.

"I find it hard to believe your words, sir." she said, not caring that her voice sounded cold. "You barely tolerated my company when we first met. You refused to dance with me when at the Meryton Assembly, and later you ignored me. And after Netherfield ball, you left so suddenly…"

"No, no." he whispered. His hand touched her cheek, before sliding down to her neck and finally coming to rest on her arm. "It was not like you think… I fought this, what I felt for you, I thought you deserved better… that I should not involve you into my life which is… complicated." he said the last words slowly, with hesitation, and then added with a new found energy. "However, when we met again here in Kent, purely by accident, I thought that fate had decided for us, and that it is our destiny to be together."

Elizabeth needed to digest what he told her for a moment, before she asked warily. "You say your life is complicated… what do you mean by this?"

He strode away from her, his hand raking through his pitch black, straight, as usual dishevelled hair.

"I meant only that you are so lively, and you like company so much… while my life, and the life of my closest family is and always has been very quiet, and even solitary. I believe that

Pemberley is the most beautiful place in all the country, and if it was my choice, I would never leave it but… It is so far away from people. I have mentioned before that we have no immediate neighbours, and the closest town is twenty miles away. I was afraid that you would be unhappy so far away from your family and friends and the society."

"I have never thought about living so far away from Hertfordshire." she admitted quietly.

"You see yourself." he cried, walking back to her. "You do understand my hesitation back then. But now…" he swallowed, "Would you consider moving to the far north… with me, as my wife?"

"I am not sure. It depends..." she whispered.

He leaned to her and spoke above her ear, the tone of his deep voice giving her pleasant shivers, running down her spine. "I shall adore you. Say yes."

Strong arm wrapped around her and his face buried into her throat. The dizziness overpowered her. His scent, his nearness, his touch, all made it difficult for her to keep her composure. She felt boneless, as if her legs refused to support her. She stared at the sky above his wide shoulder, her vision unfocused.

Elizabeth gathered all her internal strength and stepped away from his embrace. "I cannot possibly answer now." she said in all seriousness. "I do not know you well enough to decide now. Marriage is the most important decision in woman's life. It should not be taken lightly."

Darcy searched her face for a moment before he gave a slight nod of his head. "I cannot argue with your reasoning. Would you agree to an official courtship then? I will ask your father for permission at the first opportunity."

Elizabeth lowered her eyes to the ground, and said in a quiet but clear voice. "I do." She raised her eyes at him. "You may ask my father for permission to court me."

He broke into a wide smile, and before she knew it, she was in his arms, lifted up, her feet dangling above the ground.

"Put me down!" she squeaked, laughing.

He twirled her around, before putting her gently to the ground and kissing her smiling lips noisily. The kiss was short, no more than an innocent peck.

As he leaned, his nose touched the side of her neck which produced a giggle on her part. She pushed from him to look into his face. "Your dog, I mean your wolf, did the same once."

He grinned. "He did?"

She smiled with a nod. "Yes, every time I met him, he sniffed me, only his nose is always wet."

Darcy's face stretched in a toothy smile. One of his hands wrapped around her waist, keeping her to him, while the other touched her rounded cheek with the pads of his fingers.

His hand moved down and found the delicate gold chain resting across her collar bone. "You have never wore this before." He pulled at the medallion which was safely tucked behind her spenser and inside the low cut bodice of her dress.

She searched his eyes, "Do you think I should not?"

The arm around her tightened. She responded by placing her hands on the hard planes of his chest. "I want you to wear it."

Elizabeth took the medallion from him and turned it in her hand. "What is written in here?" her eyes pointed to the inscription.

"I am not sure. I know only that this inscription was copied from one of the large stones founded at Pemberley's grounds. These are runes, the Vikings used them before Norman conquest."

She nodded. "I thought as much. It is a shame we cannot read them."

Darcy took the medallion from her hand and put it back into the opening of her spenser.

"Shall we walk?" he offered her his arm.

Elizabeth accepted it with a smile. They strode for a while in silence before she spoke. "I think it unfair that you have not given a name to your dog."

Darcy stopped and glanced down at her. "You do?"

"How can I play with him, when he has not got a name I could call him by?"

He smiled. "Do you want to play with him in the future?"

"Can I not?"

In response he took her hand from his arm and kissed it.

"Can I think about name for him?" she asked when they resumed they walk.

He seemed to hesitate, but agreed. "If you want to."

"I have one more question."

"Yes." she thought to hear the worry in his voice.

"How did you know that it was I who stitched your wolf?"

"Oh…" he hesitated. "I was worried when I noticed that he did not return to Netherfield for the night so I sent the servant to look for him. He saw you playing with the wolf one night when both you an your sister had stayed at Netherfield, so he thought to look for him at Longbourn. He noticed you leaving the stable late in the evening, then found the wolf, and rightly assumed it was you who helped him."

"Do you know the other dog who attacked him?" Elizabeth asked, her eyes wide. "He looked like a wolf as well, only his colouring was lighter."

"I do not think it is possible that it was a wolf, my dear." Darcy said slowly.

"Perhaps… I saw the other dog for a very short time."

"My wolf tends to fight very often. Still, I think that the other dog must have provoked him."

"Oh, I am sure that he was provoked. Such a gentle animal could not possibly start the fight without a good reason." Elizabeth said with great conviction.

Darcy smiled at her defence, and they resumed their walk.

"There is one more thing." she said after a while.

Darcy sighed and stopped again. "Yes."

"I asked Mr. Bingley about your wolf the next morning after I met him the first time. I described how he looked, but he very decidedly said to me that he kept no such dog at Netherfield, and I must have dreamt it all."

"I think I can explain that. As you know, my wolf is not a threatening to people, but still, keeping a wolf as a pet may seem to be unusual and even frightening to many people, even if he is domesticated. I believe that Bingley did not want to alienate his new neighbours. He did not want me to bring the wolf in the first place."

"Well, I am happy that you did, sir. Your wolf is adorable."

He looked at her in astonishment and then chuckled. "And this is your opinion of him?"

"Oh, yes. I cannot wait to meet him again."

"You will one day, I promise." he said, brushing the wisps of hair from her face.

***

Elizabeth was about to leave Hunsford to pursue her walk, when Mr. Darcy called. She was surprised to see him. When they parted the day before, she had assumed that they would meet again in the grove as they had done every day.

"I have not expected you to call, sir." she said when they were left alone in the parlour. "I am afraid that you found me all alone. Mr. and Mrs. Collins have gone to the village."

"I needed to speak to you without delay." he said without preamble. "I am leaving for London today and then to the north. My carriage is waiting outside."

Her eyes widened. "Has something happened?"

"Nothing unusual, but I must go. Some matters in the north demand my immediate attention. " He stepped to her. "It is not my wish to part with you though."

Elizabeth smiled bravely. "I only remain here a week longer. Jane's wedding is in only three weeks, so I must return as well."

He cupped her face between his hands. "We will meet in Hertfordshire, then." he kissed her lips chastely as his thumbs stroked her cheeks.

***

"Lizzy, Mary, Kitty, Lydia!"Mrs. Bennet shrieked through the halls of Longbourn. "Where are those girls when I need them? There is so much to be done yet before the wedding! Oh, my poor nerves!"

Elizabeth crept down the staircase and sprinted towards the back door, thankfully not noticed by anyone. Minutes later she was on the path leading to Oakham Mount.

Only three days were left before Jane's wedding, and their mother found herself in a state of utmost anxiety. Kitty and Lydia used every opportunity to escape to Meryton to visit Aunt Philips or the wife of Colonel Forster; even Mary accompanied them, though it was not her usual habit. Mr. Bennet closed himself in the library, refusing to take part in all that bedlam, as he referred to the wedding preparations of his eldest daughter.

Mr. Darcy had not come back from the north yet. Elizabeth had tried to learn something about his prolonged absence from Mr. Bingley, but he had dismissed her concerns, ensuring her that his friend would come in time.

As she stood at the top of the gentle hill, she saw a rider on a black horse, moving at great speed.

She shielded her eyes with her hand from the sun, and soon her face broke into wide smile. Her legs brought her down to the road, where she stood, hoping the approaching rider to notice her.

Her heart stopped in her chest as the horse came to a halt and the man dismounted in one smooth, well practiced movement. Covered with the road dust, Darcy approached her with great haste, but did not make a move to touch her or speak to her. He only looked down at her with an uncertain, shy half smile.

Elizabeth had no such qualms. She stepped close, so their bodies touched lightly. "I thought that you all but forgot about me." she said straight from the heart. Then she lifted on her toes and kissed his cheek.

He sighed, smiled and pulled her to him, his hands resting gently around her. "Please, forgive me." He tucked the wisp of her blond hair which escaped her coiffure behind her ear. "I thought about you every single day." he murmured against her temple.

Elizabeth stared at him happily. "I hope that all matters were resolved to your satisfaction."

"Yes." His arm wrapped around her, as he took the reins of the horse with his other hand. "I can stay in the south for another five to six weeks before I will have to go back to the north again to attend business there."

Darcy started to walk, with Elizabeth tucked tightly to his side, and his horse following closely behind them. "Will you walk with me to Netherfield?"

"Yes, but I think we should go across the fields." Elizabeth said as she looked around them.

Darcy glanced at her. "Good point. I do not want any blemish on your reputation because of me."

They were just approaching Netherfield Park, when Elizabeth stopped and turned to him. "Mr. Bingley is invited to dine with us tonight."

"You suggest I should accompany him?"

Elizabeth nodded, biting her lip. "I understand that you may be tired after the strenuous journey…"

"No." he interrupted her. "I am not tired. Are you sure Mrs. Bennet will not think it an imposition?"

She shook her head. "Of course not. You are Mr. Bingley's friend, after all. That is enough of a recommendation for her."

Darcy took a step forward. "Do you think I will have the opportunity to talk with your father tonight?"

She frowned. “About what?”

Darcy paled. “You know… about… about…” he stammered, searching her eyes frantically.

“I am not sure of your meaning, sir.” she said, her eyes downcast.

A small smile started to shape her lips, as she kept peeking at him from behind her dark eyelashes.

An audible sigh escaped him. “You are teasing me.” He was obviously relieved.

Elizabeth smiled at him openly, her eyes sparkling.

“Do not ever do that.” Darcy growled, his fingers clasping her arms. “You can tease me about anything.” he shook her gently. “Anything, but not about that…”

She raised her finely shaped eyebrow. “That?”

“Yes, that.” he said, as he lifted her up against his hard frame, so their faces were at the same level, his lips catching hers in a lingering kiss.

Elizabeth laughed against his lips and pushed at his chest.

“I will tell Papa you wish to speak to him.” she cried as she ran down the hill.

Chapter Six

"What did you and Mr. Bennet discuss for so long in the library after the dinner?" Bingley asked when the two friends got into the carriage.

Darcy looked over at the younger man and said after a moment, "I asked for his permission to court his daughter."

Bingley's sandy eyebrows arched. "Which one?"

"Bingley, do not ask such nonsensical questions!" Darcy snapped. "I think it is obvious."

"Miss Elizabeth." Bingley leaned into his seat. "I should have guessed you are somehow inclined to her. After all, she was the only lady that you danced with at the ball, and what is more important, appeared to her in your other form."

"Mr. Bennet gave me his consent." Darcy noted.

"Well, well." Bingley stared at his friend. "I presume that first you needed to gain her consent."

"Of course." The other man replied smugly.

"And pray tell me, how she reacted to the news about your… let us say, second nature?"

Darcy kept silent, and looked out of the window in the darkness of the night.

"You did tell her…" Bingley said slowly.

"No."

"But you do intend to tell her… Am I correct?"

Darcy shrugged. "Eventually."

"When?"

"In due time."

Bingley's eyes narrowed. "I see, you want to deceive her!" he accused.

"Bingley, it is not your business." Darcy murmured.

"On the contrary!" Bingley cried with much feeling. "She will be my sister in three days. Miss Elizabeth's unhappiness equals my Jane's suffering. You must know how close they are."

Darcy turned to him and looked straight into his face. "My only wish is to make Elizabeth happy. I will do everything in my power to achieve that."

"If you want her happiness, you need to be sincere with her from the very beginning."

"I cannot believe that you were so sincere with Miss Bennet." Darcy cried sharply. "Did you tell her about your out of wedlock daughter?"

Bingley straightened himself. "Yes, I did. She understood and forgave me. She wants to take the girl from my Aunt, and let her live with us."

"Elizabeth is right that her sister is too good, too good for you, Bingley." Darcy noted. "You are lucky to have her."

"Jane is good and kind, but I am not sure whether she would be so forgiving if she found out about my past after the wedding, or from someone else."

"I did not father a child with another woman." Darcy made his point.

"No, you did not, but you do change into a wolf a few nights every week." Bingley said with mock expression. "Do you think she will not notice this common occurrence?"

Darcy gave him a stormy look. "I can control myself for as long as necessary. She will not notice anything."

"Do you really believe that? Darcy, come down to earth! Miss Elizabeth is very perceptive. I cannot imagine her reaction when she learns that you deceived her on purpose."

"I will explain everything to her at the right time."

"Before of after she runs away from you screaming?"

Darcy's face clenched his fist. "Bingley, just mind your own business." He snapped, losing his patience. "Do not dare tell Elizabeth anything! It will be the end of our friendship."

"As you wish, but you are making a mistake keeping it from her." Bingley shifted away to the window. "You will regret it, mind my words."

***

"Lizzy, please give me another cushion." Mrs. Bennet pointed with her hand to the bed. "No, no, the smaller one."

Elizabeth brought the pillow and put it behind her mother's back.

"Thank you, dear." Mrs. Bennet sighed, arranging herself more comfortably on the settee. "I am so exhausted that I can barely speak." she said slowly, her eyes half closed. "The last weeks kept me on my feet all day long. The preparations to your sister's wedding tired me down so much that I can hardly think sensible anymore."

Elizabeth returned to her chair and picked up her book. "You must be pleased, Mama, with the result though. All went so well, the ceremony itself and the wedding breakfast." She looked over her book at her mother with a small smile. "I heard Aunt Philips saying that Jane's reception was incomparably more elegant than Charlotte's in every respect."

Mrs. Bennet pursed her lips. "But of course it was much more elegant, after all, Mr. Bingley is not some mere parson as Mr. Collins, and our Jane is at least ten times more beautiful than Charlotte Collins. I doubt anyone can argue that it was one of the finest wedding receptions in the neighbourhood in years."

Jane looked so beautiful." Elizabeth noted with a smile.

Mrs. Bennet's eyes lighted. "Mr. Bingley could not take his eyes from her."

There was a knock at the door, and the servant entered.

"Mr. Bennet asks that Miss Elizabeth go downstairs." the maid said. "Mr. Darcy has come to call on her."

Mrs. Bennet's eyes bulged. "Mr. Darcy?" she said, "To call on Lizzy? Are you sure? Our Elizabeth?"

The maid nodded. "Yes, Mistress. He awaits in the drawing room."

"Oh, Lizzy, what is the meaning of this?" Mrs. Bennet cried when the maid left the room.

Elizabeth sighed, knowing the time had come to inform her mother about the nature of Mr. Darcy's interest in her.

She sat beside her mother and spoke in a calm voice. "I should have told you earlier, Mama, but so much has been happening lately due to Jane's wedding." She took a deep breath and continued. "When I visited Charlotte in Kent, I met Mr. Darcy there. He stayed with his aunt at Rosings Park for several weeks. We spent some time together, he called several times on me at the parsonage… and eventually asked whether he could court me officially. He has already spoken with Papa about it, before Jane's wedding, and was granted consent."

Elizabeth looked at her mother, waiting for her reaction to the news. Mrs. Bennet stared at her second daughter in mute amazement for several moments.

Elizabeth's forehead creased with concern. "Mama?"

Mrs. Bennet blinked her eyes a few times.

What came next was an outburst of joy on the older woman's part.

"Mr. Darcy!" she shrieked, and Elizabeth was sure that it was heard in the entire house. "Such a rich man! I heard that he has at least ten thousand a year! Ten thousand a year! My Lord! Dearest Lizzy, I knew, I always knew that you were not so bookish and intelligent for nothing! What a grand lady you shall be! What carriages, jewels, gowns! Oh, and all that pin money!"

Elizabeth closed her eyes in mortification. "Mama, there is no talk about me being Mrs. Darcy. We are not even engaged. He only wants for us to get acquainted a bit better."

"Acquainted! Do not be stupid, child!" Mrs. Bennet snorted. "He is a serious man. He would not have gone to your father if he did not have marriage in his mind."

"Mama, we, I mean Mr. Darcy and I, want to take things slowly." Elizabeth said with quiet determination. "Please promise me, Mama, you will not try to push Mr. Darcy into anything he is not ready for."

"Do not fret, my child." Mrs. Bennet patted her daughter's rosy cheek. "You proved that I can trust you by catching him in the first place. Now I know why you refused Mr. Collins! You must have known Mr. Darcy admires you. My clever, clever girl! But why so secretive; not speaking a word to your dear Mama about having such a suitor?"

Elizabeth stared at her mother's beaming face. "I should not allow him to wait." she said with a heavy sigh.

"Oh, yes, yes, Lizzy. You must go. But first go to your room, and change into another dress. Perhaps the pale yellow one, it is cut lower than the one you are wearing now."

"Mama!" Elizabeth cried sharply, blushing to the roots of her hair.

"Oh, do not be silly, girl!" Mrs. Bennet exclaimed. "With no dowry to speak of, you have to recommend yourself somehow to the gentleman."

"Mama, I will not change. The dress I am wearing is perfectly suitable."

"Nonsense!" Mrs. Bennet took her arm and pulled her to the door. "Let us see whether the yellow dress is freshly pressed."

A quarter of an hour later, Elizabeth with more than usually heightened colour, entered the drawing room. Her mother had not allowed her to go downstairs till she had changed into the yellow dress, which indeed had a rather daring décolleté neckline. Elizabeth wanted to wrap a shawl over her arms, but her mother would have nothing of that.

She closed the door and supported herself against its frame, thankful that her mother did not accompany her.

"My dear." she heard a warm voice beside her. "Is something wrong?"

As she lifted her eyes, she met his concerned gaze, and stepped into his arms with a sigh.

"What is the matter?" he crooned, stroking her back.

"I told my mother about you."

"And?"

She glanced up at him. "Have you not heard her raptures from upstairs?"

He squeezed her closer to him. "I gathered that Mrs. Bennet is pleased with the news."

Elizabeth covered her face with her hands. "It is so humiliating." she murmured. "I am sorry I have kept you waiting. She made me change into another dress."

Darcy took her hand and twirled her in front of him.

"A very fetching gown indeed." he pulled her back to him. "You look very lovely." he kissed her cheek.

"Thank you." Elizabeth stepped from him, and gestured to the sofa. "Shall I ring for some refreshment, sir?"

Darcy sat in the appointed place and smiled. Before she could react and stop him, she was pulled decidedly onto his lap. "I do not want tea. I want to have a few moments with you, without interruption."

"I wonder what my father would say, should he find us like this?" Elizabeth said, trying to give her voice a serious tone, and at the same time attempting to remove his hands from her and rise from his knees.

His arms only tightened around her. "He would order me to obtain a special license and marry you by the end of the week; a possibility I very much look forward to."

Elizabeth frowned and stiffened. "We have already talked about this. I am not ready yet to make such a commitment to you."

"I know. I know." he sighed, burying his face into the side of her neck. "Let me only hold you for a moment. I could barely have a word with you in the last few days."

She relaxed into his arms, and her fingers combed through his pitch dark hair. "I love your hands, so soft." he murmured, rubbing his nose against her collarbone.

His nearness was affecting her. Elizabeth bit her lower lip, closed her eyes for a short moment, and shuddered.

"I shall call for tea." she whispered as she slipped from his lap.

When the tea arrived, and they both busied themselves with their cups, Elizabeth asked, "And how are the newlyweds?"

Darcy shrugged. "I hardly know. I breakfast alone, and take dinners in my room. For the last two days, I managed to spend the entire day in the library or on horseback. I gathered that they deserve time for themselves now, it is their honeymoon, after all."

"Jane mentioned you proposed to move yourself to the inn after the wedding."

"Yes, but Bingley scolded me for that. I try to be invisible though."

"That is very thoughtful of you."

Darcy put his tea away, took her hand, and invited her to sit beside him. "I should go to London soon. I have not seen my sister for nearly two months."

"Of course, I understand."

"I cannot bring her here because of Wickham, still I want both of you to meet. Could you come to London for a week or so? Do you think it possible?"

Elizabeth nodded. "Yes, I think it is. I will talk with my mother yet today. We will have to write to my Uncle, and ask whether he would agree to host us for a few days."

Darcy lifted her hand to his lips. "Thank you."

Elizabeth smiled at him, and then her face lit up. "Have you brought your wolf?"

"No, he stayed in the north."

Her expression dropped. "Tis a shame. I have missed him very much."

He frowned. "More than me?"

"Well, he is excellent company, sir." she glanced up at him from behind her long eyelashes. "So sociable and amiable, always ready to play with me."

Darcy shook his head. "I do not know how I could fall in love with such a teasing creature." he pulled her to him, back on his lap.

"Let me go." she whispered, as she fought with the shuddering sensation which his warm kisses on her neck created . "Papa may enter at any time… My sisters should be due back from their walk to Meryton any minute."

Darcy sighed, but allowed her to return to the chair opposite him. "One day you will have no escape or excuse from me." he said, as he reached for his tea.

***

Georgiana Darcy stood by the window in the Darcy townhouse in London, twisting the lacy curtain in her fingers. At last she was to meet Fitzwilliam's future wife. Her brother had told her so much about Miss Elizabeth in his letters. She sounded very lovely. The fact that she was a full blooded human was a great advantage in the girl's eyes. Though Georgiana did not resent what her family was, she often felt alienated among the pack, as she did not undergo the usual werewolves change. Her intimidating, broody brother was always so preoccupied with his responsibilities. She was sure of his love and concern for her, but with no female friends around, she was lonely. Now she would have a companion, someone with whom, in time, she would be able to share all her secrets and worries.

She watched as her brother's carriage stopped in front of the house. Fitzwilliam got out first, and handed down two ladies. She assumed that the older woman, who entered the house first, had to be Miss Bennet's mother. Her eyes were round and her mouth agape as she stepped on the stairs leading to the main entrance.

Georgiana smoothed her skirt, and sat on edge of the sofa, her back straight, as she waited for the guests.

A few moments passed, the door opened, and the company entered. She tried not to stare at the guests, but found it hard to take her eyes away from her future sister.

Miss Bennet was rather short, and she looked almost too small against her brother's tall frame. At first, Georgiana was a bit disappointed with her outer appearance. Her brother was very handsome, and she had always thought that he would choose to marry a woman of great beauty. The young lady in front of her, though rather pretty, was not strikingly beautiful.

As always when nervous, Georgiana found herself tongue tied, and no topic came to her head.

Miss Bennet seemed to understand her predicament, as she moved closer to her on the sofa where they both sat and spoke in a warm voice. "I have heard that you are great musician, Miss Darcy."

"I am not so sure of that. Brother takes me to concerts when he is in town, and I know that my playing is far inferior to what you can hear from professional musicians. But I do love music, and I love to learn to play new sheets."

"I can only admire your resolve." Miss Bennet kept smiling at her. "I never bothered to practice enough to be fairly proficient."

As the other woman spoke, Georgiana thought that her first impression of her brother's intended had been very much mistaken. Miss Elizabeth was very pretty, her dark eyes sparkling when she looked at her, her rounded cheeks graced with charming dimples when she smiled.

"Would you like to accompany me on my walk tomorrow?" she blurted, before she could consider her proposition.

Miss Bennet smiled widely again, showing the row of small, white teeth. "With pleasure." Her hand covered Georgiana's and squeezed it. "We will have more intimacy to speak freely. I wish to know you better."

***

After Mr. Darcy escorted Elizabeth and Mrs. Bennet back to the Gracechurch Street, they were unexpectedly given a few moments of privacy.

"You can say goodbye to Mr. Darcy now, Lizzy." Mrs. Bennet said, and without a second look at her daughter and the man beside her, she entered her brother's house, leaving the couple alone in front of it.

Elizabeth stepped as closely to him as propriety would allow.

"You never told me that your sister is so beautiful."

Darcy presented a proud smile. "Yes, she is. Even as a child, she was as pretty as a picture. Sometimes I would prefer for her own good to be less… attractive. I do not like when strange men gape at her on the street.'"

"She has not much confidence about herself though." Elizabeth noticed. "As if she was not aware of her own beauty."

"Like Mrs. Bingley?" Darcy prompted.

Elizabeth nodded. "Yes, indeed. They seem to be quite similar in that respect. Well, Georgiana and I have plans for tomorrow. We agreed that I will accompany her on her walk in the park."

Darcy's face lightened. "I shall see you tomorrow then."

She bit on her lower lip. "I would prefer to be alone with her. I want to know her better, and I doubt she would open to me with you hovering around."

Darcy made a pouting face.

"Oh, do not do that!" Elizabeth scolded him quietly. "Your sister deserves to better know the woman you will marry one day."

"Ah!" she exclaimed in a soft voice, as he pushed her back inside the carriage

"What are you thinking!" she cried angrily against his seeking lips. "We are in the middle of the street! Surely all my uncle's neighbours are observing us from the windows."

Darcy's arms only tightened around her. "You have just said that you will be my wife." he grinned.

She rolled her eyes, and sighed with exasperation. "If you will not let me free, I can very well change my mind."

He moved from her with obvious reluctance, his hands still lingering on her waist.

"You are insufferable." she announced sternly, as they were again outside the carriage.

His expression darkened and he pressed his lips together. "Sometimes I think you do not care for me at all."

"You cannot be serious saying this. Had I not cared for you, I would have never agreed to allow you to talk with my father." she reasoned.

Darcy stared at her for a moment with frown. "I do not see the reason why we should wait so long before getting married." he murmured.

"I have explained it to you." she said in gentler voice. "We must have time to know each other better."

He looked straight into her eyes. "I do not need any more time."

Elizabeth's eyes narrowed. "But I do need it. Perhaps you should reconsider your proposal, and find yourself someone more accommodating."

She did not wait for his response, only turned on her feet and entered her uncle's house.

Chapter Seven

My dearest, loveliest Elizabeth,

I must start by saying to you again how it burdens me that we have parted on such bad terms. I cannot bear to think that I left you angry and disappointed with me. I torture myself with the look on your face when you left me alone on your uncle's doorstep...

Her eyes lifted from the letter, written in tight, strong handwriting, and rested at the landscape spreading in front of her from Oakham Mount.

Mr. Darcy had needed to depart north the very next day after her visit at his townhouse and meeting his sister. There had been no opportunity then to talk about their last conversation. He wrote to her almost every other day, in each letter apologizing, and telling her how he missed her.

Elizabeth sighed. She could not understand why he was so impatient, and always wanted more than she felt ready to give him. At the same time, she harboured not a little guilt about what she had said to him when last they met. She knew that in the future, she must show more patience and consideration for his feelings.

Still, there was a little shadow, a small doubt in the corner of her heart, which prevented her from giving herself to him entirely. She could not fight the feeling that there was something missing, that something was wrong.

Again, some urgent business had called him back to the north. He travelled there so often, and almost always against his previously laid plans. He never bothered to explain to her the exact nature of his duties in the north. Even in his letters, he wrote only how he longed for her, and counted days to their reunion. He never shared with her any details of his life. She knew many landlords in person, her father was one, after all, and she was well aware of their responsibilities to their estates and tenants. Still, none of them was at the beck and call so often as Mr. Darcy.

She sighed again and folded his last letter, slipping it carefully back into the hidden pocket of her dress. As she walked down the hill, she decided she did not want to return home yet. Perhaps visiting Jane, and a private talk with her elder sister, would help to clear her mind and settle her heart.

She was taking the shortest path to Netherfield, when she heard a male voice calling her name.

"Miss Elizabeth!"

Mr. Wickham was approaching her quickly from the other side of the pasture. He must have seen her walking from the main road to Meryton.

Elizabeth frowned, and hastened her pace. Darcy had stressed many times that she should avoid Mr. Wickham, as he was not the gentlemen he appeared to be. What honourable man would have attempted to seduce and force into marriage a fifteen year-old girl?

"Miss Elizabeth! Please wait!" he called again, this time his voice much closer and stronger.

Elizabeth forced herself to stop. She turned to the man with a cool expression on her face.

Wickham bowed deeply in front of her. "Are you trying to avoid me, Miss Elizabeth?"

She barely returned his polite greeting with only the slightest nod of her head. "Excuse me, sir." she said, unsmiling. "I am in a hurry. I promised to pay a visit to my sister, Mrs. Bingley."

"May I accompany you to Netherfield then?" he asked, his voice light and pleasant.

"No. I thank you." She lifted her chin high and turned on her feet, with the full intention of walking away and leaving the man alone in the middle of the pasture.

She did not walk even a step farther when she felt a steely hand wrap around her arm.

Her eyes went from Wickham's hand on her arm to his face. "Let me go, sir." she said, her voice clear and even.

"What happened, Miss Elizabeth?" he pulled her closer. "Why so high minded? You were much nicer to me in the past."

She tried to wrench her arm away, but he held it tight. "Let me go." she narrowed her eyes. "I will not talk to you."

He laughed. "You will not?"

"No. You do not even deserve to be admitted into society, among decent people. You should thank your good fortune every day that Mr. Darcy did not reveal your misdeeds to the world."

The clasp around her arm grew stronger. "My misdeeds?" he hissed. "What about his? Did he tell you who he really was?"

Her eyes narrowed. "I will not listen to any lies about Mr. Darcy." she spat out. "Let me go now, and I will not tell him that you bothered me."

"So tis the truth…" Wickham took a step closer, "The rumour that he courts you." He searched her face. "He is after you." His free hand grasped her other arm, and he brought her closer to his body.

"I said to let me go!" She wiggled her body in his embrace, her stomach tightening in fear. "Let me go this instant, or I will cry for help."

Wickham ignored her words, and lifted her up so their faces were at the same level, her feet dangling above the ground. She twisted her face in disgust when he started to sniff her like a dog.

"I can still smell his odour on you." He inhaled sharply. "Has he made you his bitch already? Has he mated with you already? Do you carry his bairn?"

At that moment, Elizabeth produced a loud shriek, and using her sturdy leather half boot and all the strength she possessed in her leg, she kicked him his most sensitive place.

His face contorted in pain, and his hands dropped her, landing her squarely on her bottom.

She heard him curse under his breath, but did not give him a second look, busy raising herself to her feet, ready to run away.

"You bitch!" He pulled her back to him by her bonnet. "You will pay for this!" With one strike of his hand to her face, she fell to the ground.

Elizabeth saw dark patches falling in front of her eyes, and for a moment she thought that she would lose consciousness.

"You will have something to tell him!" Wickham's voice cried above her. He flipped her on her stomach and tugged at her petticoats.

Elizabeth heard the sound of tearing muslin, and screamed when she felt his hand wrapped around her ankle. She could not believe what was happening to her. Was he mad? He behaved like an animal, not a human.

Another scream died in her throat when he laid heavily on her and clasped his hand around her mouth. Her eyes bulged, looking for someone or something that could rescue her.

Tears brimmed in her eyes, and she started to pray silently, her heart banging in her chest. A second later, she heard a shot of a pistol and lifted her eyes to see one of Darcy's footmen running to her. Relief washed over her, and soon she felt her attacker's weight being lifted from her.

As she scrambled to her knees and turned, she saw Darcy's servant holding Wickham by the back of his coat. Well over six foot tall, footman directed a series of merciless blows into his stomach and face. Elizabeth's mouth fell open. She had never seen anyone as strong as her rescuer. She always considered Wickham to be tall and well built, but now he squirmed like an adolescent lad.

The next moment, the strangest thing happened. Wickham started to cringe under the blows, getting smaller and smaller, and growing… Fur? Elizabeth blinked several times, not believing her eyes. Here, in front of her, there was a yellow dog drowning in Wickham's uniform.

She watched as the footman dropped the animal to the ground and kicked him with his booted foot.

Her vision started to blur, and she fainted.

***

Four days later, late in the evening, Darcy dismounted his worn out horse in front of Netherfield Manor. Bingley waited for him on the doorstep.

"How is she?" Darcy asked without preamble.

"She is well." Bingley assured him, gesturing his friend into the house. "Bruised some, but otherwise unharmed. You know that she has been staying with us since the accident."

"I want to see her." Darcy strode into the foyer, and kept walking toward the staircase.

Bingley's hand on his shoulder stopped him. "Rest first, and eat something. Jane checked on her not long ago. Miss Elizabeth managed to fall asleep."

Darcy hesitated for a moment and nodded. "I should not interrupt her rest then."

"Let us go to the library." Bingley proposed.

Darcy ran his hand over his face. "I could use a drink."

Bingley patted his back. "Come then. I will tell Jane you have arrived, so she can order a dinner for you."

"Good, but first I need to see her," Darcy stared up the staircase. "I shall not disturb her. I just want to have a look at her to see if she is truly well."

"Go then." Bingley waved him away. "I would have you on pins and needles if you did not go to her first. She is in her old room."

Darcy leaped the stairs and walked the corridor, stopping in front of the bedroom that Elizabeth had occupied during her first stay at Netherfield.

The inside would have been dark to human eyes, as the curtains were tightly drawn, but he of course could see everything very clearly.

He sat beside her, mindful not to touch her. She looked peaceful, sleeping on her side, with her face tilted awkwardly to the side. The heavy bruising on one side of her face had to hurt, and prevented her from touching the pillow with it.

"I gave her an herb tea." He heard Jane's whisper. She appeared behind his back with a single candle in her hand. "She will sleep till the morning."

"Herb tea?" he asked. "She cannot sleep?"

Jane walked over him, and reached to adjust Elizabeth pillow. "She claims to be well, but she is afraid to fall asleep, because she dreams nightmares, even during the day."

Darcy moved the wisp of blond hair from Elizabeth's forehead. "I will kill him for that."

Jane shook her head, "No, you will not. He ran away. No one has seen him from that day on." She sighed, "Thank God your man came to her rescue, and she was spared something much worse than a few bruises. I know it would kill her if Wickham... We must thank the Lord the worst did not happen."

Darcy took Elizabeth's warm, small hand and leaned over her. His lips lingered on her forehead, and he took the opportunity to inhale her scent. She had eaten cheese and some vegetables earlier. He sniffed again, and a deep scowl appeared on his face.

"Is she bleeding?" he barked out.

"No… She had a small cut on her cheek, but it was very shallow - it bled but little, and healed well."

"I can smell blood on her." he insisted.

Jane frowned and searched his face. "She is … indisposed." she said slowly. "You must know, it happens to women once in a month."

Darcy closed his eyes and let out a sigh of relief. "Oh."

Jane did not stop to glare at him. "Let us go downstairs, Mr. Darcy." She took the candle from the bedside table and strode to the door. "Your dinner is waiting."

When Darcy hesitated, she repeated herself, her voice more decided than he had ever heard. "Come, Mr. Darcy. My sister needs her rest."

***

"Darcy." Bingley put the half empty glass of brandy on the small side table. "I hope you will not mind, but I shall retire now. It has been a long day."

Darcy nodded, staring into the fireplace. "Of course."

Bingley stood up and stretched his long limbs. "You should go to bed too, Darcy."

The other took a sip of his drink. "I will, Bingley. I shall not stay here long. I will ask you for one more thing. Could you send my man to me, please?"

"The one you left here?"

"Yes."

Bingley looked at his friend for a moment before he spoke somehow tentatively. "He rescued her."

Darcy flashed a dark look. "I would not call it that."

Bingley gave impression he wanted to say something more, but eventually he turned to the door and left Darcy alone. A few minutes later, there was a knock.

"Enter." Darcy stood up from his seat, reaching his full height.

The man closed the door after himself without a sound.

Darcy stood in front of the man, who though a few inches taller than his master, now seemed as if smaller.

"Can you tell me how this could happen?" he asked with a voice seemingly devoid of any emotion.

The man dropped to his knees. "Master…" he started.

Darcy's expression tightened. "You were to follow her everywhere whenever she was alone."

"I did, Master." The man spoke, his eyes downcast. "When I saw Wickham walking to Miss Bennet, I thought that I needed first to change into human. It took me a moment to go to Netherfield, put on some clothes and return to her. You gave strict orders she should suspect nothing. I did not think it wise to let her see another wolf."

"And Wickham?" Darcy barked. "They tell me that he escaped. You allowed that

First he threatened my sister, and now my future mate! He should be lying dead at their feet."

"I started to hit him, but then he transformed. I decided I could not leave her all alone to chase him right then. He hit her hard when she resisted him. She fainted and bled. I needed to reassure myself whether her state was not life threatening. Wickham used the moment of my distraction and escaped."

Darcy was silent for a long moment. "I see."

"I thought it was the best I could do then."

Darcy nodded. "I will think more about your conduct on this matter and announce to you my final opinion later."

The man, still kneeling in front of Darcy, took his hand to kiss it.

"You can go." Darcy flicked his wrist into the direction of the door. "Leave me alone."

***

Bingley crept into a darkened chamber. It was late, and he had no intention of calling his valet to undress him. One by one, the items of his clothing landed on the floor, sofa and his wife's vanity.

Perched on the edge of the bed, he kicked off his shoes, removed his stockings and breeches.

Jane slept on her side with her back to him, her long, honey coloured hair strewn on the pillow. All the Bennet sisters were blondes, but his Jane's hair was the darkest, with red highlights here and there. He slipped under the covers and took off his shirt.

He spooned behind his wife, his face buried in her sweetly scented waves. His hand, slipped inside her nightshift, and probed for a large, puffed nipple. She was such perfection, every single part of her. He still could not believe that this angel was his alone.

Jane murmured something and shifted onto her back. Bingley pressed himself into her soft body, his face nibbling at her supple throat, his hand moving under her nightgown, as always tangled up about her thighs.

"Charles?"

"Yes, Janie." His fingers darted into a warm place between her legs.

Jane's perfect little nose frowned. "You drank." She avoided his kiss.

"Just some brandy with Darcy. I could not refuse a friend."

She pushed away from him. "You promised you would restrain yourself with drinking."

"I am, Janie. I am. I truly am." His hand wrapped around her, and he pulled her under him again. "Kiss me, my angel."

"Charles, it has been a long day..." she started, but he interrupted her.

"Please, Janie. It has been so long. You have sat by your sister for the last few nights..."

Jane sighed and hiked her nightshirt around her waist. "Only try not to dribble all over me like the last time."

Bingley wasted no time to move on her, his hands and lips busied all over her, kissing, rubbing and massaging her sensitive spots.

His heart sang in joy and pride when she started to make those small sounds at the back of her throat, her fingers digging into his arms, her half open lips catching air in short breaths. She always attempted to behave as ladylike in bed as she did in broad daylight. He, in turn, loved to make her lose this genteel façade when he made love to her.

Without asking, he took her hand and brought it between their bodies, seeing to it that she would rub herself at the place where their bodies were joined. At first she protested and tried to remove her hand, but after a moment, she started to willingly touch herself in the rhythm of his pushes.

"Oh, yes, Janie, yes, yeeeesss." Bingley cried as he felt her tightening rhythmically around him. He drove into her the last time, growled and collapsed over her damp body.

A minute later, when he was on the verge of sleep, one of his hands on his wife's breast, the other on her lush bottom, he heard.

"Charles."

"Mhmm." he murmured.

"We need to talk."

He yawned. "We do? Now?"

"Yes, we do." There was steel in her sweet voice. "It cannot wait."

Bingley opened his eyes. "Yes, dear."

"Tis about your friend, Mr. Darcy..."

"Yes."

Jane sat up. "I am not sure whether Lizzy should marry him. He is... unusual. His behaviour baffles, and often worries me."

Bingley sighed, thinking how much he should tell her. He could imagine Jane's reaction once she learned the whole truth about Darcy, though he preferred to delay this moment as long as possible. She would rightly blame him, partially at least, for her sister's peculiar misfortune of marrying a werewolf.

"Janie, I will not argue that. He is different from most people, but he is a good man, noble, responsible, caring, and devoted to his family. He will take good care of Miss Elizabeth. He will love and respect her. You can be sure of that."

"Do you trust him?"

"Yes, I do. He saved my life, you know, when we were together at university."

"What happened?" Jane asked, her voice curious.

"It is a long story." Bingley yawned again. "I will tell you tomorrow. Now let us go to sleep."

Having said that, he pulled his wife back to him and drew the covers over both of them.

***

When Elizabeth woke the next morning, Darcy stood by the window next to her bed.

"Tis you?" she whispered, her voice sleepy.

He sat on the edge of the bed, took her hands and raised them to his lips.

Elizabeth stared into his face for a few moments, not speaking. Her lower lip began to quiver, as tears brimmed her eyes, and with a quiet sob, she buried her face in his chest.

His arms wrapped around her, and he rocked her in his embrace, placing small kisses all over her fair head.

"Say you will marry me as soon as possible." he whispered when her weeping stopped. "I shall go to London tomorrow to purchase the special license, and we shall wed next week."

"I cannot go to church looking like this!" She sniffed loudly into his shirt.

Darcy pushed her away from him to have a better look at her bruised face. "So we shall wait till you face heals." he said. The tips of his fingers touched the swollen, discoloured cheek, and the cut in the corner of her lips. As he examined her, his lips pressed tightly, his eyes darker than she had ever seen.

She rushed back into his arms, her face supported on his arm. "Do not look at me. The doctor said it will all heal, and there will be no trace in a few weeks. I must look horrible though, as Jane refused to give me a looking glass."

"I know that words will not help here, but I am so sorry this happened to you."

She shook her head. "Tis not your fault."

His arms tightened around her. "It is my fault, only mine. I did not protect you, and it is unforgiveable. I knew that Wickham would try to hurt you once he learned you belonged to me."

"Fitzwilliam…" she whispered, her eyes wide as she stared in the space in front of her, her unhurt side of face rested on his arm.

"Yes, love."

"About Wickham… he said such things about you and me, about us…"

He stroked her back repeatedly as he asked in low voice. "What things?"

"Vulgar things, and later when your man came to my rescue, I saw something which makes me doubt my sanity."

His hand on her back stopped. "What did you see?"

She straightened herself to look at him and whispered. "I saw Wickham changing into a dog, into an animal."

He stiffened. "What?"

"I saw it very clearly. Your man hit him several times, and just then he started to shrink and grow fur and then…" She frowned. "I do not exactly remember what happened next."

He pushed her hair away from her face. "Are you sure you did not dream it all?"

She shook her head. "No, I saw it."

Darcy sighed and turned her into his arms so she sat with her back to his chest. "You are not insane, sweetheart, far from it." he whispered into her ear as his arm rested under her breasts, keeping her close to him, and his other hand stroked her forearm in slow motion. "You see, I think that you were in shock after that bastard had attacked you." He kissed her rounded shoulder, bared by the loose neckline of her nightgown. "You talked and presumably thought too much about wolves in the last months… Your sister told me that they gave you herbs to make you sleep peacefully as you had nightmares. I think that all that compounded together in your mind and you dreamt it, thinking later that it was a reality. You may have too vivid an imagination perhaps, but you are not insane."

"I can only hope that you are right." She looked up at him. "It was so terrifying, seeing Wickham to change into animal." She shivered. "Like a scene from a nightmare, from an eerie fairytale about evil witches and mean werewolves I read as a child, so unnatural, so…"

"Hush…" he whispered against her lips. "It was only a dream, Lizzy. You have to forget about it, and not torture yourself by remembering it. You must focus on your recovery now so we can be together."

"Perhaps you should not marry me." she said in all seriousness, her expression earnest.

"Why ever not?"

"I may have very well developed a tendency to project such delusions… and in that case, our children might inherit it."

"Lizzy, we have settled it was just a dream, do not over think it." He shook her gently, his voice warm but firm. "I do not want to ever hear that you should not marry me."

She returned into his arms with a sigh. "I was so scared when he pushed me to the ground. He was so inhuman, so animalistic. I thought it was my end…" Her speech slurred, and she began to weep again.

"He will never come near you again." he vowed, rocking her in his arms. "And he will pay for this, I promise you that."

Chapter Eight

"Do you think I should take this one too?" Elizabeth turned to her sister, a light blue dress in her hands.

Jane sat on the window sill in her old room at Longbourn, and watched her younger sister with a slight frown of her delicate eyebrows.

"It is old, but I do like it." Elizabeth murmured to herself, as she spread the dress on the bed in front of her.

"Perhaps you should wait with the wedding a few months, at least till your trousseau will be ready." Jane suggested.

Elizabeth leaned over the dress, and smoothed its skirt, "Do you disapprove of my wedding?" she asked quietly.

Jane walked to her sister. "It only seems a rushed affair to me. Lizzy. You do not know Mr. Darcy well enough."

Elizabeth turned to face her. "I have known him exactly as long as you have known Mr. Bingley."

"Yes, but it was so different with Charles and me. He spent long months here during the winter so we could know each other better. Mr. Darcy speaks so little about himself. He will take you to some wilderness in Scotland, and we shall not see you for a year, or even longer."

"It is not Scotland, but Cumbria," Elizabeth pointed. "I heard it is so very beautiful there. Besides, I am sure Fitzwilliam will not forbid me from visiting whenever I feel homesick."

"But it is so far away." Jane said with a sigh.

Elizabeth crossed her arms in front of her. "You, yourself have said that you and Mr. Bingley have considered leaving Hertfordshire."

Jane put a gentle hand on her arm. "Dearest, I am only worried about you. We do know so little about him."

Elizabeth frowned, and her lips pressed tightly together. "I do not understand why you dislike him so much, Jane. He is your husband's best friend, after all. You told me yourself that it was

Mr. Darcy who saved Mr. Bingley's life when he involved himself in a brawl in the public house when they were at the university."

Jane shook her head. "I cannot explain it, Lizzy," she paused, "There is something strange about him."

"I cannot believe it!" Elizabeth snapped at her sister, losing her patience. "You are always so kind towards everyone! Without any hesitation you forgave your own husband when he confessed his misdeeds to you. Mr. Darcy is just shy, perhaps not very talkative and a bit withdrawn, but it is not a sin. He loves me, and he will take care of me. Had he not left his servant here, who knows what would have happened to me?"

"Do you not find it strange that he left that man here in the first place? How could he know that Mr. Wickham would attack you?"

"I do not care about that! I can only be grateful that he rescued me from a fate worse than..." Elizabeth bit her lower lip and the tears started to form in her big, dark eyes.

The sisters were silent for a moment longer, the thick, heavy atmosphere hanging in the air. It was Elizabeth who spoke first, with a sigh, her voice calmer and gentler.

"Jane, you know I cannot stay here. The whole neighbourhood has somehow learned about what happened to me. My reputation is ruined."

"It was not your fault."

"Still, it does not change the fact that people do gossip. I do not want to live another couple of months here, suffering their curious stares and whispers behind my back, when I can marry a good man and leave; start a new life and forget."

"Lizzy, I understand you want to escape and change your surroundings I agree that a change would be good for you. Still, you do not have to marry in such a hurry. You can go to London, and stay with Aunt and Uncle Gardiner for some time. They are always pleased to have you."

Elizabeth shrugged. "They have gone on a trip to Derbyshire."

"But they will be back by the end of the month. You could stay with them for a few months. Mr. Darcy could visit you there. And later, if you feel you still do not want to return to Longbourn, you could live with us."

"At Netherfield? It would not change anything for me."

Jane shook her head. "No, we are moving; it is decided. Charles wants to buy an estate somewhere in the north. Uncle Gardiner promised to look for something interesting for us in

Derbyshire. Nobody there would know that Charles' little girl is illegitimate."

Elizabeth sat on the bed. "Poor little girl… Have you seen her, Jane?"

Jane sat next to her. "Yes, when we were in London last week. She is a sweet little thing, just three years old. For now, she lives with Charles's aunt, but it is not a good place for a small child to grow up."

Elizabeth bit on her lower lip and asked tentatively. "Do you know who her mother was?"

"An actress, I understand." Jane answered calmly. "She died from fever after the birth."

"An actress?" Elizabeth's eyes widened. "Are you sure it is Charles' baby?"

"Oh, yes. She looks just like him, the same light green eyes, pale blonde curls, his gestures and expressions."

There was a knock at the door, and to both sisters' surprise, their father appeared in the door opening.

"Papa?" Elizabeth blinked at the man. "Is something the matter?" She could hardly remember her father ever visiting her bedroom. The last time, she had probably been eight, and had fallen out of a tree, in the process, twisting her ankle, so he had carried her upstairs.

"Jane, please leave us alone." Mr. Bennet said, his voice earnest, any trace of his usual humour washed away from his eyes.

***

Elizabeth sat in the luxurious carriage, opposite her husband of three hours. She was Mrs. Fitzwilliam Darcy now, and as such, she was eager to start a normal life in the north with her husband and new sister. At last she would learn more about the man who sat in front of her. Surely, all her doubts would find a perfectly reasonable explanation once she settled herself as a Mistress of Pemberley.

She watched him move from his place, and sit beside her. His arm wrapped around her back, and he whispered in a low voice. "Kiss me, my wife."

She turned her face to him, and let him kiss her, his hungry lips demanding a reaction she did not feel up to giving.

"What is the matter?" he asked when she broke the kiss and turned her face away from him to the passing countryside. They were just leaving the outskirts of Meryton.

She sighed. "It is about Jane and my father."

He stroked her arm. "What about them?"

"They seem to be less pleased with our wedding than I expected them to be. I do not have to explain to you that they are two people whose opinions I care for most. I would wish they were more enthusiastic about it."

Darcy turned her to him, reached for the ribbons of her bonnet and untied them. "They do not want to part with you, I can understand that." He put the bonnet away and tucked her under his arm. "There always comes a time for a woman to start her own family, in a new home. I think they would have preferred you to marry somewhere closer. Still, in a few months, the Bingleys will move to Derbyshire. I talked with Charles, and all seems to be arranged. It is only a little more than a day of good road from Pemberley. You could see your sister whenever you wish. Even your father, he could come to visit us… not now perhaps, but in some time when you will…" he cleared his throat, "well… adjust to life in the north."

Elizabeth smiled, but it was such a small smile that it did not reach her eyes.

Darcy squeezed her to him and kissed the top of her head. "You shall see that they will reassure themselves, when they see how happy you are with me."

She looked up at him. "You think I shall be happy?"

His expression turned serious. "It only depends on you."

She smiled. "In that case, I am determined to be."

"Good, that is settled then." he said, and kissed her this time more gently.

***

Before nightfall, they reached the inn where they were to stay for the first night. Fitzwilliam escorted her inside and introduced her to the owner's wife Then he excused himself to see to some business with his men.

The apartment to which she was led looked comfortable and very clean. It consisted of a large sitting room, bedroom and a small side room that served as a dressing room.

She was rather relieved to have some time for herself after all the excitement of the early morning and the many hours spent in the running carriage. She had slept some through the journey, supported against her husband's hard chest, but it only made her feel more drowsy and tired.

"Would you like a bath before dinner, ma'am?" the owner's wife asked as Elizabeth looked around the rooms.

"Yes, please." she smiled at the woman.

The warm bath sounded delightful after many hours of sitting in the same position. They had been travelling constantly from eleven o'clock in the morning, with only short breaks to change horses.

As she slipped into the hot, rose scented water, Elizabeth questioned herself whether she was apprehensive of her wedding night. Her mother had told her she must lie still, be quiet, and let her husband do what he wished.

Closing her eyes, she relaxed, supporting her head against the rim of the bathtub. She decided that her anticipation about what would happen this night was far greater than her apprehension. So far, all the intimacies they had shared were most pleasant. She enjoyed Fitzwilliam's touches, kisses and caresses. Invariably, his close proximity gave her sweet, tingling sensations. He was always very gentle, she reminded herself, consequently there was nothing to fear from him.

She was on the verge of falling asleep, lulled by the warm bath, when she jerked, hearing the heavy, energetic footsteps in the bedchamber and her husband's voice, crying.

"Lizzy? Lizzy! Where are you?" The footsteps were getting closer.

She did not manage to answer and explain that she was in her bath, because the doorknob turned and Darcy strode into the small room.

His black eyes widened and mouth fell agape as he stared down at her.

Elizabeth felt the hot blush spreading over her skin, from her cheeks down her neck to her chest. Her eyes followed his gaze to the tips of her pink breasts, poised just on the edge of the water. She looked around, but seeing nothing else with which she could cover herself, she reached for her own petticoats that she had on herself during the day.

"Forgive me." he murmured, still staring at her. "Had I known you were in your bath, I would have not intruded on your privacy." Having said that, he neither moved from his spot in the open door, nor averted his eyes.

Elizabeth managed a brave smile. "All is well." She stood up from the water, clutching her now damp petticoats to her chest. "You mentioned some matters you had to deal with before dinner. I thought to use this time to take my bath."

Darcy nodded. "Finish your bath then. I will not interrupt you any longer."

Elizabeth let out an involuntary sigh of relief when he left the room. A smile formed on her mouth and then turned into a giggle. Could he have seen his expression as he had stormed here, she noted wistfully. Her mother would have been shocked too, as she had stressed many times to her and Jane that a proper lady should always wear at least a nightgown in her husband's presence.

Still smiling, she threw the petticoats aside and reached for the rough washcloth. She finished her bath, scrubbing her body clean in energetic movements.

When she walked back to the bedroom, dressed properly in a nightgown and robe, Fitzwilliam sat on the chair next to the door, clearly waiting for her to appear.

Darcy stood up the moment she entered. "One more time, please forgive me…"

She stepped to him and lifted her finger to his mouth. "No harm done. I think that there is nothing wrong in you seeing me like this… You are my husband now." She smiled warmly into his eyes.

He smiled back and pulled her closer to him. "No, there is nothing wrong in that."

Elizabeth wrapped her arms around his neck, and with a happy sigh, nestled into his embrace.

"Lizzy…" he started hesitantly.

"Mhmm…?"

"Are you very hungry?"

She looked at him in surprise. "No."

He had seen to it that she would eat a hearty meal when they had stopped to change horses.

"Our dinner is waiting in the sitting room." He pointed with his head to the door. "However, would you mind if we first…" He lifted her up to his body, his large hands squeezing her round backside, and looked deeply into her eyes.

She frowned in her naivety, not comprehending his meaning at first. Only after a moment, she blushed bright red and nodded slowly. "I do not mind."

"You will not think me a brute?" He nuzzled her ear. "Rushing you so."

"No." she whispered, breathless. "Not at all."

He touched her face. "It is not night yet."

Elizabeth looked through the window at the setting sun.

Her eyes twinkled with mischief. "Do you think we can do it by day?" she asked in a theatrical whisper.

Darcy laughed out loud, picked her up into his arms and kissed her soundly on the lips. In a few steps, he was next to the bed, and laid her gently on it. Eyes wide with wonder, Elizabeth observed him disrobing himself. When he was left just in his breeches and shirt, his neck open to her view, she thought it would be wise to remove her own robe.

He sat on the bed with his back to her to pull off his boots.

Sitting on the bed, just in her thin, very revealing nightgown, she fought with the temptation to touch him. The tall boots fell with a heavy thud on the floor, and he turned his head to her, smiling.

Elizabeth smiled back and scooted behind him, flattening her breasts against his back.

She yelped as in one movement, he pulled her in front of him onto his lap.

His rough hand reached to cup her cheek.

"Will you not let you hair down?"

"Ah, yes." she reflected to herself as she busily reached to her head to remove the numerous pins. "Of course."

A moment later, the heavy, long, blond tresses fell down her back, reaching almost to her waist.

With careful hands, he began arranging her hair around her shoulders.

Elizabeth smiled at his actions, but did not protest.

He seemed to avoid looking into her eyes, concentrating on her hair.

This time, it was she who cupped his cheek, and kissed him.

From there, things happened more swiftly. He kissed her back, his arms wrapping around her, squeezing her to him.

His lips tugged persistently at hers, and his left arm supported her back, while his free hand reached to the neckline of her nightgown, opening the little pearl buttons.

Elizabeth arched with a sigh as his hand cupped her bosom, weighing it in his hand. She gasped anew when his fingers were replaced with his lips. He suckled on her like a hungry baby, his tongue swirling around the tip of her breast, teasing it.

"Now come here." he rasped as his mouth released her.

He arranged her squarely on his lap, with her back to his chest.

She glanced up at him with a hint of surprise. "Fitzwilliam?"

"Trust me," he pushed her legs apart, so they dangled on both sides of his heavily muscled thighs.

His face buried in the side of her neck, one of his hand cupped her breast, while his right hand pulled her nightgown up, baring her privates to the cool air coming from the open window.

Her protest at his action died in his kiss, and his hand cupped her womanhood.

Elizabeth's eyes popped open, and then as he stroked her, rolled to the back of her head.

She heard strange, almost tortured like moans, and was taken aback, realizing that it was she who uttered them. She strained against him repeatedly as he caressed her in places she had never dared to touch herself longer than necessary.

"Yes, Lizzy, squeeze one more time, give yourself to it." he whispered, his hot breath tingling her ear, his fingers pulling at the tip of her aching breast.

The unbearable pressure was building inside her, and a moment later, her eyes shut tightly, she cried out, shuddered and slumped in his arms, her head resting on his chest.

She was barely aware of him saying something, whispering into her ear. She felt good all over, her whole body tingling delightfully, from the tips of her toes to the tops of her breasts.

He was arranging her on the bed, and when she opened her heavy eyelids, she saw him above her. Supported on one powerful arm, he was settled between her wide spread, bent up legs.

She smiled at him before there was the slightest pain, and he was inside her.

"Lizzy." he murmured into her neck as his hand wrapped persistently around her hip, "Lizzy… Lizzy." he chanted, moving inside her.

At first tentatively, she began to meet his strokes, lifting her bottom up. He must have liked it, because he groaned deep in his throat and started to move faster. A moment passed before she caught the rhythm, and was able to move along with him.

"Yes, like that…" he panted. His hand left her hip and moved between their bodies, searching in the triangle of sparse, blonde curls.

She knew that he found the right spot when the feeling of sharp pleasure shot through her. She moaned.

He kissed her harder and moved faster.

Soon, he moved too fast for her to match his rhythm. She wrapped her arms and legs around him and accepted him into her body. She watched as he gritted his teeth, let out a hoarse grunt like sound and collapsed on her. It was over.

Elizabeth lay under him, pinned with his weight and unable to move, their bodies still locked. She stared at the canopy, her fingers slowly stroking his damp back under his shirt.

A longer moment passed before Darcy lifted himself on his arms, and carefully withdrew from her. He looked into her face for a moment before he shifted on his back and simultaneously pulled her with him.

She snuggled happily to him with her head tucked on his chest, pleased with herself, as she was a real wife to him now.

Chapter Nine

"Thank you, God." he murmured, as he combed away the wisps of hair from her temple with gentle fingers.

Elizabeth rubbed her cheek against his shoulder. "Thank you God for what?"

"Tis the last time in my life when I had to deflower a virgin."

"There was no other way." she reasoned.

"No, there was not." he agreed. "But I am most pleased it was a once in a life time experience. My heart would not survive it again." He patted his chest. "Have I hurt you much?"

"Not at all." Elizabeth nestled closer, her face buried into the curve of his neck. He was still dressed in his shirt, and as she assumed, his breeches were only pulled down his legs, and not completely removed.

She glanced up at his face. It was relaxed now, and his eyes were closed. Had he fallen asleep? Mama had said that he would have probably fall asleep soon after.

Her eyes focused on the dark patch of curly hair, peeking from the opening of his shirt. She had not seen the entirity of his naked form as he had seen hers, and she was curious. He seemed to be unusually hairy. Earlier, when he had moved against her, and her hands slipped under his shirt to stroke his back, she even felt some hair there.

She had seen other men bare from their waist up, mainly field workers in summer at Longbourn, but they had all been rather smooth skinned.

Her hand moved from his shoulder to the gap in his shirt. She pushed her fingers under the fine cotton cloth and into the thick, springy hair which covered his chest.

She amused herself with his pelt for a moment; she combed her fingers through it and pulled at it gently.

She was about to move her hand farther, to his ribcage, to explore more of him, when he stopped her hand, covering it with his

His fingers wrapped around her wrist and he pulled her hand out of his shirt.

"Let us take a nap? Hmmm?" He kissed the inside of her palm, rolled her gently to her side and snuggled against her back.

"Fitzwilliam…?" she began in a shy voice.

"Go to sleep, Lizzy." he said with unusual firmness in his voice.

Elizabeth felt that something was suddenly wrong. She thought to move away from him, but as his big strong arm was wrapped securely around her middle from behind, and she was completely encompassed by his large body, understandably she could not maneuver much.

Sleep was not exactly on her mind, though she was tired and weary. Her private area started to hurt now, and she felt a very unpleasant cold stickiness between her thighs.

"I love you so much, Lizzy." she heard above her ear.

She smiled, and closed her eyes.

***

She woke up to the sensation of something cold and wet touching her skin. Her eyes opened. It much darker than before, no candle lit the room, though the sun had set completely. There was a bright, almost full moon in the sky. The bed covers were pushed aside, the same as her nightgown, which was gathered around her waist.

Her legs were splayed apart, and her husband was busy with cleaning her privates.

A mortified gasp escaped her, and she tried to push his hands away and cover herself down there, but he stopped her hand and leaned over to kiss her nose.

"All is done." he said, and with the last stroke of the washcloth over her belly, pulled her nightgown down

"You should not…." she whispered, still flushed in embarrassment.

"There is nothing to be ashamed of." he said in a sure voice. "I thought you to be uncomfortable. Now…" he stood up from the bed, "I called for another dinner, and it has just been served. The previous one was already cold and inedible when I woke up." He reached to her and buttoned the opening of her nightgown at her breasts securely, stopping her bosom from spilling out. "For my peace of mind." he murmured before kissing her cheek.

Then he swept her up into his arms and carried her to the sitting room, seating her gently on the chair.

"What do we have here?" he uncovered the lids.

Elizabeth's face brightened when she was presented with all her favourites. Her mouth watered at the sight of the lemon tarts, thick, steamy soup, and baked, crunchy potatoes.

She started eating with enthusiasm, placing the tarts, together with white cheese and some vegetables on her plate.

After some time, she noticed he had not touched any of the food. "Are you not hungry?" she asked as she swallowed the last bit of the second tart. "You are not eating."

He shook his head. "Perhaps later."

She frowned. "Later? When?" She gave him the last tart.

He ate it obediently, but she could tell that he did not really enjoy it. Then she remembered that he usually ate little, only nibbling at the most of the dishes. At the same time, he was heavy, and far from a lanky body type. She wondered how he sustained all that hard, bulging muscle with so little food.

His eyes were on her as she finished her meal, dabbed her mouth with a napkin, and let out a satisfied sigh.

"Sleepy?" he asked with tenderness.

Elizabeth nodded as the small catty yawn escaped her. "Tired."

Darcy stood up and took her hand into his. "Should you not return to bed now?"

"I need to first clean my teeth." she walked past him to the bedroom.

"Take your time." he called after her.

A short time later, she left the dressing room and walked back to the bedroom, her hair freshly brushed and plaited into a thick braid.

There was no sign of her husband. She walked into the sitting room, but he was nowhere to be seen. She had no suspicion where he could have gone at this hour, but she was sure he would be back soon. The thought that he would not like to spend the rest of the night with her in one bed did not cross her mind.

She returned to the dark bedroom and sat on the bed, and waited. However the time passed, and he did not return.

She glanced at the clock on the mantelpiece. It was nearly midnight. She did not understand what could keep him away at such an hour. Her heart tugged in apprehension. Perhaps something bad had happened to him?

On impulse, she put on her robe and slippers and ran across the rooms to the corridor outside their apartment.

She nearly screamed when just outside the door, she walked into a huge figure of a man. With relief, she recognized it was one of her husband's servants, the very same one who had saved her life a few weeks ago.

"Do you know where your Master is?"she asked.

The gloomy looking footman bowed with visible respect. "Master thought that you had already retired, Mistress. He has some important matters to attend."

"At this hour?" she cried.

"Yes." the man acknowledged, his face like stone.

She wanted to go past the servant and look for Fitzwilliam, but something in the man's expression stopped her. It was not her intention to create a scandal, searching the place for her husband in the middle of the night.

She stood still, not sure what to do, biting her lower lip.

"Mistress." the servant bowed again and spoke calmly. "I am sure that Master will be back soon. He would be worried to find you wandering alone at night, looking for him."

Elizabeth blinked rapidly. Was he reading her mind?

She opened her lips, but no words came out of them. Her forehead frowned in growing confusion. One matter was clear for her, this well over six foot tall footman did not intend to let her go anywhere.

Slowly, she turned away and walked back, closing the door quietly after herself.

She stood for a moment next to the door, listening whether the servant was walking away. There was no sound of footsteps heard. Did he intend to guard the door the entire night?

Still worried, and very much confused, she returned to the bedroom and climbed into the cold, lonely bed.

She put down the candle on the bedside table and closed her eyes. There was only a dim light from the dying fireplace. Her body ached after a long journey, and her first loving in Fitzwilliam's arms, but she could not fall asleep. Soon, the clock struk one in the morning. It was much later though, perhaps close to two o'clock, when she heard his footsteps in the sitting room. She rolled on her side and closed her eyes, keeping her breathing even.

The door opened with a quiet click. She peered through her eyelashes to see as Fitzwilliam walked to the bed. He stared at her for a moment before she felt his gentle hand on her cheek in light caress. Then he began disrobing himself. She did not give him sign that she was not fast asleep till he slipped under the covers beside her, and very gently tried to pull her into his arms.

She slapped his hands away, sat up and hissed. "Where have you been?"

There was a moment of shocked silence on his part before he spoke. "Did my man not tell you? An urgent matter had occurred to which I needed to attend."

"What urgent matter could it be in the middle of the night?" she demanded.

"Lizzy…" he attempted to embrace her.

"Do you think me stupid?" she pushed at his chest and got out of the bed.

She took the box of matches and tried to light the candle. A few matches broke in her trembling fingers before she sensed him coming behind her. He took the matches from her and swiftly lit the candle.

She turned to him, taking in his face, visible in the dim light coming from the single candle.

"Where have you been half the night?" she asked again. "I was worried."

His hand came to rest on her shoulders. "I needed to go out for some time."

Her eyes stared into his. "I do not understand."

He sighed. "I needed some fresh air."

"At midnight?"

He nodded seriously. "Yes."

She let him pull her into his warm embrace.

He kissed her hair and rubbed her back. "It was not my intention to upset you."

She looked up at him. "And how would you feel if you were abandoned on your wedding night?" she cried with a deep hurt in her voice and expression which she did not care to disguise.

"Shush." he pulled her back into his arms. "Do not distress yourself. I want to be with you, day and night, all the time."

"So why did you go?"she insisted.

He sighed. "It is complicated." he combed the hair falling on her face which escaped her braid.

"You always say that, but you never care to explain anything to me!"

"You will understand everything one day. I promise."

She stepped away from him, her arms folded on her chest. "At least be honest with me. Tell me the truth." she probed.

He swallowed visibly, his eyes bored into her face as if he tried to read her mind.

"You are disappointed with me." She could not stop the blush creeping on her face and neck. "because of what I did... how I acted before..."

She did not finish, not knowing how to put into words her fear that he was disappointed with her performance as a wife.

"No, Lizzy. No, sweetheart." He cupped her face and murmured into her lips. "I adore you. You cannot even imagine what I felt being inside you."

"So why did you not stay with me so I could fall asleep in your arms?" she asked in a trembling voice.

"I should have. I am sorry." he whispered as he bent down to kiss her.

Elizabeth was left breathless, her whole body tingling at the touch of his warm, big hands, when he lifted his lips from hers a long moment later. He reached behind them to put the candle out with his thumb.

He lifted her up and tucked her under covers.

Elizabeth clung to him as he joined her in bed. She relaxed, hearing the steady rhythm of his heartbeat under her ear as she snuggled to him, nestled on his chest.

"I was thinking, Lizzy." he whispered some time later.

"Mhm..." she murmured on the verge of sleep, lulled by the warmth and wonderful security of his arms.

"At Pemberely..." he sighed. "I think we should keep separate bedrooms."

Elizabeth stiffened instantly.

"I will visit you, of course, some nights if you allow me, but both for reasons of practicality and propriety, it is advisable for us to have separate bedchambers."

"Of course." she said at last as she moved away from his embrace. "I understand you perfectly, sir." She rolled on her side with her back to him.

She prayed he did not to notice her tears rolling down her cheeks. How could he even suggest that after what they had shared? She had never thought him to care for such things as propriety and what others would say.

"Lizzy." She felt his hand on her arm. "There is no reason to scoot away from me."

She shrugged her arm from his touch.

"Are you crying?" he asked. "Do not cry." Another heavy sigh on his part. "It was not my wish to upset you."

"You stated your wishes perfectly well, sir," she bit out. "I shall not bother you any more with my person." She pulled the covers up, almost over her head.

"That was not what I meant." He tried to pulled her to him, but she resisted.

"I am tired." she whispered with broken dignity, "There is a long day's journey before us tomorrow, and only a few hours left till the morning. I need my rest."

She sensed him shifting away from her so she could not feel his warmth in the huge bed. She moved away from him even farther, to the edge of the bed.

***

Elizabeth did not understand how she managed to fall asleep at all after what he had told her, but she must have slipped into obliviousness at some point, because when she woke up, the sun was shining into the room through the curtains that somebody had opened.

Her eyes felt swollen, her eyelids, as if glued together. She would look a fright today.

"You are awake." she heard, and her gaze concentrated on her husband. He was fully dressed, already in his travelling clothes, including his greatcoat and tall boots.

He sat beside her on the bed and kissed her cheek. "Good morning, my love. I was about to wake you. We must hurry if we want to reach the next planned stop in our journey by night."

Elizabeth rubbed her eyes, not knowing what to say and how to take his kind behaviour.

She felt an object being pushed into her hands, and the smell of freshly made coffee teased her nose.

"I thought you would like to have some coffee to wake yourself. I have tasted it already, it is good."

"Thank you." she said as she wrapped her fingers around the cup and took a sip

She was grateful that she could concentrate her attention on something.

"The girl awaits to help you with dressing. Your breakfast is ready too." He kissed the top of her head. "I hope to see you downstairs soon."

Half an hour later, Elizabeth walked out of the inn. She certainly did not look her best this morning, not like the glowing bride she had been yesterday. It was nothing surprising, after all, taking into account all the crying she had done last night. There were dark circles under her eyes, surely both from lack of sleep and tears; her eyelids were puffed and red. Washing her face in icy cold water several times had helped only a little.

"Mistress." the footman bowed deeply in front of her. "The carriage awaits. Shall we go?"

Elizabeth followed the servant, not for the first time astonished with the way her husband's people behaved in her presence. Since the day their engagement had been announced, they had treated her more as if she was a dowager princess, at least, and not merely the future wife of their employer. Opening the door for her, and stepping from her way could be considered normal, but bending nearly in half to greet her seemed too much of subservience in her eyes. The Middle Ages had ended a long time ago, after all.

Darcy stood next to the carriage. She put on a brave face as she approached him.

He had stared at her for a long moment, surely thinking how unattractive she looked this morning, and she felt compelled to avert her eyes.

"Thank you for coming down so quickly." he said.

She nodded, still not looking at him. "I know you want to cover as much road as possible today." she said in a formal, polite voice.

She sensed him stepping closer.

"Are you well?" he whispered as his lips touched her temple below the rim of her bonnet.

"Yes, I am." she said before she turned to the open door of the luxurious carriage. "I think it is high time to go." She stepped forward and let the awaiting servant hand her in.

In the carriage, she scooted away, far from him, close to the opposite window.

She planned to enjoy the view of the passing scenery, unknown to her countryside, but very soon the weariness overpowered her. Her head hurt, as did her eyes, and she was very sleepy. She found it hard to fight her eyelids dropping every few minutes.

She barely registered Darcy moving to sit close to her.

"Let us remove this bonnet." he murmured, "It must be uncomfortable."

She hid her pride and allowed him to remove her bonnet, gloves and open her spencer. When she was freed of all these restricting garments, he tucked her against his frame. Before she knew it, she was fast asleep in the comfort of his embrace.

The next thing she heard was his voice, crooning at her ear. "Wake up, my love. We must stop for an hour or so to change horses."

Elizabeth rubbed her eyes and lifted her hands to her head. "What time is it?" she murmured, still groggy from her nap.

"Midday." he answered as he picked up her bonnet and helped her to put it on, before smoothing the wisps of hair around her forehead.

He escorted her to what looked to be the best inn in the small, busy town, the size of Meryton or perhaps slightly bigger.

He stayed with her in a quiet corner. She was surprised by that. She had expected he would go to his men.

He asked her to eat, but she shook her head and only sipped some of the strong, fragrant tea.

He did not insist upon her eating, and she stared dully out the window as he ate his lunch.

"Would you care for a walk around the town?" His voice brought her attention back to him. "We have some time left."

"Yes, I would." she smiled, perhaps the first real smile that day. A walk was always a good idea in her view, especially with the prospect of sitting for the next couple of hours.

His face broke into a boyish grin, and she could not help her heart fluttering at the handsome face in front of her.

As they strode into the main street, Elizabeth supported herself securely on his strong arm.

Her eyes swept over the shop window displays as they walked. She was first drawn to the bookshop exposition, but as she saw nothing interesting there, she stirred them forward.

Fitzwilliam followed her lead without question, even when she stepped in front of the large shop offering all kinds of female articles from ribbons and gloves to bonnets and shawls.

Her gaze was drawn by the vanity set in silver and ivory; a large looking glass to take in hand, hairbrush and comb. The handicraft was exquisite.

"Shall we go?" she heard above her ear. "I think that all is set up by now."

"Yes, of course." she smiled politely. "Let us go."

They approached the awaiting carriage ten minutes later. Elizabeth was surprised that he did not hand her in, but let the servant do that. He excused himself, saying he remembered something urgent and walked hastily away. Elizabeth frowned, her lips tightened. Without a word, she sat in the carriage.

She did not turn her head when he got in nearly a half hour later.

The carriage began to move, and she turned completely to the window.

To her surprise, she felt something heavy being placed on her lap. She turned her eyes from the window. There were two elegant packets placed on her skirts.

She looked up questioningly at him.

"For you." he said only.

Curious, she opened the first parcel. It contained a novel, by an author she had not had the pleasure to read yet, but had heard of, and a small book of poetry by one of her favourite poets.

"I noticed you did not bring any books with you." he said.

She frowned, tracing with her fingertips along the gold letters on the cover of the smaller book. "Thank you, it is very thoughtful of you."

"Will you not open the other one?" he asked after a moment.

She smiled dutifully at him and started opening the other parcel.

There was a polished wooden box inside.

A loud gasp escaped her when upon lifting the lid, she recognized the set she had admired earlier.

"How did you …?" she said as she took the looking glass into her hand.

"I noticed you looked at them longer than the other articles on display."

"You did not have to." she whispered, blushing. She did not want him to think that she stared at the mirror on purpose to induce him to buy it for her. To her embarrassment, she could not stop admiring the present.

"I wanted to." he explained simply.

"But the cost…" she started hesitantly.

"Tis not important."

"Thank you." She braved a look at him. "They are very beautiful. I will treasure them." She leaned to kiss his cheek.

"You are welcome." he lifted her hand to his mouth and kissed it.

Chapter Ten

It was late afternoon the last day of their journey from the south. Elizabeth looked at her husband's dark head as it rested on her lap. She sat close by the window, and his body occupied the rest of the seat. Still, it could not accommodate the length of him, so his legs were twisted awkwardly against the opposite wall of the box.

Her backbone hurt, the stiffness in it slowly becoming unbearable. She was afraid to move though, not wishing to disturb his rest. He had little sleep last night, and the previous two as well, she recalled with a smile. He had to be tired, the same as she. Three long days on the road had exhausted her. Three passionate nights in his arms had made her addicted to him.

All she longed for now was her own room, a bed and a good night's rest.

When she looked down, she saw his black eyes focused on her. She smiled.

He lifted himself, sat up and stretched his powerful body so that something in his bones snapped softly.

"Tis good it is the last day." He yawned. "I hate sitting in one position for so many hours."

"You could have rode on horseback beside the carriage." she said. "I told you I would not mind."

He wrapped his arm around her. "I knew you would not like to stay all alone in the carriage."

She smiled and snuggled against him.

"We will soon come upon the grounds of Pemberley." Darcy pointed to the window with unmistakable pride in his voice. His arm wrapped even more securely around her as she watched the passing countryside.

"How close to the Scottish border are we?" she asked.

"About fifteen miles.

Her eyes widened. "So close." She turned to him again. "Are you Scottish then?" she asked archly.

He shook his head with a smile. "No, I am not. Darcys originated in France. They came to live here centuries ago. They were safe here."

Elizabeth frowned. "Safe?"

"Yes… I understand that they felt endangered in the north of France, as it was becoming much too populated."

"I am afraid I do not understand." She shook her head. "Were they afraid of other people?"

Darcy hesitated for a moment. "Not exactly. It was the locals who frowned upon us. I believe that there was a kind of conflict between my family and their neighbours. My ancestors felt that it was a good idea to look for a new place to live. They already had some relatives in Scotland, and decided to come here, under the rule of the English King, who, as you probably know, was from Normandy, from the French dynasty at that time. They sold all they had in France, bought land here, and built Pemberley."

Elizabeth's eyes shone with interest. "That is so captivating and rare to know the history of one's family so many centuries back. I would love to learn more about the history of your family."

"Our family." he corrected gently.

"Our family." she acknowledged shyly.

"Actually, we still have some relatives across the border. Some Darcys had Scottish brides, but it was rather in the past. For the last generations, they married in the heart of England, like me." He grinned at her. "And my father of course."

"I see." she said, letting him play with her hand, his thumb gently stroking her knuckles.

He leaned over to her and started the kiss. Elizabeth relaxed in the caress of his lips, temporarily losing interest in the views outside.

Since their first night, when she had become so worried because of his sudden disappearance, he had been the most attentive husband she could wish for.

He saw to her every comfort by day. Every evening, he had dinner with her, then carried her to bed and loved her most attentively till she was so exhausted that she promptly fell asleep in his arms. However, when she woke up in the morning, he was consistently gone from the bed.

Now her eyes were shut as his lips kissed her neck under her ear, while his right hand brushed over her sensitive breasts. She gasped when he opened her spenser, and his warm hand slipped inside her dress.

She was lost every time he touched her in this manner. She did not care, and wished for nothing at such moments, only his hands and lips on her.

He took her mouth again, and with one decided move, raised her skirts, baring her stocking clad legs.

"Fitzwilliam..." she gasped, glancing down as his hand disappeared under her petticoats.

"Be quiet, so the driver and footman will not hear you." he whispered into her gasping mouth a minute later, as his hand started to work his magic on her.

She pushed herself into his hand, straining her back, her bottom shifted to the edge of the seat.

She turned her head and looked out of the window, gasping for air. At some point, the pleasure became so intense that she had to swallow back the tears. She bit her lower lip hard not to shout out. She would have been mortified had the driver heard her moans.

As her release came, she sagged limply against the window. From under her eyelashes, she saw as he impatiently tore at the buttons on his breeches. He pushed her down on the seat and climbed over her. He pushed her skirts higher up, together with her petticoats, and chemise and easily slipped into her.

Only a few pushes, and he dropped heavily on her; a now familiar wetness flooding her insides.

As she came to her senses, when the rest of excitement left her, she lifted her hands to her flushed cheeks in embarrassment. She did not expect that she could have ever forgotten herself to such an extent. He did not say anything, but silently cleaned her with his own handkerchief, and righted her clothes.

"Pemberley." He gestured a moment later.

Elizabeth leaned toward the window to see better. "Can we stop?"

Darcy nodded and banged at the wall that separated them from driver a few times. The carriage came to halt instantly. Elizabeth, not waiting for anyone's help, opened the door and jumped lightly to the ground, her legs still wobbly.

She ran a few yards to the edge of the hill, where she stopped and glanced down.

She was to live in that? It looked like some Medieval Castle. She frowned. No, it did not look like a castle; it truly was a grey stone built castle, or to be precise a fortress. There were hardly any windows, and all she could see were several tall towers and impressive, thick walls surrounding it.

"Beautiful? Is it not?" Darcy asked proudly from behind her, his arms wrapping loosely around her waist.

Hardly, she thought, as she leaned back into his solid frame.

"It looks very… old." she said in a weak voice.

"Yes, you are right. It was built in the last decade of the twelfth century."

Her eyes widened as she stared down at the stone monstrosity. The last thing she expected was for her new home to be a six hundred year old dungeon. She could not imagine living there, especially during the cold, long winter.

"Like from a fairy tale." she commented at last with heavy heart.

She did not want to criticize; there was no doubt how proud he was of his home, but she did not like what she saw in front. It was picturesque, to be sure, but looked rather inhabitable.

He squeezed her to him.

She lifted on her toes to see farther. There was something bluish lingering on the horizon.

"Is it a sea over there?" she cried disbelievingly, pointing with her hand to the sky line behind the castle.

"Yes."

She turned around in his arms. "You did not tell me it was so close to the sea! I have never been to the seaside. How absolutely delightful!"

He smiled. "A surprise."

"Can we go down to the beach?"

He laughed out loud. "Now? I am afraid it is not possible." he kissed her mouth lightly. "Come." he said, tugging at her hand. "We must go. Soon it will get dark. Tonight is the full moon. We should hurry." He glanced apprehensively at the setting sun. "Everyone is surely waiting for us by now."

"May we go the beach tomorrow?" she asked as he handed her in.

"If you wish to." he said calmly.

She nodded eagerly. "I do."

"Then it is settled." He smiled at her as the carriage drove on.

***

Mrs. Reynolds, the housekeeper at Pemberley manor, looked apprehensively at the carriage that approached the castle. She stood before nearly one hundred people, next to Miss Georgiana. All the servants stood in due order, according to their rank, behind them, in their very best Sunday outfits.

The next months would prove to be a hardship now that Master, the same as his father, and great grandfather, had decided on a bride who was a fully blooded human. They were all here to help him, and thus aide the new Mistress in adjusting and accepting her new life. Miss Georgiana, who had met Miss Elizabeth Bennet earlier this spring in London, was clearly enchanted with her, and overjoyed to gain a new sister and companion.

Mrs. Reynolds had been but a young girl then, but she remembered well the first months when Master George had brought Lady Anne here for the first time. In time, the Mistress had learned to love their people, and had been a good and devoted wife to the pack leader. They all had mourned her premature death together with her husband and children. However, the first year, until Master Fitzwilliam had come to the world, had been more than difficult for Lady Anne, and for all of them.

At last the carriage stopped. Master got out first, and handed down a small blonde. The young lady was dressed simply, in light pastel colours, suited well her fair colouring.

On closer look, Mrs. Reynolds observed that she had very beautiful, dark blue eyes, almost too big, which stood out in her pleasantly rounded face.

Though not very tall, she did not look like a weakling at all, Mrs. Reynolds noticed with relief. Her figure was trim but curvy, with visibly plump breasts, and she was rosy on the cheeks; it bode well. They had feared that Master might have chosen a woman of a frail constitution as his mother had been. But no, she would do fine, Mrs. Reynolds decided. She would bear many strong sons to the pack leader.

Master stood proudly behind his bride as she greeted Miss Georgiana, and later as she was introduced to the servants.

When the new Mistress walked past her to greet the footmen and maids, Mrs. Reynolds caught her scent, human, but very strongly mingled with Master's. She allowed herself a small smile. It was obvious that Master had not wasted his time on the long journey from the south. It was wise. The sooner Master's mate would become with child, the better for everyone, including her.

***

After the introduction to the staff, Elizabeth was escorted by her husband to her new apartments. To her great relief, they were not situated in any of the towers. The castle she had seen from the hill was one only, but the oldest part of Pemberley. Behind, there was a large addition, which looked as if built around sixteenth century. Even farther, the closest to the sea, there was situated the newest wing. She guessed that it must have been built no more than twenty years ago. It was a modern building, with airy, spacious rooms, full of light and with tasteful, contemporary furniture.

It looked to be mainly a family wing, as all the bedrooms, including her new rooms were located there, on the first floor.

"These are your rooms." Fitzwilliam said formally, as he opened one of the doors at the end of the corridor.

Elizabeth walked in slowly.

"It is lovely." she whispered in awe of the elegant, feminine, sitting room.

"I am glad you approve." He took her hand to his mouth for a short caress.

Elizabeth walked to the balcony door. "You can see the sea from here!" she cried, enchanted with the view.

"My father built this wing for my mother exclusively." Darcy explained. "She found the old part of the castle to be a bit gloomy. She liked the view from this room too."

Elizabeth silently thanked her late mother-in-law. She understood her completely. Thanks to her, she would be able to live in these beautiful rooms, and not in some sinister, bare stone chambers with weapons on the walls and suits of armour standing in every corner that she had passed on her way there.

Darcy took her hand to show her around.

"This is your bedroom." He opened one of the doors.

Elizabeth peeked curiously inside. The room looked as if it had been freshly redecorated. There were pastel wallpapers in delicate flowery patterns, and all the furniture, thick plush carpet, curtains and upholstery looked new as well, and had a subtle feminine touch to it.

Only the bed looked old. It was very large, almost enormous, the biggest bed she had ever seen. Judging by the elaborate carvings (which depicted some hunting scenes, she presumed) on the bedposts and headboard, it must have been brought from the old part of the house. The bed sheets looked fresh and inviting, but it was enough to imagine it covered with some animals furs, and it could easily go back to one of the towers.

"These rooms have been closed since my mother's death, over fifteen years ago." he explained. "I thought to refresh it a bit before your arrival."

Elizabeth walked to look closer at the delicate, white vanity.

"You can, of course, change whatever you wish." he assured.

"Oh, no." she protested at once and looked around. "It is all very lovely. I would not change anything…" she hesitated.

He waited patiently for her to finish.

"Apart from the bed." she said.

Darcy frowned. "You do not like it?"

"No, it is very… stylish, I guess, historical." She cleared her throat. "But so dark and imposing. And so very large. I would get lost in it." she tried to jest, but it turned flat, even to her own ears.

"Do not worry." he pulled her to him, his arms wrapping around her waist. "I will find you in it."

Elizabeth rolled her eyes at his comment.

"I am afraid the bed has to stay here." he continued. "All the Darcys were conceived and born in it." he announced proudly. "It ensures our fertility."

She laughed out loud, believing it was another attempt at a jest on his part. But when she met his expression, she thought that perhaps it was not. Her eyes rested on the bed again. She decided not to enquire about it further, afraid that she would next hear that all the Darcys had died in it as well.

She looked around. "My dressing room?"

He led her to the opposite and pushed the door, hidden in the wall panelling.

"How clever." she said, as she walked inside. It was bigger than her old room at Longbourn.

She noticed another small door. "What is in there?" she pointed.

He stepped forward to open it for her.

She gasped. “A bathing room!” she looked around with amazement. “A real bathroom.”

He nodded. “With hot water and a splashing toilet.” The pride in his voice was evident, even more than when he had spoken about the Darcy birthing bed. “Another of my mother’s ideas. I remember that the men from London were once brought when I was a child to install the pipes. It still works fine.”

As they returned to the sitting room, she found her courage to enquire. “And your bedroom?”

He stepped to the left and pushed the heavy curtain covering part of the wall. There was a massive door hidden behind it. “Over there.” he explained. “Always open if you ever need me.” he assured.

“Thank you.” she walked to him, lifted on her toes and kissed his cheek. “It is all so very lovely. I could not imagine more pleasant and comfortable rooms to live in.”

He kissed her back, but shortly. “I imagine you would like to take a bath and change yourself before dinner.”

Elizabeth nodded, and he pulled on a cord.

In the matter of a minute, a rosy, tall, dark haired girl, perhaps a year or two younger than she, appeared in the door.

“This is Heather.” Darcy introduced. “Your new lady’s maid.”

Elizabeth smiled kindly at the girl who looked scared, her eyes rooted to the carpet.

“Greet your Mistress.” Darcy ordered.

The girl plopped to her knees and kissed the end of her lady’s dress, and later grabbed her hand to kiss it as well.

Elizabeth snatched her hand away and stared in shock at the girl. “Please, stand up.” She tried to lift the girl to her feet.

Heather refused to stand up. “It is a great honour for me to serve you.” she murmured. “A great honour.”

Elizabeth stared at Darcy, her eyes big.

He walked to the servant, and taking the girl’s arm, lifted her. “Heather is from the village, and she is not particularly aware of the ways of the world.” he glared at the servant. “But she is a good girl, selected from many others, I assure you.”

Elizabeth looked warmly at the girl. “I see.”

“I will try hard to please you, my lady.” Heather assured eagerly. “I have been trained to do ladies’ hair by Miss Georgiana’s maid for the last two months, who once was trained by a lady's maid in London, who was in service for a real Duchess." she boasted.

"I am sure you will be a great help for me." Elizabeth said kindly, with a warm smile.

"Go and prepare your Mistress' bath." Darcy said.

Heather bowed and hurried to the bedroom.

When the servant disappeared, Darcy walked to Elizabeth. "I shall leave you alone now. There are some matters I have to see to yet before dinner."

"Of course." Elizabeth smiled.

He placed a kiss on her forehead, stroked her face and walked out of the room.

Chapter Eleven

Elizabeth opened her eyes to the sounds of muffled voices coming from behind closed doors. She sat up in the ancient bed, and looked around her new bedroom. She felt as if she had slept for a week. Strong summer sun invaded the room through the gap in the heavy cream curtains. It had to be quite late in the morning. How long had she slept?

She pushed the covers aside and climbed out of the bed. She felt weak in her knees as she strode to the window and opened the curtains. The sun was high in the sky. What time could it be? She glanced around the room, trying to locate a clock.

She thought she heard Fitzwilliam's voice in the sitting room, so she padded to the door and turned the doorknob.

He was there together with her maid, Heather.

Both the girl and her husband turned their heads as she stood in the open door.

She could see a warm, private greeting in his eyes as he spoke to the servant in a quiet voice.

"See to your Mistress' breakfast."

"Aye, Master." the girl bowed and hurried out of the room.

Darcy approached her and she stepped into his arms with a smile. "What time is it?" she asked, her throat dry.

He kissed her hair, which was strewn freely around her shoulders and down her back, and rubbed her bare arms, uncovered by the short sleeves of her thin summer nightgown. "Nearly one o'clock."

"I have slept so long?!"

"I was a bit worried too, but you slept so peacefully, I thought there was no reason to wake you." he said in his usual calm voice.

"I can hardly believe it." She covered her face with her hands. "What will everyone think; their new Mistress sleeping past midday on her first day here? It does not bode well."

"Nonsense. Do not fret about it." Darcy dismissed her worry. "We travelled extensively the last couple days. Moreover, you had little sleep at nights too, which was entirely my fault," he murmured, stroking her rosy cheek. "It is perfectly understandable that you needed your rest."

She shook her head with a frown, trying to recall the course of the last evening. "I do not even remember going to bed. The last thing I recall was tasting my wine at dinner."

Darcy nodded. "You literally fell asleep during dinner, and I had to carry you upstairs."

"How mortifying!" she gasped. "In front of all the servants!"

"I can assure you that they were only concerned about your well-being. But you had no fever, so I knew that you were only very tired. I undressed you, helped you into your nightgown and put you into bed. You slept like a babe."

Elizabeth rubbed her forehead. "I think that I slept too long. My head feels heavy and my stomach uneasy."

Darcy took her arm and led her to the window. His hand cupped her face, and he looked down at her with concern in his eyes. "You shall be fine." he said after a moment, relief visible in his expression. Then he hugged her to him tightly. "I must remember in the future how delicate you are." he whispered with a sigh.

She pushed from him. "I am not a fragile flower," she announced. "I am a healthy country girl."

He shook his head with a smile. "Perhaps. But still a human."

Her eyebrows raised up high on her forehead, confusion growing her face. "Are we not all humans?" she asked after a moment.

"Forgive me." Darcy shook his head with frown and suddenly changed the subject. "As far as I remember, yesterday you very much wanted to see the beach."

Elizabeth clasped her hands together. "Oh, yes!"

Darcy smiled at her enthusiasm. "I have a meeting with my steward later in the afternoon, but if you hurry with your dressing and breakfast, we will manage to go down to the beach, and have a nice walk before my appointment."

Elizabeth grinned, and without a word ran back to the bedroom, wondering whether all her dresses were still in their trunks. Perhaps Heather had already managed to unpack some of them, so she would have something to wear on her walk.

***

An hour later, Master and Mistress were seen leaving the house, walking in the direction of the beach. Mrs. Darcy walked properly supported on her husband's arm, but the moment she was sure they could not be observed from the windows any longer, she released his arm and instead snuggled closer, her smaller form fitting perfectly under his arm.

Darcy embraced her, and kissed down the top of her head, decorated with blue ribbons, as the lady had discarded her bonnet this morning. He helped her down the steep cliff till she was safely on the sand.

Elizabeth ran almost to the edge of the water, and stared at the waves for a long moment. It was a warm, sunny day and the sea was almost calm, just with the slight waves here and there.

She inhaled deeply in the breeze, tiny drops of salt water fillings her lungs. "I will come here every day." she promised herself.

Darcy advanced from behind, pulled her into his arms and rocked her in place.

They stood for a long moment, two pairs of dark eyes focused on the far horizon, wind blowing into their faces.

"Can we bathe?" she spoke first, not taking her eyes from the water.

"I do not think it to be the best idea." Darcy said slowly. "I admit that I do swim here quite often. It is not very deep, and the tide is rarely strong, but the water is rather cold, even in summer, and you…"

"Oh, I do not mind a bit of cold water!" she interrupted him, turning into his arms to face him. "You must have heard that Papa was about to take Mama and my sisters to Brighton to do some sea bathing just after our wedding." she pouted, indicating that he should recompense her somehow for the missed trip.

"Lizzy, it is not Brighton. The climate is much colder here." Darcy took her hands into his. "Even now I can feel your hands are freezing." He rubbed her naked arms where goose bumps appeared.

He took his greatcoat off and wrapped her into it. "You must remember to put on a spencer and a warm shawl every time you go out. We are far in the north, and I do not want you to get yourself ill." he said, making sure that she put her arms into the sleeves.

Elizabeth gazed down with a frown at her own person. Her husband's greatcoat was several times too big for her, and she felt drown in it. She pulled the sleeves up to uncover her hands, and sighed very quietly. He had not even noticed the pretty dress she had on herself today. It was a new one, and she had never worn it before, pale blue muslin, decorated with dark blue ribbon, perfectly matching her eyes. Heather had managed to press it nicely while she had her breakfast. Elizabeth knew that thanks to the clever cut of the gown, she looked slimmer and taller in it. She had hoped he would appreciate it.

"Can we just try one day?" she said, lifting her eyes at him. "I promise I will not insist if I find the water too cold. I could only stroll along the bank while you will swim."

He hesitated a moment. "We can, I suppose, one day, on the condition it will be truly a warm day."

"Oh, thank you, thank you!" She jumped into his arms.

Darcy returned the embrace, picking her up for a moment. Then he put her down, but did not release his hold on her. His arm curved around her waist, under his greatcoat.

His eyes focused on her lips, and he leaned to her, his hot breath on her cheek.

"I have almost forgotten!" she cried. "Where is he?"

He frowned, still staring at her lips. "Who?"

"Your wolf!"

He straightened himself up. "Oh… you still think about him."

She smiled. "Should I not?"

His expression darkened. "He is not here now. I lent him to one of my neighbours across the border."

"Why?"

He sighed, as if displeased. "He needed a good breeder."

Elizabeth's expression saddened visibly. "Tis a shame. I thought about him so often."

"You did." he said with a frown.

She nodded. "Yes, I was thinking about the name for him."

"And?"

"I do have a few suggestions…" She looked at him from the corner of her eye, battling her dark eyelashes at him. "First I thought about Fluffy."

She laughed out loud at the half disguised, half terrified look on his face. Biting on her lower lip, she continued, "But then I thought that perhaps it was too feminine, surely a better name for a cat who spends his life in the drawing room, and not for an animal who runs the forests and howls at the moon."

"I cannot disagree with that." Darcy grunted.

"What do you think about Wolfgang?" Elizabeth proposed.

Darcy presented a less displeased expression. "Prey tell what induced that?"

"Cannot you guess? Wolgang Amadeus Mozart, my favourite composer, Woofie for short."

"It is better than Fluffy." Darcy acknowledged gravely.

"But eventually I thought about King."

His chest pushed up, and he straightened. "King, just King?"

"Yes, because of Shakespeare. Do you remember King Lear?" she asked.

He shook his head.

"He's mad that trusts in the tameness of a wolf, a horse's health, a boy's love, or a whore's oath." she quoted.

"Well, what do you think?" she waited for his reaction.

"I think that..." He pulled her to him "I found myself a very clever wife."

She grinned. "And I think I found myself the best of husbands."

His expression turned serious. "I am afraid you will not think that always."

She searched his face for a moment and then sighed. "I think I know what you mean. You think that we will change in the years to come." She snuggled closer. "Fitzwilliam, I cannot imagine us ever being the same as my parents, or like the Hursts, two strangers living together under the same roof."

"I am not afraid of that." he ensured quietly. "I fear you will be disappointed with me in time, when you come to know me better."

"Tis true, you are rather… well, unusual in some ways." she admitted in a soft voice, "You speak little, and you keep many things to yourself. Sometimes you seem to be so distant, so closed in yourself. Your servants' behaviour baffles me, but perhaps the customs here in the north are different and…" Her lips formed a playful smile. "You happen to make strange sounds in your sleep."

He paled. "I do?"

"Yes." Her smile grew and then she blushed. "At nights when we finish… after we…"

"After we make love." he ended for her.

"Yes." Her blush grew deeper. "You pull me close and fall asleep, but I am so… alert still, that I lie awake for some time yet, and then you… as if growl very softly right into my ear. But it does not bother me." she ensured him. "I can only hope that in time you will want to share everything with me."

"Lizzy, dearest." He cupped her face in both hands and whispered fervently. "I want it as well. You cannot imagine how much… If there are some matters which I cannot tell you about, it is for your own good. I ask you to trust me for the time being. I love you so much."

She looked into his eyes and smiled. "I love you too."

There was such a joy in his eyes as he picked her up into his arms. She realized that she had said the words of love to him so clearly and straightforwardly for the first time ever. The kiss that followed left her boneless and yielding, slumping in his arms, her breasts tingling from the touch of his hands.

His voice brought her to reality. "You can go anywhere you wish around the house, in the park and the house. You are safe here. No one will harm you."

She lifted her face from his chest, surprised with the sudden seriousness of his voice.

"Still, since you do not know Pemberley well enough, I would wish for you to always have a companion when you choose to go for a walk."

Elizabeth frowned. She did not find the idea very appealing so far. She liked her solitary walks. Sometimes she needed to be alone. "A companion?"

"Yes, in case you get lost." he said, and produced a low whistle.

To Elizabeth's astonishment, seemingly out of nowhere, a young wolf ran to them.

The animal stopped in front of Elizabeth and waved his tail invitingly.

Elizabeth glanced from the animal to her husband. "For me?"

Darcy nodded. "His name is Wilfred. He is well trained, and will be obedient to you."

Elizabeth knelt down. "Hello, Wilfred." she patted the wolf's head gently, as he leaned into her hand. "We are going to be good friends, are we not?" she asked, and the animal barked twice.

"He is beautiful." She stroked the animal's shiny back. "He seems to be not much older than a pup." she observed. "How old is he?"

"Ahh..." Darcy hesitated for a moment. "Around six months, I believe."

Elizabeth knelt down and petted her new friend for a moment, and then stood up to face her husband. Lifting on her toes, she wrapped her arms around his neck and kissed his cheek soundly.

"Thank you." she whispered, gazing into his eyes.

Darcy's hand came to rest lightly on the back of her waist, but with less enthusiasm than before. "You are welcome." he answered formally.

Elizabeth snuggled closer, lifting on her tiptoes and intentionally pressing her full breasts into his chest. "I want another kiss." she purred in a low, needy voice. She lifted her face to him, her lips forming a perfect rosebud, ready to be touched.

Darcy let out an embarrassed sound. "We have a company." he said at last.

Elizabeth looked around, confused. The beach was empty. She took his meaning only when he glanced down at the animal, still sitting beside them.

She followed his gaze. "Wilfred?" she laughed. "Do you expect that he will go to the kitchen and gossip to the servants about my scandalous behaviour?"

Darcy still seemed to be somehow uneasy though, and did not share her laugh. Only when the wolf turned his head and ran a few yards away, did he bring her closer and let their lips meet.

The kiss was sweet, but in Elizabeth's opinion, less ardent that the previous ones and ended too soon.

She lifted her eyes to him. "Will you come to me tonight?" she whispered.

His gaze turned serious. "You wish me to?" She thought that his voice sounded uncertain.

Her body rubbed against his. "So much." she whispered. Her lips placed an open mouth kiss on the side of his neck, and rubbed against him.

Darcy moaned throatily, but soon pushed her away at a safe distance. "You are a little devil, you know." He tried to sound stern, as he squeezed her hand. "I think you enjoy torturing me like this."

Elizabeth batted her eyelashes innocently.

"Pray, tell me how I can go to meet my steward like this?" his eyes pointed down to his lap.

Elizabeth blushed, seeing the large bulge at the front of his breeches.

"I am sorry." she whispered, but the twinkle in her eyes told him she was not very sorry at all.

He shrugged. "It is enough for you to brush against me…"

Her blush deepened.

Darcy took her arm and turned them into the direction of Pemberley. "I must go, but you may stay here longer if you wish."

She shook her head. "No, I will come back with you. I want to spend the rest of the afternoon with Georgiana."

They walked slowly back to the manor with Wilfred following at their feet.

***

Elizabeth woke with the start in the darkness of the room. She looked around with wild eyes, her heart banging in her chest. She was in her room. She plopped back on the pillows, her apprehension abated. As she looked to the side, a new relief washed over her on the sight of the dark head on the pillow beside her

Fitzwilliam was still with her, he had not gone yet to his room, as he had done all the previous nights.

The prolonged, deep, torturous, group howling was heard despite the closed windows. She shivered. It was just like in her dream, all those wolves around her in the middle of the night, howling to the moon. She thought that the sound was only the creation of her mind, but no, it lasted and grew even stronger.

"Lizzy…" a warm, big hand wrapped around her waist.

As she leaned back against his familiar form, she realized that she was naked, her nightgown probably discarded on the floor, his wetness present between her thighs. They had spent a merry evening with Georgiana, who had played Scottish melodies for them. When they had said their goodnights and retired, he had shushed the frightened Heather away, and disrobed her himself before taking her to bed.

"Is something wrong?" he murmured sleepily.

"Why are those animals ~~are~~ howling so much?" she asked.

"Hush…" he pushed her on her back and loomed over her. "They are wolves, it is what they do at night." he placed gentle kisses all over her face. "It is perfectly natural."

"They are so close to the house? Why? I cannot listen to that." She covered her ears with her hands. "I cannot bear it. Please do something to stop it."

"Come here." He rolled on his back and pulled her over him. "Try to fall asleep." He rubbed her back. "Do not be afraid. They would never hurt you."

"I cannot sleep." she pleaded again a moment later as the noise outside continued.

Darcy sighed and got out of bed. Elizabeth watched with round eyes as, clad only in his shirt, he walked outside to the balcony and closed the glass door carefully after himself. The bellowing was cut in the matter of seconds; the door opened and her husband calmly returned to bed.

"How did you do that?" she whispered as he pulled her to him.

"I shall be the laughing stock of all of Pemberley." he said with a sigh, but with a note of good humour. "But at least you will have a good night's rest. Tis most important." He kissed her forehead and drew the covers over both of them.

Chapter Twelve

Heather peeked inside the Mistress' bedchamber. Mrs. Darcy was still fast asleep, her long pale blond hair strewn over the pillows. She shook her head in resignation; she always brushed and plaited Mistress' hair neatly for the night. However, in the morning, it was constantly loose and tangled as if someone had been twisting and pulling at it.

The clock on the mantelpiece showed only a few minutes after six. From the experience of the last week, she knew that Mistress would sleep for some time yet. She decided to go downstairs for tea, so when her lady woke up, it would be waiting for her.

On her way back from the kitchens, a tall young lad crossed her way.

"I shall help you." He attempted to take the tray with numerous tea accessories away from her, "Tis heavy."

"It is not." She dodged away from him, and straightened herself up. "I will manage. Should you not go about your own duties?" She did her best to glare at him.

"Mistress is still in her rooms." Wilfred leaned against the wall, showing white, even teeth and a broad smile, "I am to accompany her when she walks out, of the house."

Heather's eyes narrowed at him. "At least let me do my duties, and stay out of my way." she huffed.

Wilfred stepped aside so she could walk past him. "You have started to put on airs since Mrs. Reynolds appointed you to be the Mistress' lady's maid."

Heather chose not to comment on this, and kept walking.

"Do you know what we did last night?" Wilfred asked, clearly ready to boast.

"Let me guess." she said, without a second look at him, marching through the corridor, "You howled to the moon. How interesting."

"Master came out on the balcony and ordered us to go somewhere else because his wife could not sleep."

She stopped in place, so the china clattered on the tray. "You howled right under the Mistress' bedroom?" she asked in disbelief.

"We wanted to show how much we approve of her." he explained with a wide smile, "We are glad that Master found such a fine and kind lady."

"So you decided not to allow her to sleep." She stepped with her tray toward him. "I thought that you had became more responsible since Master decided to make you his wife's guard on her outings. But now I can see that you have not changed at all from the time when we were children. Only silly pranks in this empty head of yours!"

She tried to walk past him, pleased with her speech, but he blocked her way once again. "You will regret saying this one day."

"Oh, really?"

"Yes, you will." He stared down at her with intensity. "When I become the chief of security."

"You think Master would grant such an honour to someone who gossips about him and my lady?"

"I do not gossip, I am telling only you." he reasoned as he followed her up the staircase. "You are the lady's maid. You know more about some matters than anyone else in the house."

"If you think I will tell you anything…" she started angrily, but he interrupted her in a calm voice.

"You do not have to. The whole of Pemberley knows that Master's love for his wife is great, and that he visits her bedchamber every night. Why else would he have married a human?"

"I advise you to stop that talking!" she cried sharply, "Now let me go, please." She smiled sweetly at him. "Her tea is getting cold."

Wilfred walked her to the door leading to the Mistress' rooms and opened it for her.

"I think that my lady will not need you this morning." she said as they walked inside. "I heard that Master is to go across the border today, so my thought is that she will want to spend some time with Miss Georgiana." She put the tray on the round breakfast table, and started to unload it.

"Now go." she whispered when there was heard a characteristic noise of the flushing toilet coming from the bedroom. "She should not see you here like this."

Wilfred smiled, blushed and stepped closer, "See you later," he whispered, and before she could stop him, he leaned down and kissed her rosy cheek.

"You!" she cried, but he was gone already. She rubbed the place where he kissed her. She would have a serious talk with him later; taking liberties with her without her permission, what was he thinking?

The door opened, and Mrs. Darcy stood there in her nightgown and robe, her hair wild around her shoulders and down her back.

"Good morning, my lady." Heather greeted her with a bow, "Have you slept well?"

Elizabeth smiled. "On the whole, yes, quite well, thank you, Heather." She sat on the chair by the table. "Is that my tea?"

Heather nodded. "I thought you would like to have some before breakfast."

"Thank you. It was very thoughtful of you." Elizabeth yawned into her sleeve. "Just what I need to wake me up properly."

Heather left the room and entered the bedchamber. She opened the windows and started to tidy about a bit. The bed sheet was soiled in one place, so she stripped the bed of it. The rest of the linens looked clean, so she only picked them up and spread them on the chair opposite the window to have them aired.

She stumbled over the Master's stockings and neck cloth, abandoned next to the bedpost. As she folded them neatly and put them aside, she reminded herself to return them to Gainnes, the Master's valet. Then she collected the brush, the blue ribbon and the hair pins from the vanity and returned to the sitting room.

Mistress was reading again; a new newspaper that had been brought to the manor just yesterday.

"I shall plait your hair and put it up for your bath, my lady." Heather said as she took the brush and tried to untangle the knots in the long blond tresses. She admired her lady's pale golden hair, even envied it a bit. Most of the people in the pack had dark or red hair.

She tried to be gentle, but at one more decided pull, her Mistress hissed softly.

"Forgive me, my lady." Heather said at once.

"Tis not your fault," Elizabeth massaged her scalp. "I always had my hair in a braid or in a paper curls for the night before, but since my marriage… You see, Mr. Darcy likes it free around my shoulders."

"The curls would last longer did you wear paper curls for the night, my lady." Heather pointed out as she began to plait the heavy mass.

Elizabeth nodded. "I know, it is not the same as using the curling iron."

"And it damages the hair so much."

The older woman sighed. "But I look so unattractive in paper curls. I do not want Mr. Darcy to see me like that."

As Heather finished tying the ribbon at the end of the thick braid, she recalled her mother wearing paper curls in the presence of her father countless times. She said nothing about it though, as she thought that she was not in position to comment on that.

There was a decided knock on the door, and both women's heads turned in that direction.

"Who can it be?" Elizabeth asked.

"Perhaps, Miss Georgiana." Heather pushed the last pin into the make shift bun, securing it up.

The knock repeated, and the next moment, the Master of the house entered.

Heather knew it was time for her to disappear. "I shall see to your bath, my lady", she murmured, bowed and hurried out of the room.

When Darcy and Elizabeth were left alone, she stood up and fled into his arms. "Good morning," she whispered against his neck, standing on her tiptoes.

He kissed her temple, walked her to the table, sat on the chair and pulled her on to his lap.

His eyes swept over the unfinished cup of tea, the brush he bought for her, a few scattered hair pins and stopped on the newspaper abandoned next to them. "I wondered where my newspaper had gone."

"I thought you were finished reading it." she explained apologetically, "I always read my father's paper."

He squeezed her to him. "I must see that we order more than one copy from now on."

Her face brightened. "Thank you." She kissed his cheek, "I did not expect to see you until breakfast."

"I did not want to leave without saying goodbye."

The instant disappointment reflected in her eyes. "You are going away. Again?"

He nodded, "Our neighbour, Lord McGarth, needs my assistance. I will try to be back home for dinner, I promise."

"I thought we would spend at least some of the day together," she whispered, not hiding her disappointment. "You are gone so often." She pushed his hands away from her waist and lifted from his lap to her feet. "I barely see you."

Darcy stood up as well. "Try to understand." He pulled her back to him, burying his face into her neck.

"I am trying." she said slowly. The corners of her mouth lifted up in small, sad smile.

"I shall miss you." He kissed her mouth gently, stroked her cheek and strode out of the room.

***

Later that morning, Georgiana and Elizabeth were finishing their breakfast in the smaller, more informal dining room downstairs, when Heather entered.

"Is something the matter?" Elizabeth asked as she dabbed her lips with the napkin.

"Yes, madam." Heather walked closer. "I have just been told that last evening, the rest of your trunks arrived."

Elizabeth's eyes brightened. "At last!" She clasped her hands together as she turned to Georgiana. "Due to the haste of our engagement and the wedding just a few weeks later, my trousseau was not finished on time. I have not seen all the dresses yet."

Georgiana's face mirrored her sister's excitement. "Can I see them too?"

"Of course, if you wish." Elizabeth smiled broadly at the younger girl. "We shall look through them together." She stood up from her place and faced her maid. "Heather, do you know where my trunks are now?"

"They are just being carried upstairs, my lady."

"Excellent!" Georgiana rose too, "May we go now?"

Elizabeth nodded, and all three of them left the room and hurried upstairs.

Half an hour later, several large trunks stood wide open in the middle of the sitting room in the Mistress apartments.

"How beautiful!" Georgiana cried as she pulled out the gauzy, silver like, ball gown. She put the dress to herself and danced around the room, stopping in front of the large, floor length looking glass. "You have excellent taste, Lizzy." She admired the dress.

Elizabeth knelt next to one of the open trunks, a heavy frown on her forehead. She could not recognize any of these dresses. She had expected to receive three more everyday dresses, some bed linens, nightgowns, a velvet cap and two bonnets; most of the items made by the seamstress at Meryton. What she looked at now, was over a dozen mostly silk outfits, more beautiful and expensive than anything she had ever owned before.

As she reached for another dress, this time a pale pink one, decorated with delicate lace, a note fell into her hands. She recognized her mother's handwriting, and tore impatiently at the seal.

Dearest Lizzy,

I expect you are surprised to be receiving all this finery instead of the three meager muslin gowns you chose for yourself. Those went to Kitty, and one to Mary, though she argued that the décolleté of the gown was much too low for her. But I assured her we could remedy that with just more lace.
Your husband, when he was yet your betrothed, asked me to order an entire new wardrobe for you, sending the checks to him of course. You see I made good use of this opportunity. Praise me for keeping this a secret from you! Please write to me, and tell me how you like them.

Your Mama,
Fanny Bennet

Elizabeth sighed, as she folded the note. She should not be surprised. Her husband saw nothing wrong in spending outrageous sums on her so far, and she did not expect her mother to refuse an offer of an unlimited shopping excursion.

"Elizabeth, is that all you are going to receive?" Georgiana's voice brought her attention back.

"Yes." She could not imagine needing more dresses for the next two years. "I do hope that it is all." she stressed.

"But they are all summer gowns." Georgiana said, ruffling through the trunks. "I cannot see any woolen dresses, not to mention warm caps, and a fur coat, or tall, thick boots."

Elizabeth leaned over her and retrieved from the bottom of one of the trunks, a dark velvet coat with soft fur around the sleeves. "There is a lovely coat here. Together with the one I brought with me, it should be quite enough for colder days."

Georgiana took it from her and touched it carefully. "Lizzy, it is much too thin for winter here, I am afraid. You will freeze wearing this on a walk in January."

Elizabeth frowned with worry. "Do you think so? I do not wish to stay the whole winter at home."

"It is only August, and still early enough to make you a nice coat, more appropriate for the colder climate here." Georgiana suggested.

Elizabeth's face lit up. "We can go to the nearest town for a day or two!" she exclaimed. "The one we rode through on our way here, and order something there. I am sure they have some nice shops there. That would be a nice trip for both of us, I imagine."

Georgiana shook her head. "That is not a good idea." she said slowly in a subdued voice. "I do not think that Brother would allow that."

Elizabeth looked at her, surprised. The girl looked nervous.

"When I need a new dress, and we cannot go to London, I always ask Mrs. Brown from the village to sew me one." she explained.

Elizabeth frowned in concentration. "Mrs. Brown? Heather's mother? I think I saw her in the church last Sunday. Her husband is the blacksmith, am I right?"

Georgiana nodded. "Yes, you are, Lizzy. She is an excellent seamstress. It is enough to show her the picture of the dress from a fashion magazine, and she can make exactly the same one. You cannot tell the difference between her work and the one of a professional dressmaker from London."

"I have seen little of the village so far. You brother promised to show it to me, but he has been so busy, and he is gone today again." Elizabeth said as she put the velvet coat away on the nearby chair. "Heather," she turned to the girl who was busy unpacking the third trunk, containing boxes with bonnets and shoes, "Would you like to go with us to the village and see your family?"

The girl's face brightened, but then she shook her head. "I will see them on Sunday, as usual. The trunks need to be unpacked. "

Elizabeth waved her hand in a dismissive gesture. "You can do it later, when we come back. I am sure your mother would be happy to see you."

"I would like to see them very much." the girl murmured.

"It is settled then." Georgiana smiled.

***

Elizabeth had been to the village once before, on Sunday, when she, her husband and Georgiana had attended church. She had been very much in awe, not only because of the appearance of the church buildings. The village itself made a great impression on her. It could be easily qualified as a small town, being almost the size of the Meryton.

Elizabeth asked if they could stop the carriage and walk to the Browns' household, as she wanted to see more of the village. Shockingly, the main street was cobblestone, straight and broad, with neat, wooden sidewalks. All the houses were very well kept, with clean, sparkling windows, brightly painted doors, and flowers in the window boxes. People were dressed simply, but very decently, and even the smallest children wore shoes.

As they passed, all the people bowed deeply in recognition, but to her relief, only several fell to their knees in front of her. A few rosy, dark haired boys under the age of five, accompanied by a young wolf (Elizabeth had already got accustomed to the fact that the wolves were treated like pets here), stopped before them and gaped at her. Georgiana walked to them, and retrieved the sweets out of her reticule, clearly prepared just for such an occasion. The children looked hesitantly at one other at first, but then in a second grabbed the confections, and murmured their thanks.

"There is a school." Georgiana pointed to one of the buildings, when the children ran away, giggling.

Elizabeth gaped at her. "You have a school here?"

"It was founded by my great grandmother. This is only a four year school, but it is enough to teach children reading, writing and some basic mathematics. There is a small library next to the school as well."

"And what is there?" she pointed to the one storey building with large windows.

"A hospital." Georgiana answered.

Elizabeth was silent for a moment before she spoke. "You cannot imagine how impressed I am with this place."

"Brother says that because of our isolated location, we need to have everything here."

Elizabeth was so occupied with admiring everything around her, that she did not notice that they reached the outskirts of the village where the house of the blacksmith was located.

A rosy girl of six ran out of it. "Heather, Heather!" she cried and jumped into her sister's arms.

Soon, a very tall and well built (it was another thing Elizabeth had grown to be accustomed to, the size of people here) man of reddish complexion walked out from the shed.

Heather walked to him. "Papa, Mrs. Darcy has come because she wants Mama to make her a dress."

The man dropped on one knee. "Tis a great honour to us that the wife of our Master visits our home first, before all others."

"I ask you to stand up." Elizabeth said uneasily. She never knew how to behave when they did that. "Please."

Just then, a rosy, pretty woman, ran out of the house, carrying a chubby babe on her hip. "Mrs. Darcy, what an honour! And Miss Darcy! " she cried, "Heather, my child, and you, too, are here. I did not think to see you till next Sunday. What a pleasant surprise!"

"Mrs. Darcy allowed me to come with her." Heather said, kissing her mother on the cheek and taking the baby from her.

"Please, please, come in." Mrs. Brown made a wide gesture, inviting Elizabeth and Georgiana inside.

Through a smaller room, they were led into what looked to be a parlour. Elizabeth looked curiously around. The furnishings were simple, there was flowery wallpapers and nice curtains in the windows. The room looked inviting, and reminded Elizabeth of the houses of wealthy farmers around Meryton.

"I have not had the opportunity to thank you for keeping my girl as your lady's maid." Mrs. Brown said as she walked in, carrying the tray with tea and home made cake. "She was so excited with the idea of serving in the castle. She is so curious about the world."

As Elizabeth listened to the woman, she noticed that her accent was different from the others here. To her amusement, she had even noticed that Fitzwilliam's accent had transformed since they had come to Pemberley. His perfect Oxford pronunciation vanished in favour of distinct Scottish-like dialect, with strong "r's".

"You are not from here, I am guessing." she said as she took a sip of tea.

Heather's mother shook her head. "No, I am not. I am from Kent."

"Kent?"

"Yes, I served in the manor, at Rosings Park. When our Mistress, Lady Catherine, gave birth to a baby girl, Lady Anne came from Pemberley to visit her and the baby, together with her husband, the old Mr. Darcy. My husband accompanied them on this trip. Our courtship was very short, a few weeks and we were married, and I came to live here."

Elizabeth looked at the woman, thinking how similar the story of their courtship seemed to be.

"It must have been difficult for you to accustom yourself to the life in the north, Mrs. Brown."

The woman nodded with understanding. "Yes, especially at the beginning. But now I cannot say one bad word about my life here."

The little girl who they had seen outside before peeked inside with a pup wolf at her feet.

"Emmy, come here." Mrs. Brown invited, and girl ran to her and stood at her side, staring at the guests with wide eyes. The wolf found himself a place on the other side, placing his head on the woman's lap. "This is my youngest daughter, Emma." she introduced the girl.

Elizabeth smiled at the child, who after some quiet probing from her mother, dropped a proper curtesy in front of the ladies.

"I understand you have three children, Mrs. Brown." Elizabeth said, looking fro

Heather, who sat next to Georgiana with a toddler on her lap to the toothless girl still shyly snuggled to her mother's side.

Mrs. Brown shook her head with a smile and stroked the wolf's head. "Four. My son, Alistair is thirteen."

Elizabeth had not noticed any boy around that age in the house, so she assumed he was not at home. Perhaps he was helping his father, or his mother had sent him to the village for something.

She looked at the babe held by Heather. "That is your youngest then, is it not? A boy?"

Mrs. Brown nodded. "Yes, Angus, he will be one year next week. He should start walking on his own any day."

Heather put his brother on the carpeted floor, holding his hands. "Angus, show Mrs. Darcy how you walk. Will you walk to her?"

The child made a first shaky step and then the next ones. Elizabeth stood up just in time to catch the boy when he swayed dangerously. She picked up the baby in her arms and sat back on the chair with him.

The boy examined her carefully for some time before he laughed and caught her fingers in his chubby hand, squeezing hard.

She winced in surprise. "He has a very strong grip for a child." she tried to free her hand.

Heather took the boy hastily from her.

"Folks here are usually very strong, Mrs. Darcy." Mrs. Brown noted calmly. "Only when they are older do they learn to control their strength."

"I understand." Elizabeth said, not being sure whether she truly understood that. She should not be surprised though. She knew, of course, that Fitzwilliam was very strong; he could pick her up with no effort at all. The footman who had saved her from Wickham could not be called a weakling either.

"We came, Mrs. Brown, because my sister needs a warm winter coat and a new woolen dress." Georgiana said, directing the conversation to the aim of their visit. "As you know, the climate in the south is much milder, and her velvet caps and muslin gowns will not be appropriate when the cold months come."

"Well." Mrs. Brown said with energy, clasping her hands together. "There is much to do then. Do you know what pattern would you like, Mrs. Darcy?"

Chapter Thirteen

"I think we should ask for dinner to be served." Georgiana said from the piano, sheets scattered over the small tea table. "The cook will have to warm everything again if we wait much longer."

Elizabeth turned from the window. "He promised to be back for dinner."

"I doubt he will return earlier than tomorrow morning."

"How can you be so calm?" Elizabeth turned to the window again. "What if something has happened to him? Look at the skies… it is going to rain, and the night will be very dark. What if he gets lost…"

"Lizzy, he knows every tree here, every rock on the road." Georgiana protested in a calm voice, not troubled at all. "He shall be fine. His business with Lord McGarth must be serious if he needed to stay the night there."

Elizabeth strode from the window with her brow furrowed. "Who is he?"

Georgiana looked up at her. "You mean Lord McGarth?" Elizabeth nodded. "Our closest neighbour. His lands border with Pemberley."

"This I know." Elizabeth sat on the sofa next to her, "What business does Fitzwilliam have with him?"

Georgiana hesitated for a moment before she spoke slowly. "Brother does not give me the exact details of all his business, but I know that our family, for a long time now, has shared the ownership of some lands with the McGarths. Actually, Lord McGarth is our distant cousin; our grandmother was McGarth."

"So he is a relative." Elizabeth bit her lower lip. "Do you think I will meet him one day?"

"Oh, there is no doubt about it. Lord McGarth visits us quite often."

Elizabeth peered at the younger girl. "You do not like him?"

Georgiana shrugged. “I know he is a worthy man and a good landlord, very wealthy, I understand. I do not think much of him, he is… indifferent to me.” She paused and added quietly, “But you see, Lizzy,“ she sighed, “I am… his intended.”

Elizabeth frowned. “Intended? You mean… engaged?”

“Not exactly. At least not yet engaged. When Papa lived, many years ago, he made some sort of arrangement with Lord McGarth, that he would marry me when I grew up.”

“And what are your feelings about it?”

Georgiana lowered her head and murmured, “I did not know about the arrangement between Lord McGarth and my father till last year. I was in Ramsgate for summer vacation with my companion, the one brother employed when I lived alone in London to complete my education.”

Elizabeth touched her arm. “I know what happened there.”

“Brother told you? I should have guessed. Wickham is evil. He was cast out from here because of his various misgivings. In Ramsgate, he tried to talk to me every day, always in public places, so it was difficult to… get rid of him without witnesses. I wrote to Brother, who was in London then, that Wickham was bothering me. Wickham tried to convince me to elope with him, and when I refused, he became unpleasant.”

The memory of her last meeting with Wickham replayed in front of Elizabeth’s eyes. “I can imagine that.” she said, her throat tight.

“Thankfully, Brother came instantly and Wickham disappeared. However, the day before, he told me about Lord McGarth and his intentions toward me. When I asked Brother about it, he confirmed it.”

“Did it shock you?”

“At first, yes, very much so. I always thought about Lord McGarth as our neighbour and nothing else. I should be happy though; Brother promised I do not have to marry anyone till I am twenty-one.” Georgiana said, with obvious relief in her voice. “I still have almost five years.” She smiled, “I can play the piano, read, draw, spend my time with you, and Brother when he is home. I could not be happier than I am now. I will not worry about what will happen in five long years.”

Elizabeth stroked her back. “I am convinced that Fitzwilliam would never force you to marry a man you do not like.”

"It is not that simple, Elizabeth." Georgiana said sadly, with quiet resignation in her tone. "I am afraid that Brother thinks that only Lord McGarth can ensure me safety in the future. If I ever married, it could only be to him."

"But surely if you have fallen in love with someone else in the years to come, and he would prove to be responsible, appropriate and kind, loving you…"

"You do not understand, Elizabeth." Georgiana interrupted in gentle but firm voice. "There are only three families in Scotland that can be accepted when the marriage of a woman from our family is considered. The McGarths are one, and two others live even farther to the north, in the mountains. There are also another two families in Ireland, and one in the secluded island in the Orkneys. I do not know those families at all. I saw some of them a couple of times, but they are mostly strangers to us, and I do not want to live so far away from home."

"I do not understand. It does not make any sense to me." Elizabeth was shaking her head, her expression growing more and more confused. "Why would Fitzwilliam insist on taking into consideration only men from the families you mentioned when it comes to your marriage?"

Georgiana's dark grey eyes looked straight into her sister's blue ones. "Lizzy, you must have noticed that we are in many ways very different from what you have known so far. I cannot believe that some of my brother's behaviours do not surprise you, and some of our customs do not shock you."

"Yes." Elizabeth nodded. "I cannot deny it."

"The McGarths and the other families I mentioned to you are the same as we are."

Elizabeth did not speak for a moment. "But he married me, and I am not… from here."

"Because it is different with women, with brides." Georgiana said. "A Darcy male can marry a human bride, but Darcy females must marry a man from one of the families."

"I still do not understand …"

"I cannot tell you exactly how it works. Brother should be the one who will explain everything to you."

Elizabeth took her hand and gave it a gentle squeeze. "I know only one thing. Fitzwilliam will never force you into marriage to someone you cannot love, or at least respect and trust too."

"He may not have a choice." Georgiana said. "Perhaps you have noticed that there are more boys than girls here. There are families without any girls born to them. Daughters are valuable assets."

"Assets?"

"Yes. From where you come, it is a normal occurrence that the bride's family ensures her dowry when she enters the new family, am I correct?"

Elizabeth nodded. "It is expected."

"Here, it is entirely different. The future husband pays the father, or gives him something, a cow or a horse, a flock of sheep, it depends; when he marries his daughter."

"How very strange."

"Perhaps for the outsider, but when you grew up with this, it really is not. As I said, I am happy I am only sixteen. Brother promised I would not have to marry till I am of age." Georgiana smiled as she stood up and started to arrange her music sheets into a neat pile. "Let us go to the dining room. Fitzwilliam will not come back today."

***

It was past six o'clock, and she was still sleeping. She lay on her side, her hair twisted into white papers all over her head. When he had met her at Netherfield that night when she had come out to look at the full moon, she had her hair twisted in the same way. He did not understand why she bothered to keep her hair in locks in the first place. He liked it straight, cool to touch, slipping through his fingers like golden threads.

It was not his intention to interrupt her rest, but her scent today was so hard to resist, more than usual. Gently, he pushed her on her back and kissed her behind her ear, hoping to wake her up. Her eyelids fluttered, but she did not open her eyes.

His hand went to the front of her nightgown and tugged at the ribbon which secured it. As he pushed the thin material away, and stared at her bosom, he thought there was not a prettier sight in the world; full and creamy mounds, with wide, pink nipples.

He bent his head and took one velvet tip into his mouth. She arched her back up and murmured something. He smiled, and his hand dipped under the covers to find the edge of her nightgown.

His fingers dipped between her thighs, into her womanhood. She was moist, but not drenching his hand as usual when he touched her, not ready yet to be fully open.

He took his fingers away from her and brought them to his face. She smelled so different today, heady and hot. He smiled to himself; she was in heat.

He looked up at her peaceful expression and closed eyes. He could wake her, but she would like to talk first and ask questions. Finding the right answers for her enquires was getting harder and harder. She would learn the truth soon. He knew it to be unavoidable, a matter of weeks, days perhaps. Although he dreaded her tears, her anger, perhaps even repugnance at what he involved her into, at the same time, he felt relieved there would be no secrets left between them.

Darcy rolled over her, mindful not to crush her, supported on his arms, and started to kiss the way down her body. When he reached the blonde curls that concealed her femininity, he buried his nose into it and simply breathed. The sweetest fragrance he could imagine.

The pressure in his breeches began to be unbearable. Hands shaking, he tore at the buttons of his breeches, and started to rub himself against her plumpness.

"Fitzwilliam..." she murmured, and her dark blue eyes stared incoherently at him.

"Yes, my love." He gave her more of his weight, his hand moved between their bodies and he started stroking and opening her.

"When did you come back?" she asked, rubbing her eyes.

"A few hours ago." he growled as he slipped into her with ease.

He hid his face into her neck and started to move into her. She welcomed his thrusts, lifting tentatively to meet him half the way. She was still sleepy though; he noticed her yawning into his shoulder.

Soft, small hands went under his shirt as usual, and she started to touch him. He liked that, enjoyed her stroking on him very much. He wanted her to touch him in other places as well, but it was too soon for her to discover his scars. When her fingers started to wander down his sides to his ribcage, he pushed harder into her to distract her attention from his chest.

Her eyes popped open, and a slight frown crossed her face. Had he hurt her? In their previous encounters, he had been very careful not to move too deeply or roughly into her, and kept the penetration shallow.

Her expression changed then, her eyes rolled back and she moaned, biting on her lower lip. Small hands moved from the dangerous area down along his sides and dug into his backside. He smiled as her face contorted in pleasure and drove again and again, as deep as he could, each time eliciting delighted, surprised, incomprehensible sounds from her throat.

Feeling his release approaching, he gave her all of his weight, pushed into her far to the very end and whispered into her ear, so only she could hear it.

"Squeeze yourself around me again, Lizzy, squeeze that tight, sweet kitty around me again."

He lifted his face to look into her shocked eyes.

"Come on, Lizzy." He drove inside again. The next moment he felt her tightening rhythmically around him, her nails scraping his lower back.

"Ahhhh…." a deep growl rumbled from her, then she relaxed under him, her head dropped to the side as he spilled into her.

He lay partially on her for a long moment afterward, his eyes closed when he felt her moving under him, her small hands pushing him away. He thought that he was too heavy for her, so he rolled over, at the same time attempting to pull her with him.

She slapped his hands though and crawled out of the bed. "I must refresh myself." she said as she adjusted her gown and walked to the dressing room.

He sat in the bed and heard the sounds of running water and splashing toilet. The next moment, the door from the sitting room opened and Heather entered, carrying what looked like freshly ironed petticoats in her arms.

The girl was humming something as she hung his wife's underthings over the chair and moved to open the window.

She turned to the bed then, and at last saw him.

A loud shriek escaped her, and she stared at him with round eyes for a moment, before she turned on her feet and ran out of the room.

The next moment Elizabeth stood in the open door. "What was that?"

Her hair was free around her shoulders, in long blond locks, brush in her hand.

"Your maid."

She frowned as she walked to him, brushing her hair energetically, "You must have scared her." She sat on the edge of the bed, "You should not have, she is a good girl, I like her."

Darcy sat behind her and pulled her to him, his hands cupping her breasts. He wanted her again, soon, now.

"Do not." she dodged away from him.

"What is wrong?"

"Sometimes, I think you married me for one thing only." She glanced at the bed.

"Lizzy," He drew her to him, placing her head on his chest. "How can you think so?"

She sighed into his shirt covered chest. "We waited for you with dinner yesterday."

"I am sorry."

She looked up at him. "I was worried that something happened to you. You said you returned a few hours ago, which means in the middle of the night. It was such a dark, rainy and windy night, and you rode in such conditions."

"Sweetheart, it is my home, I have often returned home by night and nothing has ever happened to me."

"And what about those wolves in the woods? I am sure not all of them are domesticated like those who lived with the people around the households and in the village. They could have attacked you."

Darcy laughed. He could not help himself.

She pushed at his chest. "You are laughing at me?" she cried, red in the face. "I cannot sleep half the night, worrying about you and why you did not return, and now you mock me by laughing at me?"

"No, my heart, you misunderstood me." He did not allow her to free herself from his embrace. "I should not laugh, I am sorry. I do appreciate your concern about me. Simply, the wolves here cannot do any harm to me or to you."

There was a long moment of silence before she asked in a low, slightly trembling voice. "Do you have some kind of… power… a command over them?"

He smiled. "Yes, I have, in a matter of speaking," He kissed her brow and gazed into her dark blue eyes, "I admit I am rather tired. Let us stay in bed this morning, have a nap, then we can have breakfast in here."

"What about the servants? What will they say…"

"I do not care." He pushed the covers aside and tucked her in.

"Your duties?" she asked as she placed her head in the crook of his arm.

"They can wait," he said as he pulled the covers over them.

"Georgiana? She will…"

"She will understand," he interrupted her, "Close your eyes." He kissed her eyelids.

Sleep was not what he craved now most; her scent was making him hungry with need, but he knew she needed to feel safe now, and not used. He pulled her tighter to him and closed his own eyes with determination.

Chapter Fourteen

Elizabeth had just entered the house with Wilfred faithfully following at her feet, coming back from her every day walk along the beach, when she was addressed by Mrs. Reynolds.

"Mrs. Darcy," the housekeeper said with agitation unusual for her, and at the same time gesturing to the maid to take Elizabeth's bonnet, spenser and gloves. "Master has asked for you to come to his study as soon as you returned."

"Has something happened?"Elizabeth asked, handing her things to the maid.

"We have a guest." Mrs. Reynolds said in an unnatural, trembling voice; she paused and added in a lowered voice. "Lord McGrath is here. He may stay till tomorrow."

Elizabeth frowned. "Were we expecting his visit?

Mrs. Reynolds looked at her with a good degree of reproof. "It does not matter." she stressed, "He is our closest neighbour; his estate is on the other side of the border, and he is very influential. The Darcy and McGrath families have been close for many centuries."

Elizabeth glanced down at the soiled skirt of her old Longbourn dress. " I should change and refresh myself first." she touched her hair worriedly, feeling with her fingers that some of the locks had loosened themselves. She must have looked a fright.

"There is no time." Mrs. Reynolds manoeuvred her gently towards the corridor leading to the older part of the house. "Lord McGrath is very curious about you. Mr. Darcy gave me very clear instructions to bring you to his study without delay."

Elizabeth did not like the tone in which Mrs. Reynolds spoke to her. She was both aggravated and surprised, because the housekeeper had been undeniably patient, kind and respectful in her attitude to her. Her stomach lurched at the thought of being introduced to the enigmatic Lord McGrath she had heard so much about. She needed some time to prepare herself for the meeting.

She lifted her chin higher than was her custom and said in a clear, sure voice, "A few minutes for me to change into a fresh gown will not do any harm, I believe." she walked past the woman to the staircase, "Pray, send Heather to me."

Half an hour later, she stood in front of the dark, massive double doors. The study was located in the older part of the manor, as she had been told by Georgiana, erected during the rein of Queen Elizabeth. Fitzwilliam seemed to like this wing; he spent many hours there as both library and his study were located there. Elizabeth admitted that she did not dread it like the stone castle. The rooms here had a subtle historical touch to them with original heavy furniture, panelled walls with Dutch tapestries on them, stained glass windows, low ceilings and dark waxed floors. Sometimes when they sat together in the library she felt as if they had moved in time to the sixteenth century. Still, she much preferred spending her days in the newest part of the manor.

She raised her hand to knock, but before her knuckles touched the carved wood, she checked her appearance one last time. She was dressed in one of the new elegant gowns, sprinkled modestly with rose water, her hair freshly brushed, and elegantly pinned up by Heather's efficient hands. She looked her very best, and she refused to be intimidated like everyone else by the man she would meet in a moment.

She knocked lightly, then waited to hear Fitzwilliam's formal voice bidding her to enter, she opened the door.

"My dear." Fitzwilliam stood up from behind his desk and walked to her. She noticed at once that his behaviour was altered. He seemed nervous, less sure of himself than usual.

He took her hand and gently led her to the very tall man who stood by the window.

"Elizabeth, this is our closest neighbour, cousin and a good friend of the family, Lord McGrath." he introduced her.

Elizabeth glanced at her husband before she rested her eyes upon their guest. Had she not known him better, she would have thought that Fitzwilliam sounded exactly like Mr. Collins when introducing Lady Catherine to her. Gone was his self confidence and arrogance, even his tone had lost its usual command strike. He seemed belittled, humbled even.

Elizabeth moved her eyes from her husband to the man who now stood in front of her. She curtseyed elegantly and smiled. "Lord McGrath, it is a pleasure."

The man's pale blue eyes stared into hers for a long moment. Elizabeth held his gaze boldly, but with a kind expression, the sparkles of amusement dancing in her eyes. The man was gigantic, taller than Fitzwilliam, and more muscled. From the way Georgiana had talked about him, she thought him to be older, but no, he was perhaps a few years older than her husband, in his early thirties perhaps, though it was hard to say his exact age.

At last McGrath bowed in front of her, "The pleasure is all mine, Mrs. Darcy. I must admit that I was very curious about Darcy's bride." He looked at the other man. "But I see he chose well. A courageous wife is always a treasure."

Elizabeth raised one dark blond eyebrow. "Since we have only just met, pray tell me how you could possibly know that I am courageous?"

"You looked me straight in the eyes." he explained, and then lowered his voice leaning to her with confidence, whispering with smile, "Not many dare to."

She showed him her dimpled smile, "Should I fear you then?"

He smiled back. "Not at all."

Her smile waned and she spoke more seriously, "What if my courage has its true source in my foolishness and unawareness?"

His eyes narrowed, and he studied her for a moment. Then he turned his head to Darcy, speaking to him for a moment as if she was not in the same room.

"She is sharp as nails, Cousin," She felt his gaze on her again, assessing her from the tip of her soft light green slippers to the silk ribbon plaited into her hair, "She looks comely enough too."

Elizabeth averted her eyes, knowing it was not her face he stared at. She could not believe that Fitzwilliam stood there and allowed that. He was usually very jealous and possessive of her. She remembered on their way north, when they had made stops to change horses, he frowned and scowled at every man who dared to even look at her. Now he did not react when this strange man eyed her so rudely.

"A very good choice." Lord McGrath murmured, to her relief, taking his eyes away from her chest at last. He slapped Fitzwilliam on the back and said, "You will have intelligent, strong sons by her. God knows we have too many idiots ruling the packs."

Elizabeth gasped as she stared at Darcy. She wanted to find the anger and outrage in his eyes, in his expression, at this man's insults directed to her, but her husband looked ridiculously pleased and proud; he even smiled.

"Mrs. Darcy," Lord McGrath turned to her, again forcing her to stand next to him, "I have no doubt that your courage derives from the strength of your character only. I find it refreshing and most welcome."

"Thank you." she murmured as he took her hand into his enormous one, holding it very gently as if it was made of glass and he was afraid of breaking it. He bowed over it with gallantry. "I hear you enjoy long walks."

"Yes, I do." she answered, trying to keep a polite expression on her face. "It is so beautiful here, nature so unrestrained, so many enchanting sights. I especially enjoy the beach."

"Are you not afraid to walk all alone?" he asked. "I imagine you do not know the grounds well enough yet."

She shook her head. "I am not alone on my outings. Mr. Darcy gave me a wolf; he is a most loyal companion."

Lord McGrath turned to Darcy. "Do I know him?"

Darcy nodded. "Wilfred."

"The grandson of old Wilfred?"

"Yes." Darcy said only.

The older man nodded. "Good choice, even though he must be young. I am sure that Mrs. Darcy is safe with him."

Elizabeth smiled in almost despair, because for countless times since she had come here, she felt that she failed to grasp the real meaning of the conversation. It happened almost every day, this strange feeling that there was a double meaning to the words. Was she hearing things right, or was she going mad?

As she managed to put back a pleasant face, she graciously said, "The housekeeper mentioned you will honour us with your company at dinner."

"Yes, if you allow it, madam." McGrath bowed in front of her again. "I am on my way to Ireland."

The next question went through her tight throat, but she hoped it sounded natural. "Would you consider then staying a few days at Pemberley before such a long trip?"

"I cannot. I must leave at first light in the morning. The business in Ireland needs my instant attention. Not all my people are so reliable as your husband, madam. I even wanted him to make this trip with me, but he confessed he did not want to leave his young wife on their honeymoon, upsetting her tender feelings thus."

Elizabeth looked at Fitzwilliam, who managed to look both embarrassed and gratified.

"In this case, we will be happy to have you as our guest tonight." she said smoothly. "Please excuse me now. I shall see to the arrangements."

Mrs. Reynolds waited for her in the corridor outside the study.

"How was it?"

Elizabeth frowned, "I am afraid I do not take your meaning."

"Did he speak to you?"

"Of course. Why should he not?"

The housekeeper sighed in obvious relief. "That is well."

***

Elizabeth stared at the plate placed in front of her by the servant. Raw meat. Again.

She well remembered when during the first week of her stay at Pemberley, it had been the third day perhaps, at dinner, the meat had been served, in her opinion inedible. It had been just roasted slightly on the surface, but raw and bloody inside. She had wanted to send it back to the kitchen to cook it up properly or give it to the dogs, but to her amazement, Fitzwilliam had explained to her that it had been a local dish which they all enjoyed.

For the few next minutes, she had observed with round eyes as not only her husband, but her sister as well, had consumed the bloody steak with what seemed to be a great appetite. She had not even been sure how they had been able to bite into it. But then it had come to her that both Darcys seemed to have very strong, white teeth. Fitzwilliam rarely smiled a full smile that showed his teeth, but Georgiana laughed often when they talked together, and Elizabeth was struck by how perfectly even and white her teeth were. Sharp too, she was sure, because Fitzwilliam was always very careful when kissing her. He often deepened the kiss, pushing his tongue in her mouth, but when she tried to do the same, he did not allow it. Usually he broke the kiss, and started on nuzzling her neck or kissing her cheeks.

She looked from under her eyelashes at Lord McGrath. He ate the dish with obvious zeal. Was she the only person who considered it inedible?

She waved at the servant to take her plate, and pointed to the boiled vegetables to be brought to her.

Shortly after dinner, the gentlemen excused themselves to the library. As they were leaving, Darcy whispered into her ear so that she and his sister would not wait for their return.

Georgiana was a bundle of nerves during the dinner. Lord McGrath asked her a few polite questions about her time in London this spring, about her studies and her music, but she answered in monosyllables, not meeting his eyes. Elizabeth could tell that the man tried to put the girl at ease, he smiled at her, and his tone was gentle, but she simply refused to look at him.

After dinner, Georgiana was still so agitated that she did not want to play the piano, though Elizabeth knew that she had practised a new song for the last two days. When they retired, Elizabeth stayed with her in her room till she fell asleep. She met her husband's valet and asked whether his Master had finished his conference with Lord McGrath. When she heard that they were still in the library, she thought there was no point in waiting for Fitzwilliam to come to her room that evening. She guessed he wanted to talk business with their guest. It was late, and she was tired after the eventful day, when she had the first real opportunity to play a hostess at Pemberley. It did not take her long to fall asleep.

She woke what seemed many hours later, in the middle of deep sleep, at the sensation of her husband's hands on her.

"Fitzwilliam?" she murmured in sleepy voice. "What time is it?"

"Laaate." he slurred against her lips.

Elizabeth pushed at his chest. "You are drunk."

"Yes." he agreed as he busied himself with tugging at her nightgown. "We needed to talk of many important matters."

"Did you need brandy for that?" she snapped.

"Lizzy..." he murmured against her throat, his hand wrapping around her upper thigh.

She tried to push him off her. "Go back to sleep."

"You were so wonderful, Lizzzzy. I always knew that you would be. He was pleased with my choice." he murmured as he managed to push her nightgown up to her waist.

"But I am not pleased with his behaviour here at all!" she blurted. " Who does he think he is? How could you allow him to talk about me in such a degrading way, and in my presence? What about Georgiana? She dislikes him, and almost fears him, and I cannot blame her! Poor girl! Your own sister! Will you allow him to marry her?"

"Shush, Lizzy." he murmured into her mouth, "You do not understand who he is..."

"Fitzwilliam, stop that." she tried to push his hands away. "You must sober first."

"Do not refuse me..." he pleaded. "I need you."

"You are drunk." she reasoned.

"I will not hurt you."

"I know, but..." she started, but stopped, feeling his thick finger pushing between her private folds. He rubbed her diligently, while his other hand moved up and grasped her breast through the thin cotton of her nightgown. His technique seriously lacked the sophistication she was used to on his part, but it was quite effective, she had to admit.

"Wet already." he murmured, moving heavily on her, between her legs. "Always wet for me."

Elizabeth sighed as he fumbled for an endless moment, not being able to find the right place to insert himself. At last she helped him, guiding his hand.

"Good." he murmured as he pushed inside. "Good."

There were three unusually shallow pushes, and he spilled himself into her, partially on her thighs and belly.

It took some effort to push him off her to his back; he was that heavy, even more when unconscious. He snored a minute later. Elizabeth slipped from the bed to the bathroom to wash the stickiness from her body and change into a clean nightgown.

Chapter Fifteen

Elizabeth sat curled on the settee in her bedroom, in front of the merry fire. Almost a month had passed since she had inhabited these chambers. It was nearly ten o'clock, but Fitzwilliam was still downstairs. After dinner, he had excused himself from their company, explaining he had numerous correspondences to work upon.

She did not like to surrender herself to dark thoughts and despair; it was not in her nature. However, she could not deny any longer the fears which invaded her. She was afraid of her own suspicions about her husband and about the people here.

There were only two possibilities. The first one was that everyone around her, her new family, servants, tenants and the people in the village were involved in some sort of secret. The mystery around Pemberley was somehow connected with the Middle Ages, the times when the castle had been erected and the wolves that lived all over the area.

"The wolves..." she whispered and shivered in herself, hearing her own voice uttering the words aloud.

There was also the second possibility, that all that she found strange and incomprehensible here, had a reasonable explanation, and she was just slowly losing her mind.

Countless time she ordered herself to remember all good and worthy things that she had met here - the kindness of people, the great prosperity of the place, the friendship and company of her new sister, easy companionship with Heather, the loving tenderness and care of her husband.

Her eyes moved from the fire to the clock on the mantelpiece, now showing half past ten. She doubted that Fitzwilliam would return any time soon. Perhaps in an hour or two, when she would be fast asleep, he would wake her up with his kisses and warm hands and make love to her – twice at least – and then long before dawn, he would be gone.

She sighed and wrapped the woolen shawl more tightly around herself. She took a single candle from the nightstand and walked out of the bedroom. Outside, in the dark hall, she found Wilfred napping. He woke up instantly when she came out, wiggled his tail playfully and sniffed at the hem of her nightgown.

"I am sorry. Have I disturbed you?" she asked as she leaned over the dog. "Why have you not gone to the kitchens for the night? You have your own comfortable rug there in the warm corner." She rubbed her arms against the chill and draft in the corridor.

"Come," she started walking to the staircase, "I am going to the study, and you will go to your place for the night."

She was not surprised that Wilfred chose to walk her down right to the study door. He accompanied her everywhere, welcoming her at the door to her room each morning when she left for breakfast. Together they walked the grounds, often far outside the gardens and the park surrounding the manor. More than once she found herself in the middle of nowhere, not seeing the castle any more, not sure how to find her way back. Wilfred seemed to understand her dilemma, as he always waved his tail and barked, indicating for her to follow him. He always found the shortest, most direct way back to the house.

On her walks, she had met a few tenant families, working on the fences or tending to the sheep. They all seemed to know very well who she was, as they always interrupted their work and greeted her with respect. She still felt very uncomfortable with people bending in half in front of her, or even worse, going to their knees. They never looked at her, and never resumed their work till she had walked past them. She very much wanted to talk with them, but each time she was about to do that, their supervisor walked to her, asking her very politely whether she was lost, and how he could help. Then she felt guilty that she interrupted on their work and walked away.

She had broached the subject with Fitzwilliam, asking him whether she should not start paying visits to the tenants. He had only answered that there would be time for that, and that he would take her to visit some cottages one day.

As she reached her husband's study, she noticed the light coming from the crack under the door, proving the he was actually there, working.

She was pleased that the study was not located in the castle. She doubted whether she would be brave enough to go there at night. During her nearly month long stay at Pemberley, she had visited the oldest part not more than three times altogether, and only in the company of Mrs. Reynolds, Georgiana or her husband. The castle was unfriendly and dark, chillingly cold even in the middle of the summer. The chambers were small, with low ceilings, thick walls, smallish windows and enormous fireplaces. The smell was disturbing too. She would never acknowledge it out loud, but it reminded her of a dungeon. The only advantage of the old part was the breathtaking view from the highest tower tha

Georgiana had once showed to her. Her sister was currently drawing it, and she had promised to give Elizabeth the picture when it was finished.

"Now, go to your place." she said to Wilfred as she raised her hand to knock. She waited till the animal disappeared round the corner and rapped at the door, at the same time pushing it open.

Fitzwilliam frowned over some letter, and there was a small pile of still unopened ones on his right.

Before she spoke, his eyes rested on her.

"Is something wrong?" he asked, about to raise himself.

"No, stay where you are." she said, closing the heavy door and running to him.

She plopped onto his lap and wrapped her arms around his neck. "I have been waiting and waiting for you."

His arm brought her tighter to him, and he kissed the top of her head. "You see that I have many letters to read and answer. I must do it tonight, as I will be busy with something else for the next couple of days.

"I missed you." she whispered into his throat, tightening her hold on him, "I do not like falling asleep without you in bed."

She felt his mouth on hers in a lazy kiss. Not breaking it, he stood up with her in his arms and walked to the large stuffed sofa in front of the fire.

"Bare feet?" he asked disapprovingly as he sat down with her still in his arms. Elizabeth scooted to his side, hiding her feet under her nightgown.

"I forgot to put on my slippers."

"Forgot the slippers." he chided her, "What were you thinking, sweetheart? Do you want to develop a cold?"

Elizabeth stifled a feeling of irritation at his remark. Quite often, he treated her like a child, as if she could not take proper care of herself. It was his way of showing her that he cared for her, she presumed.

"How was your day?" he asked, bringing her close to him.

"It went well…" she hesitated.

"What is the matter?" he asked gently, combing his hand through her long tresses. She always remembered to let her hair free when they were alone in private. He had never told her out loud, but she knew that he enjoyed it like that more than when it was pinned up or in a braid.

She took his hand into both of hers. "I was thinking…"

"Yes."

She examined his palm, so much bigger than hers, "I know how busy you are, and I respect and admire your devotion to this land. I saw the village, and I must admit that I have never before seen any estate to be run so efficiently, the homes so well kept, the people so prosperous but…" she sighed.

He turned to look into her face.

"I miss you so much, and we see each other only in the evenings or at night." she complained.

His face reflected his worry. "You feel lonely?"

"No…" she hesitated, "Everyone is so kind to me, Georgiana, Mrs. Reynolds and all the servant, but I would wish I could be more often with you."

He signed and resumed playing with her hair.

Elizabeth looked up at his face. "I thought that perhaps you could choose a horse for me, and I could accompany you sometimes during the day."

"You cannot ride."

She sat up away from him, blocking his view of the fireplace, "I have never said that I cannot. Papa taught all of us horse riding when we were little. Perhaps it is not among my favourite pastimes, but I am able. Especially if I had a docile animal. I am sure…"

"That is not a good idea." he interrupted her sharply.

"Why?"

"The estate is very large. I travel many miles a day…" his voice softened but retained its firm note, "That would be too much for you physically. Besides it can be quite cold… I do not want you to get ill."

He pulled her back to him. "I need to know that you are safe at home when I am at my duties. All I think is that you wait for me at home, and that we will spend the evening together."

Elizabeth smiled, but it was a sad smile.

"I could help you with your correspondence then!" her face lit up again, "My handwriting is very neat, and I could answer some of the letters or make notes for you…"

He shook his head. "Sweetie," he kissed her temple, "Do not trouble yourself with that. It is not a work cut for you. You have home matters to tend to… you can focus on introducing some changes to the house, anything you want; remodel the drawing room or the park. And in a few years, when the children will come, you will have your entire days occupied, and then you will wish a time for yourself like you have now. Enjoy it."

Elizabeth closed her eyes tightly as she cuddled to him. His arm was around her, his fingers stroking the side of her face. He was shutting her out – from his work, from his life outside the house. Had he wanted the drawing room decorated, why had he not married Miss Bingley? Elizabeth was not used to such idleness; she needed some purpose and occupation during the day.

Even when they were intimate, he never gave himself entirely. He controlled both of them, but especially her responses during their lovemaking. His was always gentle, loving, and mindful of her needs; she could not complain about that. Still, he never allowed her to touch him as he did her. At first she had been so overwhelmed with the entire experience that she had simply lain under him and let him do to her what he wished. But as the weeks passed, she began to crave to touch and caress him too, not to just be the passive recipient of his attentions.

Every time she tried to take the initiative, he stopped her. He always took her nightshirt off, caressed, explored and kissed every spot on her body, but never allowed her the same. All she had seen was his neck, and what was visible of his chest through the opening in his shirt.

So far, her attempts to take some of the control over their lovemaking had been shy. She considered that there was a possibility he had not noticed them. Many times Mama had said to them that men needed be told the things straightforwardly, because they were not proficient at guessing games.

Perhaps it was the night to take matters in her own hands.

She counted to ten, took a deep breath and lifted from the sofa, facing him. Looking straight into his eyes, she opened the robe she had over her nightgown, and let it drop to the floor. Then, with trembling fingers, she reached for the ribbon securing her gown and untied it. Feeling the thin material slipping from her, she closed her eyes, knowing that not only her cheeks, but her neck and breasts, were flushed in embarrassment. Do not be a coward, she whispered to herself, and opened her eyes. Then before he could say or do anything, she climbed astride onto his lap.

"Elizabeth, what are you…" he started, but did not finish because she closed his lips with her mouth.

Kissing him, she ran her hands down his body, trying to pull his shirt out of his breeches with the intent to remove it completely.

Fitzwilliam was still at first, his hands resting on his sides, not touching her.

Elizabeth opened his shirt and kissed her way down his chest. Her hand managed to slide inside his trousers, the tips of her fingers reaching his manhood. She had never seen it, and she was curious what he put in her several times every night.

She slipped from his lap to the side, and tugged at the buttons of his breeches with impatient hands. He did not protest. Soon his member sprang out of the nest of black, springy hair.

Her mouth fell open at the sheer size of it. She reached and tried to wrap her small hand around it. It was a wonder that the pain was so slight that first time. It was a miracle that she could walk at all.

She was petting him absentmindedly for a moment before his fingers gently wrapped around her wrist.

"If I were you I would not do that." he hissed.

Elizabeth stared at him. His eyes were wild, different.

His mouth crushed hers. Elizabeth yelped in shock, as he lifted her up over him with no effort at all, as if she had been a rag doll. His mouth attached itself to the tip of her breast and sucked hard for a few moments before moving to its twin, giving it the same attention. Her eyes widened when seconds later, he pushed her even higher, forcing her to sit on his face. She tried to cry out in mortification of this act, but the sound died out in her tightened throat. The attempt to free herself turned useless as he held her securely over him, his hands wrapped around her hips like iron claws. Never in her life had she felt so ashamed and humiliated as now, hovering over her husband who lapped with his tongue at her secret place.

"No!" she managed to cry out, "Please stop!"

He did not stop, so she pulled at his hair. "Let me go!" she pleaded, "I do not want it like this! Please, please stop!"

Surprisingly, he did. He lowered her down, and for a moment their faces were at the same level, his mouth glistening from her wetness. Her breathing laboured, she kept gasping, staring into his eyes. They were black like the darkest night, and unfamiliar in expression.

She cried again as the next moment he pushed her down on the carpet and loomed over her. The feeling of relief washed over her as he started to kiss the path down her body, lingering on her neck, breasts and the curve of her belly. That she knew; it was safe. Her intention when she had come to him this evening had been to discover more of him during their lovemaking, but now she preferred to just lie still not to provoke him.

She stiffened again when his face buried again between her thighs. Her stomach knotted up, and she turned her face to the fire. Clearly, he was intending to kiss her private area. His hands held her thighs firmly, but his touch was gentle. When she was accustomed to the novelty of it and relaxed, it started to feel good; the sweet tingling sensation began to pulsate down in her belly.

Without warning, he stopped and soared from between her widespread thighs. She thought then that he would come over her and take her.

His arm went under her and flipped her on her stomach. She turned her head to look over her back at him. He leaned forward and kissed her again, hard. She felt his hands on her sides, lifting her bottom up. She did not understand yet what he intended.

She did a moment later when he first spread her with his fingers, and then surprisingly, gently pushed himself into her from behind.

The hot tears brimmed her eyes. It was not painful, but she felt horrible. Never had she been so miserable in his arms. She could not see his face, she could not touch him, feel his weight on her and wrap her hands around him. Even when her insides gripped him and the shocking pleasure ripped through her, all she wanted to do was to weep.

And she did when he finished and moved from behind her. She curled in a ball on the floor in front of the fireplace and sobbed. He did not say anything, just righted his own clothing before wrapping her into her robe and picking her up in his arms.

He was still silent as he carried her upstairs. In her bedroom, he put her down on the chair. She curled on it and observed as he built up the dying fire again, and walked to the bed, moving the covers aside. She gasped quietly when he picked her up again and carried her to bed. He removed her robe and naked tucked her in. She drew the sheets up to her chin and shut her eyes tight. She heard him walking about the room, removing his clothes before he climbed into the bed beside her.

She wept still as he wrapped around her body from behind.

“I am sorry.” he whispered, “I know I frightened you.” he sighed. “You must trust me next time, and not start something you cannot control. Especially so close to the full moon.”

She did not answer. The fear gripped her, and for the first time, she wondered whom she had really married.

Chapter Sixteen

As Elizabeth opened her eyes the next morning, she was surprised to find herself enfolded in her husband's arms, her head nestled on his chest. He had stayed with her for the entire night; it was a rare occurrence. The heavy arm around her was relaxed, and his breathing was even. She closed her eyes again, wishing she would not have to rise and face the new day. What she would give now to wake in her old room at Longbourn.

"You are awake." His voice rang in her ears.

She glanced up at him. She thought he was still fast asleep, but he was not. He stared down at her.

Elizabeth freed herself from his embrace and sat up, supporting her back against the headboard. She was naked, so she drew the covers up her body, covering her breasts.

"What are your plans for today?" he asked as he got out of bed. He still wore the shirt and breeches he had on yesterday.

She shrugged, looking to the side. He acted as if nothing unusual had happened yesterday, or in the last weeks.

"As usual," she answered in a subdued voice. "I will go for a walk, then spend the afternoon with Georgiana."

He did not comment on that. After the rough adjustment of his clothing, he walked around the bed and sat heavily on the edge of it by her side.

Elizabeth clenched her hands together so her knuckles turned white. Her throat squeezed in an almost painful sensation, and she wanted to weep again, the tears were just there, she could feel them. All she knew was that she could not stay silent any more. She did not care. She needed to wash out all these doubts and fearful thoughts which had haunted her heart and mind almost from the beginning of her marriage.

"What else can I do?" she cried at last in a voice full of hurt and rejection. "Mrs. Reynolds runs the household, and she does not need my help with it. I cannot even introduce changes into the menu because you do not like the dishes I know. I cannot ride a horse, I cannot visit the tenants, I cannot take a carriage and go to the nearest town. I cannot help you with your duties, or anything else." As she spoke, her voice gradually raised to a high pitch before she paused and added brokenly, "You never tell me anything. You disappear all the time."

He tried to touch her face, but she dodged away, "Tis not true."

Her dark eyes flashed at him. "Is it not? You are gone for entire days and nights, and you never tell me exactly where you go and what for."

Darcy said nothing, only took her hand in his, but she snatched it away.

He sighed. "I know that you are disappointed about last night, but you started it yourself." He sat closer, "You cannot expect I will not react the way I reacted when you behave in such a …" he stopped, trying to find the right words, "provocative manner."

She paled, then turned bright red. "I did that out of desperation! I wanted to be closer to you. You never allow me to touch you, or to see you. I wanted to participate more, yet I did not expect to be treated like a…" she pressed her lips tightly, "like a whore."

Darcy hung his head down.

"You say nothing, I see." She narrowed her eyes at him. "Where were you two nights ago?" she demanded.

He looked up at her in surprise. "In your bed." he answered calmly.

"Yes, you were, but earlier in the night. However, closer to dawn, I woke up because those wolves were howling again so terribly, and you were gone. I could not go back to sleep, so I walked to your bedroom. I thought that perhaps I could stay with you till the morning. Your room was empty, bed covers untouched. You never slept there that night."

"I needed to get up earlier that day." he explained in calm voice.

She leaned towards him, clenching the sheet to her bosom. "How silly must you think I am? It was three o'clock in the morning, still dark. No one gets up so early."

"I do." He looked straight into her eyes. "My duties require that."

She dropped back on the pillows. "What duties?"

His expression tightened. "I should not tell you. Not yet."

Elizabeth's eyes narrowed at him in two dark slits, "Does it have something to do with Lord McGrath?"

"Yes."

"Who is he?"

"Our distant cousin and neighbour."

"Is that all?"

"No," Darcy stood up, and walked to the window. "I am obliged to follow his advice."

"You are?"

"Yes, I am."

"I see that you do not only have to follow his advice, and be at his beck and call, but also allow him to offend your wife in your presence."

Darcy turned back to her. "What are you talking about?"

"Are you blind? Do you not remember the way he stared at me that day in the study? He talked as if I was not in the room, calling me something just short of a brooding mare of yours."

"Elizabeth, you do exaggerate!"

"Do I?"

He sat back next to her. "His attitudes are different than you are accustomed to." he spoke in a sure and gentle voice, "He is the most honourable man after my father that I know. He would never think to take another's wife for himself. I believe he simply wanted to compliment you."

"By undressing me with his eyes right in front of you!"

He put his hands on her bare, rounded shoulders. "Lord McGrath certainly did not want to offend you, I dare say he likes you very much. I admit that he is rather old fashioned."

"Old fashioned!" Elizabeth raised to her knees in bed, "Old fashioned could perhaps describe you. He is positively Medieval in his attitudes."

Darcy did not respond to that.

There was a very long silence, both of them avoiding the other's eyes. When Elizabeth asked the next question, it seemed to be in an emotionless voice.

"Do you have a mistress?"

Darcy's shocked eyes met hers, "I cannot believe you asked that." His voice grew angry, "How can such a possibility even come your mind?"

"What else can I think?" the long held tears brimmed her eyes, the sob choking her throat. "I know that wealthy men do keep lovers when a wife does not satisfy them. And I am clearly lacking to you."

He grabbed her by the upper arms, and lifted her up so the sheet dislodged, exposing her breasts, "Do not ever say such things." He shook her, "It is insulting to you, me, and most of all, to my feelings for you."

He released her slowly from his hold and walked away from the bed. He ran his hand across his face and stared out the window.

Elizabeth drew the sheet up over her chest again. She stared down at her hands, placed on her lap. They trembled.

"Are you aware that you are with child?" he asked unexpectedly from the window.

Her eyes widened, and she looked up at him. "What?"

He turned to her. "Your monthly bleeding has not come for the month, at least, certainly not since our wedding. Am I wrong?"

"No, it has not come… but how can you know about such things?"

"I am not an ignorant." He sat beside her again. "You are with child. There will be a baby next spring."

"How can you be so sure of that? You are not a midwife or a doctor." She frowned at him.

He presented a wide smile. "No, I am not, but I do know that you carry my child."

"How?"

He pulled her into his arms and she did not protest. "I can smell it in you." he whispered.

She stilled and pushed her hands in front of her, "Please, cease that." She was shaking her head, her expression pleading. "Pray stop saying such strange things. It scares me when you do that."

His big, warm hand, cupped her cheek. "Do not fret so much. There is explanation to everything." He kissed her hair. "I love you. Never doubt it."

She sighed into his neck. "Stay with me today." she asked. "Let us spend this day together."

He closed his eyes. "I cannot." he said as he raised himself and walked to the entrance. "Today is the full moon." he added before disappearing out the door.

Elizabeth sat in the bed a while longer after he left her. Full moon, yes, he had always been gone somewhere when it had been full moon. Those trips to London when they were engaged, and even earlier, when she nursed Jane at Netherfield, and later in Kent. He had always had urgent business in town around that time of the month.

She rang for Heather to prepare her a bath, and breakfast. She was in hurry to finish her dressing and go downstairs to the library. She needed to discover the secret surrounding her, and learn the entire truth, hoping to find her answers in the books.

To her relief, the library was empty. She doubted she would be disturbed there at this hour. She presumed Fitzwilliam would be out till the evening. First, she decided to learn more about the phases of the moon, so she picked up the thick academic treatise on astronomy. However, after an hour of reading it, she found nothing which could explain her husband's unusual behaviour.

She started to look in other sections, till she encountered the slim brochure about witchcraft in Medieval England, written a few years ago by some parson from Yorkshire. Having read the first two pages, Elizabeth decided that the book was poorly written and silly, the kind of thing that her cousin, Mr. Collins, could have penned out of his dull sermons. However, as she leafed through the pages, she found a separate chapter devoted to the effect of the full moon on people and animals. She read it three times before, with trembling hands and her heart rapidly beating, she put the brochure away.

She started to feel sick, and more frightened than she had ever remembered.

"This cannot be." she whispered to herself, rubbing her forehead, "It is only a legend."

Her feet brought her to the window.

Her hands went to her face. "Cannot be, cannot be." she kept repeating.

She looked at the skies. It was a sunless day, and the clouds hung low over the manicured gardens. Her hand went to her chest, to the medallion Fitzwilliam had given her almost a year ago. She had never taken it off since the day of their engagement, a few days after Wickham had attacked her.

She paled abruptly, her eyes widened in terror, remembering the last time she saw George Wickham. What if what she had seen had been real, not just a figment of her imagination as Fitzwilliam had convinced her?

Elizabeth took the medallion off her neck and looked at the landscape pictured there, reflecting very much what she could see through the window, the mountains, the forests and the lake. She turned the piece in her hand to the other side to examine, as she had countless times before, the signs engraved in the gold surface.

ᛒᛁᛋᚲᛚᚨ ᚱᛖᛏ

She knew that it was an old runic alphabet, used in England in the early Middle Ages. Her father had a treatise about it in his library. Why had she not tried to translate the inscription from the medallion back at home?

"Fitzwilliam surely has this book." she murmured to herself.

She found the needed volume without much problem, Runologia by Jón Ólafsson of Grunnavík, published in 1732. The scholar who penned it had been from Iceland, and he had written his work in his mother tongue. Elizabeth stared at the text in concentration, but recognized only a few words similar to German. She wished her father had been here, he would have helped her to decipher it. She was about to close the book and put it back on the shelf, when on one of the pages she noticed the table with runic symbols one by one translated into Latin letters. She ran to the desk, opened the first drawer and took out a clean sheet of paper. She dipped the pen in the ink and carefully rewrote the runes from the medallion. Then, glancing at Mr. Ólafsson's translation, she deciphered letter after letter, so a word came out.

"Bisclavret" she mouthed, "What does it mean?"

She slumped back into the leather chair and frowned over the paper in her hand.

"Bisclavret" she repeated.

The word sounded like English, especially the first part. Bisclavret must have meant something in Old English. She sighed. Now she needed to find a book about the Medieval English dialects and try to translate the word Bisclavret into Modern English.

"A dictionary of Old English would be the best." she murmured to herself as she looked around the room for the place where the dictionaries were shelved.

She found dictionaries translating from English to almost every European language she heard of, but nothing remotely close to what she needed.

"There must be something..." She moved into the English literature section, looking for old English books.

"Chaucer..." she read one of the authors, and shook her head, "No, something older."

Then a small, leather book fell to her feet, it must have been placed somewhere behind the The Canterbury Tales. She bent down to pick it up, and her hand froze over it when she read the title in gold letters Bisclavret.

She leafed through the book, and to her relief it contained some poems written entirely in English. She chose the comfortable chair by the window, curled on it and began to read.

The preface stated that the author was a woman poet, Marie de France, who probably had been born in France in 12th century, but had lived her life in England. The poems were translated into Modern English by an Oxford professor from an Anglo-Norman dialect Marie de France used when writing her works.

Elizabeth bit her lower lip as she read again the short note about the origins of the poems. Fitzwilliam had mentioned to her that the Darcy's had come to England from France, exactly in the 12th century. Perhaps Marie de France had been somehow connected with the family, or even had belonged to it, so Fitzwilliam had purchased the book during his university times.

She started to read.

In Breton, "Bisclavret"'s the name;
"Garwolf" in Norman means the same.

She swallowed, her eyes widening; Garwolf? She forced her eyes back to the text.

A garwolf is a savage beast,
While the fury's on it, at least:
Eats men, wreaks evil, does no good,
Living and roaming in the deep wood.

She read further. Bisclavret was the protagonist of the story, a wealthy baron from the north of France. He disappeared often without telling anyone about his whereabouts. His wife begged him to tell her his secret.

My lord, I'm in terror every day,
Those days when you've gone away
My heart is so full of fear,
I'm so afraid I'll lose you, dear—
If I don't get some help, some healing,
I will die soon of what I'm feeling!
Where do you go? Now you must say
What life you live, where do you stay?

Elizabeth felt cold sweat running down her spine as she looked at the wife's words. She could ask her husband almost exactly the same questions.

She began to read the next stanzas. Bisclavret revealed to his wife who he was.

"My lady, I turn bisclavret;
I plunge into that great forest.
In thick woods I like it best.
I live on what prey I can get."[1]

Elizabeth closed the book. She did not want to read more of the story. She had learned enough. Bisclavret had meant a man who turned into a wolf, hiding the truth of his nature from his wife. A werewolf.

She began pacing the room, her agitation growing. She needed to clear her mind. Some fresh air would do her good.

She turned to the door first, but then she remembered that Wilfred was surely waiting for her in the corridor. Thankfully the library was situated on the ground floor, so all she had to do was open the window and jump lightly straight into a well kept flower bed.

It was cold, and she did not have on anything more than a thin muslin dress. The ground was wet from the rain which had drizzled from yesterday morning.

---

[1] Translation: Judith P. Shoaf, http://www.clas.ufl.edu/~jshoaf/Marie/bisclavret.pdf

Her home slippers were completely wet by the time she ran out of the courtyard and in the direction of the seashore. The wind blew out her thin muslin dress as she ran as fast as she could away from the house.

Soon, she could see the sand of the beach when she heard a bark behind her back. It was Wilfred. He encircled her a few times and kept barking, jumping out and pointing with his head in the direction of the house.

Elizabeth's eyes narrowed at him. "You are one of them, are you not?" she cried, the cold raindrops intensified by the breeze from the sea hitting her cheeks.

Wilfred stilled and stared into her eyes.

She began to walk again. The wolf followed her.

"Go away!" she cried. "Leave me alone! Do you hear me? Go away!"

She ran till she reached the soft, wet sand on the water's edge. A small wave came to her and washed over her feet and petticoats. She heard barking again. This time stronger and louder. She turned around.

"I told you to leave me alone." she cried angrily, thinking it was Wilfred again. But it was not him.

"Tis you." she whispered. Although many months had passed, she recognized him immediately.

The animal approached her.

There was no sound, and no light, no smell, and the transformation happened very quickly. Her husband stood in front of her, stark naked.

She felt the cloying sensation in her stomach, coming up to her throat and she fainted.

Chapter Seventeen

When she opened her eyes, she was in her own room, in bed, under the covers, dressed in a nightgown. Her hair was down, around her shoulders. It was dark outside the window.

"You are awake." Georgiana's voice caught her attention. The girl sat on the chair next to the bed. "We were so worried, you were unconscious for so long. He said it was from the shock. Brother called the doctor, who is waiting now in the sitting room. Let me tell him you are awake." She stood up, about to turn in the direction of the door.

"Georgiana, wait." Elizabeth sat up, "Where is…," she swallowed, "Where is he?"

The girl's dark grey eyes stared into hers, "You mean, Brother?"

Elizabeth nodded slowly. "Yes," she said through her parched throat.

"He is not here. It is the time of his change, but he should be home before morning." Georgiana said calmly, "He very much wanted to stay and wait till you awakened, but I think he considered it to be too early for you to see him in his wolf form again."

Elizabeth lay back on the pillows, and Georgian left the room. What she had read in the library and seen on the beach was all the truth. She found herself right in the middle of the most unthinkable nightmare.

"Mrs. Darcy." The sober looking doctor entered her bedroom together with Georgiana, who went to sit on the chair in the corner. Elizabeth remembered him and his family well from church. He had even dined once at the manor together with his son, who had just finished medical school in Edinburgh, and now took his place beside his father at the hospital in the village.

"Doctor." she acknowledged him weakly.

The man sat beside her on the edge of the bed, and took her hand to check her pulse.

"Does your head hurt?" he asked.

She shook her head. "No."

He touched her forehead and found it cool. "There is no fever, and you seem fine to me."

Elizabeth lowered her eyes and said nothing.

Doctor sighed. "How are your spirits after finding out the truth?"

She looked up at him. "Doctor, is it true? How is it possible?" she paused. "The werewolves?"

"I cannot answer that." The doctor stood up and reached for his bag, "It has been like that for centuries."

She lifted her wide eyes at him. "You are…" she swallowed, "You are as well…"

The man smiled and whispered, "A werewolf?"

Her mouth fell open and she nodded.

"Yes, I am… which means that now when I know you are well, I must go. I am afraid I cannot postpone my own change any longer. Miss Darcy will keep you company."

Elizabeth only paled more, hearing this.

The doctor leaned to her and spoke in a kind voice. "My child, there is no reason to be so frightened and devastated. Everything looks much worse to you now than it really is, I assure you. All will turn out well, and you will be happy."

"How can you know?" she asked in a hollow voice.

"My wife is human too, you know. She learned the truth six months after our wedding. After nearly thirty years of life together, she does not consider me a monster and is, I dare say, quite fond of me."

The doctor walked to Georgiana, who now stood at the foot of the bed, said something to her in a hushed voice, then left the room hastily.

"Are you hungry, Lizzy?" the girl asked, walking closer. "Doctor said I must see that you have dinner."

Elizabeth stared at the girl with an intense expression.

"Will you transform?"

Georgiana shook her head, smiling. "No, I will not. I never change. I still am a werewolf, though. I have all the other traits of our kind, I am stronger than humans, I have keener senses, and I do understand Fitzwilliam when he communicates with me in his wolf form. The only difference is that nothing happens to me when the full moon comes."

"Why?"

"Doctor could explain it better to you, I think. My mother was human, and my great- grandmother too; it happens sometimes that a female does not change at all when she is partially human. However, if I ever had a son, he would undergo a change like my brother and all the others."

Elizabeth was shaking her head, her hands on both sides of her face. "It is all impossible. It is a dream."

Georgiana touched her arm gently. "Tis the truth."

"Such things do not exist." Elizabeth insisted.

"You cannot doubt it now. Brother told me that he changed right in front of your eyes."

Elizabeth hid her face in her hands. "No, I cannot believe that."

Georgiana moved closer, sat on the edge of the bed and put her arms around the other woman. "I would wish to help you in some way."

"He deceived me, you all did." Elizabeth whispered, freeing herself from the embrace.

"We hardly had a choice." Georgiana said gently, "What would you have thought if he had told you before the wedding who he was? Would you have believed him? Would you have agreed to marry him in the first place? Besides, he was forbidden to tell you earlier than now by our laws. Men are allowed to have human wives, but they cannot reveal the truth to them until a certain time."

"What time?"

Georgiana frowned. "I am not certain. There have been no human brides in recent years, and I never asked about that. I think that the wife always finds out some time after the wedding on her own, or perhaps she is told only when she is already well ingrained into life here."

Elizabeth leaned back against the pillows and said nothing.

Georgiana gave her a worried look, and after a moment of hesitation, spoke with feeling, "Brother loves you very much. We all do."

Elizabeth pulled the covers higher over herself and said indifferently. “I want to be alone.”

“But first you need to eat your dinner.” Georgiana said promptly.

“I am not hun…”

“You must.” the girl interrupted her, firmly. “Doctor said you must have a meal. I will go and talk with Mrs. Reynolds now. Heather will keep you company.”

Georgiana left, and Heather came in. Elizabeth looked at her shortly, very much relieved to see the crispy white cap and rosy cheeks instead of fur. Perhaps her maid did not change, the same as Georgiana. Her mother, Mrs. Brown, was from Kent, so she was probably a human too.

She turned her back to the girl and stared at the fire. She was not in a mood to speak with anyone.

They came with dinner, and she forced herself to swallow a bowl of steamy, thick soup, knowing they would not leave her alone till she ate something.

When they left her at last, some of the tension eased off, and she could think more clearly about her situation.

The next few hours were the darkest of her life so far. She lay in the monstrously large bed, curled into a tight ball, wide awake for most of the night.

The only bright side of the situation was that she was not insane, as she had previously thought. She was married to a werewolf, and even though she had seen a visual proof of it, her mind refused to believe it.

She considered what her life would be now. Perhaps if she had left the place, and returned home, she could have pretended that none of this had happened, that the werewolves did not exist and that she had not married one of them.

Yes, she had to escape as far from here as possible. What would she tell her parents? No, she could not return to Longbourn; Mama would not understand why she had left such a wealthy and generous man.

She could always say that he had mistreated her. Her father would have not refused her his home in such case, for instance had he known that she had been hit. However, to make it believable, Elizabeth would have needed to present heavy bruising on her person. The only way of acquiring marks from the beating on her skin, could be jumping against the chest of drawers or banging her head against the oak door. Her husband could be a despicable liar and half animal, but he would never raise his hand to her.

Telling the truth to her parents was out of question, they would lock her in the mad house, and with good reason.

"Jane." she whispered.

Yes, it was the best solution, she would go to live with Jane and Charles. Only a few days ago, she had received a letter from her sister, informing her that they had established themselves in Derbyshire completely. Jane would never refuse her help, even when she confessed the entire truth. As for Mr.Bingley…

She gasped. Why had she not thought about it before? Mr. Bingley had to know everything from the very beginning. He and Fitzwilliam had been together at the university, even shared the same quarters, so he must have known for years. That morning at Netherfield when she had asked him about his unusual looking dog, and he had pretended not to know anything about it, he had been protecting his friend.

Even though Mr. Bingley knew for sure, Jane did not. Her sister must have suspected something though. She had even tried to convince her to postpone the wedding till she knew Darcy better.

Oh, why had she not listened to her sister's sensible advice. She had been blinded by his sweet words, his kisses and embraces, and had not been thinking straight.

Elizabeth glanced out the window to see that the sky was turning greyish; dawn was upon them.

What about Fitzwilliam? Would he allow her to leave? And what if… she truly was with child? It was possible. Her courses were rarely late. But what, exactly, would she give birth to? Will it be in human form or…? Would it be a litter?

She started to breathe heavily, and moaned, "Oh, Good God, this cannot be happening to me…"

The sudden sensation of sickness went up to her throat. She crawled out of the bed, but did not manage to reach the bathroom, and the contents of her stomach, all of what Georgiana had forced into her the previous evening, ended up in the middle of the dressing room.

As she knelt over the hard wood floor, new waves of nausea overpowering her, warm, big, familiar hands came on her shoulders, and when she finished, her face was dabbed with a wet cloth.

"Oh! Oh, my lady!" she heard Heather's voice as she slowly raised herself, supported by the strong arms of her husband.

"Clean it." his voice ordered.

Heather bowed and ran out of the room.

Elizabeth kept her gaze on the level of his chest, and did not look up into his face. She did not want to look at him ever again.

"I need to go to the bathroom." she said weakly.

He allowed her that, leaving her alone there. She brushed her teeth and washed her face. She nearly screamed when she saw her own reflection in the mirror; a ghostly pale face, tangled hair, tightly pressed lips and black circles under her eyes.

She sat on the edge of the bathtub, afraid to leave, to see him. She knew that he was on the other side.

A moment later, there was a light knock and the door was pushed. "Elizabeth, darling." He stepped inside, and she felt his eyes on her.

She stood and walked past him, careful not to brush against him.

Heather was plopped on the floor, hurrying to clean the mess Elizabeth had made before.

"Heather," her voice trembled, but she tried to control it, "Could you please prepare one of my travelling dresses, high boots and the dark blue velvet pelisse?" she asked, feeling Darcy's presence just behind her, "I would like you to also pack underwear for me for the two days of travel and my toilettes into the smaller carpet bag."

The maid lifted from her knees, a wet, dripping cloth in her hands. She glanced at Darcy, her eyes wide, unsure.

Elizabeth took a deep breath. "Heather, I want my travelling clothes." she paused, and added using her most commanding tone, "Now."

She felt the heavy hand on her shoulder. "Heather," he said, "Mrs. Darcy will not need you this morning."

Heather looked from Darcy to Elizabeth, her eyes stopping for a moment on her Mistress.

She bowed deeply and said, "Yes, Master." Then she collected her things, the bucket and the broom, and hastily left the room.

Very slowly, Elizabeth turned to face him. She did not care to read the expression on his face, so she focused on his chest. He wore only a plain shirt, with no neck cloth, so it was easy for her to open it. His chest was covered with thick black hair down to the waistband of his trousers. She reached to the right, and just under the third rib, she found the moon shaped thickness.

"Do you recognize it?" he asked, "Your own handicraft."

In response, she lifted her right hand and slapped his cheek as hard as she could. He did not even flinch.

He caught her hand and asked in worry. "Have you hurt yourself?"

Elizabeth ignored the sharp pain in her arm and hissed, snatching her hand away, "Do not touch me ever again!"

She ran to the first closet, opened it, and took out the first two dresses she could grab. She picked some petticoats, a nightgown and warm stockings, and started to pack everything into the carry bag she found at the bottom of the closet.

The iron grip on her waist stopped her actions. He brought her to him, wrapping her in his arms completely. Elizabeth dropped the bag, and it tumbled to the floor, letting some of the things fall out.

"I love you most in the world," he whispered into her neck, trembling all over his body, "I will never allow you to go. I had been so very lonely before you came. Please stay with me, do not leave me."

"Let me go." she whispered, her eyes lowered.

His arms only tightened around her.

Her clenched fist hit his chest. "How could you?" Now she hit him with both hands, "How could you do this to me?"

Darcy bore her outburst without much visible reaction. He held her only to him, allowing her to strike him.

"It is not normal!" she shouted, not looking where she smacked him anymore. "It is not natural! You are all freaks of nature! I will not stay here another day longer!"

He caught her wrists in one hand, the other wrapped around her waist. "Stop it." he commanded. "I know you are upset, but you will only hurt yourself."

Elizabeth was out of breath, exhausted by her attack, staring steadily into his black eyes. "Please, let me go." she rasped weakly.

He did.

She turned around and walked a few steps away from him, into the bedroom.

She blinked her eyes repeatedly, and it came to her that she did not feel at all well. The lovely, white and blue room, spun in front of her. Her head swirled, and felt heavy; she reached her hand forward and supported herself against the doorframe to gain some balance. She wondered whether she had a fever. The day had been cold yesterday, and she had run from the house only in her muslin gown.

A moment later, as she dropped into unawareness again, she felt his arms catching her before she fell.

***

Darcy moulded her limp body against him. She was tucked in bed, but he could not let her go, and he sat on top the covers ~~beside,~~ her back supported against his chest.

"What have I done to you, Lizzy?" he whispered, stroking the wisps of damp hair from her forehead.

His father should have told him how hard it would be, warned him somehow, prepared him.

He leaned forward to kiss her forehead. She was so hot.

"Lizzy," he cupped her face and shook it gently, "Open your eyes, darling. Talk to me."

She did not respond. He wanted to weep for the first time since his mother's death.

"What have I done to you?" he repeated, placing kisses all over her feverish face, cuddling her to him.

The doctor entered the room with one decided push of the door. Georgiana, Mrs. Reynolds and Heather followed him, their faces drowned in worry.

"I would prefer for everybody to leave." he said, putting his bag on the bedside and opening it. "I need to examine Mrs. Darcy."

The women left immediately, but Darcy did not move from his place beside her.

Doctor did not comment on that, nor did he try to convince him to go.

"Put her down, Master." he said, because Darcy still held her to him.

Darcy nodded, and with utmost care, he laid her down, pushing the covers away from her.

Doctor started his examination with heavy frown, but soon his face relaxed.

"Could you lift her up?" he asked, taking out his ear trumpet, "I want to listen to her lungs."

Very gently, Darcy brought her to a sitting position, supporting her limp body on his chest and arm.

The doctor raised the nightgown, baring her back, and listened for a long moment.

"You can put her down now." he stood up, and began arranging his instruments neatly into his bag.

Darcy wanted to hold her to him, but thinking of her comfort, he laid her down as he was told. He placed her hands on the covers and adjusted the pillow, making sure she was comfortable.

"It is only a cold." the doctor said, "She will be well in a few days."

"But she is so hot." Darcy put his hand on her forehead. "And unconscious."

"Fever is good, her body is fighting the infection. It is none of those malicious fevers people die from in the cities. She must have gotten chilled yesterday when she went for a walk. It was a very cold day for September. Her system is accustomed to a much warmer climate. Not to mention, she should not have left the house in such a thin dress and without the proper shoes. I noticed that her slippers were completely drenched yesterday when you summoned me, the cold could have started from there."

Darcy took the small hand, and closed it in both of his. "But she will recover?"

"Oh, I am sure of it." The doctor's voice was rich and optimistic. "She is young and healthy; just exhausted and still in shock, which is understandable. The fever is not that high, and we can easily bring it down. Changing the cold compresses often should be enough."

Darcy was not convinced, "She fainted again and returned her food."

Doctor nodded, "Yes, you should be prepared for that in the next few weeks. These are the signs of the early confinement. Moreover, we have to take into consideration another notion. Because, she is a human, her body reacts very strongly to the fact that she carries one of our kind. Her system is trying to adapt. Over the years, I have noticed that especially the first pregnancy, and the first months of it, are much more difficult for human brides. My assumption is that her blood mixes with the blood stream of the child, and her body reacts more forcefully than in the case of normal conception, when both parents are of the same race."

"Is it dangerous for her?" Darcy cried, his terror plainly written on his face. "Nobody told me that the child may be a threat to her life."

"No, no, nothing like that." The doctor assured soothingly, "There was never a case of a human bride dying or getting permanently ill from impregnation only. They were, of course, cases of death in childbirth," The doctor paused, seeing Darcy's suddenly whitened face, "But it happens rarely, and the complications during a labour are never the result of the child being of mixed race." he finished quickly.

Darcy was not calmed. "What could be the cause of such complications then?" he cried in alarm.

The doctor shrugged. "Usual problems like too narrow a pelvis, or too big an infant. But there is absolutely no reason to think that it will happen to Mrs. Darcy." he said with firmness. "Do not think about the birth now, Master. We have many months too prepare for that. At this point, we must focus on fighting the cold and keeping her safe."

Darcy ran his hand over his face.

"Thank you, Doctor." he mumbled, his eyes on Elizabeth's limp form.

"I must go now to see other patients, but I will be back again later in the afternoon to check on her. I will give instructions to Mrs. Reynolds about the proper diet for her."

Darcy nodded absentmindedly.

The older man gave him a long, thoughtful look, hesitant to leave, "A word of advice, may I, Master?"

Darcy tore his eyes from Elizabeth, "You may."

"I know it must be difficult for you to believe it, but she will forgive you, come to terms with everything, and you will have a good life together."

Darcy shook his head, "You did not see the way she looked at me before she fainted, and what she said."

"I did see that look many years ago, and I can very well imagine her reaction and her words. You must remember that my wife is human too."

Darcy's frown deepened. "My father never told me how my mother reacted."

"It is hard to describe." The doctor said slowly, "You have to be strong. She will try to escape, you can be sure of it. My wife tried three times. The last time she even managed to get as far as her own family in Edinburgh."

"What happened?" Darcy asked with open curiosity, "How did you manage to convince her to return to you?"

"It was not that difficult. I was in the north then, the old Lord McGrath needed an additional doctor for his pack, because they had major smallpox epidemic – nothing deadly, but serious enough. When I got back home after three weeks' of absence, and found it locked and empty, my very first thought was that my Lucy must have returned to her family. Thankfully, she did not tell them the real reason for her escape from me. They were very happy to give her back. She was big with our first child then, and otherwise well kept and well dressed, even had money with herself, so they did not see the reason to support her idea of separation from such a good husband. She had no one else to stay with, and came back home with me."

"I will never let my wife go away from me." Darcy announced, his expression strained.

The doctor looked at the determination written on Darcy's face. He thought that their young Alpha Male would have a few very busy months, trying to keep this pretty blonde by him. The old man smiled inwardly, remembering the feats of his own wife from nearly thirty years ago. From the perspective of such a long time, they seemed amusing. He sobered though, when he recalled his own despair at that time, his fear that his Lucy would abandon him forever.

"I would not underestimate your wife." he said cautiously. "Make sure she will not attempt the escape till she is completely healthy. Another walk to the beach in the cold rain in her present state and she will get pneumonia, not just a cold."

Darcy extended his hand. "Thank you for everything, Doctor."

"A hand shake." the old man smirked, taking the professed hand. "Your father would have never thought of doing that." He walked to the door, "Times are changing."

Chapter Eighteen

Elizabeth slept till the evening. The awareness of all that had happened was with her, but her mind and body felt too exhausted to concentrate on it. She was so worn out, that all she could care about was sleep.

They woke her in the early evening for dinner. She swallowed a bowl of chicken soup, and did not even protest when Fitzwilliam fed her with a spoon. She was too weak, sleepy and tired to push him away, and the hot soup felt good on her aching throat.

The moment her husband took the empty dish away, and dabbed her mouth with a napkin, she turned to her side, drew the covers over her herself and dozed off.

She yearned to rest before she would have to face what her life had come to.

The strong, almost unbearable need to empty her bladder woke her up in the middle of the night. On her hands and knees, she crawled out of the bed. Her wobbly feet touched the thick, plush carpet, and she supported herself against the bedpost.

She could feel the fever burning in her, as she concentrated on making tiny steps across the bedroom to the dressing room door.

Strong arms wrapped around her long before she was even half way to her destination, "You should not get up."

Her head lolled against his chest. "I must go to the bathroom," she winced, crossing her legs together, "Cannot wait."

Without a word, he swept her into his arms, carrying her to the bathroom and sat her on the toilet bowl. Elizabeth was too groggy, and her head hurt too much to be embarrassed when he pulled her nightgown up so she could relieve herself.

She fell asleep again as he carried her back to the bed. When she opened her eyes the next time, it was midday. Instantly she knew that she was much better. She was hungry and she craved a bath.

The door to the sitting room was partially open, and as she leaned forward, she saw her husband and Doctor Craw, standing and talking in lowered voices.

"Should she sleep for such a long time?" Darcy asked, the tone of his voice impatient to Elizabeth's ears, "It has been almost two days. She should have awakened by now."

Elizabeth frowned and glanced angrily in the direction of the younger man.

Why does he want me to wake up? What will he do to me now that I know? Will he want me now? Does he need me anymore? The questions staggered her mind.

"He has got everything he wanted from me." she said the last words out loud, wanting them to hear.

The door was pushed open, and Darcy strode into the room.

"Darling," he sat beside her, one of his hands on her shoulder, the other cupping her cheek, "We have been so worried, you slept so long. How are you feeling? Better?"

His voice was so tender, his big hands on her so gentle, his eyes genuinely distressed when searching her face; it was all a lie, a deception. All she felt now was cold fury.

Very slowly, she wrapped her fingers around his wrists, pushing his hands away.

"Lizzy," he leaned toward her, but she turned her face from him, her lips pressed in a thin line, "I can explain everything to you, I know you will understand," he whispered, his eyes begging her to look at him. "My love, please. " He tried to envelop her in his arms, but she kept pushing him away.

"Do not touch me." she said in a clear voice.

He drew back slowly. "Elizabeth."

Her lips pressed even tighter; the last thing she cared for now was his dejected, as if heartbroken, voice.

"You want me to be well?" she looked straight into his dark eyes.

"Of course." His hand lifted to touch her, but then dropped back on his muscular thigh.

"Then go!" she cried, "Go from my sight, because when I look at you, it makes me ill!"

She averted her eyes, turned her face away, focusing on the blue skies outside the tall windows.

He stayed as he was for a moment or two, before he lifted himself and left the room, dragging his legs.

Elizabeth closed her eyes. She would not cry; she was too angry for that.

"Mrs. Darcy."

"Doctor Craw." She forced herself to smile at the man who had just entered the room. He must have heard everything.

One bushy eyebrow cocked up. "Even without proper examination, I can see that you feel much better today." the man said with a smile.

Elizabeth sat more comfortably against the headboard, "I do, Doctor."

The doctor moved a chair closer to the bed, sat on it and opened his bag.

"Headache?"

Elizabeth shook her head.

The doctor's warm, rough fingers touched her neck on both sides just under the jaw line.

"Say O."

"Oooo." She presented the inside of her mouth.

"Your throat could look better." he noted.

"It hurts still," she admitted.

With quick efficiency, the doctor checked her temperature, pulse and listened to her lungs.

"I am very pleased with your recovery, Mrs. Darcy." he said as he packed his instruments back into the bag. "You will be like new in a week, but only on the condition that you follow my instructions. You will stay in your rooms, no outdoors for now. Eat three full meals a day, drink a lot. You do not have to stay in bed, you may rest on the sofa, but warmly bundled up."

Elizabeth sat quietly, biting on her lower lip.

"Any questions?" The doctor asked kindly. "I imagine there are many matters you want to know more about."

She took a deep breath, "Am I with child?"

"Yes.

"Is it absolutely certain?"

"Yes."

Elizabeth closed her eyes.

"To tell the truth, it is a bit too early to say, just judging by the symptoms," he continued. "I would need to perform a very embarrassing examination to confirm it, but it is not necessary, as your husband can already smell his baby in you."

She hid her face into her hands.

Doctor Craw patted her back, “Do not worry, child. You will not give birth to a pup.” he assured.

Elizabeth uncovered her face, her eyes lit up with hope. “Are you sure?”

Doctor smiled, “Yes, absolutely. Even if both parents are of our kind, the child, when it is born, resembles any other infant born to human parents. The first change into a wolf comes around the age of eleven, twelve, sometimes even thirteen; usually much earlier for girls than boys.”

Elizabeth’s hand went to her chest, “I must say I am very much relieved to hear it.”

Doctor nodded. “I understand.”

Soon, Elizabeth’s eyes widened in distress again, “Would it be one child? Not four or five, I hope. Not a litter?”

Doctor allowed himself a chuckle, “No, no, again everything is very similar like in human families, there is usually one child, rarely twins. Actually, two babies are very often born from mixed couples, and in such cases, I think that it is the human side that decides. We could expect twins in this case, had there been twin babies in your family.”

Elizabeth nodded, “My mother has a twin brother, Uncle Edward.”

“Well, then it is a large possibility that you can carry twins, but it is too soon to tell.”

Elizabeth stared down at her hands.

“Do you know the symptoms of the early confinement?” he asked. “Do you know what to expect?”

“I guess that I do. My elder sister and I stayed with my aunt three years ago, when she was expecting her youngest child.”

“Good, but you must remember that all those symptoms, like unusual tiredness, early morning sickness and the dizzy spells will be intensified. Your body needs to adapt not only to the pregnancy itself, but also to carrying a baby of a different species. ”

She shook her head in slow motion. “I still cannot believe in it.”

The doctor interrupted her, “Just wait till the baby starts to kick, you will feel entirely different about it.” He took the chair that he had occupied and put it back where it had stood. “I must go now, I must visit a sick tenant’s child today before going to the hospital. I will come to check on you tomorrow, of course.”

"Is it something serious with that child?" Elizabeth asked with earnest worry.

Doctor Craw smiled at her concern. "The girl had pneumonia, but she is on her way to a full recovery, just a routine visit, to ease her parents' worry."

He was near the door when she asked.

"Doctor?"

"Yes?"

"I want to go back to my family. Will you help me to….?"

He walked closer, all the pleasantness wiped out from his face. "Mrs. Darcy, you should not even ask me that, or any other person here, unless you wish to bring trouble to them. You are the mate of our Alpha Male, and for us, it is like treason to help you abandon him and us. You can compare it to convincing someone to betray the King of England. No one will help you escape."

Elizabeth looked down at her hands. The doctor took a step closer and spoke in a low voice, "Attempting to escape has no point, he will look for you till he finds you, no matter how far you manage to go. I am saying this for your own good."

"Cannot you see that it is wrong?" she whispered.

The man shook his head, "No, I cannot." he answered flatly, "Nobody mistreats women here, men do not keep mistresses, the wives are loved, cared for and protected. Can you say the same about your world?"

Doctor Craw did not wait for her answer, but left the bedchamber.

Elizabeth's hand curled into a fist. There must be a way to escape. Other women had tried in the past, they must have attempted, some of them surely succeeded, they just were not telling her that.

A soft knock on the door, "Lizzy." Georgiana peeked inside.

Elizabeth smiled brightly. There was no reason to take it out on Georgiana; the girl should not be burden with the responsibility for her brother's misdeeds.

Encouraged by the welcoming smile, she entered. "Feeling better, I heard?"

"Much better, thank you. I would very much like a bath."

"Your maid is waiting to help you with everything. Heather!" she called into the sitting room.

The maid appeared a moment later, "Good morning, my lady!" Heather cheered, producing a toothy smile from ear to ear. "So good to see you back to your old self."

Elizabeth could not stop another smile at her enthusiasm. "Thank you, Heather."

"My sister wishes to take a bath." Georgiana said.

"Aye, at once, my lady," Heather bowed and hurried to the dressing room.

"Just build up the fire well in the bathing room." Georgiana reminded.

"Aye, Miss Darcy." Heather's voice was heard from the bathroom.

"What is that noise?" Elizabeth asked when she got up from bed, Georgiana helping her into her robe.

The girl walked to the window. "Folks came to ask whether you are better. They came yesterday too."

Elizabeth frowned. "Someone ordered them to come?"

"Of course not." Georgiana cried, "They are worried about you."

Elizabeth stepped to the window as well.

On the lawn, directly under her windows, stood about three dozen people, strictly speaking, wolves and people, mostly small children with mothers.

Elizabeth recognized Mrs. Brown with Emma, and many other faces that she had remembered from church and the village.

"They would be very happy and calmed down if you came closer to the window." Georgiana suggested. "So they could see that you are truly better."

Elizabeth gave her an uncertain look. "You think?"

Elizabeth pushed the lacy curtain away stood in front of the glass. A child noticed her, and started jumping up, tugging at its mother's sleeve. All at once, the heads lifted up and she could hear cheers and see smiling faces.

"They all seem happy to see me." she said as she waved one last time and closed the curtain.

Georgiana stepped closer, taking her hand. "They like you."

***

Darcy sat in his study, surrounded by piles of unopened letters. He was supposed to work, but so far he had managed to stare with glossy eyes into the space in front of him.

Nearly two weeks had passed since the last full moon, and as the doctor had assured him, his wife was now completely recovered from the cold.

The bad news was that she neither spoke nor looked at him since then.

When he had come to her bedroom the day after she had ordered him out of it, she had completely ignored his presence. He had not tried to start a conversation. She had still been weak, and he had not been sure how she would react to his attempt at communication. He could anticipate everything from weeping, to shouting, fainting and kicking or hitting him. He had not wanted her to exert herself in her delicate state. He had stood by her bed for a minute or two like an idiot, feasting his eyes with her lovely sight; long, pale, shiny hair, smooth, translucent skin, gently rounded face, graceful hands. But when she had not acknowledged his presence with even the smallest gesture, he had left.

He had observed her from afar since then, as she interacted with his sister, Heather, Doctor Craw and Mrs. Reynolds. She did not seem to be angry at them, and was her usual kind and charming self to everyone except him. *God, will it be like this forever?* He knew it was unreasonable to think that, but he was beginning to doubt whether she would ever speak to him again. He did not want to pressure her into something she was not ready for; in her newly awakened rage, she could harm herself or the baby, but they needed to talk.

There were matters that he must explain to her which was impossible for the time being as she refused to listen to him or even stay in the same room as he.

Darcy stood from the desk and walked to the window. Perhaps she was taking her daily walk now. Yesterday, the doctor had allowed her to go out for the first time, to take a stroll, but only in the gardens near the house. The day had been beautiful, sunny and warm for September, and she and Georgiana had tilted their faces to the sun with obvious pleasure. Understandably, Wilfred had accompanied them, this time in his human form. Heather had been with them as well, carrying Elizabeth's things, a small umbrella and an additional woollen shawl, had the Mistress got cold or overheated.

He could not stop himself, and had changed into a wolf, and followed them, maintaining a safe distance, hiding behind the bushes. Elizabeth must have been unaware of his presence, and it had been Georgiana who had sensed him being near, and called him to come to them.

Elizabeth had recognized him instantly as he approached the small group. He had hoped his lupine form would soften her heart, after all, she had always seemed to be more willing to show affection to him when he had met her as a wolf. However, this time the trick had not worked. She turned on her feet with her back to him, and suddenly announced that she had been tired and wanted to return home.

She had left him there alone, seething with anger, perhaps more humiliated than ever. He was the Alpha Male here, and she had acted as if it had not mattered to her at all, as if she had not acknowledged his power. She could act as she wanted and speak to him as she wished when they were in private, (and she had) but to degrade him like that in front of his people; it was unthinkable for nobody else ever dared ever to treat him that way. Her behaviour could have been compared only to slapping him in the face right in front of his pack.

Yesterday, when she had walked out on him, he had wanted to shake her, make her listen, make her understand that he had had no other choice but to keep his real identity from her. But most of all, he had wanted to transform back into a human, throw her over his shoulder, take her somewhere where nobody would bother them, and lie with her.

He had done nothing of the sort; only watched as she had walked briskly back to the house, small upturned nose high in the air, with a befuddled Georgiana, Heather and Wilfred keeping her pace.

Patience and understanding, yes, that was the key. Above all, he needed to show her his love and consideration; in time she would accept the situation and forgive him. She loved him, after all.

There was a light knock at the door. Without taking his eyes from the view outside the window, he said absently,

"Enter."

The moment he heard the soft slippered steps, he knew it was she.

"Sweetheart," he whispered, turning to her.

She closed the door, walked closer and smiled politely, "I would like to talk with you." she said softly. "Could you find some time for me now, or should I come later?"

He barely registered what she had just said, she looked so lovely. She wore a gown he had not remembered; pale yellow silk that moulded to her body like a second skin. His eyes were glued to her chest, the gown was cut low, showing the upper curves of her pretty breasts.

"Of course we can talk." He gathered her to him, and she did not protest. "My love, I was so afraid you would not want to speak with me ever again," he murmured into her neck.

She put her small hand against his chest and pushed gently, "I needed a few days to think about our situation."

"Come, sit down." He took her hands and led her to the sofa. "Elizabeth, I want explain everything to you, why I hid the truth from you."

She freed her hands and clasped them on her lap, her posture straight, even a bit stiff.

"You do not have to, I think that I understand."

"You do?"

"Yes, according to your laws, the human brides cannot know until they are fully embedded into their new life. It has been like that for centuries, I am told, and it is for the protection of the entire pack, so the outside world would not learn about its existence." she recited like a well taught lesson.

"Exactly." he cupped her face, "I am so relieved you understand," he leaned to kiss her, but she averted her face. Perhaps it was too soon for intimacies. He could wait as long as necessary; most important was that she seemed less angry with him, and came to him on her free will.

He wrapped his arms around her back and pulled her closer. She allowed that, leaning into him lightly.

"How are you feeling?" he lifted her hand to kiss it, "Have you been sick this morning?"

She nodded, "Yes, I threw up my breakfast."

"But no fainting?"

"No."

His hand went to her midsection and rested there. "How is the baby?"

"Fine, I guess. I cannot feel it yet, it is too early. Doctor Craw says everything is well."

He pressed his hand more firmly, "Yes, and what else did he say?"

"That it should be born at the beginning of May, and that there might be the possibility of twins."

"Twins, really?"

She nodded, "Because there are twins in my family, my mother and Uncle Gardiner are twins."

He could not help himself, and hugged her to him, wrapping his arms around her, "That is wonderful news, sweetheart, two babies at once," he drew back to stroke her cheek, "My only worry is that carrying twins will be much more taxing for you."

A shadow of a smile crossed her face as she pulled away from him completely.

"Yes." She cleared her throat, "I have received a letter from Jane." She reached to the hidden pocket in her skirt and took out the folded paper. "She and Mr. Bingley invite us to see their new home."

Darcy's eyes narrowed immediately. "Yes, I got a letter from Charles. He confirms the invitation, and he wants my advice on the changes he should introduce into his new estate."

"I thought that perhaps we could go together with Georgiana." she said calmly. "I wish to see Jane very much. I miss her."

Darcy stood up and walked to the mantelpiece, leaning against it, "We cannot possibly go now."

"Why?"

"You must remember that Lord McGrath is in Ireland, and during his absence, I am fully responsible for both packs."

"I forgot about it," she acknowledged quietly.

Darcy sat back next to her, "I know that you are disappointed, but at present time the trip is simply impossible."

She was silent for a moment, but he could see that she was about to say something, gathering her thoughts.

"Would you then agree to let me go alone, or with Georgiana, if she would be willing to accompany me?"

"Alone?"

She looked to the side, "Yes, it is no more than a day and a half of travel from here."

He stood up and his hand curled into a fist. "You want to go alone."

Her dark blue eyes raised steadily at him, "Yes. I want to see my sister."

"I am sorry, but you do not have my permission."

"May I hear your reason?"

He looked down at her, "Because I cannot trust you at this point – that you would not try to leave me permanently."

She rose to her feet as well and walked to him, "And if I promised, if I vowed not to try to escape, and come back to Pemberley before, let us say, before Christmas."

He wanted to say yes to her; she looked at him with such hope written all over her face. He could pretend he needed to think about it, give her that hope, but he did not want to sway and deceive her any more.

"I will write to Charles, explaining we cannot go now because of your condition. But you are free to invite your sister here, after the baby is born. I have nothing against visiting the Bingley's in a year or two, when our child will be big enough to travel with us."

Elizabeth listened quietly, then stood up, and without one look in his direction, left the study.

Chapter Nineteen

After Elizabeth had gone, Darcy tried to return to his correspondence with no result. As he raked his hand through his hair, he realized he was facing the onset of a great storm that could set off at any moment. His tempest at a little over five foot of height, blue eyed, with sunny hair and a sweet voice, but no one should be swayed with her pliable outer appearance.

He hated to say no to her, but allowing her to visit the Bingleys was out of question now, when the discovery of his true self was still fresh and painful to her. He was scared to death of losing her, as he had little doubt that Jane Bingley would have done everything to free her little sister from her monster husband, had she seen Elizabeth unhappy or worse, learnt everything. Darcy had little doubt that the eldest Bennet had never been particularly fond of him; every time she had looked at him, it had been with a judgemental and calculated appraisal in her pale blue eyes. He even had a strong suspicion that Jane had tried to convince Elizabeth not to marry him at all, or at least postpone the wedding.

What was his wife thinking now? What was going on in her mind? She came here to plead with him, and he turned her down flatly, but what else could he do? She should not go away from Pemberley during her pregnancy as it was the only place she and the baby were safe. Outside, there was always a possibility of her encountering some werewolf outcast, rightly expelled from his pack for misbehaviour, forced to dwell among humans. The bastard would have felt the baby to be of their kind the minute he stood next to her. Then he would have surely tried to find out who the father was, and had he learned that she was the Alpha Female, and the mate of a large pack's leader… God, he preferred not to think what could happened then, she could have been killed, the baby literally ripped out of her body to blackmail him, or even to try to overthrown him, having his heir. Wickham was still free; should he learn that she had abandoned him, he would have done everything to use the situation to his advantage.

Darcy briefly considered going to her and explaining the dangers of her leaving the pack's territory now, but he rejected the thought. She was frightened enough. Undoubtedly, she would have grown even more terrified, had she learned that without his protection, she would be hunted like an animal for the baby she carried. God, he could not allow that, she must stay here with him, safe and protected.

He felt an overpowering need to see her, to put his hands on her, ensure himself that she was safe.

He stormed out of his study and dashed through the manor to the new wing, and up the staircase. He found Wilfred, languishing next to the door to her rooms. The youth sprang up, alerted the moment he sensed him coming.

Darcy looked at the young wolf. *Is my mate inside?*

Wilfred growled in low voice. *She came back half an hour ago, and has not left since then.*

Darcy nodded. *Go now, you are free from your duty till dinner time.*

Wilfred ran away without a second glance as Darcy entered his wife's apartment. The sitting room was empty.

Understandably, he loves Pemberley, every single stone of it had been built over the centuries, but since his marriage, those were the rooms he cherished the most. Not that his taste was in light blue, yellow and white, flowery upholstery and curtains; he favoured less bright colours, like brown, and dark green. Simply, those were her chambers now, and that was enough to make him be partial to them.

In only a few weeks of residence here, Eliizabeth had put her own feminine touch to the rooms. There were numerous pictures on the walls depicting nothing in special, but some water washed flower bouquets. He had asked her once who had created them, and she had answered that they were her sisters' works. There were vases with fresh flowers on every flat surface, both from the conservatory and the common wildflowers she liked to pick up during her walks, creating a stuffy atmosphere in his opinion. Only added to it, the numerous pots with green, ivy like plants, she had brought with her from the south. The ivy thrived in here, because it climbed up, winding around the picture frames, covering the walls.

He remembered the plants well, because those damn little pots had travelled with them in the carriage, and she had watered them by herself, constantly checking whether they had been in good condition.

Another change was the presence of books, the ones sent from Longbourn, and the others that she had annexed from the library. The third day of her stay, he had showed her the library. She had innocently asked then whether she could borrow some books. Understandably, he had agreed, happy to please her with such a small thing. He had not expected though that the whole novel and poetry section would be methodically cleared up within just a few weeks. Now, he knew that 'borrowing' meant taking for keeps. A small cabinet had been moved from one of the guest rooms, and now it was already completely filled, with another pile of volumes cluttered on the desk ready to be stored.

The door to the bedroom was ajar, so he pushed it forward.

Elizabeth rested curled on her side with her back to him, dressed in the same yellow gown she had worn to the study earlier.

As he walked closer, he heard a quiet sniffing. Was she crying?

"What is the matter?" He knelt beside the bed. "Have I upset you so much?"

She sat up and shook her head. Her carefully arranged locks had loosened themselves and her pretty eyes were rimmed red. "No… I felt sad, so I started to weep."

He lifted himself to sit next to her, "Elizabeth, what can I do? Tell me?" He wrapped his arms around her.

"I am not crying because of you... I mean, I am still angry with you, and have not forgiven you, but I weep because lately I feel like I need to weep, at least twice a day." She sniffed into his shirt.

He rubbed her back, "I do not understand."

"Neither do I." she hiccupped.

The sight of his beloved in tears was not something he enjoyed, but he appreciated the opportunity to keep her close to him, all warm, soft, yielding and not argumentative.

At last her sobbing ceased, and she allowed him to dry her face with his handkerchief.

"Could you please help me with removing my dress?" She pulled away from him and scrambled to her feet. "I am so tired," she said listlessly as she walked slowly to the dressing room, "I want to take a nap."

He followed her, and stood behind her, "Where is Heather?" he reached for the tiny clasps at the back of the gown, "She should be here to help you."

"I gave her a day off."

"A day off?"

"Yes, her little sister has a birthday today."

Darcy frowned, irritated with the inability to undo the clasps of her dress with his suddenly too thick fingers, "She should not have asked you for a day off." he scolded. "Her duty is to serve you every day, and she has Sundays after church free, sometimes Saturdays as well."

"She did not ask me, I gave her an order to go home."

He smiled, "And she listened."

"Yes, I was a bit surprised that she just did so without any kind of protest." Elizabeth pushed the gown down her arms, stepping out of it carefully.

"She is duty bound to follow your orders." Darcy stated casually.

Elizabeth gaped at him, "She is?"

He nodded.

She walked closer, tilting her head to the side, "And the others?"

"They as well. You are my mate, the Alpha Female. They follow your orders, but my command stands above yours, so they must obey me first."

With a frown of her own, she smoothed the yellow dress and hung the dress carefully into the closet.

With hungry eyes, he watched as she removed her petticoats, sat down only in her chemise and started rolling down the silk stockings. She had many pairs of them now, but still treated them with great care, because as she had said to him, once she had owned only one pair when still being Miss Bennet.

His wife had nice legs, pale and smooth, with almost no hair; rather short, but perfectly proportional to her height. They were strong and well muscled from all the walking she did daily. She may have little power in her hands and arms, but when she locked her legs around him when he made love to her and held tight, there was no way he could easily free himself from the clasp till he gave her exactly what she wanted.

He found himself aroused more than he should have been with the vision of her pinned under him, her legs wrapped around his hips. The sight of her bare thighs under the short chemise did not help much either.

He sighed out loud and met her puzzled gaze, which stopped being so confused when her eyes rested on the front of his breeches.

He actually blushed in embarrassment. He knew their marriage was not what it was supposed to be at present, but it had been two weeks since he had touched her, and the incessant pain in his breeches demanded some release.

She stood up and stepped to him, her barely clad body touching him lightly.

Her eyes steady on his face, she took his hand and placed it on her breast.

He squeezed it.

"Just gently, they are tender." she whispered.

The next few minutes blurred in front of him, his frantic undressing, his quick caresses to make sure she was ready, his gasp of relief when he finally was engulfed within her.

She was very calm and quiet when he moved against her. And she did not try to kiss, touch and stroke him like usual. He looked for some signs of discomfort on her face, showing that she was in pain, but found nothing, though she avoided his gaze. He reassured himself, remembering that she had been moist, her womanly flesh pink and swollen when he had pushed inside. He would have never allowed himself to enter her when she was dry, no matter how he needed it, that would surely hurt her. There were days when it took him longer to make her well prepared for him, and he wondered why; perhaps it had something to do with her womanly cycle.

He found his release, but she did not, and later he stroked her with his fingers till she trembled into the ecstasy. Then she took her nap, nestled against him, breathing softly. When she woke up an hour later, he took her again, and this time he managed to control himself till she had her pleasure when he was still sheathed inside her.

After the second time, he wanted to pull her into his arms so she could rest again, but she resisted and turned on her side with her back to him, the sheet barely covering her.

As he looked at her, he knew that she did not doze off again, the muscles in her back were too tense for that.

He sat, supporting his back against the headboard.

His hand reached to her and he stroked the silky smooth skin of the shoulder blade with the back of his fingers.

"I want to go to live with Jane for some time." she said very clearly.

His hand dropped.

"So you allowed me in to your bed only to get my permission."

She shrugged. "I thought you would be in a better mood to discuss it."

He curled behind her.

"Lizzy, listen to me." He kissed her shoulder. "I fell in love with you at Netherfield, and I tried hard to resist you then, because I knew how difficult our union would be. Then we met again in Kent, purely by accident, I realized that it was our destiny to be together, and that I should not act against it. I knew that we could overcome all the obstacles, and in time succeed in a happy marriage. I still believe in that."

There was a long moment of silence before she spoke, "You did not tell me that you were not human."

He turned her to him, cupping her face, "I could not tell you. Would you believe me?"

"No."

"Would you have married me had you known who I really was?"

"No."

"So what else could I do?"

Elizabeth pulled out from his embrace and sat up. "Leave me alone, and find yourself someone of your own kind."

Darcy sat behind her, "You are now of my kind, because of the baby, his blood running in you binds us together."

She turned to him, her eyes narrowed, "The baby is mine." She pressed her lips in a thin line, "Every day I pray for a girl, because she will be normal like your sister, and then I could raise her alone, away from here."

"Alone and away from here?" he pushed from her, standing up next to the bed, his voice authoritative, "I will never allow you to go away from me, especially with my child, no matter if it is a girl or a boy."

Elizabeth crawled across the bed towards him, clenching the sheet to her front, "But if the baby is a girl and it is very possible that it is, because my mother gave births to girls only, you will not need her. You could let us go, give me a divorce and take yourself another wife of your kind who would give you a son. Then I could live away in some cottage with the baby, or perhaps with Jane and Charles."

He did not answer at first; he even refused to look at her. His hands trembled as he dressed himself; he was so enraged with what she had just said.

"Elizabeth, I will tell this only one time." he said as he picked up his coat and neck cloth from the floor, trying to control his voice, "Remember it well. Werewolves mate for life, there is no such possibility as separation or divorce, it is entirely a human notion. Any child you have is mine, no matter what gender, it will stay here with me, the same as you. Forever."

Elizabeth dropped on the sheets, burying her face into the pillows.

Before leaving the room, he stepped to bed and reached to stroke the hair from her face, "I know you suffer now, but nothing can change the fact that you and the baby belong to me."

***

Darcy kicked his horse's sides to make the animal go faster. He was on his way back from the three day long trip to Lord McGrath's lands, and he would see the house in a minute or two. He had left Pemberley with a heavy heart, afraid that Elizabeth would try to escape, but he could not postpone his duty any longer. Lord McGrath was still in Ireland, and Darcy had made a promise to oversee his lands and people during his absence. He reasoned with himself that there was no possibility for Elizabeth to get away. Before he left, he had made sure that his people understood that she was to be watched every hour, day and night.

His racing heart slowed down only when he noticed Elizabeth standing with Georgiana next to the open carriage. They were both dressed in velvet coats and matching bonnets. They looked as if they were off to pay a visit.

He was on the ground before the horse even came to a halt.

"Brother!" Georgiana ran to him and into his arms, "You returned early."

Darcy picked her up and kissed her cheek. Every time he returned home from a longer absence, it struck him that his little sister was a woman now, tall, beautiful and all grown up.

"Where are you going?" he asked, letting Georgina down. They walked to Elizabeth who barely acknowledged his presence. He was not surprised; he did not expect a warm welcome from his wife. She had not talked to him or looked at him since that afternoon they had made love in her room.

"We have been visiting the tenants for the last two days." Georgiana explained, pointing to the baskets covered with white cloth that Wilfred and Heather carried to the carriage.

Darcy glanced at Elizabeth, who chose to look in the other direction, "You have."

Georgiana nodded, "We are almost finished, only four families left to visit today. After that, we must go to the village because Elizabeth must try on the new winter dress Mrs. Brown is making for her."

Darcy gestured to the baskets cluttered at the back seat of the carriage, "Whose idea was that?"

Georgiana grinned. "Elizabeth's. She said she wanted to know everyone more closely."

Heather and Wilfred were already seated on the coachman's box, and Darcy handed his sister in, "When will you come back?"

"Well before evening. We should be done with the tenant visits by early afternoon, but the dress fittings may take some time."

He turned to Elizabeth, who stood, unsmiling, a few feet away. Darcy stepped to her, took her elbow and walked her aside.

He could not see her eyes because she lowered her head, and they were hidden under the wide rim of her velvet bonnet.

"Are you well enough for this?" he asked quietly.

She adjusted her fine leather gloves, not raising her eyes to him. "Yes."

He leaned to her; God she smelled even better than he remembered. "You will take care of yourself." he whispered into her delicate ear.

"Yes." she repeated, and walked away to the awaiting carriage.

Georgiana moved aside, making room for her.

Darcy did not ask for permission, but came behind his wife, put his hands on her waist and lifted her up to the high seat of the barouche.

Georgiana waved at him as the carriage pulled off. "Bye, Brother!"

***

Elizabeth was more than surprised how normal her visits to the tenants' cottages proved to be. Had she not known that the families she met were werewolves, she would have thought only what kind, decent and hardworking people they were.

Now she stood in the middle of the small sewing room, at the back of the Brown household.

"Mrs. Darcy, I think it fits well around the arms," Mrs. Brown murmured through the pins in her mouth.

Elizabeth turned to see her back in the tall looking glass, "It is excellent. I see that Georgiana did not exaggerate when she talked about your skill. I like the way you altered the pattern we chose. It looks much more elegant now."

"Well, it is to be an ordinary woolen day dress, but it does not mean it must look like a potato sack." The older woman frowned, looking at the front of the dress, "It reminds me… I found a lovely piece of brown ribbon, and I thought we could put some around the sleeves. It will go nicely with this dark blue and brown tartan." She walked to the window sill where the box with all kinds of ribbons was placed. "I am not sure whether I should burden Miss Darcy with my little devils." She glanced worriedly at Georgiana, who stood with the youngest child in her arms, while the older two were running around them, chased by Heather and Wilfred.

"She will be all right. Georgiana is good with children," Elizabeth smiled, "And Heather is with them too."

Mrs. Brown walked to her, her eyes sparkling, "We have heard the good news, that next spring there will be a little one at the castle that Miss Darcy can play with."

Elizabeth's smiled waned. "Yes, there will be."

The other woman gave her a long, thoughtful look. "I should not pry, Mrs. Darcy," she hesitated. "But you do not seem very happy with the news about the baby."

Elizabeth gasped. "You should understand me! You are not from here either."

Mrs. Brown opened the dress on the back and started to pull it off carefully, not to damage the basting threads. She glanced at the younger woman, "You want to know how I felt when I found out that I married the werewolf."

Elizabeth turned to her abruptly, "Did you try to escape?"

Mrs. Brown shook her head with a smile. "No."

Elizabeth stared at her unbelievably, "No?"

"Well, I ran from the house once when I accidentally saw my Hugh transform from a wolf back into a human. I was so scared with what I saw that I just kept running and running. But later, when he explained everything to me, I understood.

"You did?"

Mrs. Brown took the dress and put it back on the form in the corner, "My situation was a bit different than yours. My family was very poor, we went hungry more often than with full stomachs. My father drank and hit my mother. When she died from exhaustion, he started to hit us too. My two eldest brothers ran away from home, and then Sir Lewis de Bourgh took my little sister and me to the manor. Mary was just six then, but they allowed her to play around when I worked in the kitchen. She was a good child, and very quiet."

Elizabeth looked at her compassionately. "You had a very difficult life."

Mrs. Brown shrugged. "It was a long time ago. I was not aware of the seriousness of our situation back then. Now I know that had not Sir Lewis taken us to the manor, I think that my father would have killed one of us."

Elizabeth nodded with a thoughtful frown. "I understand that in comparison to the life your mother had, your marriage seems something much better."

"Much better? It is heaven!" the other woman exclaimed. "My husband has never even raised his voice at me, not to mention hit me, though you must know how strong they all are. He brought up my sister as his own child, and when the time came, he arranged her marriage very well to a wealthy carpenter from Lord McGrath's pack."

"You allowed your sister to be married to one of them?"

"My sister's husband is a very decent man." Mrs. Brown said firmly. "He makes very elegant furniture, and sells it to towns in the south."

Elizabeth glanced at her with sudden interest, her eyes narrowed. "Does he?"

"Oh, yes." Mrs. Brown nodded proudly, "A few times a year, he travels to Manchester, and once he even made furniture for a family in Bath."

"Bath, really?" Elizabeth bit her lower lip, "It is far away from here."

"They were a very elegant family; the gentleman was a baronet." Mrs. Brown added. She brought Elizabeth's dress and helped her into it. "I have never known poverty since I came here, Mrs. Darcy." she continued, buttoning the dress at the back. "I have a good husband, hard working, kind, loving, and a better house than the parson's wife had at Rosings Park."

Elizabeth turned to her, and asked with feeling, "But your husband is a werewolf, not human, does it not bother you?"

The older woman waved her hand in a dismissive gesture. "So what that he is a werewolf? He is just like a dog running around and barking. Werewolves are not some bloody creatures killing people, or stealing infant children under the disguise of night. They do not do anything unusual when they are wolves."

"They do not?"

"No, they just run around and play like… like little boys."

Elizabeth took her bonnet and walked to the looking glass to put it on.

Mrs. Brown stepped behind her with her coat. "Mrs. Darcy, you may very well try to look at the situation like I do." she said in a rational voice. "You have a good husband, who does not drink, does not gamble or chase other women. He works hard for you and your future children and he does not beat you, never that. I remember three years ago there was a man who got drunk and hit his wife on the face. Master ordered he be put in the dungeon with no windows in the old castle, on bread and water for three weeks. His wife was offered to live separately from him."

"And what happened?"

"His wife took him back, but he never touched her again… I mean that he never hit her again: they have a new baby now and they get by. But you see that such behaviour towards women is not tolerated here. As I said, the only strange thing is that every second night he changes into a wolf and runs around the forest with his friends, howling to the moon, hunting for rabbits and squirrels. It is very good exercise, I dare say, very healthy, and keeps them fit." she paused. "Do you know what is the best thing of all?"

Elizabeth shook her head.

"He feeds himself outside the house, and all you have to cook is for you and the children, even not so much for children, because he brings the dead animals for them too."

Elizabeth felt her stomach coming up to her throat. "That is repulsive."

"I agree. It was a bit of a shock the first time I saw my Heather, when she was still a scrap of a girl, chewing on a dead squirrel which Daddy brought especially for her. You do not have to watch that. I just leave the room."

Elizabeth stared at Mrs. Brown, her expression doubtful and puzzled.

The woman smiled at her. "The dress will be ready in a week's time. I will send it to you through Heather when she has her next day off."

Elizabeth smiled back. "Thank you, Mrs. Brown."

Chapter Twenty

It was a full moon night, closer to dawn. Darcy had hunted with his men for most of the night. He carried a freshly caught rabbit for Georgiana, just as she liked it, young and fat. He would leave it at her doorstep so she could eat it just as she woke up to the smell of the raw, juicy meat. He entered the manor through the back entrance and ran straight upstairs. He dropped the animal at his sister's bedroom, and went across the hall to the Mistress' rooms. With one flick of his head, he dismissed Wilfred, who was already on pins and needles, ready to do his night's howling.

Through the sitting room, Darcy paced into his wife's bedroom. He hopped on the bed to ascertain that she was all well, resting peacefully.

His heart stopped for a moment and then started pounding as he stared at the empty bed.

Darcy forced himself to calm down and think. *She must be somewhere in these rooms*; Wilfred had guarded the door the entire night, and she could not break out through the window as they were not on the first floor.

Bathroom! Why had he not thought of it? She used it more frequently nowadays because of her condition. The bed covers were roused, so she had slept here this night. In one long leap, he was in the dressing room and adjacent bathroom. He smelled the place carefully, but she had not been there for the last couple of hours. He trotted back to the bedroom and started sniffing around. She had to be somewhere, she could not evaporate. He traced her scent back into the sitting room, and to his surprise, into his own bedroom.

He realized that he began breathing again when he saw her curled on his bed under the covers. He hurled onto the bed, sniffling her all over in his happiness. She turned to him on her back, her eyelids fluttering.

"Fitzwilliam?" she murmured.

He licked her hand, and nudged her with his head.

"No," she frowned, pushing from him, "You are all wet and dirty," she sat up, "Where have you been running all night long?"

He started licking her grumpy face and barked out joyfully. "Do not." she kept pushing him away, "Go wash that mud from you and first of all change into a human, please." she dropped back on the pillows.

When he returned a quarter hour later, his hair still damp, she was curled in the same position as before, her eyes closed.

Naked, he slipped under the covers.

"What are you doing here?" he asked, snuggling to her, inhaling her own, sweet scent, that he was already addicted to.

She pressed to his chest. "You are leaving tomorrow." she murmured with a sigh, her eyes closed.

He cupped her face. "And?"

Dark, expressive eyes opened and she bit on her lower lip. "I am afraid that I will miss you when you are away." she wrapped her arms tightly around him, and hid her face in his neck.

"You are clingy tonight, are you not?" he asked, shifting on his back, and pulling her with him, "Lizzy, I will be back in a few days. We have been separated for longer before our marriage."

She sighed and held onto him.

He stroked her hair. "You know, you can go with me, you have never seen Lord McGrath's castle before."

"No!" she cried out, sitting up abruptly, "I do not want to go there." she said, emphasizing each word.

"Lizzy, you do not have to." he nuzzled the side of her neck, "I am not asking you to go there now, perhaps some time later when you will feel ready." He manoeuvred her to lie beside him in the crook of his arm, then touched her delicate, puckered lips with his finger and kissed her.

"Does this mean that you are not angry with me any more?" he asked cautiously against her lips, when the kiss ended.

Her hands dipped into his hair, and she kissed him back, pushing her small tongue into his mouth.

"Mhmm." he murmured, surprised with the ferocity of her embrace. He allowed her hands to glide over his body, and obediently rolled on her when her arms attempted to pull him over.

Her mouth got attached to his neck, nibbling and licking, while her hand ran down, resting on his backside. Her soft, warm thighs wrapped around his hips and she drew him in.

Darcy squeezed his eyes tight and a low growl rumbled in his chest as he prayed for self discipline. He did not want to frighten her like the last time when they had loved during the full moon, but she was driving him insane, especially when she rubbed herself against him like that.

"Oh God." he breathed, and lifted above her on his outstretched arms. "Lizzy, we must talk about this."

In response, she grasped the end of her nightgown, which was already hiked around her waist, removed it completely and tossed it aside.

Her soft palms began stroking his stomach and chest. "You do not want to?"

"Of course, I want to." he laughed in strain, glancing down at his engorged manhood dangling between them.

"Then come." She lifted up, hooked her arms around his neck and pulled him down on her pliant, curvy body.

"Ahhh," his eyes rolled to the back of his head, and he cupped her face, "Love, I want to try something different."

She stilled and narrowed her eyes. "Different?"

"Yes." he swallowed, searching her eyes, "I know you were frightened the last time when I ..."

Her frown grew more severe, "Oh, no." She pushed from him and turned on her side. "I do not want the wolf way."

"Lizzy..." He tried to turn her to him, but she resisted, "I did not hurt you back then, did I?"

"No, you did not, but it is not the point,. She glared at him over her shoulder. "I do not think that people do it in this way."

"They do." he said, but seeing her sceptical look, added more firmly, "It is absolutely certain."

"How can you know?" Her expression tightened and she looked at him with accusation. "You said to me that I was the first."

"You were." He took her hand and kissed it. "But I heard stories from other men in London, and during my university years; and I have read some... educational books on the subject... Trust me that people make love in many ways, including what we did that night."

Elizabeth moved back on her back, and snuggled to him, "I like when you are on me. I can touch you and see your face, kiss and embrace you, feel your weight."

"Just from time to time then?" He kissed her temple. "Please."

She inhaled deeply and let the air out slowly. "Oh, very well." She rolled on her tummy and raised her round bottom up.

An ear to ear grin stretched his face as he stroked the smooth, pale globes of his wife's backside.

"Do not worry, my mate," he spoke into her ear, hovering over her back. "I will make you feel good." he murmured against her shoulder blade, his hand moving under her, down her body. He could already feel the differences in her body; her breasts were fuller, and though her stomach was still flat, it was more firm to the touch, and her midsection had thickened visibly when he put his hands on both sides.

As his fingers reached the delicate, slick flesh between her legs, and began to caress it, she strained against him; muffled sounds came from her face buried in the pillow.

When he felt that she was ready, he positioned her bottom just at the right height, and with a grunt of pleasure, pushed inside, her warm body taking him in a tight grip. As he moved against her, minding her earlier words, he remembered to touch and kiss her, caressing her swaying breasts, stroking her back and sides.

"You have not answered my question yet," he reminded her, as they lay entwined together a long moment later, spent and tired with their loving.

Her eyelids lifted shortly and dropped again. "A question?" she yawned.

"Yes, I had asked whether you are still angry with me for not telling you the truth."

She was silent for a minute or two before she answered. "Of course I am angry with you." She sat up, wrapping her hands around her legs, her chin supported on her bent knees, "I should be angry, I have every right to be angry, but…" she sighed, "I like you, and yearn for you, despite everything you did. You make me dizzy with your touch and your presence. I miss you when you are gone. It is so difficult for me to keep my distance from you when I want to be close."

He pulled at the end of her braid. "I wanted to be close. It was you who avoided me for the last weeks, not talking to me, not even looking at me."

"You deserved it." She snuggled back to him, but did not speak more.

Darcy did not try to start conversation anew; whatever reason brought her into his arms tonight, he intended to enjoy, and not ruin it.

"Fitzwilliam?" she whispered a long time later, when he was sure that she was deep in sleep.

"Yes, dear."

"Who is Lord McGrath?"

"You know who he is, Lizzy. You met him, talked to him."

She lifted on her elbow, and tilted her head to the side. "Why are you obliged to listen to him?"

He reached over to comb away the hair falling on her face. "You can say that he is the king of the werewolves, and I am one of his... well... barons or better knights."

"Georgiana mentioned other packs to me, living in Scotland and Ireland."

"Yes, there are several."

"Are there werewolves in other parts of the world?"

He nodded. "In North, Central and Eastern Europe, in the areas where the human population is low."

She laid down on her back, her wide eyes unfocused and staring at the canopy."I understand that your family needed to leave France because you were hunted down there."

"Yes, people started to know about us. You read Bisclavret, am I right?"

She turned to him, so they lay sideways, facing each other. "Just the beginning. I stopped when the baron reveals the truth to his wife. I was not in a state to read more then, but I am curious now what happens next."

Darcy shifted down, and lay against her, nestling his head onto her middle. "The wife knows Bisclavret's secret, and she convinces the knight that loved her for a long time to steal her husband's clothes so he cannot change back into a human. Bisclavret must stay in his wolf form for years, while his wife marries the knight who took his clothes."

Elizabeth frowned. "Could he not find some other clothes? It does not make sense."

"I do not know, Elizabeth. I did not write this story." he pointed out rationally.

"I am sorry." her hand dipped into his thick, slightly too long hair, and she combed her fingers through it, "What happens next?"

"Bisclavret goes into the king's service as a wolf. The king is very much impressed with his gentleness, cleverness, politeness and nobility."

She glanced down at his dark head, resting on her chest, her eyebrow raised. "He is?"

"Yes, indeed, he is. One day the wife comes to the court with her new husband. Biscravlet attacks the husband, then later attacks the wife and tears her nose off."

"Her nose? Truly?"

Darcy smiled, "Yes, truly. In the end, she confesses everything that she did, Biscravlet is given back his stolen clothes. They led him into the King' chamber, where he has the privacy to change into a human. The King is happy to see his old friend, welcomes him warmly and gives all his lost lands back to him."

"What happens with the wife?"

"She is expelled together with her husband, and their many daughters are born without noses."

"That could not be a pretty sight."

"No, indeed."

Elizabeth moved her hand down across his hairy chest. "The moral is that the wife is the true monster here."

Darcy yawned, and shifted from his back to the side, his cheek pressed against her stomach, one hand resting on her breast, his thumb stroking the soft nipple. "It is just a story, Lizzy."

"Is it not a true story?" she asked. "Does the author, Marie de France, describe her own experience? Was she from your family?"

He sighed tiredly, not opening his eyes, "The family legend says that she indeed was a human married to a werewolf, just like you are. Although there is no written evidence for it, because some two hundred years after the family moved from France to England, there was a great fire here, and all the papers were destroyed."

"Fitzwilliam..." she started, but he interrupted her.

"Let us have some sleep, love." He moved up to lie beside her. "I had a very industrious night, and I need some rest before tomorrow's journey."

"I only want you to know that I love you." she said.

Not opening his eyes, he smiled, kissed her hair, and pulled her against him, "Oh, sweetheart, I love you too, you and the baby."

His hand moved to her stomach and rested there as his breathing evened, and he fell asleep.

"Forgive me then." she whispered a long moment later, as she closed her eyes, a single tear running down her cheek.

***

Elizabeth lay in her large bed, eyes wide open, glancing from time to time at the face of the clock she had purposely put on the bedside before retiring.

If she was to escape, she needed to get up now, or it would be too late. Fitzwilliam would return tomorrow, so it was now or never. Her limbs refused to move though, and she lay still. She was scared of what she was about to do; she loved him, and did not want to leave him. At the same time, she needed to do something; to take the responsibility for her own fate, and for the child she carried under her heart. With a little bit of luck, she would succeed, and return to the normal world. She had to do that; living with werewolves could not be good and natural for people.

"No, doubts, Elizabeth." she commanded herself in a furious whisper. "You must do it, and this is your only chance."

She threw the covers aside and dove under the bed to take out a human sized doll made of sheets and pillows, dressed in one of her nightgowns. She arranged it under the sheets, and drew the coverlet over the doll.

She ran to the dressing room and opened the trunk where for the last weeks, she had stored all the things she would need for her escape. She removed her nightgown, and began to bind her chest, wincing at the pain of flattening her tender, swollen breasts. She put on the warm cotton pantaloons and thick, woollen stockings. Next, she pulled on the plain white shirt, and reached for the breeches. They were a bit too tight, as her tummy was already starting to round from the child within, but as she took a deep breath, and managed to button them up. At last she pulled on the warm, thick sweater she had knitted herself in the last weeks.

The final touches to her outfit were her own ankle high, sturdy boots, a coat, scarf and a cap. She tried to squeeze her long, thick braid inside the hat, but it was too small, designed more for a boy than a grown up person. For a moment, she considered taking a hat from Fitzwilliam, but then discarded the thought. When they discovered the missing hat, they would know she made her escape dressed as a man. In desperation, she reached for the scissors and cut the braid at arms length. Considerably shorter, her hair fit under the hat easily. Still, it was long enough to be able to pin it up later, when she would change back into women's clothing in Manchester.

She crept out of the room and into the corridor. To her relief, Wilfred slept soundly, and did not react when she walked past him. To the last moment, she was afraid the herbs she had added to the servants' meal would not work. Now, most of the house should be fast asleep.

Through the darkened house, she crept into the library, carrying the small carpet bag in her hand. She thought that leaving through the window was safer than using the front door, which was closed, and surely safely guarded.

As her feet touched the damp ground outside, the cold wind blew right through her. She shivered all over, and pulled the leather gloves out of her bag. She did not expect it to be so cold, it was just the beginning of November, it should not be freezing. She well remembered talking to Darcy outside Netherfield almost a year ago. She had worn only a velvet cape then, thrown over a thin ball gown, and her teeth were not clattering like now. She was not in Hertfordshire though; it was almost Scotland, she reminded herself.

She bounced up and down in place for a minute or two, waving her hands, and clasping them together to make herself warmer. Feeling less cold, she sprinted across the lawn in the direction of the lake, dragging her nightgown on the ground behind her.

She prayed only that she would not meet some of her husband's wolf patrols on her way to the village.

Chapter Twenty- One

Elizabeth moved the coarse blanket higher over her head and rubbed her hands up and down her body to create some body heat. She was already in the furniture cart, to which she had thankfully managed to slip unnoticed by anyone. It was so cold that she was tempted to forsake her entire plan of escape and return to her own warm bedroom with a built-up fire and hot water in the bathtub. Through the crack in the cart wall, she could see that the sky was turning grayish, so why were they not going? Heather had clearly told her that her uncle and his brother planned to stay for the night at her parents' house and leave early in the morning continuing their journey to Kendal, a large market town in the south Cumbria.

She was worried about the baby. If she felt so cold, it could not be good for it.

"Hold on, little one." she whispered, placing a hand on her stomach. "It will surely get warmer later. We should be grateful that we have such a comfortable sofa to rest on, and do not need to sit on the cold, hard floor, between the chest of drawers and the table."

At last hearing voices, she sat up and moved closer to the hole in the wall. The Browns were saying goodbye to the carpenter, Mr. Connery, and his younger brother. From what she understood from the conversation, Heather's younger brother, Alistair, was to accompany them on the trip.

She froze when the tarp, t the back of the cart moved up, and the younger Mr. Connery put a large basket on the floor next to the sofa she occupied.

Dropping the tarp, the man walked away, and she started to breathe again; he did not notice her. The last goodbyes were heard, and when the cart started to roll, she allowed herself to relax. Once they reached Kendal, she would find a quiet place, perhaps in some stable, and change into the dress she had in her carpet bag. Then she would rent a room in the inn for the night and the next day, catch the first post to the south. All would be well.

***

Darcy left his horse to the stable hand in front of the main entrance and strode into the house. Those three days in the north had been sheer torture. He had thought about her constantly, and missed her, not being able to focus on the matters they had talked through with Lord McGrath. He had received a good deal of teasing remarks about his distracted behaviour from their overlord.

He noted that the house was strangely quiet as he climbed the stairs to the family wing. The first person he saw was his sister, leaving her apartment.

Her grey eyes lit up when she saw him, "Brother!" She ran to him. "You were supposed to come back tomorrow."

He leaned down and kissed the girl's cheek. "Are you well? Has everything gone smoothly during my absence?"

"Yes, I am well; and nothing unusual happened while you were away."

"How is Elizabeth?"

"Well." Georgiana looked up at him, raised one dark eyebrow, imitating to perfection Elizabeth's expression. His sister was clearly becoming influenced with his wife's mannerisms. "Elizabeth was very quiet for the last few days. I think it was because she missed you." She grinned.

Darcy shook his head and pulled her to him, tugging gently at her black, glossy locks.

"No!" the girl screeched, pushing from him. "You will ruin my hair!" She lifted her hands, with careful fingers checking the damage to her coiffure.

"Elizabeth is still in her rooms?" he asked.

"Yes, I think that she is still sleeping. She had a headache yesterday, and she went to bed early."

Darcy observed her with a proud smile as she walked past him to the staircase. She was becoming a strikingly beautiful woman and the company of Elizabeth was certainly helping to overcome her inborn shyness. Lord McGrath had asked many times about Georgiana during his stay, and Darcy was afraid that he would insist on marrying the girl earlier than was initially planned, in a year or two. Darcy understood McGrath very well; the overlord was a few years older than himself, and had not children from the marriage to his first wife, who had died in childbirth many years ago. He needed the heir, and soon, otherwise his now strong position among the packs would become endangered.

Darcy did not want to push his little sister into marriage and motherhood too soon. He knew that she would be well cared for and lack nothing as Lady McGrath, but she was not ready for that yet. Georgiana was very childish still, despite her mature, womanly looks, she thought about nothing more than her piano, drawings, and fashion. He had promised to her that he would not marry her before her twenty-first birthday. On the other hand, he doubted whether Lord McGrath would be willing to wait five long years.

Darcy pushed open the door to his wife's sitting room to find a blushing Heather, industriously stitching something, with Wilfred sitting opposite her and staring. Darcy rolled his eyes at the dreamy expression written all over the youth's face. He should consider moving the lad to some other position. There was no doubt that he was doing a good job accompanying his wife, and Elizabeth liked and accepted him, but his attitude toward Heather was not what it was supposed to be. These two were too young for such looks, and spent too much time together; nothing good could come out of it. Heather would be ready for marriage in a year or two, and her father would surely want some reliable farmer, or a merchant, for her; someone older and financially secure, not a boy her age without position or a penny to his name.

Heather saw him first and jumped to her feet. "Master," she bowed deeply.

"Is my wife still in her bedroom?" he asked without preamble.

"She did not feel well yesterday, and asked me not to wake her up in the morning."

Darcy frowned and glanced at his pocket watch. "It is after ten. She never sleeps this late unless she is sick."

He knocked at the bedroom door, but there was no response. He turned the doorknob and walked in, his eyes resting on the bed. Something was wrong, he could sense it. The shape on the bed looked unfamiliar, and he could not feel her presence. He stepped to the bed and threw the covers aside. Instead of the comely form of his wife, there was a makeshift rag doll.

He turned back to the sitting room. "Where is she?"

Heather and Wilfred stood in the doorway, staring at him with round eyes.

"She is not there?" Heather mumbled, running past him into the bedroom, checking the bed and under it.

Darcy's hand curled into a fist, and in a matter of a second he had Wilfred, pushed up high against the wall. "Where have you been?" he barked.

"By her door in the corridor, Master, as you ordered," the lad answered, trembling as a child.

"Then where is she?" Darcy shook the boy, pinning him to the wall, "How did she get out? You were supposed to be her shadow." he hissed through clenched teeth.

Wilfred stared down at him, his face white and terrified. "I was by the door all night long. I do not know what happened," he cracked.

Very slowly, Darcy took his hands off and the boy slumped onto the floor. "Go to Mrs. Reynolds," he ordered, "Tell her to search the house, everywhere, cellars, attics and the old castle. Then go to the chief footman so he can start searching the gardens and the park."

Wilfred dashed out of the room.

"Heather!" he barked.

The girl stepped to him, eyes wide, hands trembling. "Yes, Master."

"What time was it yesterday that you saw Mistress the last time?"

"Ahhh…" Heather bit on her lower lip, her eyelids fluttering.

Darcy put his hands on her shoulders, "Heather, when did you last see my wife?"

The girl took a deep breath. "About ten o'clock yesterday evening, I brought her hot milk she asked for."

"You will check now what clothes are missing from her wardrobe, and tell me immediately when you find out."

The girl ran to the dressing room, and he could hear the clatter of the opening closets. He stepped back into his bedroom, hoping to find a farewell letter.

He looked through every surface in his bedroom, and on the floor in case it fell down, but there was no note.

"The study," he whispered.

As he walked through the house, he registered the shouts and the alarmed servants running in all directions.

"Brother!" Georgiana approached him near the library, "Has Elizabeth escaped?"

He gave her a heavy look. "It seems so."

She looked up at him, shaking her head, "But why?"

He took her arm, "I need you to go upstairs and help Heather look through Elizabeth's personal things, perhaps you will find something that can help us."

Georgiana ran upstairs, and Darcy stormed into his study. As he expected, there was an elegant note placed on his desk, with his name written on it in Elizabeth's hand.

Fitzwilliam,

I do not know what to say to you, whether I should apologize or try to make you understand. I decided to leave. You may not believe me, but it was a very difficult decision for me; I have my doubts, even now, when I am writing this note, but I feel that I must do it.
Do not try to look for me at Jane's, I am not going there. Do not blame your people. No one helped me. I put the herbs into Wilfred's meal so he would sleep undisturbed through the night.
I have taken fifty pounds from the case in your desk. Together with the pin money from you, it should be enough to rent some place where I could stay till the child is born.

I hope, you will forgive me one day.

Elizabeth

He crumpled the letter in his hand. What was she thinking? Did she really believe he would ever let her go, and did not look for her till he found her, brought her back?

"Brother! We looked through Elizabeth's things." Georgiana ran into the room, with Heather following her closely.

He looked up. "And?"

The maid stepped forward. "She took the woollen dress my mum made for her, boots, stockings, bonnet, gloves, a nightgown, and the small carpet bag." Heather enumerated on her fingers.

"We found this in the trunk." Georgiana pulled out the thick, blond braid.

Darcy took it in his hand, and stared at it. "She cut her hair? Why?"

Georgiana gasped, her eyes widening, "She dressed herself for a boy." she whispered.

He looked at her sharply. "How can you know?"

"I was with her in the store in the village when she bought many things, including a coat, hat and shirt well suited for a young lad. She said she wanted to send those things to some poor tenant family at her father's estate."

Darcy smashed his fist on the desk. "She could not go far."

There were heavy footsteps in the hall, and the chief footman entered.

"Master." He bowed.

"Have you found her?"

"No, but…" The man's expression tightened. "Master, the boat is floating, empty, in the middle of the lake, without paddles attached."

Darcy sat down heavily, the horrifying image of his beloved lying drowned on the bottom of the cold lake in front of his eyes.

"Send people to search the lake." Darcy said weakly.

"I already have."

Darcy stood up slowly. "Then let us go there."

When they reached the lake, and Darcy saw the small boat in the middle, the fear that she might be somewhere in the water overpowered him anew, a crushing pain shooting through his chest. He forced himself to kneel on the ground, and began to sniff, terrified to detect the trail of her scent.

He looked up at the footman, "She was here just a few hours ago."

The man nodded. "We thought the same."

One of the wolves emerged from the water, dragging a white cloth with him.

Darcy ran to him and snatched his wife's nightgown.

"Oh, God." he dropped to his knees in the shallow water close to the lake's edge, clenching the dripping nightgown to his chest.

The footman bent down over him. "I do not think that she has drowned herself in this lake, Master." he said in calm quiet voice. "We searched around the lake earlier, and I think that we found her track on the other side."

Like a madman, Darcy ran on the other side of the lake and dropped to the ground. To his relief, her scent was still strong there, and it could be traced along the path leading in the direction of the park.

He stood to his feet, his eyes on the lake. "Why did she do that?" he asked the footman.

The man gave a thoughtful look. "You were supposed to come home tomorrow, Master. My thought is that she wanted us to think that she had drowned herself, or at least make us lose her track. She got into a boat, rowed across the lake, dropped her nightgown and the paddles into the water, then pushed the boat from the edge to let if drift. She knew we would follow her trail to the lake, and start to search it, seeing the boat in the middle. Clever."

"Clever!" Darcy cried indignantly. "I nearly died of a heart attack when they fished that nightgown out."

"I will order the people to look in the village." The footman proposed. "At least we know in what direction she went. She could not go far."

The footman barked orders to the men standing nearby to move the search to the village, and then turned to Darcy again. "She did not take a horse; all the animals are still in the stables."

Darcy raked the hand through his hair. "She rides poorly. She could not go on foot though."

The other man frowned, thinking for a moment. "It was a market day yesterday."

Darcy looked at him through narrowed eyes. "Yes, do you suggest…"

The footman nodded. "My guess is that she could hide in with a merchant driving to sell his goods outside our territory."

Darcy nodded slowly, "That is possible…"

"Master." A white faced Heather, who so far had stood a few steps behind them, walked closer. Her chin started to tremble, as she spoke, her voice high and cracking, "It is all my fault, but I did not mean for this to happen. Lady asked many questions about my uncle's furniture cart, but I did not think that she could…" She burst into tears, and hid her face in her apron, "Oh, what have I done?"

***

Elizabeth looked through the crack in the cart's door. It was late in the afternoon, and they were on the outskirts of Kendal, the town she remembered well from their trip from the south. She felt stiff all over, the result of lying in the same position for so many hours. She was still cold, but somehow less than in the morning.

She urgently needed to relieve herself as well. She had been careful not to drink much the day before, but even so, her bladder was bursting. Soon the cart would stop, she would wait for the right moment, and get away unnoticed.

A man's shouts were heard mixed with the sounds of galloping horse hooves. She lifted herself up from the sofa to see better what was happening, but the cart came to stop so abruptly that she rolled to the floor, landing right on her arm.

"Ouch," she hissed at the pain in her wrist.

The tarp lifted up, and her eyes squinted at the bright sunlight.

A man jumped inside the cart, causing the vehicle to shake and the furniture to rattle, and cried out, "Elizabeth!"

She closed her eyes, and laughed silently; that was a voice she could not mistake for any other.

"That was some escape," she murmured to herself, raising slowly to her knees.

"Sweetheart," he was beside her, pushing the cap off her head, "Are you all right?"

She looked up at his concerned face. "I am well." she said in a defeated voice.

His hand moved from her face down her body.

"Ouch!" she cried softly when he touched her hand.

"Your hand!" he exclaimed. "Have you hurt yourself?"

She snatched her hand away, and murmured. "I am fine. I just fell on the hand when the cart stopped so suddenly."

His arms wrapped around her and he lifted her up. "Let us get out of here."

She sighed, "You will not let me escape, will you?"

He leaned and kissed her cheek. "No."

"I knew that." she mumbled, and allowed him to help her move to the front of the cart.

Darcy jumped down on the ground, and before she could do the same, he scooped her into his arms, holding her tight.

Elizabeth glanced around at the five men and a boy, all staring at her. Three of them were from the pack.

"She was in our home!" The Browns' boy exclaimed, pointing at her, "She is our Alpha Female!" he proudly informed his uncle and his brother.

Elizabeth rolled her eyes and hid her face into her husband's chest, away from curious eyes.

Mr. Connery, the older, bowed in half in front of Darcy. "We knew nothing of that." he said. "We would never have even considered helping your mate to…"

"I believe you." Darcy interrupted, "We will not postpone your journey any longer."

The Connery brothers moved aside, as Darcy walked past them with Elizabeth cuddled in his arms.

They were close to the horses when she gasped and looked back, "My bag, I left it in the cart."

Without a word from Darcy, one of his men turned and walked back to the vehicle.

Darcy lifted her up on his big, black horse, and before she could became frightened of sitting so high, and on such an intimidating animal, he was in the saddle behind her.

"All is well?" he whispered into her ear.

She leaned against his chest, "Are we going back to Pemberley?"

He kicked his horse into a trot, and brought her closer to him, his arm wrapped securely around her middle, "No, it is too late today, and you are in no state to travel horseback for many hours. We spend the night in the inn in Kendal."

"The one we slept at before?"

He nodded, "The same one."

She winced, "I need to use a private place. "

"Now?"

She moved in her seat, "Yes."

"There are some bushes over there, will they suit?"

"Yes."

He reined the horse to a halt, jumped to the ground and reached for her, "You must promise you will not try to escape."

She shrugged, "I have no chance anyway."

He put her down and kissed her temple. "We will talk about it later."

Chapter Twenty-Two

"I want the best room you have," Darcy barked as he strode into the inn with Elizabeth in his arms.

The young girl, enveloped in a large apron, holding a heavy looking tray with dirty dishes, walked to them. She gaped at Darcy, accompanied by three giant footmen for a moment, till her attention was drawn to Elizabeth, still dressed as a boy.

"I will call my father, sir." the girl stammered, bowed, put the tray on a side table and hurried to the back of the large eating area.

Elizabeth glanced around the crowded place, filled with numerous travellers, both single gentlemen and families with small children. As she realized they had become the centre of attention, collecting curious stares, she hid her face in her husband's chest.

Not a minute had passed when the anxious looking innkeeper rushed to them from the back room.

"Mr. Darcy!" He inclined his head, "We were not expecting you. You always inform us about your visit well in advance."

"It is an emergency, I am afraid." Darcy explained, "My wife had an accident, and we need your best rooms and privacy."

Without waiting for an answer, he started walking towards the staircase.

"We have so many guests now, sir. We are full this week, and I am afraid that your usual rooms are taken at the moment." The man stuttered as he followed Darcy, trying to cross his path.

Darcy stopped and looked down, his black eyes not leaving the man's face.

"But I am sure that we will find something appropriate for you and Mrs. Darcy." he conceded promptly.

"Good," Darcy began to climb the stairs. He adjusted Elizabeth in his arms, bringing her closer to him. "Now, show us to the room; my wife is tired. She needs a warm dinner and a hot bath."

***

Fitzwilliam put her on a single bed, kissed her on the cheek, assured he would be back soon and left. The room was much smaller, not even half of the size the one they had occupied before; but it was very clean, and had a large window pointing to the main street of Kendal.

Even though she was left alone, she had no intention of trying another escape. She was not so naïve as to doubt that Darcy put a guard outside the door.

She shivered uncontrollably and rubbed her arms. She still felt cold, very hungry and tired. She hoped that the servant would come soon to build up the fire. What had she been thinking when she had planned her escape, believing it possible? It had not been one full day, and she had little energy left to continue.

"God, I am exhausted." she whispered, adding silently in her thoughts, *It is because of the baby, I am not usually such a weakling.*

She reached to the waist band of her too tight breeches and unbuttoned them, sighing in relief. Then she kicked off her shoes, stockings and removed the jacket. She lay down, but was still uncomfortable – the pain caused by the cloth binding her bosom was too acute and becoming unbearable. She sat up, lifted her shirt and sweater and began to untangle herself.

Freed from the bandages, which followed the rest of her clothes in a heap on the floor, she curled on the bed, drew the coverlet over herself, and closed her eyes.

"Lizzy," she heard some time later, a warm hand stroking her cheek. "Wake up."

Her eyelids fluttered, and her gaze focused on Darcy.

"Have I slept long?" She sat up.

"For over an hour," he answered.

"That long?" she looked around the room, blinking. There was a bathtub filled with steamy water, and a meal on the small table. She had not even heard the servants bringing all that inside. She must have slept quite soundly.

"Do you prefer to eat something first or take a bath?" he asked.

"A bath." She shivered. "I am still cold."

If she had lifted her eyes to him, she would have seen his lips pressed tightly together, his eyes narrowed, his fist clenched as he looked down at her.

"What were you thinking, Elizabeth?" he snapped. "How did you image this?" He raised her hands not so gently and pulled on the sweater she still had on herself, "You can barely stand. How would you survive this night, had I not found you in time?"

She helped him to remove her breeches completely, "I thought I could rent a place in some inn, not here of course, some smaller place. I have money."

He took her arm and walked her to the tub. "Rent a room?" He took off her shirt, so she stood in front of him naked.

She gave him a weary look. "Yes."

He scooped her into his arms and lowered her into the water. "You think that any inn owner would rent a room to a young woman dressed like a boy?" he asked sharply.

She brought her legs to her chest, "I planned to change into my own clothes before going to the inn," she murmured defensively.

"Oh, you did."

"Yes, I have a dress and bonnet in my bag."

"Yes, I saw the clothes you took." He pulled a chair over next to the tub and sat on it , "They speak money, Elizabeth. Do you think that no one would find it suspicious that a young woman, dressed like a respectable wife, sister or a daughter of a wealthy man travels all alone, with one small bag and an enormous sum of money in notes?"

Elizabeth stared at the water and said nothing.

"What did you intend to do later?" he asked after a moment of tense silence.

"Rent some cottage in the south under the assumed name till the baby is born." she whispered.

"How would you accomplish that? You have no experience in procuring a lease of a house. You have never managed such matters.

"I am not stupid!" she bit out. "I accompanied my father and uncle a couple times in London when they worked on their business deals. I know how it is done."

"So you must know as well that as a woman you have no power to sign any kind of legal documents, such as a lease for a home." He spoke matter of factly. "You would have to pretend to be widow to make any deals, and have papers stating that you can manage your deceased husband's fortune and bank resources. It is hardly believable that such authority would be given to a young woman, looking not more than twenty years old. Widowed, you would go back to the authority of your father, uncle or a brother if you had one."

Elizabeth pressed her lips in a tight line, and looked to the side.

Darcy stared down at her for a moment, before kneeling next to the tub. "What if you were robbed?" he asked more gently, "What if someone discovered you had nearly one hundred pounds, and attacked you to take the money from you?"

She shrugged, "I had not thought of that. I would be very careful."

"Careful." He ran his hands over his face "Good God, Elizabeth!" he exclaimed. "You are too pretty and gentle looking to go unnoticed. What if you encountered Wickham?"

Her pupils dilated, and her soft mouth fell open. "Wickham?" she swallowed, "Why Wickham?"

"And why not?" he asked, his voice sharp. "He is still free, living somewhere, and for sure he is not finished with you or I."

"England is a big country." She lifted her chin, trying to control her cracking voice

"It is not very probable that I would meet Wickham, of all people."

"What about others?"

She blinked repeatedly. "Others?"

"Yes, others. The werewolves who were expelled from their packs and now are forced to live among people. Do you think that they became outcasts without a very good reason? Do you know what they would do if they smelled a werewolf baby inside you, or worse, learned who the father is?"

She shook her head.

He leaned into her, his face inches from hers, "They would take the baby from you to blackmail me. They would not even wait till you gave birth to our child, they would rip it out from your body, cut you in half and leave you to die somewhere in the back corner of the street or by a country road."

Elizabeth stared at him for a moment, eyes wide open and horrified, before two single tears rolled down her cheeks.

"I did not know..." she whispered, her lips trembling, "I did not..." she choked up.

Darcy stood up, raked his hand through his hair, and looked down at her form shaking with sobs with concern written all over his face.

"Do not cry," he cracked, kneeling back beside the tub, "You are safe."

"It is so horrible what you said…" she sniffed.

He sighed deep from inside, "I would never allow someone to harm you. Do you believe me?" he said evenly. "Elizabeth?" He touched her wet, bare shoulder, "Do you believe me?"

She nodded and burst into even more tears.

Darcy sighed again, took the washcloth from her, lathered it and began to clean her

She kept weeping quietly when he washed her back, arms, legs, breasts, sides and belly. At last, he dried the tears from her cheeks with the back of his hand.

"Are you angry with me?" she asked as he helped out of the water.

"For what?" he wrapped her in a large sheet. "Should I be angry because you ran away from me in the middle of the night?" he asked calmly, drying her, "Even though I never purposely did anything to hurt you; I never mistreated you. Should I be angry because you lulled me into a sense of security, coming to my bed and telling me you loved me? Should I be angry because you made me believe you drowned yourself in the lake?"

She lifted her eyes to him. "I am sorry. I did not lie when I said that I loved you."

He met her eyes with accusation, "You said that, and still left."

She nodded, "Yes. I needed to try to escape. I hated to think that I had no other choice but to stay with you."

"Elizabeth," He looked directly into her eyes, "You have no choice but to stay with me if you want to live, both you and the baby," He cupped her face in both hands. "You must promise me that you will never again do something like this. I would not survive if anything happened to you or the baby. That would be the end for me, Elizabeth. Do you understand?" He squeezed her arms.

She searched his eyes for a moment before she stepped to him, throwing her arms around him "I promise not to run away again. I do not want to be away from you either."

He closed his eyes as he kept her close. "It is behind us." He whispered into her ear and rocked her in place, "We will return home, and all will be well."

***

When Elizabeth woke up the next day, it must have been late in the morning, because bright sunlight shone through the curtains onto her bed. The room was empty, but there was a note on the small table beside her bed.

Dearest,
I need to manage some matters for our return to Pemberley, but I will be back with you shortly. Ring for breakfast, and do not rush with getting up from bed.
F.

She yawned, stretched out, and climbed out of the bed, wondering where Fitzwilliam had slept. This narrow bed was too small for both of them, certainly too narrow to accommodate him alone. She did not remember exactly the moment when she had fallen asleep, she had been so exhausted. She only hoped he had not slept on the bare floor.

Still groggy from sleep she stumbled to the window, wearing a simple shift that Fitzwilliam had borrowed from the owner's daughter.

She pushed the curtain to the side and looked down on the busy street. People were working in front of their shops, horsemen passing by, carts rolling slowly down the street, children running around. She smiled at the boys doing handstands on the green near the blacksmith, opposite her window.

Her eyes enjoyed the view of the playing children before her gaze moved to the tall man standing by the tree a few yards from them. Her fingers gripped the curtain as her eyes fixed on the man, and her heart began to pound. His blond hair looked untidy, and was much too long; he was unshaven, and his clothes gave the impression of not being washed for several weeks.

The cold feeling enveloped her when the man looked directly at her, lifted his hand in a gesture of greeting and smiled.

She shoved the curtain closed, and stumbled from the window. She wanted to go back and check whether he was still there, but could not make her feet move.

The door opened quietly and Fitzwilliam peeked inside.

His face broke into a smile. "You are awake."

Elizabeth ran to him and pulled him inside. "He is here!" she whispered, her face washed of any colour.

Darcy frowned, putting a calming hand on her, "Who?"

"Wickham." It came from her tight throat. "He is standing there," she pointed to the window, "On the green by the tree."

Darcy strode to the window and tore the curtain away. Elizabeth hid behind his back.

They observed Wickham together for a minute or so, though he did not look in the direction of the window. When he raised his eyes again, but saw Darcy instead of Elizabeth, he lowered his head, pulled on a deformed hat, and walked away quickly, hands in pockets.

"What is he doing here?" she asked. "How can he know that we are here?"

"I am not surprised that he dwells somewhere near Pemberley." Darcy stepped from the window, his expression tense, "A werewolf always returns to his territory. Kendal is a small town, and they know me here, as I always stop here on my way to or from Pemberley. News travels fast, and I am sure everyone here talked about us arriving in town on horseback, with you in man's attire. He could even have seen us yesterday when we rode through town." He explained in a sure voice before turning towards the door, "You will stay here and wait for me. It will not take long."

"No!" Elizabeth grabbed at his hand, "You cannot go there to see him!"

"Elizabeth, I must. We can finally get him." He tried to push her away, but she only clung to him more furiously.

"No, he will kill you!"

"Elizabeth." He pushed her at arms' length, "Wickham is a low creature, a coward, and I am twice as strong as he. You will stay here, have something to eat, and wait for me. One of my men will guard the door."

She was still shaking her head, and mouthing no, when he excited the room.

She tried to run after him, but her attempt proved impossible as the huge footman crossed her way in the door's opening.

The man bowed deeply. "Should I tell them to bring your food, Mistress?" he asked politely.

Elizabeth sighed in resignation. She knew that the big man in front of her would never allow her to go past him. She looked down at her body, clad only in a thin nightshift. Her face flushed bright red, and she wrapped her arms in front of herself protectively. She glanced at the man, but his eyes were focused tactfully above her face.

"I would like breakfast, and the bag with my clothes." she said with as much dignity as she could manage.

"This minute." The footman bowed again and closed the door.

Elizabeth hurried to the window and opened it, so she could lean out of it and see better to the sides. But she could see neither her husband with his men, nor Wickham.

"Fitzwilliam is right, he is surely faster and stronger than Wickham." She said the words out loud to calm herself, "And he has two people with him, while Wickham is all alone."

She stepped to the water basin in the corner to clean her face, teeth and brush her hair. She cringed at her own reflection in the looking glass. Her hair was uneven, and as it was straight now, she could easily see that it was a good three inches shorter on one side of her face.

She turned from the mirror and again walked to the window. The breakfast was brought soon, together with her own freshly ironed dress and bonnet. There were other articles as well, which she assumed, Fitzwilliam had bought earlier in the morning; new, elegant shoes, a warm velvet cap, a woollen shawl, and some undergarments.

She dressed herself, pinned her hair up in a simple, smooth style, and ate her meal with appetite. She was pleased to notice that she did not feel as though she wanted to vomit; hopefully the morning nausea had passed. Then she sat on the chair next to the window and observed the street. At last, some two hours later, she saw her husband and his people walking towards the inn. The heavy weight left her heart; he was unharmed.

He entered the room minutes later and she leapt into his arms.

"We have not found him." He answered the question before she asked it. "Perhaps if we changed into wolves, it would be easier to get him, but it is impossible here, too many people around, too risky."

"I am afraid" She looked up at him. "When he stood down there, he looked as if he had nothing to lose."

Darcy cupped her face. "He will never hurt you again." His black eyes bore into her blue ones. "Do you not believe me?"

"Yes, but…"

"You doubt my ability to protect you?" he interrupted her angrily, and there was genuine hurt in his voice.

"No, of course, not!" she assured him, "I do believe in you, and I know that you can protect me." She touched his cheek, "But I also know that he will come after us at Pemberley; I fear that he will."

He took her hand from his face, and turned it to kiss the inside of her palm. "I agree, my mate. And when he does, that will be his end."

Chapter Twenty-Three

Elizabeth shifted on the sofa and adjusted the pillow behind her back to find a more comfortable position. She put her hands on both sides of her well rounded stomach. Nearly three months had passed since her escape. She remembered how stressed she had been on her return from Kendal. She had not been sure what the pack's attitude would be toward her now after she had attempted to abandon their Master. To her astonishment nobody had said anything about her escape. They had welcomed her warmly as if she had returned home from a short visit to friends or family members. Initially she had thought that her husband ordered them not to speak to her about it, not to upset her. However within a few weeks, she noticed that everyone, not only the servants in the manor but the people in the village, treated her now with even more respect and courtesy than before. She even dared to believe that they looked at her with some new found admiration. She had asked Fitzwilliam why nobody seemed to be disappointed with her after what she had done. He had explained to her then that with her clever plan of escape she had impressed everyone, and assured them that their future leader that she was carrying would be strong, courageous and of quick mind.

According to both hers and the doctor's calculations she was now well into her sixth month, but as she was told the size of her tummy suggested her being at least one month farther along.

Fitzwilliam had been at first understandably very much excited when the small bump had become visible shortly after their return to Pemberley from Kendal. He had never missed the opportunity to touch and talk to their child whenever they had been alone. He swore that the baby made them a surprise and appeared one morning after they had woken up. He seemingly thought that the baby had grown over night and caused the swelling. She had rolled her eyes at his reasoning but said nothing, not wanting to diminish his joy and enthusiasm.

However, when with each day she grew bigger and bigger, and hearing that she looked too advanced in her pregnancy than most women at this stage, he had quickly become alarmed that the baby she carried was too large. Doctor Craw reminded them again that there was a strong probability that there were two babies instead of just one, especially taking into consideration the history of twins in Elizabeth's family. Moreover, now when she could feel the child's movements, she thought it too active for one baby, stirring and pushing in too many directions at once.

Understandably Darcy wanted to know how much more dangerous was it to carry and give birth to two babies in comparison with one. Doctor Craw assured him that bearing two smaller children one by one should be less strenuous and life threatening for the mother than giving birth to one very big child.

Elizabeth was not sure whether Darcy was calmed with Doctor Craw's explanations, but he tried to hide his anxiety. She knew that he feared the time of the delivery, because every time she tried to initiate the conversation about it, or discuss names for the babies, he changed the subject. She tried to understand how he must feel about her condition. All his life he had been used to being able to control his environment, help his loved ones when they needed him and protect them, even fight for them when necessary. Now he found himself in a new position where he could do nothing at all but pray and hope for the best while waiting for the outcome.

She glanced from her protruding tummy to her husband, sitting by his enormous dark desk, who for the last hour had been answering the correspondence with determined diligence.

"Fitzwilliam?"

"Yes, dear." he said, not raising his eyes from the letter he was writing.

She let out a puff of air. "I am bored."

He smiled, but still did not look at her.

"You can read a novel."

She frowned and wrinkled her small upturned nose. "I do not want to read a novel."

"Then you can read some poems."

She rolled her eyes, "I do not want to read poems either."

"You can ask Georgiana to play for you."

"The baby starts to kick my back every time music is played near me," she complained.

"I see." he said, and dipped his pen into the ink.

Elizabeth narrowed her eyes at him and slowly lifted herself to her feet. She waddled to him and stood by his desk.

"I am bored." she repeated, this time with steel in her voice.

His dark eyes at last met hers.

"You are spoilt." he stated putting the finished letter on the side to let it dry.

She shrugged. "And whose fault is that?" she crossed her arms in front of herself. "You spoilt me."

She did not know how he had done it, as his moves were so swift, but in the next second she was safely nestled on his lap.

He sighed dramatically and shifted his legs under her added weight, "You are too heavy for me."

She punched his arm with her small clenched fist, "I am not!" she cried outraged, "Nothing is too heavy for you, and you know it very well."

"I am not sure, perhaps you have grown too heavy to bear even for a werewolf in his prime!" he grinned at her.

"You..." she muttered through clenched teeth, "If I may remind you it is your ba..."

She did not finish her attempted tirade because he began a long and very thorough kiss.

"I want to go for a walk to the beach," she said after a while, nestling her head on his shoulder.

He rubbed her tummy, "It is too cold for that, and it will rain." He pointed with his eyes at the gray heavy clouds outside the window.

"It is not that cold and it will not rain." she contradicted him.

"It is too cold and it will rain." he said calmly.

"It is not and it will not." she argued back.

He took her hand and kissed it. "I promise we will go tomorrow on the condition it gets warmer."

She did not answer to that, but attempted to climb astride on his lap, a feat in which her tummy was a major obstacle.

"What are you doing?" he laughed, straightening his legs farther under the desk so he could support her bottom against them.

It took her some effort till she maneuvered herself as she wanted, facing him, her bent legs resting on both his sides.

He kept her securely to himself, his hands on her bottom, so she would not roll back.

She made a pouting face.

He raised one black bushy eyebrow.

"I still need some exercise."

He laughed out loud, his voice rich and full. "You had your exercise this morning.

He patted her bottom suggestively.

She tugged at his neck cloth, peering at him from behind her eyelashes. "It was many hours ago."

He smiled and leaned forward, his lips tugging gently at hers. "Let us go upstairs then," he kissed the path to her ear.

"Why not stay here?" she purred, "You could return to your correspondence right after."

"Oh, sweetheart, are you not afraid that the desk will collapse under your weight?"

Her fist met his collar bone.

"Ouch!" he cried out laughingly, "That really hurt." he assured her.

Her lips began to quiver, and the big tears gathered in her eyes, "You are making fun of me, you think I am fat," she sniffed, "Your remarks are cruel…"

His face reflected her anguish momentarily, "Oh, Elizabeth, I am so sorry, I should not, I should not," he pulled her tighter to himself, "I am so worried about you that sometimes I do not know what I am saying."

She tilted her head to the side. "Worried?"

"I wish it were already summer , you safe, unharmed and feeling well, and the baby in its crib in the nursery."

She stroked his hair compassionately. "All will be well."

He touched her face, "I feel so helpless, I cannot do anything to aid you in this matter."

"Then let us not worry about it in advance," she reasoned, "We have almost three months before my time comes."

"You are right." He kissed her nose, and ran his hands down her back, "Now Mrs.Darcy, may I have the honour of accompanying you to your rooms?"

***

When she woke up from her slumber over an hour later, Darcy was dressing himself, picking up one by one their scattered clothes on the floor of her bedroom.

Her eyes glued themselves to the wide planes of his chest, then moved to his lean waist, hard, muscled stomach, and powerful thighs in tight breeches. There he stood, looking like the statue of some Greek hero, unusually hairy hero but still beautiful and perfect. Here she was blown up, with swollen breasts, fingers and feet, every day growing larger and rounder all over.

She sighed, "You will not stay longer with me?" she sat up, her back supported against the headboard.

Darcy buttoned his shirt, and sat on the edge of the bed.

"There are still matters I need to attend today." his hand reached to stroke her hair away from her face. "You should stay in bed till dinner time."

She nodded, "I think that I will. I was not aware that being with child can be so exhausting. There are moments when I suddenly feel so tired that I could fall asleep exactly where I stand."

He leaned to kiss her cheek, "We shall see each other at dinner then, just make sure that someone is with you when you descend the stairs."

Elizabeth rolled her eyes, but nodded her agreement. "I will ask Georgiana or Heather."

He kissed her again, "Do."

"Could you please bring me my nightgown before you go, I do not want to get up for it."

He stood up and walked to the dressing room. "Which one?"

"It does not matter." she answered, staring with unseeing eyes at the space in front of herself.

"Fitzwilliam?" she started hesitantly, when he handed her the white simple shift and helped her to put it on.

"Yes." he said, as he moved around the room to pick up the clothes she had previously discarded; the dress, petticoats, chemise, the silk stockings and the ribbon she had in her hair.

She looked up at him and said with a sigh. "I received a letter from Jane yesterday."

Darcy frowned as he hung the collected items over the back of a chair.

"Does she want to come here?"

Elizabeth put one hand on her tummy, and with the other one reached to her husband. “I think that she does. She did not write it directly but she asked when we would see each other again.”

He sat next to her and took her hand. “But you explained to her that you cannot go now because of the baby?”

Elizabeth bit on her lower lip, “She is with child too.”

“She is?” Darcy relaxed, “Bingley did not mention anything in his last letter.”

“I think he did not know then. Jane wrote that she was almost certain and that she could not wait to tell Mr. Bingley. Her baby will be born not earlier than in August though, and I think that she wants to come here to be with me in May.”

“I am not sure, Elizabeth, whether it is a good idea for your sister to come here at that time.” Darcy said, with a heavy frown.

“Fitzwilliam, cannot I simply tell her the truth?” she pleaded. “Mr. Bingley knows already and…”

“Sweetheart you know the rules.” he interrupted her in a gentle voice, “The less humans know about us the better.”

“But she is my sister. I think that she suspects something already.”

His eyes narrowed. “You did not tell her, did you?”

She shook her head, “No, of course not.” Her worried eyes met his, “When I found out about everything, I wanted very much to write to her about it and tell her everything, but I was sure that you would not allow me to send such a letter to her. I ceased writing to her and answering her letters for over a month. I simply did not know what to write to her and I did not want to lie.”

Darcy nodded, “Charles wrote to me asking about you on Jane’s behalf. She was worried that you were not answering her correspondence for such a long time. I wrote to him that you were sick because of the baby and did not feel well enough to write.”

“I am sure that Jane still thinks that something is wrong with me.” Elizabeth continued, “Even though I have assured her many times that I am well now, and apologized to her for my silence in the last letters. I hate lying to her like this, Fitzwilliam, she knows that something was not as it should be and she worries about me. Can we not invite Charles and Jane here and tell her the truth? She will be shocked at first, but then I am sure that she will understand.”

Darcy lowered his head for a long moment, "I must think about it and consider everything," he said at last, "Give me some time to give you my answer."

Her face broke into a smile and she threw her arms around his neck, "Thank you!"

"I want you to be happy, Lizzy." He squeezed her to him, "I hate to think that you are unhappy here with me."

She pulled away from him, "I am happy." She smiled, "You are every woman's dream after all."

He actually blushed and murmured defensively, "You are making fun of me."

"No, I am serious, the only real flaw, and true drawback I can see is that I will never be able to live among people, or be close to them. Our children will always be different and forced to live in secrecy, hiding their real identity. The fact of you being a werewolf does not bother me so much any more. I feel more and more settled with it. These days I am so sleepy and tired that I find very little energy to ponder over the fact that my husband runs in the forest and catches rabbits at night."

***

A week later, Greystone, Derbyshire, Mr. Bingley's estate,

"Charles," Jane Bingley said when her husband entered her bedroom, "We need to talk."

Bingley removed his trousers, threw them into the corner and then clad only in his shirt climbed into the bed next to his wife.

"Yes, Janie." he pulled off the ridiculous wifely cap, similar in fashion to the one his mother-in-law wore, off her head so the fragrant honey locks fell around her shoulders. He kissed her cheek, and neck, "How is the baby?" he pushed his hand under the covers and touched her still flat stomach.

Jane smiled. "Well."

"Do you think it will be a boy?" he asked, the image of himself teaching a young boy horse riding filling his mind.

"I cannot say," she glanced at him, her delicate eyebrows frowned, "Will you be very disappointed if we have a girl?"

"No, not at all." Bingley smiled blissfully at the image of a little copy of his Jane with bouncing curls in a pink dress, "My parents had two girls before I was born. I could buy her a pony."

"A pony?" She frowned. "You will spoil her."

"If she looks like you, I will not be able to refuse her anything." Bingley smiled happily, not at all discouraged with the idea.

"Charles," Jane snuggled to him, "I am worried."

"Worried?" he wrapped her into his arms securely, "What is troubling you?" he crooned.

"Lizzy."

Bingley rolled on his back with a sigh, his eyes fixed on the canopy. "We have talked about this many times already. Your sister is fine."

"I have a feeling that something is not as it should be, there is something very wrong." She lifted up on her elbow, "I have just received another letter from her."

Bingley glanced at her. "Does she complain about anything?"

"No, apart from feeling uncommonly tired but it is expected in this condition, even more that she is over three months farther along than me. Still her letters are different."

"Different how?"

Jane sighed, "She sounds like some other person, not my sister."

"Everyone changes." Bingley noted philosophically.

"She is my most beloved sister, I know her and I can feel when there is something lacking." Jane insisted.

He did not comment on that, considering how long he would be able to keep the Darcys' secret from Jane. He would write to Darcy tomorrow, and try to explain to him that he had no choice but to tell his wife what he knew.

"I am sure it is all your friend's fault!" Jane cried indignantly.

"Nonsense, Darcy loves her. He would give his own life for her without any hesitation."

Jane narrowed her eyes. "He did not allow her to visit us."

"That is not true. He explained in his letter that Elizabeth was very sick in the first months of her pregnancy and could not travel."

"I do not believe it," Jane sat up, and beat the pillows behind her back, "Lizzy has always been very healthy, rarely even had a cold. I think that he forbade her to come here."

"Forbade her, Janie, you cannot seriously consider it." Bingley sat up as well, "Your sister is the last person to be ordered around, it is not so easy to simply forbid her to do something. You remember how she rejected the offer of your cousin, that parson from Kent, despite the fact your mother insisted that she accept him. When she agreed to marry Darcy last summer after just a few weeks long engagement, she did it against yours and your father's advice to postpone the wedding till Christmas"

"We were right about him!" Jane cried out with a feeling, "He is not like other gentlemen; so cold, brooding, unsocial and possessive of her. How can you explain that last autumn I did not receive a letter from my sister for nearly six weeks?"

"Because she was sick." Bingley answered calmly.

"If she was so sick that she was not able to even write a short note to me they should have called me there so I could take care of her. Lizzy walked three miles through muddy fields to take care of me when I had a cold; I would gladly travel a hundred miles to the north to nurse her."

"I am certain that she had the best medical care, Janie. I think we should not interfere." Bingley said in a firm voice.

Jane glared at him, "You do?"

"Yes, I do. Those are their private matters and their marriage. Even if they have had some problems they should solve them on their own." As he spoke his voice raised louder than ever; "If your sister does not ask specifically for your help and advice you should not impose it on her."

Jane pressed her lips in a tight line, "I will not stand by calmly and look away while Lizzy suffers."

"You cannot be sure that she suffers." He tried to reason again, his voice calmer and gentler. "From what you said, in her last letter she wrote that she was well and content, so perhaps it would be wise to respect it."

Jane huffed, blew the candle out and turned on her side with her back to him.

Bingley sat quietly for a minute or two before he put the light out on his side of the bed and laid down.

"Janie," he snuggled behind her, his hand slipping inside the opening of her nightdress, searching for her nipple. "Let us not quarrel." He turned her on her back, and pushed one side of her nightgown down, baring her shoulder and one full breast.

His mouth attached itself to her neck, and slowly he kissed a path toward her breasts.

"Charles," her hands rested on both sides of his head and she pulled him up so they could see each other's face, "I want to go to Pemberley and make sure that my sister is well."

Chapter Twenty-Four

"Elizabeth! Elizabeth!" Darcy cried as he strode into his wife's apartments.

Elizabeth slowly emerged from her bedroom, one hand on her back, the other on her protruding tummy. "Has something happened?"

"I have just received an express from the south, from Bingley."

She paled instantly and lowered herself slowly on the chair. "Has something happened to Jane?"

"On the contrary. Charles writes that she is determined to come here and see you. We should expect them in two days." Darcy dropped onto the opposite chair, and handed her the letter, "Here, read for yourself."

Elizabeth skipped through the letter, folded it neatly and spoke cautiously, "I must say that I am pleased with the thought that I will see Jane so soon."

"Do you not understand how dangerous her visit can be?" He stood up and started to pace the room. "The next full moon is in three days. I am not talking only about your sister and Charles being here, but the servants they will bring with them. If they notice anything, we will have to keep them here forever, or..." he hesitated.

"Or?"

He made an offhand gesture. "Some five hundred years ago, I would have ordered them killed if they refused to stay here and live with the pack."

She gaped at him, eyes round. "Fitzwilliam," she mouthed.

He gave her an apologetic look, "I will not do that now, of course. Good old times..."he added wistfully, "The hell with Charles! He cannot control his own woman. He does exactly what she wants."

"Interesting," Elizabeth raised one eyebrow, her hands resting neatly on her tummy. "Are you absolutely sure that you can control me?"

"Well, not exactly," he faltered quickly. "But you are my mate, and you are… rational... to some point at least."

Her eyes narrowed, "To some point?"

He stepped to her chair, and reached for her hand to kiss it. "I can trust you." He walked a few steps away. "I cannot trust her!" He smashed his hand against the door frame. "She never accepted me. She tried to turn you against me."

"How can you know that? Did Charles tell you?"

"He did not have to. Your nosy sister never liked or accepted me. I am not blind."

Elizabeth stood up. "Jane is not nosy! She worries about me!"

"Dear, sit down, please." He assisted her gently down on the chair. "I used the wrong word."

Elizabeth gestured for him to sit. "I still think that we should tell her the truth," she said when he joined her on the other chair. "Jane and I were always very close, and took care one of another. When you married me, you must have perceived that such turn of events would eventually come. I cannot cut myself off from my family completely."

Darcy reached for her hand. "I do not want you to break the bonds with your family." He stroked the top of her palm with his thumb. "When the child is old enough to travel, we will go to visit your family, perhaps next spring. I want our children to be able to live in both worlds as much as it is possible, even more than me. You could stay at Longbourn for a month, or even two; though it will be difficult for me to part with both of you for such a long time." He touched her tummy. "I cannot stay away from Pemberley for more than a few weeks." He paused, and looked directly into her eyes. "Elizabeth, we cannot invite your family here."

She covered his hand resting on the baby bump with hers. "I know that I will never be able to invite my parents or younger sisters to Pemberley, and I do understand why I cannot. I do not wish to do anything to endanger the pack."

"Thank you." He moved his chair closer to her, and lowered his dark head, putting his ear to the baby's bulge.

"Jane is not a gossip." Elizabeth continued gently as he tapped at the wall of her tummy, whispering hellos to the child. "She would never harm anyone on purpose. She will understand. Please, allow her to learn about us."

Darcy dropped back on his chair, pulling his long legs in front of himself. "I guess we have little choice now, when she is determined to find something." He sighed, "Perhaps she will not notice anything unusual?"

Elizabeth gave him a long, thoughtful look, biting on her lower lip. "It took me a month to guess, but you did not try very hard to hide the truth from me. I think that if you give orders for folks not to transform during the day for the time of their visit, not to run around the village and fields as wolves, and not to howl near the manor at night, she should not have any suspicions. You and Georgiana will have to eat what I eat at the table, or at least pretend to."

Darcy's face brightened, "That is a wonderful plan, Elizabeth. It may work. It will work!" he cried with energy. "We are perfectly able to live exactly like humans for those few days."

"Fitzwilliam," she looked at him with pleading in her dark eyes, "I want Jane to know. Mr. Bingley knows, so what harm would it be if Jane does too…"

"Lizzy," Darcy interrupted her gently, "Bingley knows because he learned accidentally, not because I told him. And over the years, he proved that he can be trusted with the secret."

"You never told me the exact circumstances of how he learned." She winced slightly at the pain in her back, and shifted in her seat, trying to find a more comfortable position. Instantly, Darcy pulled out the footrest for her, and put a small pillow behind her back. She gave him a grateful smile, and continued, "Yet when we were engaged, you mentioned you helped him during a fight in the public house during your university times."

"Yes, I was in my second year then, and Charles was a freshman. It was very difficult for me, because I was the first Darcy to go to university. I had to leave home for many months and live among people only. I was young and very stressed not to appear different, and act like a human. Then I met Bingley, and he was also the first from his family to access the higher education. We got along well; I helped him with his studies, and he introduced me to his numerous friends. One day after end of term exams, we went out for a drink, and some vile types started to pick on us. They grabbed Charles first, started to kick him, I defended him…"

"And?" Elizabeth asked, her eyes wide and curious.

"One of those drunks ended up with broken leg… in several places after I threw him over the length of the entire room and he hit the wall. I was not very good at controlling my strength. I think that was when Charles started to suspect something."

"What happened next?"

"Three stray werewolves, outcasts from their packs came upon me when I was on my way home after dark. I tried to fight them as a human. I was too afraid to change into a wolf there in the street; someone could always see me transforming."

"You were alone?" She interrupted him, "Did your father not send someone from the pack to protect you? You always have your guard when you travel, the same as Georgiana, and even me; you gave me a bodyguard before our wedding.

"Nowadays, yes, we never travel alone without strong back up, but back then, my father thought I should go alone, that if I had other werewolves with me, the people would more easily discover who I was. The times seemed somehow safer then, for years no one had heard about outcasts. Those three who attacked me were not even from England, but somewhere in Romania, and had been expelled from the pack there. They dwelled in France for some time, later moving to the south of England. My father blamed himself that he had sent me all alone to Oxford."

"He could not have known about the danger," she said. "He thought he acted in your best interest."

"He thought he failed to protect his only son, his heir. He felt terrible guilt about it. I tried to explain to him that he could not have possibly perceived such a turn of events. Before me, Doctor Craw was actually the first man from the pack to go to university. All the years in Edinburg in medical school, he was all alone and nothing happened. Nobody knew. He even got married there, and his wife did not know until he brought her here. I admire him for that. Once he told me that during the nights of his change he closed himself in his room, and could not run outside and hunt…"

"Did you not do the same in Oxford to avoid being discovered?"

Darcy nodded. "Yes, I did. But it was always easier for me as half human, to control the urge to change. Most werewolves need to change almost every single night. They can wait for an hour or two after dark, but not for long."

Elizabeth shook her head in slow motion, a pensive expression on her face. "I am sorry I interrupted when you were telling me how those three werewolves attacked you…"

"Ah, yes… Charles came upon us, and managed to somehow frighten them away. I do not remember how exactly, because I transformed and lost my conscience. Charles took care of me."

"You transformed in front of him?"

"Yes, I could not really postpone it any longer then. When we are injured, and it is life threatening, we change into our wolf form, even against our will. I think it is because we heal faster as wolves."

"What about the bandits who attacked you?"

"I sent a message to my father as soon as I was able to pen a note. Lord McGrath, actually his father, sent a small troop to deal with them. I know only that they were eliminated."

She reached up with her hand and smoothed the hair over his forehead. "I cannot like thinking how you must have suffered when they attacked you there."

"It was many years ago, Elizabeth. There is always a risk for us when we are outside our territory. Today the danger is far less than centuries ago when people still believed in us and hunted us down."

Elizabeth was silent for a long moment, deep in thought.

"You said that you were the first from the family to leave Pemberley for school," she said slowly.

He nodded. "Yes."

"How did your parents meet then? Colonel Fitzwilliam mentioned to me that his family spent most of the year in London. I always imagined that your father met your mother during a season in London."

Darcy chuckled. "My father in London for the season? If you knew him, that thought would never have crossed your mind. My parents met here."

She gaped at him, "In Pemberley?"

"Yes, in the north part of our territory, on the Scottish side, actually. You have not been there yet. We must go when the baby is old enough."

She shook her head, "I do not understand how your mother got there?"

"One summer, my mother travelled to Scotland with her brother, his wife, their son, not Colonel Fitzwilliam, because he had not been born yet, but their firstborn, and their sister Catherine."

Elizabeth smiled. "You mean Lady Catherine from Rosings Park?"

Darcy smiled back. "The same one. Apparently one day they went on a day long trip across the mounts to see the views. I think that my Aunt Matlock stayed in the house they rented, so there were only my uncle, my cousin, who is the Earl of Matlock today, my mother and Aunt Catherine. I understand that Catherine and my mum quarrelled, and as a result, my mother walked away from them for some time. She lost her way, it started to rain and she slipped into a valley."

Elizabeth clasped her hands, "Your father found and rescued her," she said with dreamy expression on her face. "How romantic!"

Darcy grinned at her enthusiasm. "Her arm was broken, she had a bump on her head and both ankles were twisted, so she could not walk. Father took her to Pemberley, and Doctor Craw set her arm. When she woke up, she did not remember who she was or how her accident happened. All she knew was that her name was Anne. The doctor explained that the loss of memory was because of the head injury."

"They fell in love." Elizabeth guessed.

He nodded. "My father had already decided that he would claim her when she recovered."

She frowned, "Claim her?"

"It is an ancient law." He explained proudly, "When a werewolf finds a human woman on his land, he has the right to claim her and mate her, if he has not mated already."

"That is barbaric." she gasped. "Would you have done that to me if I happened to cross your land with, let us say, my Aunt and Uncle Gardiner."

Darcy's black eyes twinkled, he reached for her, motioned her to stand up and pull her onto his lap, "Of course I would," he squeezed her to him.

"It is not civilized," she stated in a firm voice.

"Perhaps, but it is much better than all that courting I had to go through to get you."

"You did not get me," she stressed. "I agreed to marry you." She tried to lift from his lap without success. "And that was not much courting."

He kept her to him, his arms around hers and one hand on her tummy. "Yes, I did get you."

She rolled her eyes. "You must change your attitudes. I do not want our sons to be taught such nonsense. How can you say that, as you put it, 'claiming' a woman, is better than courting her, learning first who she is, what she likes and dislikes, becoming friends with her."

He looked up at her. "You do not understand."

"I do not?"

"It is a fate that puts a particular female, especially when it comes to human women, on a werewolf's life path to claim her. As it is their destiny to be mated, they are perfect for each other, so the courtship in not necessary."

Elizabeth gave him a long, incredulous look. "You really believe that?"

"Of course I do. One should not fight destiny either; if you do, something dangerous may happen. I fought my fate to be with you too long, and Wickham almost got you. Had I clai…"he started to say the word, but seeing her expression, corrected himself, "Had I decided to court when we first met, you would not have suffered from Wickham."

"In other words, you think it was fate that brought us together," she summed up.

"Yes."

"Well I believe that it was just a set of circumstances, which has nothing to do with fate."

"Then why did you leave your room that night at Netherfield when you first saw me as a wolf?"

She shrugged. "It was a full moon, I could not sleep."

"Has that happened to you before? Did you sleepwalk? Did you feel like going for a walk at night?"

"No…" she hesitated, "No, I do not remember. I have always slept soundly."

"Something told you to go downstairs, to get out of the house to meet me."

She shook her head, "It was only an accident. You put too much to it."

"No," he took her hand to kiss it. "It was our destiny."

She said nothing to his words and changed the subject. "You did not finish telling me what happened next with your parents. How did they get married?"

"My mother recovered steadily, but still had problems with her memory. Only after a few weeks, did she remember who she was. My father sent a message to London, to her family, who by that time almost lost all hope of ever finding her. Her brother came for her, and she spent the rest of her recovery in Matlock. My father went there to visit her, and asked for her hand. My mother agreed, because she had fallen in love with my father when she had not yet remembered who she was. Her family had some objections at first, because no one had heard of such a family as the Darcys. However, when my father presented his financial situation to them and assured them that he was ready to resign entirely from accepting her dowry, they agreed. My parents were married by the end of the year."

"How sad." she whispered.

"Sad?"

"She did not know who he was."

"No, she did not." he agreed quietly.

Elizabeth slipped from his lap and stepped to the window.

Darcy rose, and walked to stand behind her. "You can tell your sister, but it is imperative that we must convince her not to tell the rest of your family." he whispered into her neck.

She looked up at him, "Thank you."

He ran his hands over their baby and he kissed her softly. "When they arrive, I will ask Charles to send their people back home the same day, or the very next one. Later, we will give them a carriage and a few of our people to drive them safely back to Derbyshire."

"That would be for the best." Elizabeth said, turning to him, "I am sure that Charles will understand the situation, and I will try to explain everything to Jane."

***

Elizabeth sat close to the window in the drawing room, staring at the road leading to the manor. When she saw the carriage at the turn of the road, she cried out.

"They are here!" She stood up. "I can see the carriage." she called, waddling to the door as fast as she could.

"Elizabeth, wait!" Darcy sprang from his seat, throwing the newspaper away. "You should not run."

He caught up to her in the next room, and taking a firm hold on her arm, accompanied her to the spacious foyer, where they waited for their guests.

Chapter Twenty-Five

Elizabeth and Georgiana sat together in compatible silence in the smaller drawing room, each of them occupied with her own amusement. Elizabeth was knitting a tiny yellow bootie using the softest of wool. While her sister, spread on her stomach on the carpet in front of the fire, waving her shapely silk clad calves in the air, frowned in concentration over music sheets.

"I cannot figure out this composition," the girl murmured, chewing on her pencil.

Elizabeth counted the rows in her sock and said, "That difficult?"

Georgiana made a note on the margin, "No, not so much, but the rhythm and pace are uncommon. I have doubts how to play it properly. It is from some new German composer."

"I think that you should trust your own instinct, and I am sure you will play it beautifully."

The girl sighed. "We shall see."

Elizabeth looked at Georgiana, and the sudden, painful, heart-tearing sadness overpowered her when she remembered her own sister. She had held such high hopes for Jane's visit. She had thought that her sister would understand, support her and share with her, the joy of upcoming motherhood. She had imagined Jane coming to Pemberley every summer, their children playing together in the gardens.

Contrary to what she had expected and hoped for, Jane had not taken the news well.

At first her sister had not believed them, and when Fitzwilliam had changed into a wolf in front of her to prove their words, she had gone into hysterics. Elizabeth had expected a reaction, she had been prepared for her sister to be in shock, but Jane's reaction exceeded her imagination.

Jane had said that her husband was a monster, that everyone around were monsters and beasts. What hurt the most was that she had called the baby Elizabeth carried a creature, and plainly told her that she should get rid of it as soon as it was born.

Elizabeth had tried to convince Jane how wrong she was. She had invited her to the village to show her that the pack was a peaceful, God abiding community, and that her husband worked hard for the well being of his people. Jane had refused to go or to listen to any argument.

Jane and Mr. Bingley had left Pemberley the next day at dawn, without even a proper goodbye.

Elizabeth had written several letters to her sister since then. She had hoped that in time the shock would wane, and her sister would show understanding and accept, or at least tolerate, Elizabeth's new family. Jane had answered only once with a short note. She had stated that Elizabeth was always welcome in her home, on the condition that she would come alone, and forget about the monsters.

Elizabeth was devastated by Jane's attitude; deeply hurt, severely disappointed and most of all, ashamed. She had tried to hide those feelings from her husband, but Fitzwilliam was not a fooled with her forced smiles during the day. When she had cried at night after Jane had left, he kept her in his arms, and kissed her tears away.

He had not said a word of reproach to her for her sister's behaviour. He had not mentioned that it had been she who had insisted in the first place that they share their secret with Jane. Only once had he referred to what had happened. Darcy had showed her a letter from Mr. Bingley, who wrote that Jane did not want to hear about Pemberley and refused to speak about it. Bingley assured them that they should not be afraid of his wife revealing the truth to anyone. Jane had convinced herself that she must be silent, because otherwise the wolves would come to kill her.

Deep in her heart, Elizabeth still hoped that her sister would change her mind. After all, Jane had forgiven Mr. Bingley his illegitimate child; she had accepted the girl, and agreed to raise it as her own. Fitzwilliam was a good and honourable man; he had not chosen who he was, but otherwise his life had been exemplary. Could Jane not see it? Could she not accept it?

A knock at the door interrupted Elizabeth's painful thoughts.

Elizabeth waited till Georgiana sat herself properly on the sofa before she spoke calmly. "Enter."

"Mistress," the servant entered, "Lord McGrath is here."

The women looked at each other in complete surprise.

"What is he doing here?" Georgiana whispered. "Brother did not mention that he would visit."

"I am surprised too." Elizabeth glanced down at her extended, now eight month pregnant belly, "I am not presentable now to take any calls."

Georgiana leaned to her, eyes wide, "Lizzy, please do not leave him alone with me. I never know what to say to him."

"Calm down, my dear, I will not." Elizabeth squeezed the girl's hand. "It would not be proper anyway to leave him with you all alone. Lord McGrath must know I should not admit callers so late in confinement."

Georgiana shrugged, her chin high in the air. "I doubt whether he is sensitive at all to such basic norms of civilized society."

The servant at the door cleared his throat.

"We are talking and he is waiting there," Lizzy gasped. "He is the overlord, after all. Fitzwilliam would be unhappy if we refused to see him." She turned to the servant and spoke in a raised, sure voice, "Please show Lord McGrath in."

"Bring me the shawl, please." Elizabeth pointed to an elegant shawl draped over the nearby chair. "It should hide my condition, if just a little," she murmured as Georgiana helped her to arrange the soft material over her shoulders and across her protruding stomach.

Energetic, heavy footsteps were heard from the hall.

"It is well, leave it, it will not hide the baby anyway." Elizabeth straightened herself up, and Georgiana returned to her seat.

The door opened and Lord McGrath entered. He bowed deeply.

"Pray forgive me for this unannounced visit." he said, his eyes on the younger woman. "I hoped to discuss some matters with your husband."

Georgiana lifted herself gracefully and then waited for her sister to rise as well. So late in her confinement, Elizabeth was forced to develop a special technique of sitting and standing up. Both women performed a simultaneous, elegant, perfectly practiced over the years curtesy.

McGrath rushed to them through the room. "Mrs. Darcy, please do not exert yourself on my behalf."

Elizabeth gratefully plopped back on the sofa. "I am afraid you found us all alone, your lordship. My husband had to ride unexpectedly to the east border of the estate this morning, but we hope that he will return for dinner." She gestured to the opposite sofa. "Please take a seat."

McGrath sat down. "Do you know what happened to make him leave so suddenly?"

Elizabeth nodded. "From what I understood, some unfamiliar wolves were spotted on the border."

"The farmer, who sent the message about it through his son, had his animals slaughtered two nights ago." Georgiana added softly.

McGrath's heavy gaze rested on the girl. "You say slaughtered."

"Yes, ripped apart and left behind the barn," Georgiana admitted worriedly.

"Has something happened to the family?" McGrath asked.

"Thankfully no. They locked themselves inside the house during the attack." Elizabeth explained, "It is the farthest situated farm on the estate. They lost all their animals."

"I would like to talk with the farmer's son, the one who brought the message." he announced more than asked.

"He is not here; he returned to his parents with Fitzwilliam." Georgiana said.

The man shook his head. "That does not sound well."

"We are very worried as well." Elizabeth assured.

"Nothing like that has happened here for a long time," Georgiana mused. "Not in my memory."

McGrath stayed silent for a prolonged moment, his face drowned in lines of deep worry, before he spoke.

"Mrs. Darcy," he faced Elizabeth directly, "Please allow me to wait for your husband here. I would like to hear more about the outcome of this unpleasant affair."

Elizabeth smiled gracefully, "Of course, my lord, it will be our pleasure. I know that Fitzwilliam will be very pleased to hear that you offered to keep us company."

Georgiana looked at the other woman, "Brother was very reluctant to go."

McGrath glanced warmly at Elizabeth's rounded form, the shawl doing little to hide it, "Because of your condition, madam."

"That too," she placed a hand on her large stomach, "But he is still afraid to leave us alone because of Wickham."

"Ah, yes, he mentioned to me that you saw him in Kendal."

Elizabeth paled considerably at her last memory of Wickham, and what could have happened if she had reached Kendal alone, before Fitzwilliam had caught up to her.

"Let us not talk about such unpleasant matters." Elizabeth forced a smile, "We were about to have some tea; would you care to take it with us?"

McGrath returned her smile, "Yes, please."

Georgiana stood up, "I will see to the refreshments."

Elizabeth smiled at the girl, "Thank you, my dear."

When Georgiana left, Elizabeth wondered on what subject she should direct the conversation. What should she talk about to the king of werewolves? What would be a safe question?

Her guest, however, solved her dilemma and spoke first. "I hope you will not find me rude, Mrs. Darcy, but when do you expect the happy event?" His eyes rested on her bulging belly.

Elizabeth blushed, and ran her hands self consciously over her stomach. "The first days of May; so I expect to have nearly one month before me. I know that my size may suggests an earlier date, but the doctor thinks I may have twins."

McGrath's eyebrows arched high on his forehead. "Twins?"

She nodded, "There were cases of twins in my family, from my mother's side."

"I can only envy Darcy his good luck. I wish you and your husband that all will go well when the time comes," he said sincerely.

"Thank you."

Elizabeth picked up her earlier abandoned work, concentrating on knitting the heel of a little bootie.

"For the baby?" he asked, his eyes pointing to the tiny article.

She smiled, and reached to her sewing basket, taking out the other, already finished bootie to show it to him. "Yes, it is a tradition in my family that a woman should make the baby's clothes by herself."

McGrath took the tiny yellow sock, which looked lost in his big hand and examined it. "My wife made similar items."

Elizabeth raised her astonished eyes at him. "Your wife?" she repeated.

"My late wife." he clarified. "She died in childbirth ten years ago. She sewed every single thing for the child, but it died a day after her, both from fever."

For the next minute, only the sound of the cracking fire could be heard in the room.

"I did not know." Elizabeth spoke first, her voice not more than a whisper, "Nobody told me that you were married, sir, and that you lost your wife in such tragic circumstances. Pray forgive me if I had brought sad memories to you, it was unconsciously done."

McGrath looked at her, "It is I who should apologize. I unnecessarily scared you with such sour tales." He leaned forward and returned the bootie to the basket.

"No, no, I am well, I am well." Elizabeth tried to smile, but tears were too close to her eyes.

She lowered her head for a moment to compose herself, and started to busily arrange her knitting inside the basket. When she looked up again at Lord McGrath, his face bore no expression; he stared into the space in front of himself with empty eyes.

"It is hard to imagine how a human... "She began gently, "How a person can rise from such a tragedy."

"There is no other choice but to live; there are responsibilities, there is a duty to those who rely on us with their lives and wellbeing." he answered in a hollow voice.

She bit her lower lip, and spoke with hesitation, "My husband mentioned to me that his father arranged the marriage between you and Georgiana."

He nodded. "That is correct. Yes, when she was yet a small girl."

Elizabeth tried to read his expression for a moment, but she could not guess what his thoughts were. "Georgiana is a wonderful companion. She is kind and sweet, perhaps a bit too shy and lacking in confidence though."

"I do not understand why she should lack the confidence." McGrath noted boldly, "She is very talented and beautiful."

"She has had no female friends, no young ladies of her position and age that she could compare herself with. She was raised all alone, without a mother, and in the formative years without a father too. All she had was a brother, a loving one, but also very busy, and much older. I think that those circumstances explain well why she can be easily intimidated by strangers."

There was a long silence when McGrath spoke again, murmuring grouchily. "You mean to say that she is afraid of me."

"She does not know you. I think that she does not fear you, as much as being married to you too soon."

"Too soon?" He glared at her, "She will be seventeen in September. Plenty of girls marry at this age."

"She may look a woman, but she is not ready," Elizabeth insisted, "Do you want to have a child for a wife, or an adult?"

"Mrs. Darcy, I cannot possibly wait." McGrath stood up and walked to the fireplace, "You have lived with us long enough now to understand that my position demands from me to marry. I need heirs. I have waited many years for Georgiana to grow up. I could have married someone else by now and already have sons."

"She will not defy you on the earlier marriage because she loves her brother too much to do anything which could harm him or affect his position. But she will not be happy."

The man's face tightened. "Life is harsh." He returned to his seat opposite Elizabeth and leaned comfortably against the back of the sofa, speaking in a confident voice, "She may be a bit sulky and sad at first, but in time she will come to terms with her new situation. I will care for her as she deserves. I will treat her well, as my honourable mate, the mother of my children and the Alpha Female above all the packs."

Elizabeth shook her head, and spoke in a decided voice. "Lord McGrath, with all due respect, you do not understand my point. She is not ready. Wait at least till she is eighteen."

McGrath gave her a long thoughtful look. "Eighteen, but not a day longer." He smiled, "I cannot promise you more than that, Mrs. Darcy."

The door opened, and Georgiana entered with the servant carrying the heavy tray loaded with tea accessories and a variety of pastries.

Georgiana was serving the tea, when Lord McGrath pointed to the music sheets, scattered on the floor, next to the fire place.

"Are they yours, Miss Darcy?"

"Oh, yes," Georgiana blushed, clearly embarrassed, and put the teapot back on the tray. "I was looking at a new composition that I am learning now, and must have dropped them there."

She made a move to bend for them, but Lord McGrath was faster. He knelt down and picked up the scattered papers.

"Allow me." He handed her the sheets. "Here you are."

The girl looked up at him nervously, "Thank you, sir." she whispered.

Georgiana walked to the corner by the window, and started to busily arrange her music sheets on the pile on the top of the pianoforte.

Her movements slowed down as she gave a sharp look in the direction of the window. She thought to see a shadow, running across the lawn. Her feet brought her to the floor length window, leading to the terrace outside. The day had been cloudy, and now it was getting darker with each minute. She could barely make the outlines of the park and the lake.

She turned from the window, "Lord McGrath," she spoke in a sure voice, "May I ask you to step to me for a moment or two?" She sat by the pianoforte and opened the sheets in front of her. "I would like to show something to you."

Both Elizabeth and Lord McGrath raised their heads from their tea cups at her words, the surprised expression written on their faces as they looked at one another.

"Certainly, Miss Darcy, with pleasure," Lord McGrath said warmly, and with one final pointed look at Elizabeth, put away his tea cup, stood up and walked to the instrument.

Georgiana shifted on her seat to make a place for him. He sat down close to her, crowding her on the slim bench with his bulky body. She played a few chords, then pointed at the music sheet.

"I have seen someone creeping under the window," she whispered, not taking her eyes from the notes front of her.

He looked sideways at her profile, "What?" he murmured incomprehensibly.

She ran her hands over the keys with grace, practising the scale, "I saw several wolves crossing the lawn and hiding behind the rose bushes at the edge of the terrace. I could see them just for a moment, but they did not look familiar to me." She began to play a quiet, sweet melody. "No one from our pack would behave like that, creeping like thieves under the windows of the drawing room."

McGrath lowered his head and whispered. "Who protects the house?"

"Brother took his second, and most of his guard with him." She turned the music sheet page with one hand, the other one still playing, "There are only a few soldiers left."

She looked up at the man, eyes wide, "I am afraid. How could they come so near the house?"

"I arrived alone on horseback." His fist clenched on the smooth, polished surface of the instrument. "Idiot! I never thought that anyone would dare to enter our territory."

Georgiana leaned to him, "I am worried for my sister. I heard Doctor Craw saying to Brother last week that the baby may come any day."

Simultaneously, Lord McGrath's and Georgiana's heads turned to the window.

"Someone is there." she whispered, and looked back at the keys, her pupils dilated.

"Is there a room nearby without windows?" he whispered back.

Elizabeth, who had been glancing at them curiously for several minutes, stood up and began to slowly walk in their direction.

Georgiana thought for a moment. "There is a small side room connected with the hall and dining room. Servants put dirty dishes there before taking them down to the kitchen." She pointed with her eyes to the opposite wall, "The door is hidden within the panelling."

"When I give you the sign, you and Mrs. Darcy will run and hide there," he said, his voice surprisingly calm.

Georgiana nodded, and started playing again.

"Are you playing the new composition to our guest, Georgiana?" Elizabeth asked with a smile, as she stopped by the instrument.

Georgiana and McGrath looked at her but said nothing.

"Is something wrong?" Elizabeth asked.

"Now." McGrath barked.

Georgiana stood up and ran around the instrument to the other woman.

She put her arm around Elizabeth and energetically moved forward, "We must hide."

"Hide? Why?" Elizabeth mouthed, but obediently started to walk.

They had not walked far, when the window in front of them broke into pieces, and the large, silver-white wolf leaped on the polished hard wood floor.

Elizabeth screamed. Georgiana stepped forward and hid her sister behind herself.

The animal bared his white teeth. His eyes glistened, and he began to growl menacingly.

"There is another one." Elizabeth exclaimed from behind Georgiana, pointing to the other animal, of similar colouring, who just hurtled inside the room.

Georgiana made a step sideways with Elizabeth closely attached to her back.

The wolf in front of them made a move, readying himself to attack. What happened next seemed to last only a split second.

Georgiana reached for the heavy, stuffed armchair her brother usually liked to sit in, effortlessly raised it above her head, and threw it, just as one of the wolves leaped into the air. The furniture hit the animal on the head, and effectively shoved him to the ground.

The other wolf ran toward them, but before he managed to reach them, his neck was needled with the iron poker from the fireplace in the hand of Lord McGrath, who suddenly appeared by their side.

Elizabeth gaped from her sister to her guest and to the wolf, dying in a puddle of blood at her feet.

"Run," McGrath screamed, as the heads of several other wolves appeared in the window opening.

Georgiana grabbed her sister's hand, and they both started to run in the direction of the wall as fast as Elizabeth was able. With her slippered foot, Georgiana kicked the door in the wall wide open, and not so gently pushed the older woman inside.

Elizabeth scooted against the opposite wall of the small, narrow room, and with wide eyes watched as Georgiana shut the door closed in front of the bared teeth of a barking wolf. She reached for the large cabinet, and pushed it across, blocking the doorway.

"No, Georgiana, we left Lord McGrath all alone there!" Elizabeth protested.

"He shall be fine." Georgiana said, only slightly out of breath, "Are you well?"

"I am well, but Lord McGrath…"

Georgiana placed the calming hand on her arm. "Soon the servants will come to help him." She looked around the tiny space, her eyes stopping at the other two doors, one leading to the dining room, another to the hall.

"Elizabeth, step aside, please," she said, and when her sister did, she moved the other two smaller cabinets, blocking the remaining exits. "To make sure no one will enter."

Elizabeth gaped at her, “How did you do that? This is very heavy furniture.”

Georgiana smiled, “You forget who I am.”

Elizabeth shook her head, “But you are so slender.”

“I rarely use my strength.” The girl acknowledged shyly. “I usually do not have to.”

Elizabeth screamed again when the blast of the pistol was heard.

“You see. They came to Lord McGrath’s rescue.” Georgiana smiled at her, “We must wait till it ends. We are safe here.”

“Georgiana.” Elizabeth mouthed, full of admiration.

“Now, sit down.” The girl gestured to the empty space against the wall, “You should not be on your feet so long.” She helped her to lower herself onto the floor, and soon sat beside her.

For long minutes, they spoke nothing, only holding hands and listening to the sounds coming from the house; running, screams, animal cries, barking, and pistol shots.

There were no shouts or running heard for some time, when Georgiana shifted in her place.

“What …?” she lifted to her knees, “Is it wet here?”

“Oh, God.” Elizabeth felt her soiled, wet gown. “It started.”

Georgiana stared at her incomprehensibly, “What started?”

“The baby is coming, my waters broke” Elizabeth touched her belly with both hands, “It started.”

Chapter Twenty – Six

Georgiana touched her strained belly. "What should we do?"

Elizabeth shook her head. "I do not know."

The girl patted her hand. "Do not worry. They will come for us soon".

"I hope so." Elizabeth panted in the darkness. "Ahhh...." she moaned.

"What?

Elizabeth squeezed her eyes tight. "Hurts!

Another two hour passed, and Elizabeth's pains started to grow in strength every ten minutes. Georgiana held her hand, dabbed her sweaty forehead with a handkerchief, and spoke soothingly to her. Most of all, she prayed ardently so that she would not have to deliver her niece or nephew all by herself in the storeroom.

At last there was a loud banging at the wall, and the unmistakable baritone of Lord McGrath's voice was heard.

"You can open up! It is safe now."

Georgiana sprang to her feet, and with one push of her arm, moved the cabinet, bigger than herself, away from the door.

The door fell open, and a stream of light broke in. Lord McGrath was covered with blood, his clothes were torn in places but otherwise he looked unharmed.

"Elizabeth." Georgiana pointed to the panting woman, resting against the wall, her legs wide spread under her gown.

McGrath leaned against the door frame, and did not speak for a moment. "We must take her upstairs. Now."

A new pain came on Elizabeth and she howled, clenching her teeth, her fingers gripping the silk of her skirts.

The man placed his hand on Georgiana's shoulder. "Run to Mrs. Reynolds so she may call the midwife and the doctor, and prepare the room. I will carry her upstairs."

Georgiana darted through the demolished drawing room, sprinkled with blood and strewn with the bodies of the killed wolves.

McGrath knelt beside Elizabeth, took her hand, and held it through the contraction.

"Is it gone?" he asked as Elizabeth's face relaxed and her head fell listlessly onto her shoulder.

She nodded, eyes closed.

"Clasp your hands behind my neck." He put her arm on his shoulder, and effortlessly picked her up.

***

Darcy wiped his dagger clean from the blood of the last of the three outcasts they had found in the forest near the farm.

"We should stay in the area for the next few days," one of his men said from behind him, "There may be others."

Darcy sheathed his weapon. "You shall stay; I will return to Pemberley."

"Now, Master? Wait till dawn, at least."

"Yes, now. I will go with one man. The rest of you are to stay here," he said, and no one dared to say a word to oppose him.

"Bring my horse," he ordered, and once again walked to the dead animals. "They were not English," he murmured, touching the wolf with his booted legs. "They remind me of those who attacked me years ago when I was in Oxford. We must learn more about their motives. I refuse to believe that their aim was only to kill a few pigs, chickens and a cow."

He turned and stepped to his mount. "Bury the bodies and do everything you can to help the family." He mounted, and spoke into the direction of the farmer, who stood with his wife nearby, "Tomorrow I shall send animals from Pemberley to replace those that you have lost."

"Thank you, Master! God bless you! Thank you!" The farmer ran to him, bent in half, ready to kiss his boots.

"Leave it. Tis not necessary." Darcy shoved him away. He kicked his horse's sides and rode away.

He and his man were a good half way on their road to Pemberley, when they saw a wolf running straight at them at great speed.

They stopped their horses and reached for their weapons.

"Master," his man said, his eyes narrowed. "He looks to be from our pack."

"It is Wilfred." Darcy whispered, as the young wolf collapsed in front of them, so exhausted that he could not even let out a single bark.

His man dismounted, knelt down by the animal and touched its side. The young wolf's fur was matted with blood.

The man lifted his head at Darcy, showing his hand stained in red. "Good God, Master, something must have happened there."

***

The new day was breaking dawn when Darcy reached Pemberley. He dismounted his horse, still in a gallop, and rushed inside the manor.

Lord McGrath was waiting for him in the foyer.

"She is upstairs," the man said.

Not waiting for more, Darcy climbed the stairs, taking three steps at once.

He saw Georgiana, pale and tired, leaving Elizabeth's rooms.

"Brother!" Her face brightened and she ran to him.

Darcy could not speak, and merely looked down at her.

She put a calming hand on his arm. "Elizabeth is well, very tired though, and she is resting now. She was very brave. Her pains started just as Wickham attacked us."

He ran his hand over his face. "My God."

"Thankfully Lord McGrath came for an unexpected visit earlier today," Georgiana continued. "We were taking tea together when it started. He hid us in the spare room adjoining the drawing room, and we sat there safe through the entire time of the attack. Oh, Brother, there were so many of them! At least twenty outcasts came into the house."

Darcy searched her face. "Wilfred told me that no one was killed."

Georgiana shook her head, "No, no one from ours. There were many injured, but they have already been taken to the hospital." She took his hand and presented a big, ear to ear grin. "But they are so beautiful, Brother!"

Darcy blinked repeatedly. "They?"

Georgiana nodded, her whole face beaming. "The boy is strong and big, and looks just like you. He was born first. The girl is much smaller, and we were worried because she did not cry at first. Doctor Craw assured us though, that in time she will be well too."

Darcy exhaled slowly, and his face relaxed as his hand cupped her cheek. "Go to bed now. You look tired too."

Georgiana kissed his cheek and stepped across the corridor to her room.

As Darcy entered his wife's apartment, he saw Doctor Craw, talking to Mrs. Reynolds in a low voice.

He did not stop to speak with them, but strode straight into the Mistress' bedroom.

Heather sat beside the bed.

"Leave us alone," he said, and the girl instantly obeyed.

Elizabeth was sleeping, her face pale, her hair combed smoothly from her forehead and tied to the side with a simple blue ribbon.

Two identical cribs stood next to her bed, with two babies wrapped in soft white blankets.

The bigger one had its dark, round eyes open now. Darcy could see that his legs kicked inside the blanket. His face was red, and he had a mop of black, thick hair.

Darcy's eyes were drawn to the other child though. She was considerably smaller, so small that he could swear that she would easily fit his outstretched palm. Her eyes were closed, and unlike her brother, her skin was very pale, almost translucent; and she had no hair. She did not move either. Darcy leaned over and touched her cheek. It was warm. He put his ear to her face for a moment. She was breathing.

"Fitzwilliam." Elizabeth whispered.

He rushed to her. "Dearest." He took her hand and raised it to his mouth. "How are you feeling?"

"Tired." She winced. "Please, help me sit up."

He helped her to lift, and supported her against the pillows.

"Are you in pain?" he asked, taking in the strained lines on her pale face.

She managed a small smile, "Some, but it does not matter. Are they not beautiful?" she asked softly, pride and love in her eyes as she gazed at the babies.

"Yes, they are." He raised her hand to his mouth again and murmured his quiet thanks.

"Please give me the smaller one," she asked.

Darcy reached for the tiny bundle, and with the utmost care, lifted the baby from the crib.

"It is a girl," Elizabeth said with a smile when he put the baby in her arms.

"I know, Georgiana told me."

Elizabeth unwrapped the girl from the blanket and touched her tiny hand.

With her free hand, she tugged at the opening of her gown. "Help me. I need to nurse her; she ate so little at their first nursing."

Darcy untied the ribbon and pushed the nightgown open, revealing a heavy, swollen breast tipped with a dark, extended nipple.

Elizabeth kissed the babe's head and stroked the pale cheek repeatedly. The girl did not react, so she nudged the nipple against the rosebud mouth.

At last the girl's eyelids fluttered, deep blue eyes showed for a moment and she started to suckle.

"Good, my precious," Elizabeth crooned. "Excellent," she added when the child pulled harder.

Elizabeth raised her eyes at Darcy and whispered. "She is very quiet, unlike him." She looked warmly at the other crib.

Darcy looked for a moment as she nursed the girl, till the loud, impatient scream came from the other child.

Elizabeth grinned. "I told you."

Darcy stood above his son and looked at the spasming red face, furiously waving little fists, and strong legs kicking inside the blanket.

He took the boy out of the crib and stared down at him. His heir. The baby kept screaming, steadily rising in volume.

"She will not have more." Elizabeth wiped the tiny mouth, and moved the girl on her arm to burp her.

Darcy put the boy on the bedcovers beside his wife and took the girl from her arms. The baby had already managed to drop back to sleep.

He nestled his daughter safely in the crook of his arm, and sat with her on the bed next to Elizabeth.

The boy was silent now, firmly attached to his mother's breast, suckling strongly and loudly.

"I am sorry," Darcy whispered. "I have failed you."

She lifted her eyes from the baby. "Failed me?"

He hung his head down. "Yes, you, our children, Georgiana, everyone."

"Fitzwilliam… it was not your fault."

"I promised to protect you from Wickham."

"You are not a God; you cannot control everything. We should be grateful that nobody was killed."

They waited till the boy finished pulling, and Darcy put the babies back into their cribs. The girl slept undisturbed, but the boy was wide awake.

"You should sleep now." he helped her to lie down.

"Will you come to us later?" she asked, her eyelids already dropping.

Darcy leaned to kiss her forehead. "Yes, darling, I will. I need to talk with Lord McGrath and see to everything, but I will be back when you wake up. I love you."

Darcy left the room quietly, and met the Doctor Craw outside.

"I would like to leave now, Master. I am needed with the injured at the hospital," the man started without preamble.

"Yes, I understand, of course, you should go. Tell me only, Doctor, whether she is truly well?"

Doctor Craw nodded with a smile. "A brave mate you have. She did very well for the first time, and with two babies at once. I will check on her later today, but I do not perceive any problems."

"And the babies?"

"The boy is very strong. I was briefly concerned about the girl. She had breathing problems after she came out, but she will be fine, although she will require more attention than her brother, especially in these first weeks."

"I understand." Darcy shook the Doctor's hand. "Thank you."

Before going downstairs, he checked one more time on Elizabeth and the babies.

She slept peacefully, the same as the little ones. As he looked at the faces of his children and wife, he wondered what he had done to receive so much from God.

***

"How is Mrs. Darcy?" Lord McGrath asked when Darcy entered the library.

Darcy smiled. "She is well, sleeping."

"And the children?"

"Simply perfect," Tears brimmed Darcy's eyes, but he quickly blinked them away. "The girl is smaller and weaker than the boy, but the doctor thinks that with the proper care, she will steadily improve in the next weeks."

McGrath walked to him, shook his hand and smacked his shoulder soundly, "My congratulations."

Darcy lowered to his knees. "Thank you." He tried to kiss the other man's hand, but McGrath did not allow it. "I owe you their lives."

"Nonsense." McGrath pulled him up to his feet, walked him to the armchair in front of the fireplace, and motioned to sit down. "I came here all alone, on horseback, without my people. We were having tea in the drawing room when they came near the house. And you must know that it is your sister who you should thank to for your wife and children's lives, rather than me."

Darcy gaped at him disbelievingly. "Georgiana?"

"Yes, your little sister." McGrath confirmed in a firm voice. As he walked aside to pour two tall glasses of brandy, in short words he described the girl's behaviour during the attack.

"I can hardly believe this." Darcy shook his head, taking a long gulp of his drink.

"She is usually so quiet and shy."

McGrath took his seat in the opposite armchair. "You did not see her when she hit one of the attackers on the head and shoved him to the ground." There was the unmistakable pride in the man's voice when he spoke the words. "She protected your wife with her own body."

"I will have to thank her dearly then." Darcy paused for a moment, "She did not say a word about it when we talked upstairs. I will speak with her when she wakes up. I ordered her to bed; she was very tired."

There was a long moment of silence, both men sipping on their drinks.

Darcy spoke first. "What became of Wickham?"

McGrath smiled in satisfaction, "Dead and torn into pieces. When the folks from the village got him in their hands..." he paused, "Let us just say that I did not try to stop them."

"He planned it well." Darcy's face tightened. "Bastard! If I could, I would tear him to pieces one more time!"

"I know it is hard to look at what happened here like that, but actually, Wickham did us a favour. He collected all the outcasts from England, Scotland, Ireland and even, I believe, several from the Continent."

"Yes, that is correct." Darcy nodded. "Those who I found on the east border were certainly not from England, or Scotland."

"And now they are all killed." McGrath continued, "We should have peace and quiet for the next several years, till the next ones begin to appear. You cannot stop outlaws forever."

"How did Wickham manage it?" Darcy snapped. He stood up and started to pace the room. "He thought that he would conquer the entire pack with twenty men?"

"I do not know what Wickham thought. I did not manage to ask him, but I do believe that they wanted to kidnap Mrs. Darcy, and probably your sister too. He would gain a lot of power and influence having in his hands the closest family of Darcy of Pemberley."

Darcy's fists clenched and his eyes flashed dangerously, "Over my dead body."

"He sent you to the far end of your territory, making sure that you would be busy there the entire day. They used boats to get here from the sea, which was very clever, and crept unnoticed from the beach straight to the house. That could not work, of course, in the long run, but it was a good plan. We should give it to him."

McGrath raised himself slowly and walked to the other man. "Well, it is high time for me to depart. I must go home, check if Wickham has not prepared a surprise for me too."

Darcy took his hand and held it in a tight grip. "Thank you, I will never be able to repay you."

"As I said, I have done nothing. Your people would have managed very well, even without me. They are very devoted to you; they would give their lives for you and your family. Not every Alpha Male can say that."

The men hugged briefly, and McGrath walked to the door. "Give my respects to your wife, sister," he smiled, "and the children."

Epilogue

"Fitzwilliam, give him to me." Elizabeth tugged at her husband's sleeve, her concerned gaze entirely focused on her son.

"Lizzy, they must see him." Darcy lifted his three month old naked son even higher above his head.

The boy screamed at the top of his lungs, and several hundreds of werewolves howled in response. It was the night of the full moon and earlier today the Christening of Darcy's twins had taken place.

Elizabeth raised her arms to take the baby. "Fitzwilliam, he is scared!" she cried worriedly.

"Darling, they must meet their future Alpha Male." Darcy stepped closer to the balcony's balustrade.

"They have already met him." Elizabeth pulled at his arm, her heart tearing up at the sight of the crying baby, "Give him to me at once!" she ordered, "He is scared to death and will surely get cold!"

Darcy sighed and gave the baby back to his mother, who instantly wrapped the boy in a blanket, and hurried inside the room.

"I must have showed him to the pack." Darcy explained as he closed the balcony door.

She flashed him an angry gaze. "They have seen him already at the Christening." she kissed the baby's dark head, "Shush, little one." She spoke to her baby boy in a soothing voice, "Mama is here, shush, do not cry."

The baby gradually calmed down, as Elizabeth carried him around the room in her arms.

Darcy came behind her, "My dear, it was expected to present him during the full moon. The boy is fine."

"You frightened him." She said, and cooed over the boy, "My poor baby."

Darcy glanced at the boy, who squirmed in his mother's arms, his head turning toward the direction of her ample bosom. "I think he is hungry. He always cries when he is hungry."

Elizabeth sat in the stuffed armchair, opened the top of her loose, every day dress, and directed the baby to her breast. The boy started to suckle instantly.

"Please, tell them to go away from here and make sure that all the windows are closed." Elizabeth put her legs on the footrest that Darcy placed near her, "I do not want Annie to get upset with all that noise, or worse catch a cold because of the draft."

Darcy walked out on the balcony again and soon the howling stopped, the pack began to disperse.

He closed the balcony door carefully and drew the curtains.

After the babies had been born, Elizabeth had decided to change the sitting room next to her bedroom, into the nursery for the time being at least till the children when older. Darcy had not opposed the idea, he understood her concern and her need to be close to the children. They were especially concerned about their baby girl, who was still not as strong and animated as her brother. They wanted her near them at night in case anything happened.

He walked to the crib, and smiled at his daughter. She was still much smaller than her brother, but her wide, blue eyes, Elizabeth's eyes, looked at him with intelligence and understanding. This springtime had been unusually cold and windy so they had postponed the Christening till the babies were three months old, and the girl could be safely carried outside to the church.

Lord McGrath and Georgiana had stood as godparents for the twins. After the ceremony in the church a feast had been thrown on the main courtyard for the entire pack. The godparents had carried the babies around so everyone could see them.

Little Thomas, named after his grandfather, Mr. Bennet, had been very active and not at all intimidated. He had not cried, and in his own way interacted with everyone around. His sister, however, Anne, named after Darcy's mother, had not born with the large crowd that well. She had hidden her head shyly into Georgiana's arm, avoiding curious eyes and smiling faces. Soon she had begun to cry, trying to reach out her small hands to her mother, who had instantly taken her back inside the manor.

Darcy leaned over his daughter, and made what he thought to be a funny face. The girl waved her tiny hands and gurgled something.

He gently blew air into her face; the child blinked her eyes, kicked her legs and giggled in joy. He repeated the act several times, his daughter laughing and squeaking, clearly delighted to be entertained by her father.

Darcy sat with his little girl in a chair next to Elizabeth, just when his son finished his nursing. After burping him, Elizabeth put him back into his crib, and Thomas who was probably exhausted after such an eventful day promptly fell asleep.

When she started nursing Annie, Darcy pulled his chair closer to them.

"Do you think she will start to grow some hair one day?" he asked, touching baby's head with a finger.

Elizabeth flashed her eyes at him, "She has hair." She said grudgingly, "Cannot you see?" she blew on the soft down on the baby's head.

Annie's wide eyes looked curiously from her mother to father, both of them staring at the top of her head.

"She is perfect." Darcy took one tiny hand and kissed it, but the baby soon pulled her hand free and laid it against her mother's breast, entirely concentrated on her meal.

The child was nursing steadily, and Darcy dipped his face into his wife's neck, and kissed it.

"I must go."

Elizabeth turned her face to him and they shared a slow kiss. "Go." She stroked his cheek, and gave him a long, warm look, "Do not hesitate to wake me up when you come back."

He kissed her once again, and hastily walked to his room, his hand at his neck cloth, loosening it.

Annie stopped feeding, and Elizabeth was about to put her into the crib, next to her already soundly sleeping brother.

Suddenly a large, black wolf ran into the room and nudged against Elizabeth's skirts.

"Look, Annie, look," Elizabeth knelt down, shifting the baby, so the girl could see the animal, "Papa came to say goodnight to us."

The girl smiled and pulled out her tiny hand, which Darcy gently nudged with his head.

"Say goodnight to Papa, Annie." Elizabeth took her hand and waved it at the retreating wolf.

The End

The blouse, recently white, reminds Frank of the day so long ago when her dog ate Frank's pet rabbit, right on the front porch. The rabbit's name was Buttercup. Frank saw the dog rip Buttercup's head off. Ma threw a white bedsheet over the pet crime scene to hide it from Frank, but the blood seeped through.

While Ma attends to her breast stain, Frank is up apologizing about the broken plate. Frank gets on all fours between the legs of guests and begins sweeping cracked porcelain with her bare hands,

"So sorry about the plate, I'll get this cleaned up..."

One moment Ma is silent in the corner. Then, in an act of magic or witchcraft, she disappears completely. Maybe she has moved into the backyard, or wandered off in the night. Frank doesn't know. She's on the ground sweeping a broken plate with her hands. The host offers Frank a broom.

Frank runs in a loop around the house looking for Ma. She makes a wider loop around the block, calling Ma's name. Ma often disappears on long walks to clear her mind. She ascribes to the philosophy that any problem can be resolved, any sadness dissolved, through walking. She will pace in circles around the backyard mumbling the mantra, "*solvitur ambulando,*" which translates from Latin to "it is solved by walking." Sometimes she leaves for hours at a time, but she's not usually high and stained with blood in a strange town. Frank runs back to her house and checks the car, her room, the bathroom, the porch—no Ma. She runs back to the party—no Ma. She calls Ma's phone one, two, three, four, five, six, seven times in a row, waits a bit, then calls three more times. She sends a series of angry and distraught texts to Ma:

"Where the hell are you?"

"I'm worried about you, answer your phone or come home!"

"What the hell????"

"I didn't mean to make you mad, please come back"

"Please pick up your phone mom"

She runs back to the party, and—wiping snot and tears on her shirtsleeves before entering—asks her friends if they have seen Ma. The host chuckles and asks,

"You lost your mom? Dude, she's hilarious. She's so cool and laid back. My mom would never come to a party with me, let alone get high with my friends."

Frank feels betrayed somehow that her friend doesn't acknowledge Ma's insane behavior. Did Frank imagine it? Is Frank overreacting? Is Ma actually cool? Fun? Is Frank the crazy one? Who is more embarrassing: the druggy, drunk, ebullient mother or the anxious, Type-A, grumpy daughter? Back in her own house, Frank curls up in a fetal position on the floor and cries herself to sleep.

She dreams that she and Ma are walking along an empty urban street at night. Frank has a tiny house strapped to her back—a Victorian dollhouse that she wears like a backpack with leather straps. Ma finds various objects on the curb: a teakettle, a vacuum, an ironing board, a broken chair. She stacks every object she finds on top of Frank's house. Frank follows along with her leaning tower of furniture as Ma rummages through trash cans, dumpsters, and boxes for more objects.

Frank wakes to find Ma kneeling next to her on the rug. She takes Frank's head in her hands, delicately, as though she were holding an ostrich egg or porcelain vase. She moons over Frank with wide, worried eyes:

"What's wrong, sweetie? Why were you on the floor?"

"Where the hell have you been, Mom? Why didn't you answer my phone calls?"

"Oh, no—I turned my phone off while I was on my date, my poor baby! Didn't you remember that I had made a plan to meet with that man from the restaurant? At the party, I realized I was late for my date, so I slipped away. We just got a few drinks and walked around town a bit. You must have been so worried, poor girl. Oh, my poor, sweet baby."

Ma lifts Frank's head into her lap—into the folds of her perfumed black dress—and strokes Frank's hair with painted nails. Frank melts under Ma's fingers. She shrinks smaller and smaller until she is a little girl in Ma's lap, before Ma left Frank's dad for good, before Frank became a sleep-sex-insomniac, before any road trip breakdowns, before boyfriends. Just Ma's hands in her hair and the tickle of Ma's humming diaphragm on Frank's cheek.

*

Ma leaves me alone in Iowa. I feel off, unhinged. When I feel it the most, I call Mom, but then just as quickly, I hang up and leave a pretend message to myself. I write emails to Mom—long, elaborate, articulate emails about my depression and my physical ailments and my loneliness. Then I delete the emails and write in their place little pithy quotes and puns. I write my own private stories and doodle horses and rabbits in the margins. Something about the project grounds me.

*

Winter settles in gradually, like an incipient mold creeping into the beams of Frank's inner house. Whatever foundation she has worked to build within herself—for safety, comfort, structure—it now sags. Her shelter is limp, wet, full of holes. It smells. Rain slips in and drips into Frank's nostrils while she sleeps. She wakes in a muddle of her own juices, her own sweat mixed with the slush of Iowa City. Her shelter has seen too many storms and floods. Frank is exhausted. She is depressed. She is self-destructive, deconstructive. She keeps this destruction hidden. She is falling apart in secret.

One day in early December, when the grey of an afternoon storm blends seamlessly into the grey of dawn and dusk, I call Mom seven times in a row. My sadness feels urgent now. If Mom picks up this time, I'll confess. I walk in loops around my block with the phone plastered to my cheek beneath the wet flap of my rain jacket hood. I circle my apartment, then expand the circle to include the nearby baseball diamond, then the handful of church courtyards, then the cemetery, then the park on the edge of town. Mom must be busy teaching. Or maybe she's on a date. Maybe she's fucking some new Tinder dude, a carpenter with a mustache and smelly toes, or a taxi driver with a potbelly, or a bartender with a law degree and three children. Every time Mom's voicemail beeps, I hang up. In the spaces between calls, I leave secret messages to nobody. I remember a passage that Mom once copied in a letter to me from one of our favorite books, *Oranges are Not the Only Fruit,* by Jeanette Winterson, which describes this moment perfectly, "It is not the one thing nor the other that leads to madness, but the spaces in between them." The spaces between my failed phone call attempts drive me into a tooth-grinding panic. I hope that there are no neighbors hiding in the bushes, listening to my audible sorrows. I hope that nobody is taking notes.

"Hi Mom. I've been meaning to tell you that I'm depressed, thought you should know."

"Mom. What would you say if I told you I'm dropping out of grad school?"

"Mom. Pick up your goddamned phone. I'm finally ready to talk to you about real shit."

"Where the fuck are you when I need you, Mom? Your baby daughter is calling."

"I'm really in bad shape. Pissed off. I'm seriously considering dropping out of grad school. I know, I know—I won't do it, I'd feel like I had wasted so much time only half-assing it, but I can't do it. I've thought a few times about how similar a writer's retreat is to a mental ward. I've considered checking myself into a loony bin, just to have some rest, and to separate myself from the madness of all of this."

"I feel sick. I may have broken a rib coughing. I think my body is aging at twice the rate it should. I look and feel like an old woman. My face is full of wrinkles. Maybe that's why everyone thinks I'm older than I really am—I just look old. My joints hurt. Most of all, I'm fatigued. My lymph nodes are swollen. Nobody wants to fuck me."

"I think I'm becoming an alcoholic. I've been sucked into the never-ending vortex of drinking nightly in dive bars here in Iowa, like all the other washed up, depressed poets. We all go out just to get warm and feel the false hope of intimacy, but it makes us feel more hollow. And, of course, there are the hangovers, and the guilt, and showing up late to seminars."

"I drink too much coffee. It makes me super anxious but I crave it and it comforts me, until it makes me anxious all over again, and I run around town like a rabid racoon."

"I think I'm manic depressive, just like you."

"Anyway, I'm ready to throw in the towel. I'm exhausted and need a fucking break. I kind of just want to run away and check into a cheap motel and watch movies for a month. Or maybe I'll fly to India to go backpacking in the Himalayas, where I'll probably pick up another fucking parasite and die alone."

"Mom. I feel like I'm a virus stuck in the throat of the Midwest. I need to get out of here."

When Mom calls back a few hours later, I don't feel like picking up. I'm exhausted by the prospect of repeating myself. I'm not ready to confess how low I have fallen. Mom leaves a few messages that I ignore. She sends little urgent, worried texts like "you ok?" and "call back, I'm here!" but I turn off my phone so that I can take a nap. I'm afraid to talk. I make a cup of tea that I don't bother to drink. I gather a massive armful of blankets from my closet and curl up in a nest on the couch.

I dream that Mom and I live in an old, colonial plantation mansion in the Louisiana bayou. It's just the two of us, alone in a house surrounded by swampland and gators. The house is so big it's hard to heat, and we wander through dark, cold rooms in silk nightgowns. Mom calls out to me from one end of the house, and her voice echoes around the spiral staircase to where I sit on a chaise lounge reading outdated periodicals. She sings, "Why don't we take a bubble bath to warm up?" In the bathroom, there is a clawfoot tub which could fit a hippopotamus or two. Mom fills the tub with salts, soaps, foams, and loofahs as though she were a witch tossing ingredients into a voodoo porridge. We climb in at opposite ends, and our bodies soon disappear under the cover of bubbles, all the way to our noses. During our bath, the lights flicker out and a hurricane tears the roof off. Balls of hail—white and large as human skulls—smash through the windows. Wind and sideways sleet flatten the structure of the house, and the tub is swept up by a black wave. We float in our tilting clawfoot ship on floodwaters that carry us to the sea.

I wake from my dream sweating in my nest of wool quilts. I brew a cup of coffee and stir up some motivation to grade my students' final essays. When I open my laptop, I find a tome of an email from Mom with the subject line, "ARE YOU ALIVE?"

Frances, I hope that you're ok, you called so many times yesterday while I was teaching and then you didn't pick up. Did you get into an accident? Did you crash your bike? I'm so worried about you, you get hurt so easily, and catch all the colds and flus, my poor baby. Call when you have a chance. Promise me that you are taking care of yourself. I would be devastated if you were to get hurt.

Not to put too much pressure on you at a time like this, I know you're in the midst of wrapping up your semester, but I'd love for you to come visit for Thanksgiving. I feel like I haven't had you girls for the holidays in a while—you always go to your Dad's. I am learning patience. I am learning to enjoy my own company and the friendships I have here in Vermont. But I miss my baby! Why don't you fly to Vermont for the break? You can escape Iowa City for a little while. We'll snuggle on the couch without a care in the world. Let me know. I love you, hope you're alive and well and not in the hospital or in a coma!

Love,
Mom

*

My apartment feels cold no matter how high I crank the heat, nor how many socks I layer on my feet or scarves I wrap around my head like wool turbans. Maybe I am cold-blooded. I need a warm rock in Arizona or some perpetually sunny, hot landscape on which to lay my tired, reptile body. I can't seem to rid the house of shadows, even when I assemble a personal army of lamps around my desk—the arsenal of buzzing filaments brings more distraction than comfort and illumination. One of the lamps is a SAD lamp that Mom sent in the mail, for sufferers of seasonal affective disorder, another item for me to add to my ever-growing list of diagnoses. I'm not the only sane one in the family, as Mom suggested in my teenage years. Instead, I belong to a lineage of crazies. I call Mom. Without even saying hello, I blurt,

"Sure, why not. I'll come to Vermont."

"YIPEE! I get to spend Thanksgiving with my baby!"

There is a long pause during which Mom prances along the sidewalk and I stir a dust bunny around with my foot.

"Also, just so you know, I think I've inherited your manic-depressiveness."

Mom's already primed for good news so she takes this statement with cheer.

"Oh, sweetie—well, you're in good company! The whole family is depressed. Do you need a prescription for antidepressants? I can fax mine over."

"Whatever. I'll just come to Vermont in November, and we can figure it out there."

I hang up without saying goodbye and slouch over my notebook at the little, crowded desk in my room. I write,

> Frank is like Ma after all, a shapeshifter. She transforms into a small, shivering rabbit, a dust bunny, wanting nothing more than to hide in a bush or to be held in Ma's lap. She has lint for ears, toenail clippings for teeth, and a hairball belly. She cowers in the shadows under the couch and nips at the feet of passersby. As a bunny, she doesn't have to worry about writing a thesis, or filing taxes, or getting tested for STDs. Now Ma and Frank have truly merged: both ill-in-the-head, shapeshifting rabbit and pony. Family at last. Unpredictable, feral creatures, trying to survive in civil settings. Scratching and clawing at their bunny cages, their horse stalls. Choking on pellets and hay.
>
> Frank dives back into the swamp only one month to go till Thanksgiving. Only one wibbly-wobbly melancholy month. Frank eats all the chocolate in the

house and the bread too, then drinks only bone broth for a week. She dances on every living room dance floor she can get her feet on. Drinks too much. Sleeps too much, then not enough. Sometimes she gets lonely, and sometimes she gets overwhelmed by having too many friends. Mysterious bruises appear in strange places on her body. She's always itchy, but she can't find the source. She catches all the colds and her butt hurts from sitting too long in one spot with papers to grade, books to write. Ma is witness to all of these ups-and-downs because Frank calls her every day, sometimes twice a day. They console each other in their mutual solitude. Frank's glad to have another sick friend who gets it— who understands what it feels like to be crazy. Sick. Wobbly.

The last thing I do before flying to Vermont is fill my first prescription for antidepressants, on Mom's urging. Pill poppers together, mother and daughter. Is this the beginning of the end? This is all I can think about on the plane. I can no longer deny it: I've inherited my mother's manic depression.

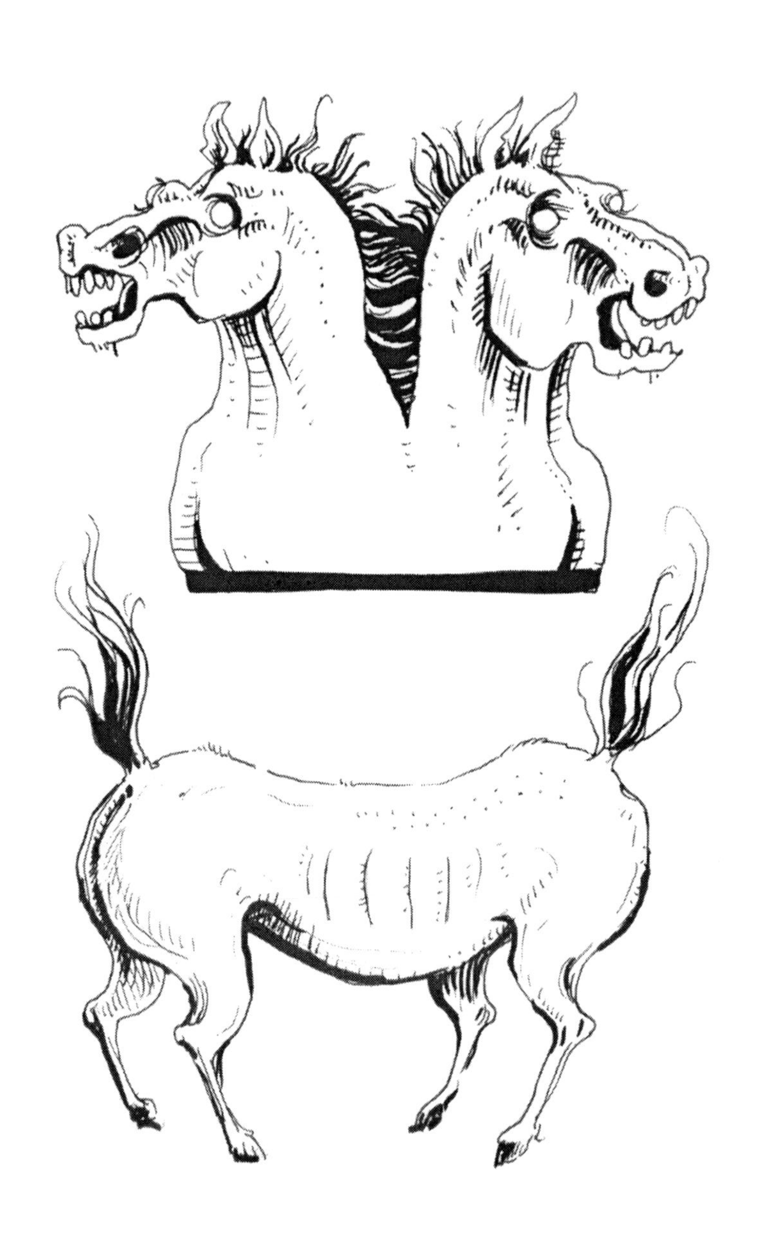

*

Frank wakes in Ma's bed in Vermont. Ma sits on the edge, stroking Frank's hair, a glazed and clownish grin on her morning face. Ma asks, "How are you doing, sweetie?" Frank stiffens and turns away, "Fine, fine." There are new conversational taboos—touchy subjects that may trigger a meltdown—either her own or Ma's.

Eliza, her boyfriend, and another friend join the feast, but Ma insists on cooking everything. The turkey, the pies. "You girls can make a vegetable side dish or something." After Ma pops the turkey into the oven, she lets loose and indulges in a few eyedropperfuls of pot tincture. She also serves herself several glasses of champagne and a few glasses of wine as they wait for the bird to brown. As everyone else sips their *first* glasses of champagne, Frank observes Ma sneak a few extra pours from the bottle. While Frank dresses the salad, Ma takes a sip from Frank's glass.

"Mom, that's mine."

Ma giggles, "Oops!"

Smoke begins to spill out through cracks in the oven. It fills the kitchen and wraps around the ceiling lamp like a ghost's shawl. Ma shouts to nobody in particular and runs around the house opening all the windows. She opens the oven repeatedly to examine the burning bird and laments her ruined rolls, the ruined turkey. She howls that she has "*ruined Thanksgiving!*" Everyone sings back in a cheerful but insistent chorus,

"No, no, no, you haven't! You're wonderful! Take a seat, chill out, relax, everything is lovely."

Ma plops down at the head of the table to more properly indulge in her sobs. With tissues flying, she reaches for the bottle of wine to pour herself another glass of wine. Frank—as quietly as she can—whispers, "Mom, don't you think you should slow down a bit on the wine?"

This breaks Ma. Her face reflects the tragic masks of Greek theater, singing of betrayal. Thanksgiving is over. She retires upstairs to her bedroom to whimper alone while the girls scrape blackened skin from the turkey to salvage what meat they can. Eliza's boyfriend reclines on the couch with a pillow over his head, as though he can block out the noise of these crazy women with a little cloth.

That night Frank sleeps with Ma in Ma's bed. Ma tries to snuggle with Frank but Frank rolls to the edge. Ma tries to caress Frank's foot with her own snaggly, calloused toes—she never trims her toenails—and Frank retracts her feet. She's trying to teach Ma a lesson: if Ma drinks too much and falls off her rocker and burns the turkey and throws a tantrum, she doesn't get to snuggle her toes on Frank. Frank is fragile enough these days. Eventually Frank falls asleep and dreams that Ma has organized a mutiny on a cruise ship overseas somewhere: France, Norway, Greenland.

The next day Ma throws bits and pieces of the meat into a cast iron pan with a few eggs and calls it brunch. Eliza and her beau and friend return to their respective apartments and jobs, leaving Ma and Frank alone together to clean up the residue of the "party."

Ma is upbeat. Maybe she's trying to make up for the fiasco of the night before.

"What do you feel like doing tonight? Anything. Anything you want. Want to get dressed up and go out on the town? I'll take you out to dinner if you want, or we could go dancing. I'll buy you a drink, my treat. What do you think? You flew all the way out here to visit, it's the least I can do."

Frank shrugs and suggests they take a walk. They hike around dirt roads past a dilapidated barn, a handful of donkeys, and a maple sugar bush. Frank begins to cry, silently, and can't stop. She's still crying when they loop back to Ma's doorstep.

Ma notices Frank's silent tears and asks, "Can I draw you a bath?"

Frank nods, snotting.

"Can I boil you some cinnamon milk?"

Frank nods, sniffling.

"Can I sing you a lullaby, and tuck you in for a nap, and read you a story, and give you a shoulder massage?"

Frank nods and begins to strip her clothing off, one item at a time, dropping a sock here, a sock there, as she slinks towards the tub. Ma brews a steaming bath of lavender salts. She leaves and returns with a mug of sweet milk, just like she used to do when Frank was little and couldn't sleep. She mops Frank's forehead with a warm facecloth and hums old Welsh lullabies. Frank becomes a blob in the tub. She watches her white limbs rise and fall in and out of a film of soap foam. When the water grows tepid, she steps from the tub as Ma offers her a fresh towel. Ma wraps her up, "like a burrito, just like when you were a baby," tucks her under the covers and sits on the edge of the bed. "Want to talk about anything?"

Frank scowls without opening her eyes.

"Want me to leave you alone?"

Frank shakes her head and burrows her wet hair into Ma's lap. She wants to be small again, before language, prescriptions, rent, before bills, responsibilities. Ma lies down around Frank, curled around her daughter like the hull around a seed, stroking Frank's temples until she falls asleep.

*

I return to Iowa. Only one semester left to finish my degree. Here, I fall into a dull routine. Wake, drink too much coffee, try to write something intelligible, scramble to prepare for class, show up late, pay tribute to the dark hole of my windowless office, celebrate my minimal efforts with some obscenely unhealthy dinner, drink too much beer, curl up for a night of psychologically disturbing dreams about a lover or my mother or both, and repeat.

Within this routine, I often walk the same loop through a neighborhood park in Iowa City to take a break from grading papers. Today I linger on a hilltop, watching a mother deer and her fawn trace the edge of the woods. They're keeping an eye on me, but they remain in sight even as I inch closer and take a seat in the grass. I used to sit with Mom and James on our deck in Montana, watching a similar mother and daughter—doe and fawn—munch on apples that we tossed for their breakfast.

Many years into living with James as my stepfather, I finally started to take a real interest in his spirituality and to invest myself in a more serious way in his culture, language, traditions, and philosophy. As soon as I learned about his affair, my idealization of this holy man deflated. I became protective of my mother. My concept of James fractured into irreconcilable parts: James as a human with his bundle of flaws and secrets; James as the image he perpetuated of a medicine man and as a dignitary of his culture; James as the person capable of wrecking my mother. I hadn't spoken to him since the divorce two years ago, but something about the sight of the deer moves me to call him.

He answers a little too cheerfully, practically shouting into the phone. We toss around a bit of trivial small talk, weather and health, then dip into more interesting subjects of our work: he's an artist and is working on illustrating his own children's book. I'm spending more time doodling than writing my thesis. We try to make light of the country's political quagmire and looming apocalypse, and we connect over books that we're reading. By coincidence, I happen to be teaching a book by one of his favorite Native authors, a book which has a permanent home on his bedside table. I do miss him—we have a great rapport, always have, and a bit of the original flavor of the fourteen years of our friendship seeps into our conversation. There's a barrier, though, and after an hour of chatter, I cut him off,

"Real talk, James. We haven't spoken since the divorce, and... "

I choke on the sentence and can't finish. There's a long pause, and I can hear car engines passing by on his end—I picture him on a bench in Red Lodge, Montana, where he moved after Mom sold the cabin. Now he's crying; I can tell from the uneven quality of his breath, and I can't help but follow suit. He tells me he's sorry, over and over again, in a half whisper. I ask him how he could hurt my mother so heartlessly. I tell him his actions put a stain on my trust in men, a stain on my trust in all my lovers, and may have ruined my ability to engage in a healthy relationship. I ask him, point blank:

"You left Mom for a younger woman and lied to me about it. Why?"

There's another pause. I watch the deer family disappear into the woods, and I lie back in the meadow, spiders be damned, mud be damned. James finally speaks,

"Because I'm weak. I fucked up."

"Is it anything Mom did? Did she do something wrong? Did you just fall out of love with her? Is it because she's bipolar?"

As soon as I've spit out this last question, I regret it—I don't want to know the answer. I want to hurl my phone into the trees. Instead, I keep it plastered to my sweaty cheek. I feel as though I'm interrogating James on behalf of my mother's well-being, acting as her page or knight. I am Frank the Defender. I am the Achilles of Relational Reparation. Below my armor, though, I am a soft, vulnerable body by association with my mother. If James responds against her, he will be attacking me. She and I are of one flesh, and I've never felt more aligned with her in the James-Mom-Frances triangle. Am I hyperventilating? Is that the sound of my breathing, or James's?

"You and I both know that your mother isn't easy to live with."

"So it's her fault."

"No, no—that's not what I mean and you know it. It just—it was hard. Exhausting. I'm not strong enough to help her. She's not like you—she can be irrational, and very needy. I just wasn't capable."

This is no comfort to me. What I don't tell him is that I *am* like my mother— I *am* irrational, I *am* needy, and I *am* difficult. In his accusation of her difficulty in the relationship, I hear a critique of my own behavior, and, instantly, I am calculating what that might mean in my own relationships. If I finally find a long-term companion, will my mood swings grate slowly away at their patience? Will my mental illness and insecurity prevent me from sustaining a long-term relationship? Will I end up alone at my mother's age? Will I, like her, obsessively check my online dating profile?

We speak for another hour, accusing, apologizing, crying, and in doing so we harvest some of our old love. By making himself tender and claiming his mistakes, he returns to me an ounce of my former trust, and I offer him the tentative companionship of a long-distance, part-time, ex-step-daughter who still cares for her old man, as long as he never lies again and treats my mom with respect. I'm afraid to tell him that I may be bipolar, just like Mom. We're *both* hard to live with.

After we hang up, I fall asleep in the grass, exhausted by the effort of mending. I wake to the sound of the mother and daughter deer duo chewing weeds near my head.

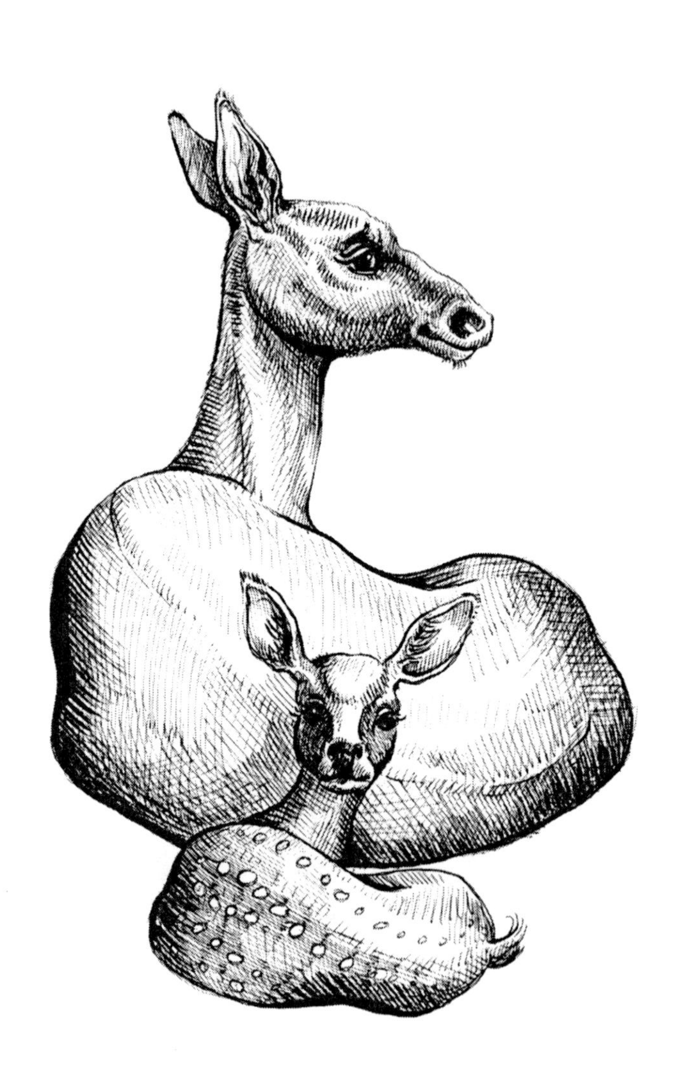

*

As with so many of my intellectual pursuits, my research begins with my mother. I call her on my way to the library, and I offer her only a half-hearted confession about the subject of my investigation:

"Mom, do you know any good books about symbology, ancient folklore, or the shapeshifter or trickster motif?"

"Sure, dozens. Sounds like a fun project, what are you writing?"

"The book about us. I mentioned it awhile ago. You're a horse, remember?"

"Oh. Right. I'd love to read it! Can you send me a draft?"

"When it's done."

She happens to be in her office in Vermont, and she rambles off a list of books from her own shelf, a handful of trusted anthropologists and literary theorists: Judith Butler, Joseph Campbell, Donald Kalsched, and once again, Carl Jung. At the end of our conversation, Mom catches me off guard by asking,

"Why am I a horse, in your book?"

I give her the only answer I have: I'm not sure. That's why I'm gathering research. Perhaps she's a horse so that I can have something more interesting to draw than my own mother's face when I illustrate the book. Or maybe it's because she's always been obsessed with horses, since her days as a cowgirl growing up on a ranch in Utah. Maybe she isn't human to me, more of a super creature, a magic being. I have an inkling that the our relationship is just too complicated and difficult to confront head-on. I'm taking a circuitous path, pursuing a tangential route. I'm dissociating; it's easier this way.

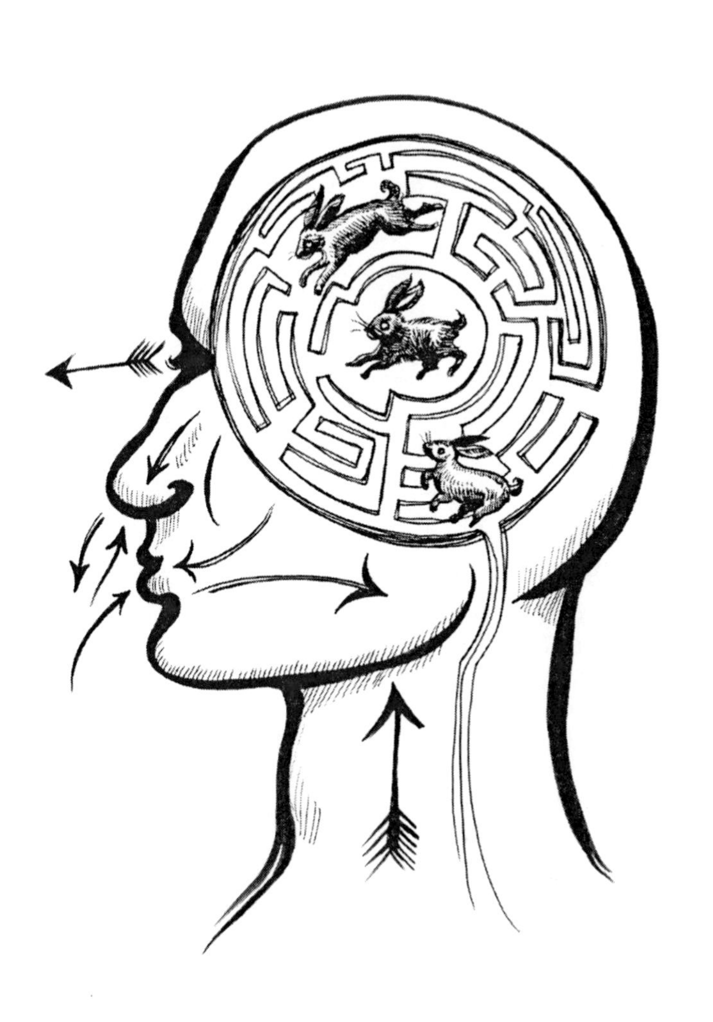

In the library, I situate myself at a table far removed from the hub of library activity, and dig into my pile of books, one by one. I scribble pages of notes, grinning furiously at the treasure trove of information which I have stumbled upon. An hour or two into my study, Mom calls. I whisper with my hands cupped around the phone as I hurry outside, my notebook tucked in my armpit.

"Mom, I figured out why you're a horse. Why we're shapeshifters in my book."

Now I'm off, strolling down the pedestrian mall with my notebook opened to a page of scribbles. I read little bits and pieces to Mom, and I loop in a circle around the block once, twice, thrice—I lose track.

"Did you know that Carl Jung's primary research began with bipolar disorder? He called this a 'mixed mood state', which stems from ego dysfunction. He associated this state of oscillation between mania and depression with the archetypes of *puer* and *senex*. Have you heard of these?"

"Sounds like a type of tea or medicine."

"Sure. Anyway, *senex* is cold, slow, like mud, or leftover porridge. Melancholy. Depression. *Puer* is the wildfire of the psyche: hot, capricious, unpredictable, youthful, energetic..."

I'm practically skipping down the street. A mother with a baby stroller sees me coming like a fireball down the walk, and she swerves out of my way.

"We can consciously strike a balance between these opposites. Through myth-making and symbol analysis, we can form a union between manic and depressive, sensual and spiritual. An equilibrium."

"This all reminds me of Joseph Campbell and the power of myth to transcend pain and trauma. Did you read any of his work?"

"Of course! What do you think I've been doing all afternoon? Yes. Yes. The imagination. If we actively process our psychic split through art and writing, we can achieve equilibrium, and heal ourselves!"

Mom agrees heartily, then steers the conversation towards her love life, and I take a seat on a nearby bench. I pretend to listen to her story about a Grateful Dead concert with Harold-something-or-other, some new boyfriend, while I process my own thoughts. I think I've found it—the reason why we shapeshift in my story. I write,

To name the symptoms is to acknowledge them and take steps towards healing. Symbols give shape to the unknown. By mythologizing my relationship with my mother, and by turning her into a shapeshifting trickster, I admit to myself her dual nature. I can more clearly see the effects of her manic-depressive behaviors when I outline them and sketch them in my notebooks. And similarly, as I write myself into my own story as a shapeshifter, I can define the disparate aspects of my character: young, old, fragile, strong. I'm reaching deep into the cave, extracting the shadow figures from my unconscious, and examining them in the full light of day. Unless I give symbolic shape to these shadows, they will remain stuck in the dark caverns of myself. I'm recreating myself from my fractured parts. I'm reconstructing my psyche where it has split. I'm writing myself back to stability. Jung calls this the "transcendent function," in which the individual actively engages with his or her unconscious archetypes to transcend their neurosis and unlock the shadows stuck within the psyche. I am transforming my life through the process of making art.

MYTHICAL DEVIANTS

Frank is an unconventional hero. She is a millennial artist, distracted by twitter, fearful of the looming environmental apocalypse, and gearing up for political revolution. She follows a more complicated trajectory than the narratives described by those forefathers of myth and psyche: Freud, Jung, and Campbell. She does not trot the linear path of conflict, tension, resolution, nor does she blossom ever forward towards success. Her path is more circuitous— an infinite loop of exploration and confusion. She is not the darling of a heteronormative patriarchal literary structure. Yes, Frank is the hero, but so is her mother. Yes, Frank is on a journey to battle her shadow demons, but she also craves her own interior darkness, and relishes her own fucked-up-ed-ness. She is fascinated by illness. And Ma is more than the mother archetype of Frank's heroic journey, Ma is also the hero. They are both tricksters, both mothers, both children. They cannot decide whether to progress forward into battle, to confront the shadows and obstacles ahead, or to retreat into the warm and gooey egg-womb from which they spilled.

*

After three impossibly long winters in the Midwest, after finally completing my master's degree in Iowa, I move in with Mom in Vermont. On paper, I appear to be regressing—I leave the nest to pursue a professional path only to return to live in my mother's house in my late twenties—but it feels right, comfortable, even thrilling. For now, I'm sleeping in her bed, and I've thrown all of my belongings—clothes, books, art supplies—into a clawfoot tub that sits in the corner of her room.

We get along just fine, and we follow pretty similar schedules; she commutes to teach full-time at Northern Vermont University, and I'm working at an art gallery while I apply to teaching jobs. We balance our mutual guilty pleasures for chocolate and beer with a shared passion for cross-country skiing and hiking. We're both still single-ish, testing the waters of polyamory. I tease her for being a sex addict and she teased me right back for being a love-addict. It's never really that funny to either of us, but we have to laugh to keep from crying.

Living in Mom's bedroom is only awkward when we have to negotiate who gets to bring a date home. Since we're both out on the prowl, casually juggling lovers, there is no predictable sleeping schedule to tack onto the fridge, such as "Mom gets bed Tuesday-Friday, Frank gets bed Sunday-Monday." Instead, we communicate with as much fair warning as we can while on our dates, with text messages like "going well, might take him home, do you have a place to sleep tonight?" We also buy an extra set of bedding so that we can more frequently rotate the sheets between "shifts."

*

One afternoon I pass by the only sex shop in Burlington. I've never stepped inside, and I pop in out of curiosity. I'm thoroughly disappointed to find that the shop is tucked in the basement of the mall and is stocked primarily with gaudy "heteronormie" junk. I ask the cashier if she has "anything for alternative couples?" Perhaps she misunderstands and thinks I mean "hippie" couples, because she leads me to the very meager shelf of organic lube. "It's biodegradable!" she chirps. While I'm examining the double-sided dildos, Mom calls to invite me on a hike up Camel's Hump mountain, and I hop up the stairs to escape this sticky dungeon, panting,

"Mom, do you know anything about sex toys?"

"What? I can't hear you, you sound out of breath."

"Yeah, sorry, I was in the sex shop."

"Oh, you did say sex toys, I thought I had misheard. What do you want to know?

"Nevermind, I'll ask you in person. Want to pick me up downtown in an hour?"

Something about the landscape outside of town dissolves my interest in sex advice, and Mom and I chat instead about the future of my career. We strategize which schools I should attack with my CV, daydreaming about nonexistent tenure-track positions. Back in her garden we light a bonfire and read each other's Tarot. I draw myself a bubble bath, and she sits on the edge of the tub reading from a book of Mary Oliver poems. We cuddle up together in her massive brass bed, floating on an extravagant pile of pillows.

I always sleep later into the morning than usual at Mom's house. Perhaps the bed's too comfortable. Perhaps *I* am too comfortable, floating in the odd womb of Mom's care. I wake late enough in the day that Mom's roommates have already shuffled off to work. The birds have already spilled out their morning songs, and the midsummer heat has pooled in my armpits. Mom sits on the edge of the bed and rouses me with a hand on my shoulder,

"Time for breakfast! I've put out a few items for you to choose from. There's granola and fruit, or if you want an egg I have toast and greens, and I've left you some coffee in the French press..."

She disappears down the stairs I drift after her like a delayed shadow into the kitchen.

Mom has set the breakfast table for me—and in front of an array of foodstuffs and orange juice, there is a small gift bag. I raise my eyebrows at Mom, and she shrugs,

"I didn't buy any of the items, a friend gave them to me, but I thought you might find them more useful. I'm too old-fashioned, too vanilla."

I reach into the bag and pull out a string of pink plastic beads. Mom knows I don't wear much jewelry, particularly not pink necklaces. Mom giggles, watching me. I reach in again and pull out a strange little wired device—a sort of remote control, with a rubber ball attached by a wire. I empty the bag out onto the table next to my breakfast plate and am horrified to realize that Mom has given me a collection of sex toys. A purple dildo with an extra finger-sized lump on one side, a set of palm-sized metal balls, and a small bottle of shimmering lube. I drop everything as soon as I realize what I've been handling.

"MOM!"

"I told you, I didn't buy them, a friend gave them to me for my fiftieth birthday and I have no idea what to do with them! I thought, after you asked me yesterday about sex toys, that you would enjoy them more than me. Can't teach an old dog new tricks and all that."

"Who gave these to you?"

Mom blushes and shuffles over to the counter to grind more coffee.

"Doesn't matter."

"Who?"

"My sex-lab partner."

"Ew! You didn't *use* these, did you? Jesus Christ!"

"Of course I didn't, I wouldn't give you *used* sex toys, I'm not that weird. Calm down, I thought you would be grateful, I take it back, forget it."

She shoves the toys back into the bag and throws the bag to the floor on the other side of the counter, as though by hiding it from my sight she could also erase my memory of their existence. Once you've seen and held anal beads, you can't wipe the vision clean. I think Mom has dissolved my curiosity about props for a time. She busies herself around the kitchen, wiping crumbs from the stove.

"So, do you want me to make you a fried egg?"

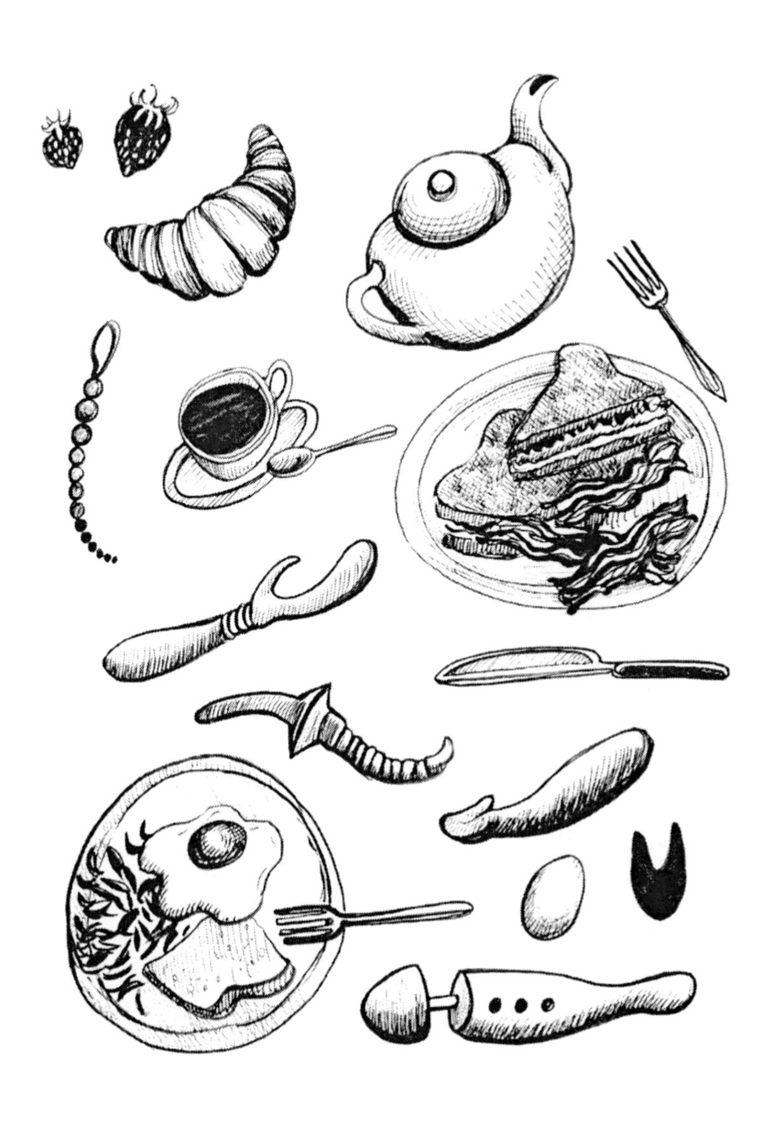

*

I spend many a morning up in my art studio—a shared space on the second floor of the downtown gallery where I work—cross-hatching the shadows of a drawing of a horse. Or, rather, it is my mother mid-metamorphosis, trapped between human and equine forms. Just as I trace my pen around her bulging eyes, my phone buzzes in my pocket: it's Mom. She wants to meet me for a treat. I stack my drawings in the corner with my stories about Mom, hidden under a book in case she comes snooping around the studio. She hasn't read anything yet, nor has she seen her skeletal, drooling likeness with horse-face.

We meet at my favorite cafe, where she and I often split an almond croissant. Mostly I just need coffee, and she's buying, but we treat it like a date. I cherish these little dates with Mom—they feel secretive and indulgent. There are certain things about my life that I don't want to talk about with anyone else: my sex life, my romantic pursuits, my anxieties, my insecurities, my depression.

The baristas recognize my mother as their only regular customer who drowns her coffee in cream, and as we walk in today they holler, "Check the dairy reserves, she's back!" I order a pourover, black. We sidle in next to one another at the window seat, and in a confessional tremor Mom tells me that this morning her other roommate suggested a sex intervention. Too much sex with too many strangers. I glance down as Mom adds another spoonful of sugar, and a slurp of milk, and yet another spoon, and another slurp. Something about these gluttonous spoonfuls remind me, once again, of our pet horse of yore, Mochachica—that violent, unbridled horse who ate herself to death on sweet alfalfa.

I agree with Mom's roommate, but I can sense Mom is in a sensitive mood—her zig-zagging intonation, the way her volume fades at the end of each sentence—so I hold my tongue. I refrain from asking how many men she's brought home in the last month and suggest instead that she shift her dating pool away from online platforms and toward more natural venues for meeting companions like hiking trails, restaurants, acoustic concerts, the grocery store. Halfway through my rant, she interrupts by pulling her phone out and scrolling her text messages.

"Mom! I'm talking to you."

"Sorry sweetie, I have to run, I'm late for lunch."

"Lunch with whom? Is this a date? Are you cutting your daughter date short for someone you met on Tinder? Which one is this, Steve? Paul? Joe? Fred? Kevin?"

"Don't be so mean. I had a disappointing breakfast with someone who lied on his profile so I'm meeting with one of my regulars."

"One of your regulars? Did you start an escort business or something? Wait—you went on a date *this morning?* I'm glad you could fit me into your busy schedule."

"Don't make fun of me, but I also have a dinner date tonight, with my sex-lab partner."

"Sex-lab? What...maybe I don't want to know. Too much information, Mom. I just hope you're being safe. When were you last checked out? And have all of these men been tested? Do they have sex health resumes or something?"

"We use condoms."

"MOM! That's only half of it! Think about it: if you're going on three dates in one day, how many dates are each of these men going on, and how many dates have their dates been on? One bad apple..."

This feeds into my perpetual half-sardonic, half-serious diagnosis of Mom as a sex addict. I have given up trying to prevent any disaster in her personal life because I see that my efforts are futile and that I might as well cheer her on instead and join her team. I have shifted, therefore, from attacking to teasing her habits. She concedes that perhaps her sexual life is more active than most, but that if she's a sex addict, I'm a love addict. She calls me a "heartbreaker," and I retort, "bedbreaker." I'm more prone to collecting emotional infatuations, while Mom collects physical intimacies. I'm just as much of a juggler, but I'll usually just make dinner for my crushes, kiss them on the cheek, and send them home. Mostly. Sometimes, though, I tease Mom to deflect being examined myself. She loves to analyze me—psychologically, socially, physically. I fear that I'm following in her footsteps; we both have addictive personalities, and though I pride myself on being the more rational and restrained character in our duet, too often our overlaps offer me a view of myself in the future. I am my mother, albeit with smaller breasts, more tattoos, shorter hair, and women at my hip instead of men.

What I don't mention to Mom in the cafe is that I *also* have a date this afternoon. Someone I met at a cocktail party—a nurse, or a pharmacist, or an engineer, or some other profession alien to my experience. I'm not too enthused but I have to indulge my curiosity. My date suggests that we meet for a drink at a new brewery downtown.

We soon find that we have nothing in common. After a few awkward drinks, on our way out of the brewery, I spot Mom crossing the street. I know exactly where she's headed: the yuppie wine bar on the corner, where she takes all of her first dates. Part of me wants to avoid catching her attention—if she sees me on a date the teasing will never stop. Or maybe she'll be angry. She'll whine something along the lines of "practice what you preach" or "get off your high horse." I'm a bit buzzed from the second beer that my date insisted on buying me, so I whisper to my date through a giggle, "That's my Mom." My date is shocked at how young my mother looks.

"That can't be your Mom, she's too hot. I'm kidding, but she could definitely be your sister."

"Everyone says that."

Am I bragging about my mother? Or jealous of my her easy good looks? Am I embarrassed that we're tracing and retracing one another's footsteps? I steer my date around the corner. We exchange awkward goodbyes, and as soon as she disappears into the crowd, I call my long-distance lover, Jack. My unsuccessful date made me feel more lonely than loved, and I know that Jack—a trans male, barista, farmer, poet, activist—will return to me a sense of connection. We've been in a passionate open relationship for almost a year. We talk for an hour, processing our longing for one another, planning tentative visits, and daydreaming about buying an airstream trailer in which to travel around the country. During our conversation I make my way towards Molly's house for a dinner date.

Molly is sweet and timid. Apparently I'm the first girl she's kissed. She works on a farm and wears her overalls all over town. She plays the cello, an instrument that to me is like a drug, or a siren's call—I'm under the spell of that deep, human moan.

While Molly pulls a roasted chicken out of the oven, Mom texts me that I should find another place to sleep for the night, "wink wink." Here I've found myself in a pickle: I can't presume to stay the night at Molly's—we just recently met, she has a sensitive temperament, and I don't think we've achieved that level of intimacy in our interaction. So I send one of my more significant flings, Sally, a flirtatious text, hoping that perhaps she'll invite me to stay at her house. Sally responds and invites me over for a digestif, which I know will turn into a sleepover. Meanwhile, Molly is oblivious. Though I've told her that I'm poly, I'm a bit ashamed to reveal my promiscuous love life in its entirety to anyone except my mother. Not yet.

Molly and I finish dinner early since she has to work at six the next morning on a vegetable and berry farm. We swoon and cuddle under the moonlight on the sidewalk, I kiss her goodnight, and I make my way to Sally's.

Some guttural magnet draws me a block out of my way towards Olivia's house. As I follow my feet toward yet another lover, I fear that I have inherited Mom's excessive love habits. So many lovers in so little time. It's not about the sex, it's something different—a restlessness or a quest for home in a companion. I'm caught between dissatisfaction and insecurity. I don't feel particularly comfortable nor enthusiastic about any of them, yet I crave their attention. I want them to obsess over me and write me love letters to affirm my sense of worth.

Olivia is a confident woman a few years my senior—a queer, feminist, bicycle activist who teaches pottery and figure drawing in the art school across from my studio. She happens to be lounging on her porch in a silk kimono as I pass by. She puts down her book—*The Heart of Tantric Sex*—and asks me to join her for a cup of tea. I wasn't planning on lingering, but she insists, "Let me give you a little shoulder massage. Just stay for a bit." I nod, and drift inside after her like a pup on a leash.

Maybe Mom and I are both falling into the same dangerous trap. I preach to Mom about open communication and polyamory while condemning her loose sexuality as dangerous. I like to pretend that my approach is more alternative, healthy, sane, modern. In truth, we're both insecure and afraid of ending up alone. We crave attention and it feels safer for both of us to form a web of multiple lovers in order to weave safety nets for ourselves. If one lover falls away, we'll have a backup lover, or two, or three.

While Olivia brews the tea, I remember that I've forgotten my toothbrush, pajamas, and journal at Mom's. Of course, I could do without, but there is something symbolic and comforting about these items—they give me a sense of home wherever I lay my head, as my physical home shifts too often to keep track of. I can't sit still while Olivia tries to massage my shoulders. I'm agitated not knowing where I'm going to sleep, and it makes me all the more uncomfortable without my little talismans by my side. Maybe I don't want to spend the night at any of my lover's houses—I just want to go home. I'm flooded with social and romantic fatigue. The one bed I can't sleep in tonight is my own. I thank Olivia for the tea, wish her a good night, and decide to drop by Mom's briefly to grab my sleepover kit on my way to Sally's. On the walk, I text Mom warnings about my arrival:

"Hey Mom, hope things are going well with what's-his-face, I found a place to sleep, but I need to swing by quickly to pick up my toothbrush. ETA 15 minutes."

No response, so I call her every three minutes along my walk. Finally, I reach her house, and I lurk on the street while I call her again. I'm hesitant to walk up the steps onto the porch, and I certainly won't knock for fear of interrupting her date. For some reason she seems particularly hesitant to introduce me to this man. When I've pressed her, assuring her that I harbor no judgement, insisting on my open-mindedness about her love life and her companions, she squirms and huffs, "Not this one, not this time." I'm not sure how to feel about this. Is she more in love with him than she wants to admit? Or maybe he has a lackluster sense of humor? Maybe he's got bad teeth or he's balding and she's embarrassed? Whatever the reason, I respect her wishes and remain on the street, calling her. Maybe I don't need my symbolic comforts tonight. I'll borrow Sally's toothbrush. I'll ask to wear her pajamas. I'll write my morning diary entry on a napkin. Whatever. I start to walk away when Mom finally picks up.

"What's wrong, baby?"

"Nothing Mom, I just need to grab my backpack. It has my toothbrush and stuff.

Sorry to interrupt. I'm outside."

"Bad timing. *Really* bad timing."

There's a shuffling noise in the background, and I assume it's the sounds of her mystery man, re-arranging his position in the bed.

"Oh, ok—sorry, *weird*— I mean, don't worry, I didn't mean to interrupt, continue"

"—I don't need it, I'm walking away, forget I called..."

"No, it's too late now. What do you need? I'll bring it out."

"Just...my backpack...it should be on top of my pile of stuff in the corner...Mom, I'm so sorry..."

She hangs up, and I shrivel into a knot on the front step, one hand on the railing to keep me from curling up entirely. This is strange. I don't want to know what Mom was doing when I called. I can assume, but I try to push it out of my mind. I wait long enough for the windchill to sneak up my shirtsleeves. Finally she cracks the door open, sees me clutching the railing, and steps barefoot onto the porch. She pads halfway down the steps and reaches my backpack down to me as though I'm stuck in a well and she's offering a rescue package of food and water. She's wearing nothing but a leopard-print robe. Her lipstick is smeared sideways, and she squints her bloodshot eyes through the shadows towards me. Pot. Or maybe she's been crying. Now I'm mad. I'm not sure why, but I feel the need to run.

"Mom, are you high?"

"Yeah, maybe. So what?"

"Never mind. Sorry again, my bad. Have a nice night."

I turn away into the dark and walk towards Sally's place without looking back. What hurts the most is that she hasn't chosen *me* as her companion for the evening. She'd rather hang out with this strange, nameless, faceless man.

Everything will be different in the morning. I'll call the friend to whom I can complain and confess my secrets, the friend who knows me best: Mom. Only Mom can offer the type of secure, eternal love that I seek, but am unable to find in any of my romantic pursuits. I'll tell her to meet me at the neighborhood bakery. She'll order the cheapest cup of black coffee, whiten it with cream and sugar, and maybe I'll get an Americano. She'll tease me for trying to be sophisticated with my expensive espresso drinks. I'll tease her for forgetting the top three buttons of her shirt. "Boobs, Mom, if you're not careful they'll pop out into your coffee."

We'll share a croissant and wordless smiles of recognition, then we'll tell each other other about our nights with our lovers, sparing no details. We will laugh about it, all of it, together.

the ANDROGYNE

In the universal mythological hero's journey, the hero is pulled from a safe space and launched into danger and eventually returns to a sense of wholeness. The hero confronts her inner shadow figure, overcomes external obstacles, crosses a perilous bridge, and forms a union of psychological opposites which had split apart when the light of consciousness entered the hero's awareness. This newly achieved wholeness is similar to the egg-womb from which Ma and Frank emerged, but somehow *more* whole, *more* warm and pleasant than before. It is a super-egg, like those fresh farm eggs with glowing yolks and blue shells. It is an egg that Ma and Frank have built together as writers. They have initiated the transcendent function of their own mythological artistry: they transformed their struggle into a beautiful work of art. An enlightened egg.

Both Ma and Frank have achieved individuation: they have each unified their own psychic opposites. Ma's highs and lows, her horse and human selves, have merged. Sometimes Ma is a horse. Sometimes Ma is Frank's teacher, a true anthropologist, a psychoanalyst. Sometimes she is a sex addict.

Sometimes she's high and obnoxious, but she can also be pretty cool.

Frank's wise grandma-self, her naive child-self, and her vulnerable rabbit-self have joined forces. Sometimes she's the mature caretaker of all the fragile, fucked-up humans in her vicinity. Sometimes she's an agoraphobic baby rodent too afraid to leave her bedroom den. Sometimes she's just Frank, the cocky poet-artist who can't decide between polyamory and monogamy, women or men, city or country, academia or anarchy. She is an androgynous hero: male, female, and everything in between. She takes after her mother and thinks too much, about *everything*. She has finally ripened into contradiction.

Here, the two archetypes of mother and daughter float as two complementary halves of a whole. Ma and Frank are two opposed ideas who have found the ability to function as one family unit. They're both the same humans and completely different beasts. They're sane *and* crazy. Strong *and* fragile. They have merged, and they share so much: mental illness, creativity, academic drive, loneliness, passion, neurosis. They're both sick in the head and the body, ailing, aging, driving one another and the world mad, dropping husbands, juggling lovers, road tripping around the country in beat-up junkers.

A mom and a daughter, strange as they are, multifaceted enigmas, shapeshifting writers, surviving together in a home they've built in their imaginations.

ACKNOWLEDGEMENTS

To all those who helped me during the writing process: reading, editing, making suggestions for research, encouraging me, and inspiring me while I wrote. To name a few: Janet Bennion, Helen Cannon, Bonnie Sunstein, Robyn Schiff, Craig Kelchen, Charles D'Ambrosio, Inara Verzemnieks, John D'Agata, Patricia Foster, Jeff Porter, all of my NWP colleagues, Jennifer Kerns, Anna Ready-Campbell, and countless others: thank you.

ABOUT GOLD WAKE PRESS

Gold Wake Press, an independent publisher, is curated by Nick Courtright and Kyle McCord. All Gold Wake titles are available at amazon.com, barnesandnoble.com, and via order from your local bookstore. Learn more at goldwake.com.

Available Titles:

Erin Stalcup's *Every Living Species*
Glenn Shaheen's *Carnivalia*
Eileen G'Sell's *Life After Rugby*
Justin Bigos' *Mad River*
Kelly Magee's *The Neighborhood*
Kyle Flak's *I Am Sorry for Everything in the Whole Entire Universe*
David Wojciechowski's *Dreams I Never Told You & Letters I Never Sent*
Keith Montesano's *Housefire Elegies*
Mary Quade's *Local Extinctions*
Adam Crittenden's *Blood Eagle*
Lesley Jenike's *Holy Island*
Mary Buchinger Bodwell's *Aerialist*
Becca J. R. Lachman's *Other Acreage*
Joshua Butts' *New to the Lost Coast*
Tasha Cotter's *Some Churches*
Hannah Stephenson's *In the Kettle, the Shriek*
Kathleen Rooney's *Robinson Alone*
Erin Elizabeth Smith's *The Naming of Strays*

ABOUT the AUTHOR

Frances Cannon is a writer and artist of hybrid mediums. She has an MFA from the Nonfiction Writing Program at the University of Iowa, and a BFA in poetry and printmaking from the University of Vermont. She has a book of poems and illustrations, *Tropicalia,* through Vagabond Press, and a book of poems and prints, *Uranian Fruit,* through Honeybee Press. She was born in Utah and has since lived in Oregon, Vermont, California, Maine, Iowa, Italy, Guatemala, France, and Mexico making art and writing books. She has also worked as an editorial intern and contributor at *McSweeney's Quarterly, The Believer, The Lucky Peach*, and *The Iowa Review*.

CPSIA information can be obtained
at www.ICGtesting.com
Printed in the USA
FFOW02n2247130817
38724FF